XERXES

XERXES

Ren A. Hakim

Copyright © 2006 by Ren A. Hakim.

Library of Congress Number: 2005910460
ISBN : Hardcover 1-4257-0349-6
Softcover 1-4257-0348-8

All rights reserved. No part of this book may be reproduced or transmitted in any form or by any means, electronic or mechanical, including photocopying, recording, or by any information storage and retrieval system, without permission in writing from the copyright owner.

This is a work of fiction. Names, characters, places and incidents either are the product of the author's imagination or are used fictitiously, and any resemblance to any actual persons, living or dead, events, or locales is entirely coincidental.

This book was printed in the United States of America.

To order additional copies of this book, contact:
Xlibris Corporation
1-888-795-4274
www.Xlibris.com
Orders@Xlibris.com
31685

SCRIPT DEFINITIONS

The following was (and still is) intended for the screen. While it has been slightly "novelized", you will find it is more technical in style than a book and, like all screenplays, written in the present tense. For those unfamiliar with script elements, here is a little tutorial on a few of the key ones:

A **SLUG LINE** sets the scene's location and time of day.

EXT stands for "exterior", meaning the shot is outside.

INT stands for "interior", meaning the shot is inside.

O.S. stands for "off screen", meaning the character speaking, while IN the scene, is not in the shot.

V.O. stands for "voice over", meaning the character speaking is talking OVER what is on screen.

"CUT TO" is a sharp transition to the next scene, generally used to put emphasis on the end of the one preceding it.

"DISSOLVE TO" is a slow transition to the next scene, which often insinuates a significant amount of time has passed.

A **MONTAGE** is a series of different scenes/images, usually set to a soundtrack. I like to think of them as mini music videos.

Side-by-side dialogue means the characters are speaking at once.

A **BEAT** is a brief moment of silence.

A **PAUSE** is a longer span of silence.

Sound effects, such as **THUNDER** and **LIGHTNING**, are capitalized.

All scripts begin with the words **FADE IN** and end with either **FADE OUT** or **FADE TO BLACK**.

CHARACTER LIST

ACHAEMENES .... Persian; satrap of Egypt and commander of the Egyptian fleet

ADALIA .... Persian; advisor to the king

ADEIMANTUS .... Greek; commander of Corinth's fleet

ADMATHA .... Persian; advisor to the king

AESCHYLUS .... Greek; Athenian; author of *The Persians*; cameo appearance

AMESTRIS .... Persian; Xerxes' wife and queen

ARIABIGNES .... Persian; commander of the Phoenician fleet

ARIDAI .... Son of Haman

ARIDATHA .... Son of Haman

ARISAI .... Son of Haman

ARISTIDES .... Greek; Athenian; statesman

ARTABANUS .... Persian; Brother of Darius the Great; Xerxes' uncle; prime minister

ARTABAZUS .... Persian general

ARTAYNTA .... Persian; daughter of Masistes and Suraz

ARTAXERXES .... Persian; Xerxes' youngest son

ARTEMISIA .... Persian ally; queen of Halicarnassus and commander of its fleet

ASPATHA .... Son of Haman

ATTAGINUS .... Persian ally; wealthy Greek

CARSHENA .... Persian; advisor to the king

CIMON .... Greek; Athenian commander

CLEOMBROTUS .... Greek; Spartan king

DALPHON .... Son of Haman

DARIUS .... Persian; Xerxes' eldest son

DARIUS THE GREAT .. Persian; Xerxes' father

DEMARATUS .... Persian ally; deposed king of Sparta

DIENECES .... Greek; Spartan soldier; Leonidas's second in command

EGEUS .... Persian; eunuch in charge of the virgins

EPHORS .... A board of five Spartan officials

ESTHER .... "Persian"; Xerxes' second wife and queen

EURYBIADES .... Greek; Spartan fleet commander

GERGIS .... Persian general

GORGO .... Greek; queen of Sparta and wife of Leonidas

HAMAN	"Persian"; later named prime minister
HATHACH	Persian; chamberlain
HEGISTRATUS	Persian ally; Greek soothsayer
HYDARNES	Persian; commander of the king's "Immortals"
LEONIDAS	Greek; Spartan king; commander of Thermopylae forces
MARENA	Persian; advisor to the king
MARDONIUS	Persian; head of the army
MASISTES	Persian; satrap of Bactria; general; Xerxes' best friend
MASISTIUS	Persian; commander of the cavalry
MEGABYZUS	Persian general
MEHUMAN	Persian chamberlain
MEMUCAN	Persian; advisor to the king
MORDECAI	"Persian" connected to Esther
OLYMPIODORUS	Greek; Athenian general
ONOMACRITUS	Persian ally; Greek oracle monger
PARMASHTA	Son of Haman
PARSHANDATHA	Son of Haman
PAUSANIAS	Greek; Leonidas's nephew; Spartan regent; leader of army at Plataea

PERICLES	Greek; Athenian; cameo appearance
PORATHA	Son of Haman
SHAASHGAZ	Persian; eunuch in charge of the women
SHETHAR	Persian; advisor to the king
SMERDOMENES	Persian general
SOPHOCLES	Greek; Athenian writer; cameo appearance
SURAZ	Persian; wife of Masistes; mother of Artaynta
TARSHISH	Persian; advisor to the king
TIGRANES	Persian soldier; youngest son of Artabanus
TRITAN	Persian general; eldest son of Artabanus
USTANU	Persian satrap of Babylon
VAIZATHA	Son of Haman
ZERESH	Wife of Haman
ZOPYRUS	Persian; father of General Megabyzus
ZOSTRA	Artaynta's attendant

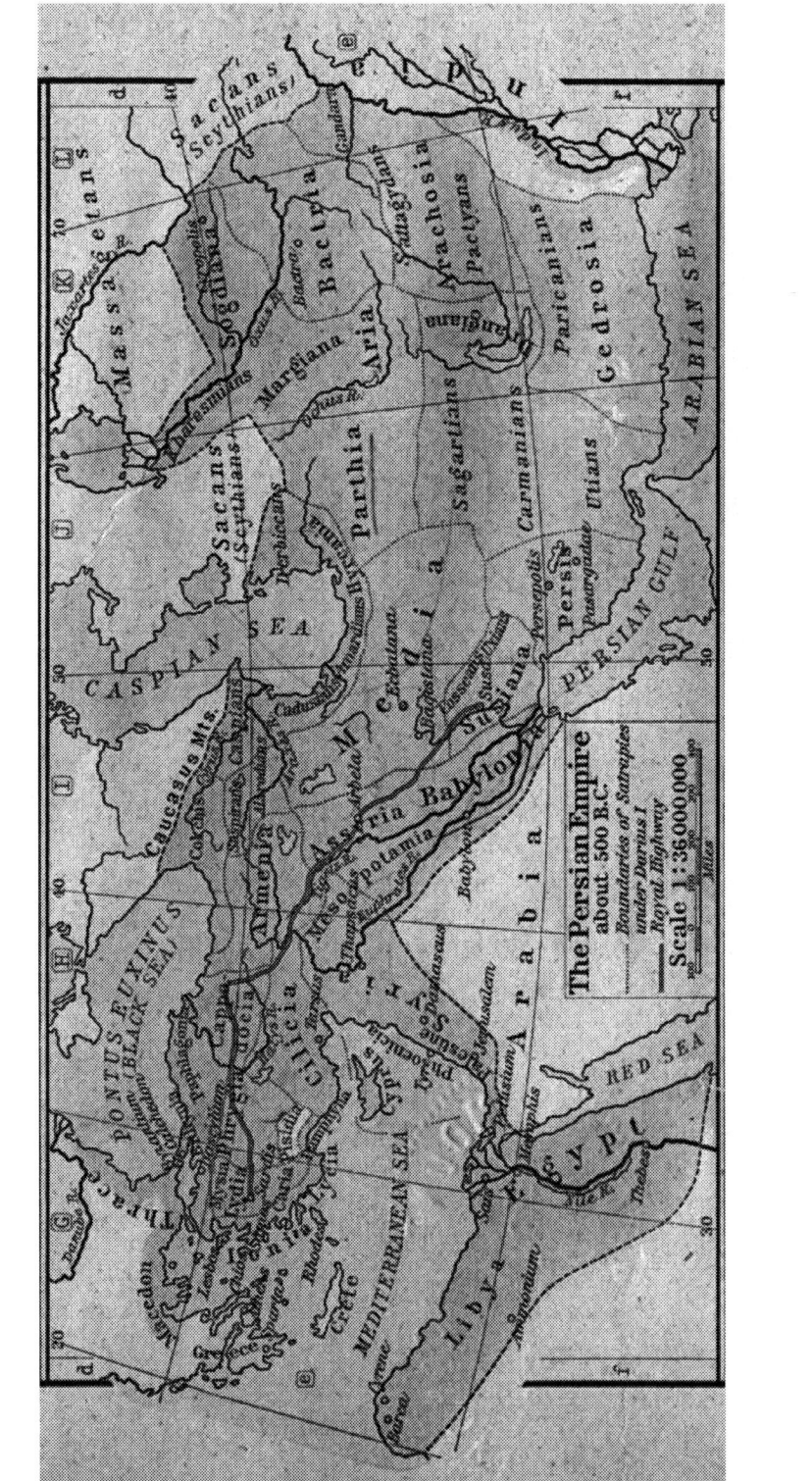

FADE IN:

EXT. MESOPOTAMIA—DATE PALM GROVE—DAY

533 B.C.

Everything is a bewildering blur, a fractured prism of color and light, heralded by the dissonant RASP of BREATH caught short in panicked lungs and the echo of SNAPPING LEAVES. It is a frenzied montage of bounding sandaled feet, sailing robes, and widened eyes set against the indiscernible backdrop of the grove. This is a state of fear, chaotically spiraling, till finally cued to focus by a desperate, strangled CRY.

One of two TRIBESMEN has fallen.

Dark, curly locks bounce as he jerks his head to search the maze of trees and brush from which he has just emerged. Shadows mimicking the trunks seemingly breathe, expanding and retracting as rays of light roll through the dense canopy of green above. A lazy breeze shuffles through the surrounding bushes, coaxing gleaming leaves to dance, and a butterfly soon flutters past to join the waltz.

While all may seem calm, the man remains guarded and dares not look away as he rolls off his belly, scoots a few paces backward and grudgingly rises to stand. Seconds pass as the survey continues and, with each, the rise and fall of his chest begins to slow. Each blink lasts just a moment longer, too, till his eyes, at last, close.

It is in this moment that a hand comes crashing down on his shoulder, spinning him around. What he now faces is not what he has run from, but, rather, a frightful look which mirrors his own.

> TRIBESMAN 2
> It's only me!

> TRIBESMAN 1
> Did you . . . did you see?

> TRIBESMAN 2
> No—

                    TRIBESMAN 1
              Nor I, but . . . this quaking—

                    TRIBESMAN 2
              What of Daniel?? Where is he? Was he
              following you?

                    TRIBESMAN 1
              No . . . I think Daniel . . .

                    TRIBESMAN 2
              What??

                    TRIBESMAN 1
              I think Daniel might yet still be on the
              river's edge.

EXT. MESOPOTAMIA—BANK OF THE TIGRIS—DAY

On the opposite side of the date palm grove, along the bank, a light gloriously shimmers, much like the undulating currents of the Tigris itself. Semi-translucent, the profile of a man is seen standing within, becoming all the more defined as the scene begins to spin, bringing us closer and closer with each rotation till we are—

INSIDE THE LIGHT

—where the elderly, biblical DANIEL, dressed simply, skin tanned and dried from the sun, hair long and grayed from the years, stands immobile in a state of reverent awe. Panning around, he appears to be alone, for what his sights are set on can only be found reflected in his dark eyes. That is where we find the shrouded face of a clandestine MESSENGER whose lips, though moving, utter words we cannot initially hear.

So, round and round Daniel we spin, seeing what he sees, seeing nothing . . . finally hearing what he hears.

                    MESSENGER
                 (as if continuing)
                     (MORE)

                    MESSENGER(cont'd)
               . . . and now I will show you the truth.
               Behold, there shall stand up yet three
               kings in Persia and the fourth shall be
               far richer than they all; and by his
               strength through his riches he shall stir
               up all against the realm of Grecia.

Back on Daniel's eyes, the messenger's form has been replaced. Now, peering back is what appears to be war imagery, a battlefield as we . . .

                                                DISSOLVE TO:

EXT. SUSA—PRACTICE FIELD—DAY

486 B.C.

The sands of time are ripped away by the powerful hooves of horses, cascading about their legs like glitter dust as they furiously gallop. The sun burns brightly; the animals' nostrils are wide, their coats washed out. Manes and tails glide through the wind like war banners.

The riders remain a mystery, only alluded to by glimpses of their bodies. One, riding a white horse, clutches a spear.

The man's hands are strong, as are his arms and torso; wrists are fashioned with cuffs of gold. Every muscle is drawn tight as the focus of his attentions draws closer with each stride.

He pulls the animal in, causing it to rear, and launches the weapon. It SCREAMS before perfectly burrowing into its intended mark: a makeshift target.

Only now, as thunderous APPLAUSE and CHEERS resound, is the "battlefield" revealed to be nothing more than a staging ground for drills. What had seemed to stretch for miles is suddenly dwarfed by breath-taking splendor.

ONLOOKERS, comprised of OFFICIALS, NOBLE FAMILIES and other DELEGATES, line the perimeter of the terrace above. They enthusiastically lean over walls which bear militaristic basreliefs and, though their sights may be set on the scene below, it is the monumental architecture which towers over them that is nothing short of awe-inspiring.

Multi-tiered palaces, imposing lamasu statues (winged bulls with the face of a man), the columnar edifices and mammoth, crouching bull capitals of the forums . . . they all appear luminescent as the glazed brick, marble and precious metals from which they are constructed are bathed in the light of the sun.

Still, it is the field which commands attention. Dispersed along the walls' inner perimeter, below the chiseled depictions of military might, armed GUARDS are posted and, before them, a group of ATTENDANTS stand in wait with refreshments.

They bow their heads and part as the spearman rides between them. He leaps from his horse, tosses the reins to a GROOM, and heads for a basin of water to cool down. The attendants brush him off and, after doing so, he turns.

Thirty-two, tall, handsome; the epitome of presence. Wearing a Persian chiton, a collar of gold, and other finery, his royal status is clear. This is XERXES: Crown Prince of the Persian Empire.

Xerxes, according to the records of antiquity, is charismatic and moody, benevolent and cruel, an admirer of beauty and an architect of war, both revered and feared—a multi-faceted fusion of contradictions.

HAMAN, an advisor and friend, approaches. He is only in his thirties, but already an old-hand elitist. He is also an opportunist, always looking to ingratiate himself before those with more power than he—like now—as he smooths his courtly robes and raises a cup.

> HAMAN
> To Prince Xerxes, may all the Great
> King's soldiers be as quick of mind and
> skilled of eye as he!

The crowd APPLAUDS. Xerxes acknowledges the compliment with a smile, but quickly turns away from Haman. A horse shaking its head, thus causing the metal parts of its bridle to RATTLE, has called his attention.

MASISTES, Xerxes' closest confidant and friend, wipes his jaw and quietly laughs as he dismounts. Though a man of nobility, he comes across like a joker, animatedly dusting himself off.

> MASISTES
> I'll be gritting sand between my teeth
> for the remainder of the day.
> (they clasp hands)
> Well done.

EXT. SUSA—TOPOGRAPHY—SUNSET

Now, we see Susa, the capital of the empire, in all its glory, sprawling before the distant, southernmost ramparts of the Zagros Mountains and bordered east and west by the courses of two rivers: the Dizful, an affluent of the Pasitigris, and the Kerkha. Lush, green fields and groves of date, konar and lemon trees drink from these waters, as well as a third source, a small tributary of the Dizful that runs through Susa, named the Shaur.

It is the Shaur which separates the citizens, whose suburbs and businesses stretch to the Kerkha, from the officials' quarter, citadel, and palace complex. The edifices of the latter rise up from the plain as if beacons to the sun. Even now, though shadow capped, their westward facades continue to beam amber as it lazily makes its descent.

EXT. SUSA—PALACE GARDEN—SUNSET

Located within the heart of the palace, bordered on each side by a portico walk-way, is a garden large enough to entertain hundreds, if not thousands, of guests. Fluted, marble pillars are fixed with silver rings and from these, bound by purple and white cording, linens of blue and white cascade and pool atop a most extraordinary pavement . . . a mosaic of porphyry, marble, mother-of-pearl and jewels, lined with couches of gold and silver.

It is in a secluded nook of the garden, surrounded by lush flora, that Xerxes is reclined. Attendants stand behind him. One keeps a parasol leveled above the prince, the other waves a fan. Haman and Masistes sit across the way, partaking in the fruit set out before them on a marble table.

With a hand, Xerxes dismisses the attendants. They bow and promptly leave.

>XERXES
>Tell me, Haman, how are my guests finding Susa?

>HAMAN
>The delegates are very impressed by the complex—

>MASISTES
>(interrupting)
>After this morning's display, I think their women are more impressed by its crown prince.
>(a beat)
>I noticed Amestris was not present.

The mere mention of his wife's name makes Xerxes weary.

>XERXES
>Perhaps if she had come, it would not have been so unbearably hot.
>That woman could turn the sun to ice.

>MASISTES
>Still at odds, eh?

>XERXES
>I often wonder if my father wanted to punish me for some forgotten trespass. There are days that I cannot fathom why this marriage was arranged, but then there are nights that make me exceedingly pleased it was.

MASISTES
So, she's not always as cold as you say.

Haman, seemingly born without a sense of humor, is not amused by the joke. Xerxes, on the other hand, laughs as he raises a cup to his lips.

HAMAN
Speaking of women, what has become
of your wife, Masistes? Did you finally
let her off your tether?

The prince pauses, intrigued by the new topic of conversation.

MASISTES
My wife? What of yours?! Don't tell
me she's pregnant yet again.

HAMAN
No, she's not—

Smiling in relief, Masistes interrupts by raising his own drink, as if to make a toast.

MASISTES
Now that is news to drink to!

Downing the contents in one gulp, he slams the cup down and grins yet again at an incredulous Haman.

HAMAN
Oh, how I wish you weren't leaving us,
Masistes.

MASISTES
Of course you do. If you must know,
Haman, Suraz has been busy preparing
for the trip. She's been a little
melancholy about the move actually,
but I know, once we get to Bactria,
she'll see it was for the best.

> **XERXES**
> It is.
> > (a beat)
> With my uncle accompanying the army, the council requires a level head such as yours to help it along.

> **MASISTES**
> I know it's a great responsibility. I'm rather anxious to begin. There are many ideas which this level head of mine has conjured, ones I'm determined to see benefit the province.

> **XERXES**
> That kind of tenacity is the reason why it must be you who takes the post. That and, truth be told, I'm tired of seeing your face.

Nearly choking on his drink, Haman looks from Masistes to Xerxes and back again, unable to decipher whether that was intended to be a joke.

Masistes loudly sighs.

> **MASISTES**
> Already? Seems like it was only yesterday that you returned to Susa. Surely it's yet too soon to be tired of such a fine countenance.

Xerxes tries to remain serious, but can't control the laughter.

> **XERXES**
> No—Masistes, truly . . .
> > (laughter ebbs; serious)
> There is no other who will miss you more than I.

MASISTES
(emotional)
I know . . .
(jokingly)
Well, except for Haman.

Both Xerxes and Masistes chuckle. Haman can't help but do the same.

MASISTES
(gritting sand)
Why did I even bother to accept your invitation? Are you sure you didn't mean to challenge Masis-tius? General of the cavalry Masis-tius? No. Wait. That can't be right. He's in Parsa with your father right now, isn't he?
(off Xerxes' nod)
Now that would be quite a match to see. When things are settled with Egypt and Greece—

The mood suddenly turns earnest.

XERXES
It is only a matter of time.

MASISTES
Has word been sent?

XERXES
They'll be leaving Parsa for here by the end of this week.

MASISTES
How long do they plan to stay?

HAMAN
Just until plans are finalized.

XERXES
There are many in store.

Xerxes gets up and thoughtfully grazes his hand against the wall-climbing leaves.

MASISTES
What are you thinking?

XERXES
That I should be going with them. I know my father has everything under control, it's only that, it feels somehow wrong not to march by his side, be there as a witness to what will be a defining moment in history. Believe me, I know he has already secured his place in it. One only has to take into account what he has already done. If not for him, Persia would have slipped into the darkness after Cambyses' passing. But he rose up, wrested control from imposters who would have destroyed it. He stabilized us, codified our laws, established the measures which have made this empire what it is today.
 (a beat)
I want, so much, to be like him.

MASISTES
You always have. I understand why you feel the way you do, why you think you should be with him on the field, but you are his successor, Xerxes. That means he's put his trust in you to uphold all the things of which you spoke should he not return.

> HAMAN
> For once, I agree with Masistes. If-

Xerxes whirls around, clearly angered by the insinuation.

> XERXES
> There are no 'ifs'. He will see to it that
> our honor has been avenged and, then,
> he will come home.

> HAMAN
> Of course. You're right.

An uncomfortable silence takes the scene. Haman peers into his cup as if it is the most interesting thing on earth. Masistes, however, keeps his sights set on Xerxes until he realizes how low the sun has crept. He gets up, absentmindedly rubbing his neck.

> MASISTES
> Speaking of home, I hadn't realized
> how late the hour was. I must be
> going.

Xerxes and Masistes clasp hands and exchange a pat on the back.

> XERXES
> Alright, my friend. I'll see you at the
> banquet tomorrow?

> MASISTES
> That you will.

> XERXES
> Till then.

> MASISTES
> Till then.

The noble starts on his way, exchanging a parting nod with Haman, but just as he's about to exit the nook, he stops and turns around.

                    MASISTES
                Xerxes?
                    (off Xerxes' look)
                King Darius really is an exceptional
                man.

                    XERXES
                More than that . . .

Masistes knowingly bobs his head and leaves.

EXT. PARSA—TOPOGRAPHY—DAY

The grassy plain of the Marv Dasht speeding below us, we see the western face of the Kuh-e-Rahmat, the "Mount of Grace," begin to peer over the horizon. With ramparts that stretch for miles, it serves as the guardian of Parsa and the paramour in whose embrace the ceremonial complex is nestled.

The complex, a sight to behold, is held aloft some forty feet and spans nearly fifty acres. Access to it is granted north and south by a prodigious, double-winged staircase. One hundred-eleven steps ascend to the terrace, carved from massive blocks of limestone, each nearly seven meters in length and shallow enough for guests to ride up. Bordering the stairs and appearing to climb them themselves, are basrelief figures of delegates bearing tributes for the king.

Gates, firmly bolted into the floor, loom at the top of the stairs. Once past these, guards' apartments and storage areas are seen. It is on this level that, during times of celebration, guests drop off tokens for the king and await audience with the court.

Two meters higher, the uncompleted Apadana and Hall of One-Hundred Columns are found. The latter has just been started, while wooden scaffolds scale the Apadana's facade. Mounds of earth, blocks of stone, marble pillars and beams of Lebanon cedar lie along the otherwise immaculate courtyard between the edifices.

Another two meters up, and we come to the heart of the complex, the palaces:

Tachara, or "Winter Palace" of the Great King,

Tripylon, or "Central Palace," used for council meetings,

and a third still under construction,

Hadish, the palace of Xerxes.

The Tachara and Tripylon sit across from one another behind the Apadana and Hall of One Hundred Columns. Spaced back from the other palaces by a central, royal courtyard is Xerxes' and behind it is the "L" shaped building known as the "Harem."

Running north and south alongside the mountain is the lowest level of the complex. This is the administration quarter. The treasury, accounting offices, and royal chancellery are all found here. Also located beside the mountain are the royal stables, domestic quarters and yet more guard apartments.

This is Parsa, yet another jewel in Persia's illustrious crown, where, like Susa, more often than not, all that glitters really is gold.

EXT. PARSA—TACHARA—AFTERNOON

Like many of the citadel's buildings, access is by a doubleramped staircase, decorated with intricate reliefs of Persian and Median nobles bearing gifts. The stairs lead to an immense, columned porch, where, atop a mosaic floor, guards are posted. They stand statuesque, holding staffs, each resting their weapon's weighted end upon an upturned foot.

Behind them is the main entrance to the palace—two gargantuan, gold doors.

INT. PARSA—TACHARA—KING'S STUDY—AFTERNOON

Carpets are sprawled on the floor. Tapestries hang from the walls, interspersed between unlit candelabras, onyx benches and gold couches. Two pillars flank a desk scattered with documents and maps. On the opposite end of the room is another table, this one lined with a wash basin, a pitcher and goblets.

One of the double doors opens, GROANING ever-so-softly before CLANKING shut.

The entrant is ARTABANUS, forty, muscular; the king's younger brother. Cold and cynical are the words which best describe this man. Genuine smiles are a rarity, as they are more frequently used as expressions of sarcasm. Now, however, standing before the doors, as if at attention, he does nothing but frown.

                ARTABANUS
        They're ready to begin when you are.

Artabanus glances toward the window. Standing there is a dark, imposing figure, peering out into the distance where work continues on the Apadana and the Hall of One-Hundred Columns. With a hand pressed against the window sill and brilliantly aglow, he looks like he could be the mythological Zeus preparing to throw a thunderbolt, but this is not the case.

He turns and the "lightning" is revealed to have merely been the sun playing off a gold signet ring.

Backlit, the man himself remains a mystery, but, drawing away from the window, less and less of a shadow he becomes. With each step, another detail emerges—like the intricate embroidery work of his prestigious robe, the abundance of jewels and gold adorning him, the loose curls of his gray beard and moustache, the subtle crook of his nose. By the time he stops before Artabanus, every feature is defined.

Sixty-four, tall, menacing, eyes as intense as those of the crown prince and framed by brows as black as pitch; this is DARIUS THE GREAT, King of Persia, the legendary hero Xerxes puts on such a towering pedestal.

                DARIUS THE GREAT
        I'm ready now.

                ARTABANUS
        Are you, brother?

                DARIUS THE GREAT
        Artabanus, we have been over this.

ARTABANUS
And my opinion remains the same.
Our only concern should be regaining
control over Egypt. This obsession
with the Greeks . . .
        (shakes head; a beat)
Every day, I sit silently and listen as you
and the rest of the council go on about
armament and training, strategies and
costs, and each night I wonder for
what? Why should-

DARIUS THE GREAT
You know why!

Offended, he goes back to the window. Artabanus follows a few paces behind.

ARTABANUS
Truly, I don't know if I do. I think
back on all that has happened and it
still makes little sense to me.

DARIUS THE GREAT
Then why don't you recite your history?
Perhaps you don't remember as clearly as
the rest of us. Perhaps I can point out
what it is you can't seem to grasp.

Darius turns, daring him to go on, but Artabanus remains steadfast and does not back down.

ARTABANUS
Alright, Darius. As I remember it, it
began with the Tyrant of Miletus,
Aristagoras. He went to Sardis, stood
before our own brother, Artaphernes,
and made a fantastic proposal. He told
him that he had been petitioned by
wealthy, Greek exiles from Naxos to
(MORE)

ARTABANUS(cont'd)
wage a campaign against the island, that once it fell so, too, would the rest of the Cyclades—even Euboea. All this, he told Artaphernes, was assured if only he had more troops and resources to launch the expedition. He would increase our dominion and, thus, our fortunes—not to mention his own— and he would do it all in your name. So, by your sanction, our brother granted Aristagoras an army and fleet. Alas, the Naxians were prepared and, for months, the island was besieged with no success. Aristagoras failed before he had even yet begun. Many men were lost, his wealth had been spent and he believed if he were to return and stand before the royal court, he would do so as a shamed man whose life was all but forfeit. He thought it better to turn traitor instead and, with what was left of his own troops, incited Miletus to revolt against Persia. They took prisoner our appointed officials, did away with our establishment and declared war on our garrisons. All the cities on the Ionian coast fell into anarchy. With great speed we moved to crush the rebellions and Aristagoras desperately sought more allies, one of them being Athens—which, before then, was nothing to us but some insignificant Greek polis. They sent ships and soldiers and as our forces were busy along the coastal cities, Sardis was sacked and burned. That was the day you proclaimed, that for their complicity, you would forevermore—

DARIUS THE GREAT
Remember the Athenians.

ARTABANUS
And not a day has gone by that you've let yourself forget.

DARIUS THE GREAT
That statement is false and you know it.
(a beat)
You think it all so simple, don't you? You think the catalyst of this campaign is a single offense when, in reality, Athens' crimes against us are many. They did, indeed, have a guilty hand in the revolt, a revolt which took years to put down entirely, and I did desire revenge and I took it—on Miletus—where it all began. You see, brother, in the grand scheme of things, Athens' role—was—minor.
If I were possessed with such enmity for them after the whole affair, why then, when I sent Mardonius to bring order to Thrace and Macedonia, did I not also command him to continue south to Athens when his work was done?

Artabanus takes a seat on one of the benches and shrugs.

ARTABANUS
Perhaps you would have . . . had many of our ships not been destroyed by that storm which came along.

DARIUS THE GREAT
After Mardonius returned, before Datis led the second Aegean expedition, I sent envoys throughout Greece, even to Athens. I offered them my friendship,
(MORE)

DARIUS THE GREAT(cont'd)
despite what they'd done. I was
prepared to absolve them of their crime
and all I asked in return was a pledge of
earth and water and what did they do?
      (a beat)
They killed the messenger.

ARTABANUS
The Spartans killed the one sent to
them as well.

Darius scoffs, goes to the table and pours himself a drink.

DARIUS THE GREAT
The Spartans. They murder their own
children if their elders deem them
flawed. Sparta. Now, Athens?
Athens is supposed to be a center of
education, a city of philosophers. They
should have known better than to
insult us again.

ARTABANUS
Which brings us to Hippias.

DARIUS THE GREAT
Yes. You know, it all would have been
so fitting. Datis would succeed where
Aristagoras had failed. We would gain
control of the Aegean and then return
Hippias, the exiled king of Athens, to
his people. I was told he had many
supporters, that once he finally
returned they would rise up and
overthrow the leadership. It would
have been so fitting . . .
      (sitting beside Artabanus)
You heard the reports. Everything was
      (MORE)

                    DARIUS THE GREAT (cont'd)
          going according to plan. The islands
          were made ours, the Aegean.
          There was only one task left to
          complete.

                    ARTABANUS
          But that is where things went wrong.

                    DARIUS THE GREAT
          On a plain named Marathon. Hippias
          thought it best to dock the ships off its
          coast. He told Datis it was a nice, flat
          stretch of land and well-suited for the
          cavalry. There they waited for Hippias'
          supporters to revolt, but no word came.
          The only Athenian army raised was the
          one blocking the road to the city and it
          grew day by day. By the fifth, it was
          clear that Hippias didn't know his
          people as well as he thought. So, Datis
          decided to pull back. They were this
          close—
                    (motions with fingers)
          —to setting sail when the
          Athenians attacked the rear-guard.
          We lost a respected general that day.

Abruptly, Darius gets up, his face now twisted in anger.

                    DARIUS THE GREAT
                    (ranting)
          Can you now understand?? Not only is
          this reprisal necessary, but it is also long
          overdue! You were right when you
          called Athens insignificant, but by
          permitting their disrespect to go on
          unchecked? Do you not brush off a fly
          when it lands on you? Or do you hold
                         (MORE)

DARIUS THE GREAT(cont'd)
still and let more gather?! No—because
you breathe, Artabanus! If we do not
go to war, others will see that
complacency as a weakness!

At this point, Darius is so upset that he is nearly shaking. Something more is wrong, though. He briefly closes his eyes and grits his teeth. Concerned, Artabanus goes to him.

ARTABANUS
Darius? Darius, are you alright?

He takes a breath, then a sip of water, and dismisses Artabanus's concerned look with a wave.

DARIUS THE GREAT
I'm fine.

ARTABANUS
Really? Then why are we holding
tonight's meeting here instead of the
Tripylon?
(off look; sighs)
Darius, look at yourself. You are sixty-
four years old. Do you know how
much it saddens me to watch you
squander your time on this war? I
listened to all your points, all your
reasons. The Ionian revolt? As you
stated, Miletus was made an example
of what happens to those seeking to
undermine us. Aristagoras is no more
and we later succeeded in carrying out
the plan he proffered which started the
whole mess to begin with. As far as the
Athenians denying your request for
earth and water . . . well, Persia's
friendship is their loss.

DARIUS THE GREAT
And Marathon?

ARTABANUS
Marathon was a presumptuous mistake on our part and a fluke on theirs, but that does not mean it could not happen again. You know history has a way of repeating itself.
    (a beat)
Datis was a good man. I mourned him. I don't want to mourn you.

DARIUS THE GREAT
Artabanus—

ARTABANUS
Or my sons—son. Nor do I want to question if the sacrifice was worth it.

DARIUS THE GREAT
Oh, brother, Persia is worth more than any one of us.

ARTABANUS
But is that what you're really fighting for?

DARIUS THE GREAT
It's a matter of honor and tying up loose ends before . . . Artabanus, when my days are near over, I want to be able to rest easy, knowing there is no business left unfinished—that any false steps I made during my life have been amended. I want to be able to take off this ring and see no shadows of regret held in the reflection it casts before passing it on to my son. I have been a good king. Persia has flourished.

                    ARTABANUS   DARIUS THE GREAT
            I don't dispute that. You've   There are only a few things
            earned your title a thousand   which keep me up at night.
            times over, but—

                              DARIUS THE GREAT
                        And once Egypt and Athens are taken
                        care of, there will be none.

Darius's eyes flicker determinedly. He's spoken. That is that. He goes for the door.

EXT. SUSA—CITY—NIGHT

Moonlight spills uninterrupted across Susa, from the city in the foreground, to the citadel and the Zagros Mountains beyond.

The citizens' quarter remains busy. People meander throughout the streets. Others lounge on their porches, some on their roofs.

ON ONE PARTICULAR ROOFTOP

—we see a petite figure from behind. This is a YOUNG HADASSAH, no more than in her early teens. One day, she will come to be known by another name, a name which will be remembered for all time . . . one day . . .

For now, she is a mystery.

Clutching a modest shawl around her shoulders, her dark hair loosely pulled back, she stares on at the palaces in the distance.

INT. SUSA—BANQUET HALL—NIGHT

The hall is moderate in size, but lovely. Fire rises and flickers from the depths of enormous, bronze baskets. Wafting curtains drape the bordering portico. Murals span the walls.

Secluded in a corner and seated upon cushions, MUSICIANS perform an UPBEAT TUNE on their DRUMS, LYRES and FLUTES. They play to a crowded room which buzzes with TALK and LAUGHTER, where every hand, except their own, holds a drink.

Every guest is standing, and the only females to be found are the SERVING GIRLS who weave through them with trays of refreshments. This reception is for the men, but it is not the only one. As the portico curtains take flight on the breeze, we can see the WOMEN'S BANQUET HALL across a CENTRAL COURTYARD.

A small group of TEENAGE BOYS are gathered by the portico. They are all the sons of nobles and, perhaps as a result of their fathers' status, stand around as if they, too, wield significant power. Most of them leer at the girls passing by, but a few stare across the room.

Holding the boys' attention is the sight of Xerxes speaking with two men. One of them is USTANU, satrap of Babylon. The other, ZOPYRUS, is the reason for the stares. Except for his eyes and mouth, Zopyrus's face is oddly shrouded.

The young men continue to scrutinize. TEEN 1, apparently the leader of the pack, is looked to for answers.

> TEEN 1
> That's Zopyrus.

One of the boys, TEEN 3, opens his mouth to ask a question, but before he can, TEEN 2 pushes to the front.

> TEEN 2
> You really think so?

> TEEN 1
> It has to be him. Look. He's standing
> with the satrap of Babylon.

> TEEN 2
> Ustanu?

> TEEN 1
> Right. Alright, so, covered face,
> standing with Ustanu and, apparently,
> someone important. I mean, who else
> could it be?

Trying to ask his question, Teen 3 is, again, interrupted. A couple more boys round into the room through the closest curtain and join the others.

> TEENS
> C'mon . . . Go . . . Hurry up.

A good-looking young man, approximately fourteen years old, pushes his way to the front of the group, startling those still fixated on Zopyrus. This is Xerxes' son, DARIUS.

Teen 1 slightly turns toward the royal.

> TEEN 1
> Where were you, Darius?

> DARIUS
> Across the courtyard.

> TEEN 1
> Spying on the women?

> DARIUS
> Mm hmm.

> TEEN 1
> What if they catch you?

> DARIUS
> What can they do to me? I'm the king's
> grandson and namesake. So, what are
> you looking at?

> TEEN 1
> See that man talking with your father?

Darius makes a face.

> DARIUS
> Zopyrus?

Teen 2 lunges forward.

> TEEN 2
> It really is him!

> TEEN 1
> I told you!

Teen 3 now lunges forward and exasperatedly shouts the question he's been waiting so long to ask.

> TEEN 3
> Who's Zopyrus!??!!

The response is a multiple SHUSH from the others.

> TEEN 2
> You don't know?

> TEEN 3
> If I knew, why would I ask?!

> TEEN 1
> He's one of the 'eyes of the king.'

> DARIUS
> He certainly can't be his ears.

> TEEN 3
> What do you mean?

DARIUS
(to Teen 1)
You want to tell him?

TEEN 1
(nods; turns to Teen 3)
Alright. Look. A long, long time ago, there was this imposter to the throne named Gaumata.

DARIUS
But my grandfather and his friends took care of him.

Pretending his finger is a dagger, Darius draws it along his neck.

TEEN 1
After that, Darius was named king and because he was new to the throne, the wealthy nobles in Babylon thought this was an opportunity to rebel and rule themselves. One of them . . .
(turns to Teen 2)
What was his name?

TEEN 2
Nidintu-Bel.

TEEN 1
That's it! Well, he renamed himself 'Nebuchadnezzar the Third' and declared himself supreme. King Darius tried to take Babylon back, but couldn't breach the gates to the city.

Teen 1 gets so wrapped up in the story that he begins to look more and more like a lecturing professor.

TEEN 1
So, Zopyrus comes up with a plan. He mutilates his own face—cuts off his nose and his ears and then goes to Babylon claiming that Darius did it and he wants revenge. Most believed him from the start, but those that doubted his sincerity were convinced soon after when he began leading attacks against the Persian army. Little did they know, the army's retreats were arranged. Eventually, they trusted Zopyrus enough to hand control over the city's defenses to him and he, subsequently, opened the gates of Babylon to the Persians. The rest is history.

Teen 1 stops and finally takes a look at his 'student', Teen 3. By the look on the boy's face, you would think there were something terribly bitter in his mouth.

TEEN 3
He cut off his own ears and nose? That man must be insane.

DARIUS
Don't let anyone else hear you say that. They all think of Zopyrus as a hero.

TEEN 2
(nodding toward Xerxes)
What do you think they're talking about?

Darius hears an eruption of laughter from behind. He peers over his shoulder and is waved back to join the other group of teens.

DARIUS
(distracted)
Politics, war . . . I don't know.

He leaves and we turn our attention to—

XERXES, ZOPYRUS, USTANU

—in the midst of conversation.

> XERXES
> (to Zopyrus)
> You should be proud of Megabyzus.
> He is a widely respected general.

> ZOPYRUS
> I am very proud of my son.

> XERXES
> As I'm sure he is of you.

> ZOPYRUS
> Thank you.

> XERXES
> So you're staying on in Susa?

> ZOPYRUS
> (melancholy)
> Just until I see him off.

> XERXES
> The day the army marches out will certainly be bittersweet, but when their work is done, they'll return heroes, one and all.

> ZOPYRUS
> Yes. Yes, they will.

Zopyrus's lips pull to a smile between the narrow slit in his head cover.

> XERXES
> Zopyrus?

                    ZOPYRUS
          I was thinking . . . You're very much
          like your father.

To Xerxes, this is a huge compliment.

                    USTANU
          Yes, and if what you accomplished
          during your tenure as viceroy of
          Babylon is any indication, he can be
          confident that he's leaving the empire
          in capable hands.

                    XERXES
          Thank you, Ustanu.

                    USTANU
          You don't know how much it honored
          me to be appointed satrap. Do you
          miss the city?

                    XERXES
          Often. I do plan on visiting when time
          allows.

A serving girl approaches the men and they exchange their old cups for new ones. Ustanu watches her admiringly as she goes.

                    ZOPYRUS
          How is the princess? I heard she wasn't
          feeling well this evening.

Xerxes' expression falls.

                    XERXES
          I sent an attendant to check on her not
          too long ago.

Zopyrus conversationally turns toward Ustanu.

> ZOPYRUS
> She's an incredible beauty.

The prince's attentions are drawn to the portico. One of its curtain panels picks up on the breeze, partly revealing the curvy figure of a woman. Xerxes is taken by the sight. He's entranced by her. His eyes silently plead to see her face.

> XERXES
> Breath-taking.

> ZOPYRUS
> Delicate.

> XERXES
> But strong-willed.

> ZOPYRUS
> She has the most charming laugh.

> XERXES
> And the softest whisper.

> ZOPYRUS
> Oh, and her eyes—

> XERXES
> You don't dare let your stare linger on them.

The breeze obliges Xerxes' wish and the curtain curls back further to reveal SURAZ, a regal beauty in her early thirties. Standing with her are two others: her fourteen year old daughter, ARTAYNTA, and her husband, Masistes.

> XERXES
> Excuse me, gentlemen.

Abruptly, he leaves Zopyrus and Ustanu, and heads for the portico. Guests hastily get out of his way. He reaches the curtain, knowing she's on the other side, and steels himself before pushing it back.

                    XERXES
                   (smiling)
              Masistes!

                    MASISTES
              At your service, Prince Xerxes.

The friends clasp wrists.

                    XERXES
                  (to the girls)
              Evening.

Shy and awe-struck, Artaynta quickly bows. Her nervousness goes unnoticed, though.

Xerxes' eyes are now locked upon Suraz. She lowers her head in reverence, peering up at him from beneath her lashes. There is an element of intrigue between the two, but one so subtle that it is obvious—only—to them.

                    MASISTES
              So, from where am I keeping you?

Severing the link, Xerxes looks to Masistes.

                    XERXES
              What?

                    MASISTES
              Surely you didn't come over here just
              to usher me in.

                    XERXES
              Oh. No. No, I thought I might steal a
              moment to myself.

The noble thumbs backwards, silently saying, 'Don't let me stop you,' but Xerxes shakes his head and briefly glances at Suraz.

                    XERXES
              In a little while.

By the look on her face, she knows exactly what that means.

Masistes, clueless, turns to his wife and daughter and points across the courtyard to the women's banquet hall.

> MASISTES
> Suraz, you ought to hurry. I will see
> you and Artaynta later.

> SURAZ
> (nods; bows before Xerxes)
> Prince.

Suraz squeezes Artaynta's hand, cueing her once more.

> ARTAYNTA
> (bows)
> Prince.

Xerxes answers with a slight tip of the head and, feigning indifference as they go, motions for Masistes to step in from the portico.

Walking together through the hall, Masistes exchanges brief waves and smiles with guests he knows. Spotting Xerxes' son, he points.

> MASISTES
> I see young Darius. How did his hunt
> go yesterday? They still hadn't returned
> by the time I left last evening.

> XERXES
> It went well.

Xerxes suddenly stops and looks around, trying to decide which direction to go. The encounter with Suraz has left him distracted, but this comes across as anxiousness instead.

> MASISTES
> (curious)
> Are you looking for someone?

For a second, he doesn't know what to say.

       XERXES
    The attendant.
      (a beat)
    I sent one to check on Amestris.

       MASISTES
    Is she alright?

INT. SUSA—AMESTRIS'S CHAMBER—NIGHT

Pulsating candlelight offers minimal illumination, but what we can see is defined by one word: luxurious. Canopying sheets hang from the ceiling above a low rise bed. Pillows litter the floor. Urns sit atop pedestals.

Before the open balcony, AMESTRIS is stretched atop a jewel bedecked lounge. Covered only up to her waist, she lies on her stomach, head turned and nestled upon folded arms, her bare skin glistening beneath the moonlight as attendants apply body oils and brush her hair.

We hear the distant sounds of the banquet, a charming INSTRUMENTAL, the CHATTER of guests, then KNOCKING just beyond the room's door.

       AMESTRIS
    Enter.

The door opens. Xerxes' attendant steps into the room and bows.

       ATTENDANT 1
    Princess.

Amestris doesn't bother to move.

       AMESTRIS
    Yes?

       ATTENDANT 1
    Prince Xerxes has sent me—

AMESTRIS
Oh? For what reason?

ATTENDANT 1
To inquire whether or not you're
feeling well enough attend the dinner.

AMESTRIS
(mock apologetic)
I already asked for my supper to be
brought to my room.

ATTENDANT 1
Well, you—

AMESTRIS
Besides, how would it look on my part if
I only appeared when the food was served?

ATTENDANT 1
I don't—

AMESTRIS
So, no. You may tell him I will not be
attending.

ATTENDANT 1
Is there anything else you would like
me to relay?

AMESTRIS
No. That's all.

The attendant heads for the door.

AMESTRIS
On second thought. Wait.

Amestris suddenly draws herself up on her elbows. Moonlight traces her profile.

ATTENDANT 1
(stopping)
Yes?

Turning her head slightly, we see only a fraction of Amestris's face, from the corner of her mouth to the arch of her brow. Long, thick, black lashes flutter up, revealing an eye the color of jealousy—green.

AMESTRIS
There is something else. Tell my husband that I appreciate his concern.

INT. SUSA—BANQUET HALL—NIGHT

The reception proceeds. Now we see Haman, clearly drunk, speaking with a small group of noblemen.

NOBLEMAN 1
As long as we're going to Athens, we might as well expand the expedition and take Greece as a whole. If they were wise they wouldn't resist, either. Surely, they must know that joining us would benefit them.

HAMAN
Yes, but would they benefit Persia? Don't misunderstand me. I will always back the king. If he decided to bring Greece into the fold, then my support would be with him. What I'm trying to say, though, and let us be honest, is that there are some already encompassed by Persia's borders who take the kindness bestowed them for granted.

NOBLEMAN 1
For example . . . ?

HAMAN
Take for instance the Jews. Cyrus freed them from captivity a long time ago, let them return to Jerusalem, granted them sanction to rebuild their lost temple. So, why is it that, half a century later, there is still such a multitude of them here? What's keeping them from going back?

NOBLEMAN 2
It's not so simple. During the exile, many Jews chose to take root where they were planted. They started families—

HAMAN
Oh, I know. Many intermarried, too.

NOBLEMAN 2
They established communities, businesses—

HAMAN
And they could do the same in their former territory. We have already been quite generous. That province enjoys a great amount of autonomy in their internal affairs.

NOBLEMAN 2
As well as a lot of internal conflict. Much had changed over the years they'd been gone. Neighboring tribes had resettled or, in some instances, had been—made—to resettle in the region. There was quite a bit of hostility between these groups and the Jews that returned, and there continues to be today.

HAMAN
And the Jews are completely faultless in that?

NOBLEMAN 2
I never stated that they were.
Anyway, the empire is comprised of many different nations and people.
So, I fail to understand why you are so particularly disdainful of the Jews.

Haman is getting increasingly flustered. He turns to Nobleman 1, hoping he might understand.

HAMAN
What do you think?

NOBLEMAN 1
I think . . . Well, it's complicated. There is a lot of contention over the matter. I can't honestly tell you I know enough about the situation myself to feel I have the right to speak on it one way or the other. I mean, ideally, everyone would be at peace with their neighbors, new and old alike—

HAMAN
A scenario, if you will. The Jewish population here in Susa is considerable. What happens when they outnumber the Persians? Do we rename the city Jerusalem? Or do they take control and do it themselves?

NOBLEMAN 2
What?

                    HAMAN
Don't think it's impossible. I, myself,
am descended from the Amalekite
king, Agag. I know. I know what
they're capable of. Oh, if only I had the
power—

                    MASISTES (O.S.)
But, you don't.

Masistes suddenly grabs Haman by the shoulders and peeks over one, smiling at the noblemen.

                    MASISTES
Excuse us.

He pulls Haman a few steps away, his smile melting into a frown.

                    MASISTES
To think you have ten sons just like
you—

                    HAMAN
There are many, many others who
share my opinion.

                    MASISTES
Unfortunately, I know, but you should
remember that the king and Xerxes—
who you claim to be your friend—are
not among them.

Xerxes walks up, cup in hand. They drop their confrontational posturing and acknowledge him. The two noblemen also gather round.

                    NOBLEMAN 1
Prince Xerxes.

NOBLEMAN 2
Prince.

XERXES
So, are you enjoying yourselves?

NOBLEMAN 1
Yes, yes. Thank you so much for the invitation.

NOBLEMAN 2
You are a most gracious host.

MASISTES
Indeed.

In a gesture of thanks, Xerxes tips his drink.

XERXES
How are you holding up, Haman?

HAMAN
Well—

XERXES
(interrupting)
Just a moment.

Attendant 1 weaves through surrounding guests and, once before Xerxes, leans in to whisper.

ATTENDANT 1
She's not coming.

XERXES
I see. Is that all she had to say?

                    ATTENDANT 1
              No. She also wanted me to relay her
              appreciation for your concern.

Expending a rueful breath, Xerxes bobs his head. He expects this kind of thing from her, but is nonetheless upset and cannot for much longer mask that behind a cheery façade. He holds the smile for just a second longer as he turns to the group.

                    XERXES
              Enjoy the reception and I will see you
              all at dinner.

He empties his cup, only to trade it with a passing servant carrying a tray of more drinks, and pushes past the guests without a second look.

EXT. SUSA—COURTYARD—NIGHT

The courtyard is, as previously established, bordered on its long sides by the opposing banquet halls. The short sides, however, are different from one another. On one end is a running portico, connecting the two buildings, accessible from the courtyard by two brick ramps. On the other is a flight of stairs which leads to a balconied terrace. A wall stretches behind it, gated at the center and guarded by two gigantic, black, marble bulls.

Above the wall's parapet, one can just barely make out the gilded rooftops of the left, central and right wings of the king's palace. (It is between this wall and the palace that the elaborate garden, seen the day before, stretches.)

Though the courtyard's perimeter is lined with torches, Xerxes is concealed in a dark niche, staring up at his wife's quarters across the way. Sneering, he takes a drink, paying no mind to those who drunkenly pass by.

It isn't until the sound of FOOTFALL grows near behind him that he turns.

Suraz is unnerved by the glare of his eyes and backs away as if reconsidering her attempt to speak with him. He raises his drink, halting her retreat.

> XERXES
> Stay. Toast my wife with me.

> SURAZ
> I don't know how I convinced myself
> that seeking you out wasn't wrong.

She turns to leave. Xerxes' sarcastic expression wanes as he drops his arm and reaches for her. Letting out a shaky breath, she stops and stiffens under his touch.

> XERXES
> I have missed you. I—

He lets her go and recomposes himself.

> XERXES
> I wasn't expecting to see you tonight.

> SURAZ
> I hadn't planned to come, but Masistes
> thought one of the prince's grand feasts
> would cheer me.

> XERXES
> Masistes mentioned your mood has
> been low as of late . . . over leaving
> Susa.

> SURAZ
> He says, once we reach Bactria—

> XERXES
> But, it's deeper than that, isn't it . . .
> the reason behind such a wistful stare?
> (MORE)

XERXES(cont'd)
(off silence)
Isn't it?

SURAZ
Yes. But what you perceive to be
wistful, is worry . . . doubt.

XERXES
Of what?

SURAZ
That no matter the distance, I shall
never be—

Suraz stops short, reaches into her robes, and pulls out a folded letter. She hands it to him and he notes its seal has not been broken.

SURAZ
I burned the others. Your—

Xerxes moves to speak, but she keeps on going.

SURAZ
(continuing)
—your attentions must stop. You must
let go.

XERXES
'Must' I?

They both freeze as a COUPLE walks by. He surreptitiously eyes them until they disappear.

A thoughtful pause.

SURAZ
Xerxes?

XERXES
When Masistes was here yesterday, we
were discussing all sorts of things and,
at some point, Bactria came up. He talked
about how excited he is to go, how he has
so many ideas for the people there.

SURAZ
He's a good man.

XERXES
Yes, he is. He is my best friend . . . and
he's determined to see his plans come
to be. That kind of tenacity, I told
him, is the reason he's being sent there.

A pained look comes across his face. He turns away.

XERXES
Then, I joked that it was also because I
was tired of seeing his face . . . and we
had a good laugh . . . and it's good that
he's going soon, before he sees through
me and realizes that it's partly true.
Don't you realize—

Suddenly, he whips around and points at her accusingly.

XERXES
—you, Suraz, have forced me to let my
best friend go. I can barely stand to look
at him without thinking about you.

The anger ebbs and he grazes the side of her face with the backs of his fingers. Suraz leans into his touch.

XERXES
I found it easier to forget the lines of
your face while I was in Babylon, but—

She cups his hand and reluctantly pulls it away.

> SURAZ
> Then you came back.

Xerxes holds the letter up.

> XERXES
> When you decided to bring this with you tonight, were you so sure you'd have a chance to return it to me?

> SURAZ
> No, but I hoped for one.

> XERXES
> What if none came?

> SURAZ
> Then, I suppose I would have kept it. Maybe even read it one day . . . even though I know it's not meant for me. None of your letters are.

> XERXES
> Every word has been sincere.

> SURAZ
> I don't doubt that.

Xerxes stuffs the letter in his robe.

> XERXES
> So, is this to be it?

> SURAZ
> It has to be.

He takes her face in his hands and leans in for a kiss. She turns her head.

XERXES
You won't even kiss me goodbye?

SURAZ
It can't be done twice.

She draws away.

SURAZ
I have to return to the reception before
my daughter tires of her new friends
and wonders where I went.

XERXES
You should hurry. They're about to set
up for the feast.

SURAZ
And you have a speech to make.
    (a beat)
She's always been your great love.
Persia. Your world begins and ends
with her. Things are as they should be
and, one day, you will be such a great
king, as Cyrus was, as your father is.

Swallowing back the lump in her throat, she purses her lips and bobs her head.

SURAZ
Farewell, Xerxes.

Suraz waits for him to echo her words, but he says nothing and that is more unbearable to her than anything. She backs away, turns and leaves.

XERXES
(whispering)
Farewell.

He himself disappears as, one by one, the banquet hall curtains of both the men's and women's buildings are drawn back by attendants. It is time for the show to begin.

EXT. SUSA—COURTYARD—NIGHT—DINNER DANCE

With the curtains now left open, the guests begin to line up just outside their respective buildings. Men and women alike set their sights between the brick ramps of the courtyard where a MUSICAL ENSEMBLE, much larger than the one which played before, is now set up. Nearly every instrument is doubled, from PERCUSSIONS to STRINGS.

It is the DRUMMERS who begin the song with a resonant, bass driven beat. They are soon joined by the rest as . . .

PORTERS, carrying short-legged tables atop their heads, walk down the ramps. To the step of the music, they arrange the tables before the guests, leaving uniformly once empty handed.

A new song is now initiated by a lone, masterful TAR PLAYER. Each draw of the string brings forth another hypnotic note. The drummers soon join in, their rhythm subtle and tribal and the entire audience stands mesmerized, watching . . .

DANCERS cocooned in an assortment of richly colored fabrics file down the ramps. Like butterflies, the women slowly emerge. They twist, turn and spin, sending fabric awhirl before draping their "veils" on the tables and leaving.

The guests, especially the men, APPLAUD wildly.

The tempo of the music steadily rises. The porters return carrying both pillows and unlit candles. The latter are placed atop the tables, the former dropped alongside for seating.

The porters now direct the guests, beginning with the men, to take a seat. They wind through the tables and, after each has found a place, their women come to join them.

Now, all is set for the finale. Another set of dancers enter the courtyard. They are just as alluring and voluptuous as those before them, but it is not fabric that they spin and twirl. These women dance with lit torches, wheeling around the tables and lighting candles, their bodies gleaning the fire's glow, the pace building and building till . . .

The music stops with a brilliant crescendo. The dancers drop on bended knee, lining the perimeter, holding their torches high above their bowed heads.

APPLAUSE thunders again.

OFF SCREEN we hear a loud WHOOSH.

The guests look up.

ATOP THE TERRACE

Between two newly ignited fire-baskets, the marble bulls looming above him, is Xerxes. Behind the crowned prince is his son, Darius, who smiles slyly.

The young boy feels powerful standing where he is. The people, however, are focused on his father.

Masistes, Suraz, Haman, Zopyrus, Ustanu—the whole audience waits for him to speak.

> XERXES
> People of Persia, whether from Fars, Media, Assyria, Babylon or beyond, east or west, north or south, you honor me and the royal house with your presence tonight. You are our friends. You are our family. You are—one— with us. We beat with one heart, stand as one body and, soon, we will pick up our sword and become a soldier . . . a soldier in the service of the Great King.

> DARIUS THE GREAT (V.O.)
> A man.

Two scenes begin to intersperse . . .

EXT. PARSA—TACHARA—THRONE ROOM—NIGHT

Torches flicker, casting light on the grandiose surroundings. Three rows of four pillars support the roof. Meticulously carved reliefs grace the walls.

The king's WAR COUNCIL surrounds an enormous table littered with dozens of maps. In attendance: the exiled Spartan king, DEMARATUS; MASISTIUS, commander of the cavalry; HYDARNES, commander of the elite "Immortals"; Zopyrus's son, MEGABYZUS.

Also present is Artabanus and his sons, TRITANTAECHMENES (TRITAN) and TIGRANES. The latter is in his late twenties and, if not for Xerxes, would probably be considered the most handsome man in Persia.

We see ACHAEMENES, ARIABIGNES, ARTABAZUS, GERGIS, SMERDOMENES, and, finally, MARDONIUS, who, in his late thirties, is the romanticized ideal of a rugged, battlescarred general.

> XERXES (V.O.)
> A king whose name is spoken across
> the empire with reverence.

Darius the Great, standing before his throne, raises a drink. He begins to descend the steps which lead to its platform and the most prestigious bas-relief is revealed. It depicts the king battling a ferocious lion-headed beast.

> DARIUS THE GREAT
> I am a man.

CUT TO COURTYARD—ON XERXES, GUESTS

> XERXES
> A leader who has transcended the legends of a great many nations and become one himself.

CUT TO THRONE ROOM—ON DARIUS THE GREAT, WAR COUNCIL

> DARIUS THE GREAT
> I am mortal, same as you.

CUT TO COURTYARD—ON XERXES

> XERXES
> The day fast approaches that he will be proved to be even more.
> (a beat)
> There are those who have foolishly chosen to be his enemy.

CUT TO THRONE ROOM—ON DARIUS THE GREAT

> DARIUS THE GREAT
> And I say, from no enemy let me fear. Not Egypt—

CUT TO COURTYARD—ON XERXES

> XERXES
> —whose rebels will regret that they dared made move against him.

CUT TO THRONE ROOM—ON DARIUS THE GREAT, WAR COUNCIL

DARIUS THE GREAT
Nor Athens, whose people will—

CUT TO COURTYARD—ON XERXES, GUESTS

XERXES
—bend their knees as they set their sights on—

CUT TO THRONE ROOM—ON WAR COUNCIL

DARIUS THE GREAT (O.S.)
—an army—

CUT TO COURTYARD—ON XERXES

XERXES
A conqueror, the likes of which—

CUT TO THRONE ROOM—ON WAR COUNCIL

DARIUS THE GREAT (O.S.)
—they have never seen—

CUT TO COURTYARD—ON XERXES, GUESTS

XERXES
—that they thought only existed in myth.

XERXES	DARIUS THE GREAT (V.O.)
The empire stands today as the greatest the world has ever known.	The empire stands today as the greatest the world has ever known.

> XERXES
> She is an empire of many—Many nations, customs and tongues. But, in the hearts of all those who love her—from the Aegean in the west—

CUT TO THRONE ROOM—ON DARIUS THE GREAT, WAR COUNCIL

> DARIUS THE GREAT
> To the Indus in the east.

| DARIUS THE GREAT | XERXES (V.O.) |
| We are one. | We are one. |

> DARIUS THE GREAT
> One kingdom.

CUT TO COURTYARD—ON GUESTS

> XERXES (O.S.)
> One people.

CUT TO THRONE ROOM—ON DARIUS THE GREAT

> DARIUS THE GREAT
> One body.

CUT TO COURTYARD—ON XERXES, GUESTS

> XERXES
> And we will be that soldier who would risk all—

CUT TO THRONE ROOM—ON DARIUS THE GREAT, WAR COUNCIL

                DARIUS THE GREAT
          For the honor of Persia!

CUT TO COURTYARD—ON XERXES, GUESTS

                    XERXES
              For the king!

CUT TO THRONE ROOM—ON DARIUS THE GREAT

King Darius, who now stands before the council, winces in pain. He sets his cup down atop the scattered maps, steadies himself against the table and clutches his chest.

                  XERXES (V.O.)
            To Darius!!!

ON WAR COUNCIL

The men get up from their seats, concerned.

CUT TO COURTYARD—ON GUESTS

The guests all rise from their places. Those with drinks raise them.

                    GUESTS
            To King Darius!!!

CUT TO THRONE ROOM—ON DARIUS THE GREAT, WAR COUNCIL

The king buckles over the table, knocking over his cup. The wine spills across two crisscrossed maps. We can only see a small part of the bottom map, but enough to know it is one of Egypt. The other, completely ruined, is of Athens.

CUT TO:

XERXES' NIGHTMARE

We see a battlefield. Half of it is a barren plain. Undulating, transparent waves of heat roll across it. The other side is lush and green. A gentle wind sifts through the grass. Each side is empty, but we hear the sound of TWO ARMIES AT MARCH coming from both. Louder and louder the sound becomes, but just when we think the soldiers are about to march into sight, the sun is eclipsed. All goes dark.

CUT TO:

INT. SUSA—XERXES' CHAMBER—AFTERNOON

Xerxes awakens. Sunlight spills across his eyes, causing his pupils to sharpen. He is still in his clothes from the night before. Groggily, he gets up.

LATER...

We now see the room. It is multi-columned and bordered top to bottom in gold. On the walls are murals, but, unlike those in the banquet hall, these are ornamented with lapis-lazuli, carnelian, sapphires, pearls and rubies. The bed is nestled in its own nook, high upon a tiered platform. The linens are still a mess and the clothes Xerxes had worn to bed are strewn atop it, too.

Changed, he stands on the border of the inner chamber and its balcony, beside a desk where an opened, simple, metal box sits.

A breeze causes sheets of sheer fabric to billow around him as he intently regards Suraz's, sealed letter. He is deep in thought, but this reverie is interrupted by a KNOCK at the room's double doors.

Xerxes lifts a false bottom within the box, drops the letter into it, and clasps the top shut.

> **XERXES**
> Enter.

We hear soft FOOTSTEPS against the floor, but they suddenly stop a few paces away. Perplexed, he turns around.

> **XERXES**
> My ever-loving wife.

Amestris steps out from the shadows and stops between two pillars.

Though a few years older than her husband, she is as exquisite as Zopyrus had boasted. Like Suraz, her features are undeniably Persian. She exudes a different type of beauty, though. If Suraz were a swan, Amestris would be a hawk. One bird is quiet and graceful, the other cunning and fierce, but both are beautiful.

Now, however, she is more like a peacock, adorned with jewels from head to foot. They are a total contrast to her simple, thin robe, but they do go well with the smirk that draws across her lips as she takes in the sight of Xerxes' weary visage.

> **AMESTRIS**
> You're finally awake. I was beginning to think you'd sleep the whole day away.

> **XERXES**
> Like you have for the past two?

> **AMESTRIS**
> I didn't think you'd care.

He does not dignify this with an answer. Instead, he glares at her, silently conveying what she already knows.

> AMESTRIS
> I heard the banquet was a complete success. They say your speech was so compelling. Perhaps you'll recite it for me?

> XERXES
> I wanted you there.

> AMESTRIS
> I'm here now.

> XERXES
> Yes, you are. The question is, why?

Amestris saunters toward her husband. With each step she makes, her robe drops further down a shoulder.

> AMESTRIS
> Why what?

She stops a mere foot away.

> XERXES
> Why I let you get away with all you do.

> AMESTRIS
> Maybe you enjoy the challenge?

> XERXES
> Oh, really? What makes you think that?

> AMESTRIS
> I know you didn't send that attendant to inquire about my well-being last night because you were genuinely concerned.

> XERXES
> And I know there was nothing
> genuinely wrong with you, either.

> AMESTRIS
> Then why not order me to come?

> XERXES
> And let you openly defy me?

> AMESTRIS
> Would you still keep me if I did?

Not pleased by her challenging words, he closes the gap between them. She backs up against a pillar, both wary and excited by the look in his eyes. They passionately kiss as hands urgently attempt to pull clothes away.

Theirs is a fire stoked by mutual animosity, but their imminent hate sex is interrupted by the incessant knocking of a GUARD.

> GUARD (O.S.)
> Prince Xerxes! Prince!

Xerxes draws away from his wife, pulling her robe up around her shoulders.

> XERXES
> Enter.

He enters and bows.

> GUARD
> An urgent message has just arrived.

> XERXES
> What is it?

It is only now, as he looks up, that the guard realizes he has interrupted something, but there is no time to apologize.

                    GUARD
            It's King Darius. You have to leave for
            Parsa right away.

EXT. PARSA—PROCESSIONAL WAY—DAY

Members of the Royal Guard race down the main road of the city. CITIZENS of all social classes, from nobles to servants, halt their business affairs. Other residents curiously peer out their windows. This is a sight they do not see every day.

Xerxes rides at the front of the entourage. He is blind to everything except the citadel ahead. Even at the foot of it, he does not stop. Instead, the maddening pace is kept as the group ascends the monumental staircase to the terrace above.

INT. PARSA—TACHARA—OUTSIDE THE THRONE ROOM—DAY

With crossed arms and downcast eyes, Masistius, Achaemenes, Tigranes, Artabazus and Hydarnes wait. The latter looks up and quickly cues the rest to stand at attention. Xerxes approaches, flanked by guards. He marches with purposeful determination and does not even spare a fleeting glance as he dismisses his men, pushes the double doors open and enters the throne room.

INT. PARSA—TACHARA—THRONE ROOM—CONTINUING

Everything is in slow motion. Xerxes weaves through the pillars, the look on his face growing increasingly incredulous. Atop the platform, where the king's throne should be, is a veiled bed. Below, immersed in deep conversation, are Artabanus and Mardonius. The former stops mid-sentence as he sees Xerxes and promptly taps Mardonius on the shoulder, suggesting they leave.

The two depart, just as Xerxes begins to ascend the stairs. With each step, more and more of the bas-relief of the "Great King" comes into sight. It is a symbol of might, of absolute authority, and is such a contrast to the old man resting in the bed situated before it.

Xerxes grabs hold of one of the curtains, takes a breath, and sweeps it back. The king notices him right away and extends a shaky hand.

>   DARIUS THE GREAT
>   My son.
>
>   XERXES
>   (forcing a smile, but in disbelief)
> Father.

Taking his father's hand, he sits beside the bed next to a night-stand and tries to look at anything but him. Darius tightens his grip.

>   DARIUS THE GREAT
>   Xerxes, I am right here.
>   (off Xerxes' look)
>   Right here.
>
>   XERXES
>   (reluctantly nodding)
> I left as soon as word came.
>
>   DARIUS THE GREAT
>   Now, here you are and it warms my heart.
>
>   XERXES
> I spoke with your physicians.
>
>   DARIUS THE GREAT
>   They say there is nothing to be done.

Darius lets go of his hand and looks to the ceiling. Xerxes will not accept this. He reaches for his father again and beckons him to look him in the eye.

>   XERXES
>   No. They're wrong. They're all wrong.
>   I told them they were fortunate I didn't
>   take their heads for such a treasonous
>   lie. How dare they forget who you are.
>   How dare they!

DARIUS THE GREAT
And who am I, Xerxes?

XERXES
Who—who are you?

DARIUS THE GREAT
Yes.

XERXES
You are the same king I spoke of as I stood before the palace gates the night . . .

He trails off, unable to verbalize what happened.

XERXES
Who are you? You are the mighty hand of Persia. A visionary who has expanded our borders. A warrior who has defeated enemies that tried to steal our identity, and a guardian to those who came here in search of one.

Xerxes, adamant, points to the relief.

XERXES
THAT is who you are! You are the GREAT KING. You are Darius—a legend among men!! Not this . . . not—

DARIUS THE GREAT
Not this old man who lies before you?

XERXES
No, that's not what I—

DARIUS THE GREAT
It's alright. It's alright. I have been many things in my life, but no matter
(MORE)

> DARIUS THE GREAT(cont'd)
> what title may be ascribed to my name,
> it cannot obscure the fact that . . . Oh,
> Xerxes, a legend is nothing more than a
> story born beneath the moon—a tale
> that withers in the light of reality.

> XERXES
> Then it has yet to dawn for me. I will
> never accept you as anything less than
> the king whose example I try so hard
> to emulate . . . whose legacy I can only
> hope to be worthy of. A thousand
> years from now, following your name
> will be a list of so many
> accomplishments—

Darius cups Xerxes' face. The king's ring glints against his skin.

> DARIUS THE GREAT
> And here is my finest.

> XERXES
> There are yet so many more to come.
> You can't die. What of all your plans?
> What of Egypt and—

> DARIUS THE GREAT
> Athens? I still intend to see them through.

> XERXES
> You do?

> DARIUS THE GREAT
> Just because a man recognizes and
> accepts he is mortal does not mean he
> ceases to reach for the stars.
>   (a beat)
> There is a reason I am here, instead of
>   (MORE)

DARIUS THE GREAT (cont'd)
tucked away in my private quarters, and it
is not so associates may come and pay
their final respects. Look there—on the
stand.

Darius points to a neatly piled stack of documents. Xerxes turns the top one over. It is a map of Greece.

XERXES
What about your physicians?

DARIUS THE GREAT
As you so emphatically stated—they're
wrong. I am not yet finished.

Xerxes sets the map down, takes his father's hand once more and kisses the signet ring.

INT. PARSA—TACHARA—THRONE ROOM—NEAR DAWN

Xerxes quietly speaks with a CHAMBERLAIN at the bottom of the steps.

XERXES
My wife and son will arrive within the
next few days. We'll be staying on in
Parsa indefinitely.

CHAMBERLAIN
(bows)
All the necessary arrangements will be
seen to right away.

XERXES
Good. Dismissed.

The chamberlain leaves.

Xerxes sits and wearily rubs his eyes. Mardonius approaches.

XERXES
General Mardonius.

MARDONIUS
You've been with him all night?

XERXES
Yes. I fell asleep at his bedside.
Artabanus is with him, now.

MARDONIUS
Are you planning to go back up?

XERXES
Yes, but I intend to have another talk
with his physicians before I do.

MARDONIUS
Seeing you must have strengthened
him. Did you talk long?

XERXES
(nods)
We spoke of many things, and many
people—including yourself.

MARDONIUS
Oh?

XERXES
He thinks very highly of you,
Mardonius, as do I.

Mardonius places a hand atop his own heart and smiles.

XERXES
He says you've spent many sleepless
nights working on the Grecian leg of
the expedition.

MARDONIUS
That is my area of expertise.

XERXES
I'm sure your prior experience there has been an invaluable source to drawn on.

MARDONIUS
Yes, indeed, it has been. We have made quite a few allies throughout the region who not only support a move against Athens, but would even welcome Persia taking the whole nation under its wing.

XERXES
Really?

MARDONIUS
(nodding)
As it is now, Greece is an extremely fractured country, always volleying between talk of truce and talk of war. Many of its people are oppressed by corrupted leaders . . . many simply want some semblance of peace amongst the city-states. They want unity.

XERXES
And you think it is only we who can unify them?

MARDONIUS
I not only think it, I know it is. We would stand to gain much from such a mission as well.

Xerxes finds this interesting, but his response is interrupted by a loud CLATTER. He jumps to his feet.

                    DARIUS THE GREAT (O.S.)
            Artabanus . . . get . . . help.

Artabanus comes flying down the stairs.

                         ARTABANUS
                   Xerxes, go! Go to him!

With Mardonius following a few paces behind, Xerxes bounds up the steps and throws back the curtains. The floor by the bed is slick with water from an overturned basin. It was apparently knocked over by Darius. He writhes on the bed, clutching his chest, WHEEZING.

                       DARIUS THE GREAT
                        Xer—Xerxes.

Xerxes rushes to his father and gently takes hold of his shoulders in an attempt to stop him from thrashing. Darius roughly grabs hold of Xerxes' robes with one hand and, with the other, reaches for the documents on the night-stand. Many of them slip to the floor beneath his touch, but he manages to retrieve the one he wanted—the map of Greece.

Unable to control his hand from clenching, it crumples within his grasp, but he continues to pull Xerxes closer, demanding he look at it.

                       DARIUS THE GREAT
                Xerx—Xerxes . . . re-remember . . .

                          XERXES
                    Father?! What? What!?

Mardonius watches as Xerxes helplessly searches his father's face. Darius continues to shake, trying desperately to issue his last words and, finally, on his last breath, he does.

                       DARIUS THE GREAT
               Remember . . . the . . . Athenians.

Now, everything grinds to slow motion and muffled sound.

BELOW, we see Artabanus running with a trio of PHYSICIANS.

ATOP THE PLATFORM, Xerxes stands in a state of suspended shock. He is gripped by the sight of his lifeless father, while looming in the background is the timeless relief depicting the Great King.

We hear a LAMENTING melody rise . . .

DISSOLVE TO:

EXT. PARSA—NAQSH-E-ROSTAM—NIGHT

Isolated, Xerxes sullenly stands before the foot of the colossal mountain, staring up at a magnificent tomb cut into its face. Standing in the periphery is his son, Darius, Amestris, the generals, and guards.

A multitude of MOURNERS are also gathered, people of all social classes. The surrounding plain looks as though it could be the night sky, dotted by torch and candle light.

We see Masistes and Suraz amongst the crowd. The former approaches Xerxes and places a hand on his shoulder.

XERXES
(despondent)
Masistes. When did you arrive in Parsa?

MASISTES
Last night. I'm sorry I wasn't here when . . . Do you want me to stay—

XERXES
No.

Xerxes briefly turns and glances at Suraz. She looks at him empathetically.

XERXES
You have to continue on to Bactria and
you mustn't delay. Especially now, when
the council will most require your help.

MASISTES
Yes. Yes, you're right. Come morning,
we'll be on our way.

XERXES
(clasps Masistes' hand)
I wish you a safe journey, my friend.

MASISTES
Be strong.

XERXES
I am going to be whatever Persia needs
me to be.

He half-heartedly pats Masistes on the back and walks a few feet away. The nobleman lowers his head and returns to his wife.

BACK ON XERXES

Mardonius and Artabanus flank him.

MARDONIUS
Your father's memory shall carry on
through the centuries.

XERXES
Forevermore.

ARTABANUS
My brother did much for Persia. It saddens
me to say that there is no time to mourn him.

Xerxes slowly turns to face his uncle.

                    XERXES
          The rebellion in Egypt . . .

                  ARTABANUS
          It must be put down.

                  MARDONIUS
          Yes, Artabanus is right. We must shed
          our sorrow and raise our swords.

                  ARTABANUS
          The matter must be resolved, but by a
          recognized king. After your coronation—

                    XERXES
          —we will prepare for attack.

EXT. PARSA—DAY

CITIZENS from every corner of the Persian Empire are gathered at Parsa to witness the coronation of their new king. Lotus flowers, a symbol of royalty, are strewn about. Large frankincense burners emit curling trails of smoke. Musicians play decadent ARRANGEMENTS. Women cuff their mouths and cry out in ULULATION.

The crowd below is completely in awe as Xerxes stands atop the platform of the fortress's grand staircase. Dressed in common linen, he drinks sour milk from an unadorned cup—a custom which shows the people that their new king is a man conscious of Persia's humble beginnings.

Completing the ceremony, he raises the cup above his head.

                    XERXES
          I am Xerxes, the great king, king of
          kings, king of lands containing many
          men, king in this great earth far and
          wide—so shall it be written!

A thunderous ROAR of approval follows.

Amestris watches, greatly pleased and clutching the shoulders of young Darius.

>AMESTRIS
>One day, it will be you who sits upon
>the throne.

The boy is speechless.

Standing close are members of the king's COURT, including: CARSHENA, SHETHAR, ADMATHA, TARSHISH, MARENA, and MEMUCAN.

They are all older gentlemen and recognized as "wise men".

Haman, Artabanus and Mardonius are also near. To the latter two, this ceremony is merely a prelude to war. They back away from Haman to talk.

>MARDONIUS
>He looks ready to take on the title.

>ARTABANUS
>Appearances are not always reliable.

>MARDONIUS
>He is the son of Darius the Great and
>born to a daughter of Cyrus. That
>makes him the prodigy of two of the
>most powerful men to have ever
>ascended a throne and as such, you
>must concede it possible that he has it
>in him to be greater than both.

>ARTABANUS
>We shall see.

Both men return their attention to the newly appointed king as he stands tall above the enamored crowd. They can only hope the empire will stand as strong.

EXT. EGYPT—NIGHT

We see nothing but rolling sand dunes.

>   MARDONIUS (V.O.)
>   They believed the key to power slipped
>   from Darius's grasp the day he passed
>   from this world. They thought it left
>   for the taking, that there was no one
>   who could stand in their way . . . not
>   even his son.

An assortment of tracks are sunk deep in the sand. The breadth of them is impressive.

>   MARDONIUS (V.O.)
>   They thought him a distant figure, so
>   far away in body that he was only a
>   name—a newly ascended, untried
>   name. Let them try to forget it now.

Past the tops of the dunes, we see the EGYPTIAN CITY of BUTO sprawled along a green plain, surrounded by palms. It has just gone down in a last stand against the Persians.

The surviving EGYPTIAN REBELS acquiesce before their reasserted leader—Xerxes.

The king clutches a sword. On horseback, searching the sky, he YELLS in triumph. It is a sound of joy, of release. Thousands of INFANTRY, dressed in elaborate tunics and shielded by plates of gold, celebrate before the king. Among the soldiers are Achaemenes, Artabazus, Masistius and Hydarnes.

A reluctant storm looms above. The sky is scorched by heat lightning. Fires burn bright in the background.

>   MARDONIUS (V.O.)
>   He reclaimed Egypt and made a wise
>   decision in leaving Achaemenes there to
>   mind that key.
>   (MORE)

                    MARDONIUS (V.O.)(cont'd)
               (a beat)
          And what about what happened in
          Babylon with its would-be ruler, Bel-
          Shimmani, and his supporters? They,
          too, were opportunists. They, too,
          underestimated Darius's son. They
          didn't think he could affirm control of
          Persia, put down the insurgents in
          Egypt and face a a takeover in Babylon,
          too. I don't know which crime Xerxes
          punished them more for . . .

                                                  CUT TO:

INT. BABYLON—BEDROOM—NIGHT

Candles melted down to the barest of nubs flicker just long enough for us to survey the room. It is in complete disarray. A CRYING WOMAN kneels beside the bed. A rigid hand dangles over it. Looking over the body, we see the weapon, a dagger, lodged just below the heart. Panning to an upturned face, the man is revealed to be Zopyrus.

                    MARDONIUS (V.O.)
          The murder of Zopyrus—

                                                  CUT TO:

EXT. BABYLON—NIGHT

PERSIAN TROOPS race through the ISHTAR GATES, down BABYLON'S PROCESSIONAL WAY. We see the tiered ZIGGURAT, TOWER OF BABEL, and the old PALACE OF NEBUCHADNEZZAR in the background.

                    MARDONIUS (V.O)
               (continuing)
          Ustanu's capture, or Bel-Shimmani
          crowning himself as Babylon's king.

                                                  CUT TO:

INT. BABYLON—PALACE—THRONE ROOM—NIGHT

Ustanu is tied up in a corner. Lazily propped atop the throne, BEL-SHIMMANI informally converses with his SUPPORTERS. Everyone looks so confident, so indestructible, but, as General Megabyzus and his men smash through the doors, their expressions are wiped clean off their faces.

> MARDONIUS (V.O.)
> Whichever it was, they certainly did pay.

Glaring at Shimmani, Megabyzus pulls out his sword. The composition of the shot insinuates the would-be king is going to lose his head.

CUT TO:

EXT. SUSA—CITADEL—DAY

483 B.C.

As Mardonius's speech continues, we see an overview of the citadel and wind closer to the practice field. Onlookers are gathered around its walls.

> MARDONIUS (V.O.)
> The name "Xerxes" no longer evokes question. It commands and demands obedient respect. So, have you waited long enough? Don't you see? He has proved his might to the empire and he could prove it to the rest of the world, too. There is nothing to keep Xerxes from avenging his father—as Megabyzus did for Zopyrus.

CUT TO:

INT. SUSA—PRACTICE FIELD—DAY

Box seats have been erected on one of the far ends of the practice field. They brim with members of the royal court, nobles and generals.

The center box holds Xerxes. In his company are Demaratus, THESSALIAN ENVOYS, ATHENIAN EXILES, and ONOMACRITUS, an oracle monger, also from Athens.

Detached from the celebratory atmosphere, are Mardonius and Artabanus. They look like conspirators, casting glances at the king as he speaks with his guests.

MARDONIUS
(continuing)
He can finish what Darius started and even push those plans further. We could take all of Greece.

ARTABANUS
So you say—so you've been saying. Indeed, you have been doing your best to convince him that it would be in our best interest to smite Athens.

MARDONIUS
It would. It is not fitting that they should be left unpunished. He strikes them and—

ARTABANUS
No one shall ever again entertain the thought of raising a hand against Persia and he, Great King Xerxes, will be celebrated for generations to come. I have heard all of it. I have listened to you tell him how, after such a success, the rest of Greece awaits and, after that, the lands beyond—lands so rich and beautiful that he alone is worthy of having them.
(pointing to Xerxes' Greek guests)
And I have listened to them tell him, too. Our Grecian guests are an interesting lot.

ON DEMARATUS

          ARTABANUS (O.S.)
      (continuing)
  Demaratus . . . well, he has always been
  keen on a move against Athens—or
  Sparta for that matter since being
  deposed as its king.

ON ATHENIAN EXILES

          ARTABANUS (O.S.)
      (continuing)
  Members of a prominent, exiled
  Athenian house, who would be more
  than happy to see the city taken . . . if
  only to further their own goals.

ON ONOMACRITUS

          ARTABANUS (O.S.)
      (continuing)
  Onomacritus, with all his prophetic
  talk of fulfilling destiny.

ON THESSALIAN ENVOYS

          MARDONIUS (O.S.)
  And envoys from Thessaly whose
  kings are practically begging us to
  enter Greece. They have pledged their
  loyalty to Xerxes and to any army he
  may lead.

BACK ON ARTABANUS, MARDONIUS

Artabanus opens his mouth to speak, but is cut short as we hear the STACCATO BEAT of DRUMS.

IN XERXES' BOX—

The king and his guests cease their chat.

ON THE FIELD—

General Masistius rides at the head of a CAVALRY SQUADRON. In time to the drums, they BEAT swords against their shields and cue their horses to step in sync with rhythm.

BACK ON ARTABANUS, MARDONIUS

> ARTABANUS
> My mother once told me a story about a boy whose parents sent him out to gather apples. Like a dutiful son, he followed their orders and picked as many as he could hold and was quite pleased with the lot of them—until he spotted the largest apple he had ever seen perched high atop a branch. So, he dropped all the others and climbed the tree to get it.

> MARDONIUS
> Yes, yes, and later, when he presented the entire bounty, he was shocked to find that his parents were not pleased. When he asked why, they told him that he only managed to fetch one good apple, for all the others were bruised. My mother told me the same tale.

> ARTABANUS
> No, he fell from the tree and broke his arm, making it impossible to bring anything back. Do you not see how problematic such a campaign would be?

> MARDONIUS
> Xerxes is no child. He has proven to be a formidable force, both on the throne and the battlefield.

> ARTABANUS
> Let's talk of my child—you see Tigranes?

> MARDONIUS
> Yes.

ON TIGRANES

He sits with fellow generals, cheerily watching the cavalry's performance.

> ARTABANUS (O.S.)
> When Darius summoned me from my post in Bactria, I had hoped my son would succeed me as satrap. Instead, like his brother, he dedicated himself to the army.

BACK ON ARTABANUS, MARDONIUS

> MARDONIUS
> And you've resented Tritan for that ever since.

Artabanus does not respond and that in itself is answer enough.

> MARDONIUS
> Artabanus, Tigranes—

ARTABANUS
—has served Persia well and made me extremely proud. He would do nearly anything for his father—but—as much as he may love me, he would sacrifice his life for the king. You see, Tigranes is like many of Persia's sons. They will do whatever he asks without question.

MARDONIUS
Well, I should hope so. He is our commander.

ARTABANUS
And he is not omnipotent, yet many think the title means he is. They will follow, right or wrong, because they have sworn allegiance to the empire and can no longer differentiate between it and the man who happens to wear the crown.

MARDONIUS
So, what are you trying to say,
> (sarcastic)

prime minister?

ARTABANUS
That Xerxes is a man who has led them well, thus far. He has solidified our borders, enforced order within them and is now focused on building up our cities, fortifying our capitals—as he should be. This is the right path to follow. This is our empire and I could bear losing my son if he died protecting it, but how my heart would shatter if he were sacrificed on the altar of hegemony.

Mardonius scoffs.

> MARDONIUS
> Well, I have already explained why a campaign is in our best interest.

> ARTABANUS
> And so did my brother, but the threat posed is one conjured. What happened with Athens was years ago. I doubt very much that anyone finds it a weakness on our part that punitive action wasn't taken. However, if we were to stir up Greece . . . it would take an immense army to take and occupy the country. That—that— could make us vulnerable.

> MARDONIUS
> Believe what you will.

ON THE PRACTICE FIELD

While the other riders continue to circle, Masistius halts his mount at center field. Saluting the king, he cues his horse to rear.

ON XERXES, GUESTS

Following Xerxes' lead, the group applauds.

Speaking to the king, the Greeks, being foreign, have an accent.

> DEMARATUS
> He is exceptional.

> XERXES
> Masistius is one of the finest horsemen in all of Persia.

THESSALIAN ENVOY 1
We have many skilled riders in Thessaly, many beautiful horses, but none such as that.

ATHENIAN EXILE 1
(referring to Masistius's horse)
Gorgeous animal.

XERXES
Yes, but stubborn, the general tells me. Not once has he been able to get it to cross the bridge—

ONOMACRITUS
(as if realizing)
It will.

Unaccustomed to being interrupted, Xerxes turns toward Onomacritus. The expression on the man's face is peculiar.

ONOMACRITUS
It will cross . . . as will thousands more behind it and . . . you will be the one who leads them.
(off look)
'Twas fated that a Persian would bridge the Hellespont and march an army into Greece. We always thought it would be Darius . . . but he died and . . . All along . . . it was you. It has always been you.

Xerxes is clearly taken aback, but disturbed, too.

XERXES
My, Onomacritus. Have your oracles told you all this?

ONOMACRITUS
It was prophesied long ago—

                    XERXES
          Really?
              (trying to play it off)
          Then you wouldn't happen to know
          whether it is a son or daughter my wife
          and I are expecting, would you?

Everyone but Onomacritus laughs. Xerxes flashes him another look and we see just a flicker of superstitious unease behind the king's eyes.

EXT. PARSA—HADISH—DAY

Xerxes' palace, now completed, is much larger than the Tachara and Tripylon. Guards posted the entrance indicate that, despite the king's absence, the building is in use.

INT. PARSA—HADISH—XERXES' CHAMBER—DAY

The chamber is similar to the one in Susa but, though larger, it is much more personal. Just inside the doors, a pregnant Amestris secretly monitors the attendants tidying the room. Only when one of the girls picks up a vase to clean, does she make her presence known.

                    AMESTRIS
          Careful with that.

                    ATTENDANT 1
              (puts the vase down)
          My queen.

Both attendants bow.

                    AMESTRIS
          Listen, the both of you—
          Look at me!

Amestris places a knuckle beneath the attendant's chin and roughly forces her to look up. The other girl does so of her own accord, but is just as startled.

                           AMESTRIS
A box has gone missing from my
quarters and a chamberlain informed
me that you two girls were there
cleaning a little while ago.

                         ATTENDANT 1
Yes, but—

                         ATTENDANT 2
We took nothing.

                           AMESTRIS
Perhaps you misplaced it?

                         ATTENDANT 1
What did it look like, your highness?

                           AMESTRIS
My husband has a similar one.

She climbs the steps to where the bed is. Beside it is a desk. The small, metal box that he originally had in Susa sits on top of it. Amestris picks it up and holds it high above her head, admonishing the attendants to take a good look.

                           AMESTRIS
See, like this.

Amestris is suddenly overtaken by a sharp pain. She drops the box. It CRASHES at her feet and the clasp breaks.

The box tumbles down the steps and miscellaneous items, like writing reeds and wax bars fall out of it. The false bottom comes loose, too. Suraz's letter slides to the floor below. The box flips off of the last step and a corner of it smashes the letter's seal.

                         ATTENDANT 1
Queen Amestris, are you alright?

She stands tall and absentmindedly nods.

> **ATTENDANT 1**
> I'll just pick this—

> **AMESTRIS**
> No.

> **ATTENDANT 1**
> But—

> **AMESTRIS**
> Leave it!

The girl shrinks back.

Amestris's eyes are fixed on the letter. Tilting her head, she walks down the steps, picks it up and opens it. As she reads, her eyes widen, an eyebrow raises, her mouth drops open. Another sudden contraction comes over her. She doubles over.

> **ATTENDANT 2**
> Your highness?!

> **AMESTRIS**
> Help . . . get me to the bed.

The two girls take her by the arms, assist her up the steps and situate her on the pillows. Attendant 2 innocently tries to take the letter away, but Amestris jerks her hand back, grips the letter to her chest and holds it there protectively.

> **AMESTRIS**
> (through gritted teeth)
> Go . . . go get help. Both of you. Now!

Clearly worried and frightened, they do as she has ordered and run from the room.

Alone, Amestris throws her head back in pain and chuckles to herself like a mad woman.

                          AMESTRIS
            Oh, Xerxes, Xerxes, all these years and
            never did you let on . . . Ooh, my
            poor husband . . . which is more
            torture? Coveting the one thing
            denied you, or pretending you don't
            want it at all?

She writhes on the bed, still laughing . . .

INT. ATHENS—BOULEUTERION—DAY

Over four-hundred STATESMEN are gathered within the amphitheater-like council hall. Some recline on rising steps, others stand beside marble busts. All sights are set on one of their compatriots, a robust man, sporting a sardonic grin, who has taken the floor.

                         STATESMAN 1
            I tell you, walking through the streets
            of our city, one's ears cannot guard
            themselves against incessant talk of
            Xerxes.
                    (he stops; mockingly)
            Xerxes this and Xerxes that. It would
            seem their tongues are looped and
            cannot speak but that one name.

Some agree with the assessment and chuckle. Others sit bemused.

                       STATESMAN 2 (O.S.)
            Their worries are not without merit!

There is much mumbling.

THEMISTOCLES, in his early forties, aristocratically featured, challengingly takes the floor.

> THEMISTOCLES
> He is right. Before the Persian throne had even begun to cool, both the Egyptians and Babylonians were muzzled and leashed. The threat of our country befalling the same fate is one which cannot be dismissed. The kings of Thessaly have already sought Xerxes' attention in Susa, as have the sons of Pisistratus. They offer him Greece, as if they had the right to, and he just might decide to take it. Darius had many plans for us and his son might yet see them through.

Again, mumbles abound.

> STATESMAN 1
> Themistocles, from what information has been passed to me, Xerxes will soon be traveling to Parsa and the only unfinished plans that he intends to carry out are those headed by architects, not generals.
> (to the crowd; laughing)
> Yes, be wary my fellow Athenians. Right now, the Persians are arming themselves with hammers and levels.

Many laugh. Themistocles grows angry.

> THEMISTOCLES
> Will you continue to laugh when they grow bored and turn to their swords instead?

ARISTIDES, late forties, runs a hand through his thinning graying hair, rises from his seat and wordlessly suggests the first statesman sit down with the others. Reluctantly, the man does so, but not before casting an antagonistic glare at Themistocles.

> ARISTIDES
> (taking the floor)
> I see no reason to lose sight of what's
> presently before us just to consume our
> thoughts with what might never come to be.

Themistocles eyes Aristides. It is apparent that they are not strangers, or friends for that matter.

> THEMISTOCLES
> Well, Aristides the 'Just', what do you
> suggest we do? Sit around like the
> whole world, save of course for Greece,
> is nothing more than an illusion?

> ARISTIDES
> While you would rather cower to one?

> THEMISTOCLES
> You were there at Marathon. If it had
> not been for Militiades, we would be
> under Persian occupation now.

The majority agree with this, nodding their heads and quietly discussing the sentiments expressed.

> ARISTIDES
> Yes, I was there and—

> THEMISTOCLES
> Don't you realize that the victory we so
> vaingloriously congratulate ourselves
> on was over a scant fraction of their
> forces?

ARISTIDES
Xerxes—

THEMISTOCLES
—is reputed to be a brilliant tactician.
(a beat)
Remind me, someone, what became of our esteemed general, Militiades?

Statesman 2 stands up.

STATESMEN 2
(sullen)
He died a debtor.

THEMISTOCLES
And what of his son, Cimon?

ARISTIDES
(ashamed)
Cimon is paying his father's sentence to restore his good name.

THEMISTOCLES
There are some who translate Xerxes' name as meaning "King of Heroes". Heroes. I wonder, where, if necessary, shall we find ours? And, once found, will we use and discard them as we've done in the past?

ARISTIDES
Alright, Themistocles. You've made your point.

THEMISTOCLES
You must understand—

Themistocles holds up his hand.

                    THEMISTOCLES
                This is Greece.

He begins to label each finger.

                    THEMISTOCLES
                The Thessalians, Phocians, Aeginetans,
                Athenians, and a host of more, and like
                this we stand, while Persia? Persia is united.
                        (makes a fist)
                It is the fist that could strike us down.

Aristides thoughtfully paces around the floor as the surrounding statesmen grow restless.

                    ARISTIDES
                So, what would you have us do, hmm?

He stops before Themistocles, awaiting an answer.

                    THEMISTOCLES
                Be prepared to withstand the impact.

EXT. PARSA OUTSKIRTS—NIGHT

Silhouetted against the moon, a caravan flanked by mounted soldiers moves across the landscape.

INT. PARSA—HADISH—YOUNG DARIUS'S BEDCHAMBER—NIGHT

On the floor, shattered pieces of a pitcher sit in a pool of spilt wine. Candle light filters through the tousling sheets of the bed, causing the shadowy forms of a man and woman to be seen. Their drunken giggles bounce off the walls as they wrestle.

                    DARIUS
                It is your . . . umm . . . your . . . duty.

                    WOMAN
                   (amused)
            My duty?

                    DARIUS
            Mmmm, do it well and I will reward
            you.

A great COMMOTION suddenly echoes from beyond the door. The young man throws the sheets back and grows quiet, but his company continues on as if not a noise was heard.

                    WOMAN
            That so? Please tell, Prince Darius,
            what would—

The, now, seventeen year old son of Xerxes covers her mouth. Completely drunk, her eyes widen as she suppresses laughter.

                    DARIUS
            What is going on?

Darius slowly withdraws from his conquest and upon doing so, more giggles escape. He casts a stern look as he pulls on a robe, prompting the girl to draw the tangled sheets up to her lips to muffle the sound.

Staggering, he makes for the door to see what is happening.

Darius peers into the torch lit—

HALLWAY

Porters rush past his room. Curious as to why they are carrying on so, he steps out into the corridor and grabs one by the arm.

                    DARIUS
            Where are all of you go—going?

                    PORTER 1
              To assist in unloading the king's
              possessions.

This news seems to humble the boy. He loosens his grasp.

                    DARIUS
              My father? He's back?

                    PORTER 1
              Yes, sir.

                    DARIUS
              Since when?

                    PORTER 1
              Just moments ago.

INT. PARSA—HADISH—OUTSIDE XERXES' CHAMBER—NIGHT

Followed by BODYGUARDS, Xerxes enters the small 'foyer' before his room, speaking with a SCRIBE who has a large satchel slung over his shoulder.

                    XERXES
              Though the hour is late, I want a brief
              report on the state of affairs. So, have
              the records sent—

The scribe reaches into his tote and pulls out a neatly stacked bundle of documents.

                    XERXES
              Ah, you already have them. Very good.

Xerxes takes and sifts through them.

                    SCRIBE
          As you will see, all is in order. There are
          a few documents which require your
          seal, but no pressing matters to attend
          to, your highness.

                    XERXES
          I want a meeting with the treasurers
          in the morning. Be sure they're
          notified.

                    SCRIBE
               (bows)
          It will be done.

                    XERXES
               (turns to doors)
          Dismissed.

INT. PARSA—HADISH—XERXES' CHAMBER—CONTINUING

Xerxes takes his time as he walks across the room. He is tired, but so relieved. Finally, he has returned to his own, private piece of the world, a place where all formality can sink away.

He climbs the steps to his bed and, with a sigh, sits down at the desk beside it. He would love just one more moment to simply breathe, but he will not allow it. Despite what the scribe stated, to Xerxes, any unfinished business is pressing business.

With the documents before him, he reaches for the metal box.

It has been fixed. He flips the top open and goes to reach for a bar of wax, but the skewed edge of the false bottom raises question. Xerxes hesitantly pulls it up.

We see the letter to Suraz, still folded, face down. He looks at it, almost longingly.

Xerxes decides to pick it up. He flips it over, prepared to snap the seal, but is shocked to discover it is already broken.

> AMESTRIS (O.S.)
> It is a beautiful letter. Any woman would envy its sentiments.

He turns to find Amestris leaning against a bedpost.

> AMESTRIS
> I know I do.

> XERXES
> (puts letter down; confronts her)
> Amestris.

> AMESTRIS
> There's no reason to be upset. I put it right back where I found it. It's not as if I sent it along to her. I mean, I could have and I nearly did, but then, I thought, what if it were to fall into Masistes' hands? The letter may be old, but, surely, it would still be news to him.
> (a beat)
> Besides, I feel so much closer to you now that we share this secret. Why would I want to ruin that?

While he is angry, he is not concerned over her threats, either. This is the game they play. He leans in as if to kiss her, then stops a hair's breadth from her lips.

> XERXES
> You are a snake.

AMESTRIS
Then we make a fitting pair.
> (backing off; a beat)

I must admit, when I first read it, I was so furious, but now, considering everything, I'm happy I found it when I did. When you are so blind with anger, you can't feel any pain, or anything else, really . . . and that's exactly what I held onto as I gave birth to your son. Or had you forgotten you had a new—

XERXES
No.

AMESTRIS
He made a royal entrance, you know . . . right here in this room.
> (a beat)

I couldn't bear to look at him for days.
> (off guilty look)

But then, I realized, what does it matter? The king has his women, and as for Suraz in particular? Well, she's hundreds of parsangs away. Feelings numb as time passes, but, even if they haven't, she is Masistes wife and that—
> (wraps arms around his neck)

—that secures my place as yours.

XERXES
Secures your place? Amestris—

Xerxes stops short and changes tactics. She dared him by getting in his face. He calls her bluff and kisses her, much to her surprise. When they pull back, their eyes are locked.

                    XERXES
            Believe me. Your place as my wife was
            secured the day we were betrothed.

                    AMESTRIS
            And my title the day your heir was born.

                    XERXES
            And now another son.

                    AMESTRIS
            Perhaps he could establish a truce?

                    XERXES
            Is he—

                    AMESTRIS
            Flawless. Would you like to go look? I
            know it's not customary for the father
            to see his child so early on, but when
            you were finally introduced to our
            precious Darius, didn't you say you
            would never wait that long again? He's
            strong, Xerxes, so very strong.

She puts out her hand.

                    AMESTRIS
            Come see.

Xerxes takes it.

INT. PARSA—NURSERY—NIGHT

The door of the nursery CREAKS open, startling a NANNY sitting beside a large crib. Amestris leans against the frame as Xerxes hesitantly steps in. The woman, realizing who it is, quickly bows.

                    XERXES
          Leave us.

The order is expediently followed, leaving father, mother and son alone. Xerxes peers into the crib and pushes a blanket away. Upon seeing the slumbering infant, his hardened exterior softens.

Amestris joins his side as he draws a finger down his son's face.

                    XERXES
          Artaxerxes.

There is a serene lull as he regards the child. It is one which makes all other problems seem unimportant. Unfortunately, this quiet moment does not last long enough for them to be ultimately forgotten.

The sound of someone clumsily RUNNING through the hallway echoes into the room. Xerxes looks up just as the nursery door is thrown open to reveal a drunken Darius, trying to catch his breath.

                    DARIUS
          Father, I was told—told I could find
          you here.

With a sloppy grin, Darius embraces him.

                    DARIUS
          Wel—welcome back.

Xerxes pulls away stiffly. The agitation he felt before resurfaces, exacerbated by his son's embarrassing state.

                    XERXES
          Our 'precious' Darius.
              (to Amestris)
          I remember the day he was first
          brought to me. I held him close and
          whispered, 'may you be as respected as
                    (MORE)

                    XERXES(cont'd)
          the man whose name you share.'
              (sadly shakes head;
              a beat)
          I have much work to do.

Casting a disappointed look at his eldest, he promptly leaves.

EXT. PARSA—HADISH—ATRIUM—DAY

Servants stand at the ready with fly whisks, fans and refreshments as Xerxes, reclined on a lounge, indulges in a bowl of dates and speaks with an ARCHITECT. Large parchments baring floor plans litter the table which separates them.

                    ARCHITECT
          We are making steady progress each day.

                    XERXES
          How are your supplies?

                    ARCHITECT
          Abundant. We are expecting more
          naucina to be delivered within the next
          month. Detail work may commence
          before then.

Xerxes simply nods, distracted by an approaching attendant. He sits up.

                    ATTENDANT
              (bowing)
          King Xerxes, General Mardonius
          wishes to speak with you.

Looking to the entrance of the garden, Xerxes sees an expectant Mardonius.

                    XERXES
          Let him come.

The attendant signals the general to enter. The expectant expression is replaced with an earnest one. There is obviously something important he wants to talk about, but, stopping before Xerxes, all he does is tip his head.

>   XERXES
>   General, what weighs so heavily on
>   your mind?

>   MARDONIUS
>   Something which I would prefer to discuss
>   in private if possible. May we take a walk?

>   XERXES
>   (intrigued; stands)
>   A walk would be agreeable.
>   (to the architect)
>   Keep me abreast of your progress.

>   ARCHITECT
>   Yes, your highness.

The architect begins to roll-up his 'blueprints'.

>   XERXES
>   (to servants)
>   The rest of you are dismissed.

Xerxes turns to Mardonius and directs him to lead the way.

EXT. PARSA—ROYAL COURTYARD—DAY

Xerxes and Mardonius walk across the private courtyard shared by Parsa's main three palaces. Past the Tripylon and Tachara, we can see construction work continuing on the nearly completed apadana and the—far from finished—Hall of One Hundred Columns. Chisels CLINK against stony surfaces as MASONS, perched on wooden scaffolds, work on the structures.

>   XERXES
>   What did you want to talk about?

Mardonius abruptly stops at the edge of the courtyard, between the towering palaces, and sets his sights on the nearly completed apadana.

> MARDONIUS
> The apadana has turned out most
> impressive. And the hall . . . when it is
> finally finished, it will be astounding.

> XERXES
> If only my father were here to see his
> projects realized.

Xerxes turns to his right and looks at his father's abandoned palace. Though only a building, it appears cold and lonely.

Both move to stand before the double-ramped staircase to the Tripylon. It is decorated with bas-reliefs of Persian and Median nobility. These works are symbols of power, but like pictures, too, for they are moments frozen in time.

> XERXES
> He had a vision of what Parsa should
> be. He would tell me of it often and,
> Mardonius—

Slowly, Xerxes approaches the palace steps. He considerately ascends one and takes in the scope of the structure. Upon the portal of the opened entrance above, the most interesting piece of detail work is found—the most sentimental 'picture'.

This bas-relief depicts King Darius seated upon the throne and supported by representatives of twenty-eight nations. Standing behind the throne, his head level with his father's, stands Crown Prince Xerxes.

> XERXES
> (continuing)
> —it was as if every word he spoke cut
> through the mists of imagination,
> making it as real to me as it already was
> to him.

MARDONIUS
You have brought to fruition many of Darius's unfinished plans and you take more to task each day, but, I wonder, will you see to completing them all?

XERXES
(turning; knowingly)
Mardonius . . .

MARDONIUS
When you succeeded your father, you also became the enforcer of his will. You ascended the throne with a vengeance—

Xerxes steps down, knowing exactly what he is implying.

XERXES
And order has been restored.

MARDONIUS
But our foes across the Aegean remain unpunished. Why? Why, when so many, even your own court, support action against them, do you not? Why, when there are even more who believe we should mobilize an army and take Greece entirely, do you shun the suggestion?

XERXES
Why should I take it up? Persia is stronger and more wealthy than it has ever been. What necessity is outside our borders that we can not already find within them?

MARDONIUS
(disappointed)
You sound like Artabanus.

XERXES
And?

MARDONIUS
You never used to. You used to speak of legends and—

XERXES
(sarcastically reciting)
Legends are nothing more than tales which wither in reality's light.

MARDONIUS
Who told you—

XERXES
My father . . . the night before he passed on.

MARDONIUS
Do you really believe that?

There is a long, considerate pause. When Xerxes finally looks up to respond, he shakes his head and sullenly smiles.

XERXES
No. But to hear him say those words . . . it felt like a betrayal and for the first time in my life, I looked at my father and hated what I saw, and what's worse? I felt pity. I pitied that he could not see himself the way I did.

MARDONIUS
The way you still do?

XERXES
Yes.

                    MARDONIUS
          Darius told you what he did in a rare
          moment of weakness, but he was also
          right—up to a point. Legends are
          stories . . . stories of men who have
          surpassed the limitations, the
          boundaries, imposed on them by those
          lacking the courage to see what lies
          beyond. He was one of these men, as
          was your grandfather Cyrus. He built
          this empire based on a vision. One
          world. One people. He left a legacy
          which proves it is attainable. It is more
          than mere fantasy. I know you can see
          that, so, what's stopping you?

Xerxes does not have an answer to the question. He really does not know. The silence prompts Mardonius to go on.

                    MARDONIUS
          Out of all the inscriptions on Darius's
          tomb, do you know which one strikes
          me as most compelling?
               (off Xerxes' look)
          'From no enemy let me fear,' and
          though it is not an original turn of
          phrase, it is one of profound sensibility.

Xerxes takes a challenging step toward him.

                    XERXES
          I fear no one.

                    MARDONIUS
          Everyone fears someone—something,
          and while you may not fear these
          Greeks, word has it that they fear you.
               (a beat)
                    (MORE)

                    MARDONIUS(cont'd)
          Xerxes, I was there. I heard Darius's last
          words—his last order left to you to
          carry out and it has yet to be done.
          Won't you do it now? Won't you
          avenge your father and take Athens?
          Won't you do as Cyrus would and
          unite Greece?

These words strike a chord.

                         XERXES
          A campaign of such magnitude would
          take years to undertake.

                      MARDONIUS
          Yes, it could, but let me ask you this?
                    (pointing toward Apadana)
          Why be content going over
          construction plans for houses and
          banquet halls when you could be the
          architect of a single—united—world
          empire?

Xerxes turns to face the old Tachara again, as if the answer to the question can be found there. Mardonius pats him on the shoulder and backs away, knowing the seed has been planted.

INT. PARSA—TACHARA—THRONE ROOM—DAY

The large doors eerily CREAK open. The sound bounces off the walls. Light pours into the room, illuminating floating dust particles as they spin on unseen currents. Cobwebs dangle from corners. Before the entrance, a great shadow stretches across the floor, but with each step its counterpart makes, it grows smaller, till being altogether consumed.

Xerxes weaves between the towering, old pillars. There is a profound sense of melancholy expressed as he looks around, stirring echoes of the past.

XERXES (V.O.)
Father?

DARIUS THE GREAT (V.O.)
I am right here, Xerxes.

XERXES (V.O.)
How dare they forget who you are.

DARIUS THE GREAT (V.O.)
. . . who am I?

MASISTES (V.O.)
. . . an exceptional man.

XERXES (V.O.)
More than that . . . you are the mighty hand of . . .

SURAZ (V.O.)
Persia. Your world begins and ends with her.

XERXES (V.O.)
She is an empire of many.

MARDONIUS (V.O.)
Based on a vision. One world. One people.

GUESTS (V.O.)
To King Darius!!

Xerxes looks up at the ceiling. Dust continues to spiral through the room, seemingly dancing around him.

XERXES (V.O.)
There are those who have foolishly chosen to be his enemy.

He begins to ascend the stairs to the throne's platform. Each step is deliberate.

> MARDONIUS (V.O.)
> When you succeeded your father, you also became the enforcer of his will.

> DARIUS THE GREAT (V.O.)
> Remember . . . the . . . Athenians . . .

> ONOMACRITUS (V.O.)
> 'Twas fated that a Persian would bridge the Hellespont and march an army into Greece.

> MARDONIUS (V.O.)
> They want unity.

> XERXES (V.O.)
> . . . a conqueror, the likes of which they thought only existed in myth.

> ONOMACRITUS (V.O.)
> We always thought it would be Darius.

Xerxes reaches the top and bypasses the throne.

> DARIUS (V.O.)
> . . . a man.

> ONOMACRITUS (V.O.)
> All along . . . it was . . .

> DARIUS (V.O.)
> My son.

He now stands before the infamous relief of the 'Great King'.

> XERXES (V.O.)
> I am Xerxes, the Great King

> ONOMACRITUS (V.O.)
> All along . . . it was you.

> XERXES (V.O.)
> King of Kings . . .

> ONOMACRITUS (V.O.)
> It has always been you.

> XERXES (V.O.)
> King of lands containing many men . . .

> ONOMACRITUS (V.O.)
> You will be the one who leads them.

> XERXES (V.O.)
> King in this great earth far and wide . . .

> MARDONIUS (V.O.)
> . . . of a single world empire.

> ONOMACRITUS (V.O.)
> It was prophesied long ago.

> XERXES (V.O.)
> . . . so shall it be written!

Xerxes grazes the relief with his fingers. He embraces what he believes is his destiny.

> XERXES
> And it will be done.

INT. BACTRIA—MASISTES' CHAMBER—NIGHT

The peaceful slumber of Masistes and Suraz is interrupted by the insistent KNOCKING of a PIRRAZADI MESSENGER.

                    PIRRAZADI (O.S.)
                Satrap Masistes!

Drowsily, he sits up, his eyes no more than slits.

                         SURAZ
                Masistes?

                        MASISTES
                Stay here.
                    (to pirrazadi)
                Just a moment.

Mumbling, he rises and stumbles around in the dark all the way to the door.

                    PIRRAZADI (O.S.)
                I bring urgent word from the king!

Both Masistes and Suraz are jolted by the exclamation. She draws herself further up, while he opens the door just wide enough to peer into the hall. There stands the pirrazadi and the chamberlain who escorted him to the room.

                       PIRRAZADI
                    (handing Masistes a summons)
                You are to come to Susa.

                        MASISTES
                    (opening the message)
                Susa? Why—

                       PIRRAZADI
                King Xerxes has summoned the
                assembly.

Masistes thoughtfully rubs his brow. Behind him, in the shadows, Suraz bites her lip. What is meaning of all this?

EXT. SUSA—CITY—DAY

482 B.C.

ON THE ROOFTOP of her house and still only seen from the back, Hadassah, now in her late teens, peers down at the—

PROCESSIONAL WAY

—where a stream of nobility winds its way to the citadel. We see chariots pulled by horses, ox-drawn wagons brimming with gifts for the king, and other offerings carried on attendants' shoulders.

> XERXES (V.O.)
> Persians, I shall not be the first to bring
> in among you a new custom. I shall
> but follow one which has come down
> to us from our forefathers.

INT. SUSA—THRONE ROOM—DAY

Susa's throne room is the axis on which the empire revolves, the ancient world's "United Nations", and a forum so majestic that it exudes a near tangible power. The most noble of Persia's elite are gathered within, the bravest of generals, and the king's court. This is the ASSEMBLY, and every eye is set on Xerxes above.

> XERXES (O.S.)
> Since the moment Cyrus overcame
> Astyages, and we Persians wrested the
> scepter from the Medes, never, as our
> old men assure me, has our race
> reposed itself. Never have we settled,
> stood idle, abandoned our intrinsic
> desire to be more than we are.

ON XERXES

He looks like he is, indeed, the single figure in which the entire empire is personified. From head to foot, he drips with gold and jewels, standing unshakable before the throne.

XERXES
Does the mighty eagle, tethered to nothing, no one, refuse the sky when it beckons? Why, then, would we, who are just as free, refuse our calling?
    (a beat; points up)
Now, in all this we are guided, and we, obeying that guidance, prosper greatly. What need have I to tell you of the deeds of Cyrus and Cambyses, and my own father Darius, how many nations they conquered and added to our dominions? You know well what great things they achieved. But for myself, I will say that, from the day on which I mounted the throne, I have not ceased to consider by what means I may rival those who have preceded me in this post of honor, and increase the power of Persia as much as any of them.
    (a beat)
And truly I have pondered upon this, until, at last, I have decided that there is, indeed, a destined path to take—a way, whereby, we may at once win glory, and likewise, a land rich in resources while obtaining satisfaction and revenge against an enemy who has dared, unprovoked, to injure us; an enemy whose day of reckoning has been long to come. For this cause I have now called you together, that I may make known to you what I design to do.
    (a beat)
My intent is to throw a bridge over the Hellespont and lead an army into Greece, that thereby I may take vengeance on the Athenians for the wrongs committed against my father—for the wrongs they have committed against us all.

A lot of jaws are dropping. The majority look extremely pleased. This is a campaign many had been pushing for. Only a few appear wary, Artabanus being one of them.

                    XERXES
Who here can forget the day that Sardis, one of our most prestigious capitals and a long standing symbol of authority, was attacked by these evildoers? Who here will ever cease to remember the incredulity they felt upon hearing the news that her temples and sacred groves were burning? Never would we have believed it possible and never would it have been, but the cowards struck as our men were valiantly fighting to restore peace along the coast.
                    (a beat)
Sardis has since risen from the ashes, but on Athens, the mark of guilt remains. Need any of you be reminded of how they shamefully murdered the messenger sent to them by my father? Or how they viciously attacked Datis's troops on the plain of Marathon? No, because theirs is a list of atrocities that no true Persian would let slip from memory.

Many nod. Some look down in sad recollection. Others regard Xerxes tearfully.

                    XERXES
              (tone rising determinedly)
Your own eyes saw the preparations of Darius against these men, but death came upon him, and balked his hopes of reprisal. On my father's behalf, therefore, and on behalf of all Persians, I
                    (MORE)

>   XERXES(cont'd)
> undertake the war. I am bent on it, and
> pledge myself not to rest till I have taken
> and burnt Athens! Let us subdue our
> enemies there and throughout the rest of
> Greece so that we may then unify its
> people and embrace them as our own!
>   (shouting over applause)
> Cyrus believed that it fell to us, as a force
> of good, to pass through this world, from
> one end to the other, and triumph over
> the evil which seeks to destroy it. Will you
> take up the sword and honor your duty?!

This is met with a standing ovation.

Xerxes is genuinely moved by the sight.

>   XERXES
>   (taking a seat)
> I now put the business before you and
> grant you the complete freedom to
> speak your minds upon it openly.

We more closely survey the audience.

Members of the royal court continue their applause.

>   MEMUCAN
> To King Xerxes!

>   HAMAN
> Long may he reign!

The generals are up, too.

>   GENERALS
> We will fight! . . . We will be one!
> . . . No one shall withstand us!

Tigranes, standing beside Artabanus, looks inspired.

> TIGRANES
> We will not stand down in the face of evil!

Artabanus briefly turns to cast a cold look at his older son, Tritan.

The nobles are the most vocal of the lot.

Among them is Masistes. Though he claps, he clearly does not know what to make of the whole situation.

Back on the generals, we see Mardonius. He leaves his place among them and stops before the base of the king's platform.

Everyone quiets and sits.

> MARDONIUS
> Truly, your highness, you surpass not only all living Persians, but likewise those yet unborn. Everything you've stated is right, and best of all your resolve is not to let the Athenians' treacherous attack on our beloved Sardis mock us anymore.
> (to the audience)
> Should we allow them, these people who have done us such wanton injury, to escape our retribution? What is there to fear? Surely not their numbers, nor the greatness of their wealth. As for their neighbors? When I marched through Greece on the orders of Darius, I went as far as Macedonia, and came but a little short of reaching Athens itself, yet not a soul ventured to come out against me to battle. And it isn't as if these Greeks are inexperienced combatants. They fight each other all the time.

The assembly finds this amusing. They chuckle. Encouraged, Mardonius's serious expression is replaced by a grin, and he proceeds to tell them an anecdote.

> MARDONIUS
> They do so in the most foolish way, too. For no sooner is war proclaimed than they search out the smoothest and fairest plain that is to be found in all the land, and there they assemble and fight, till it comes to pass that even the conquerors depart with great loss. I say nothing of the conquered, for they are destroyed altogether. Now surely, as they are all of one speech, they ought to interchange heralds and messengers, and make up their differences by any means rather than battle, or, at least, be more sensible in the way they go about it. Otherwise, they'll be forced to resolve their arguments peacefully, as there will be no warriors left to settle them.
> (laughs; a beat; serious)
> But, despite what their ridiculous manner of warfare may suggest, these Greeks are not bereft of all common sense. They know it is better to be our friend than to stand against us in defense of the Athenians—who consider no other's interests but their own, and who would, if the situations were reversed, leave their neighbors to fend for themselves. It is little wonder—as I was saying—that when I led my modest troops to the very borders of Macedonia, no one so much as thought of raising a hand against us.

Mardonius turns to Xerxes.

                    MARDONIUS
          Who then will dare, O king!, to meet
          you in arms, when you come with all
          of Persia's warriors at your back?
                    (to audience)
          In my opinion, I do not think any one
          could be so foolhardy. Grant, however,
          that I am mistaken, and these people
          are foolish enough to meet us in open
          fight? Well, in that case, they will learn
          that there are no such soldiers in the whole
          world as we.

The assembly CHEERS, but Artabanus has heard enough. He rises from his seat and shouts above them all.

                    ARTABANUS
          O king!!

He brushes past Mardonius as he approaches to address the king, much to the embarrassment of Tigranes. He is like the chaperone of the party who has arrived just in time to deflate everyone's good mood.

                    ARTABANUS
          It is impossible, if no more than one
          opinion is uttered, to conclude which
          is best. A man is forced then to follow
          the only course offered him, but if
          opposite speeches are delivered, then
          choice can be exercised. In like manner,
          pure gold is not recognized by itself,
          but when compared with baser ore, we
          perceive which is the better.
                    (a beat)
          When you were but a child, I
          counseled your father, Darius, my own
          brother, not to attack the Scyths, a race
          of people who had no town in their
                    (MORE)

ARTABANUS(cont'd)
whole land. They were wandering tribes that he, as well as many others, thought would be easily subdued. I was not so convinced, but despite my warnings, Darius chose to lead an army against them. What followed was little more than a standoff and, in the end, it was lack of supplies which decided the campaign. By the time the troops returned, many of our bravest warriors had been lost—not to their opponents, but to the march itself.
   (a beat)
You intend, O king, to attack a people far superior to the Scyths, a people distinguished above others both by land and sea. It is fit, therefore, to consider the dangers all the more earnestly. You say you will bridge the Hellespont and lead your army through Greece on a warpath to Athens. Now, suppose things do not go according to plan and success is not obtained. It's not implausible. Contrary to what some would like to believe, not every Greek outside of Attica will welcome us with open arms. War has a way of forging alliances between former foes, and for no other reason than common nationality. They could potentially raise an army considerable in number and, even if they cannot stop you by land, what if their ships can by sea? Athens alone has hundreds. What if, having defeated us on the water, they then sail to the Hellespont, and there, destroy
   (MORE)

ARTABANUS(cont'd)
our bridge? That, sire, would be
disastrous. And here, it is not by my own
mother wit alone that I conjecture what
could happen, but I remember how
narrowly we escaped disaster before,
when your father, after throwing bridges
over the Thracian Bosphorus and the
Ister, marched against the Scythians, and
they tried every sort of prayer to induce
the Ionians, who had charge over the Ister
bridge, to break the passage. On that day,
if Histiaeus of Miletus had sided with the
other princes and not set himself to
oppose them, the empire of the Persians
would have come to not. Surely, a
dreadful thing it is to realize that the
king's fortunes depended wholly on one
man.

Artabanus takes a look around. Everyone stares blankly, even Xerxes above.

ARTABANUS
What if something were to happen to
you? Why risk so much when no need
presses? Why not, at least, consider the
matter further before declaring your
resolve?
(to the audience)
Hurry always brings about disasters
from which huge sufferings are wont
to arise, but in delay lie many
advantages, though they may not be
apparent now.

He turns toward Mardonius. The two eye each other with disdain. Artabanus can no longer control his temper.

ARTABANUS
And you, Mardonius, son of Gobyrus,
do not pretend your role in this is
minor and merely supportive. You have
hungered for war against the Greeks for
years! Since Darius's passing, you've been
a constant echo in his son's ear,
encouraging him to gloriously lead an
army against them himself; constantly
repeating why Athens going unpunished
is tantamount to inviting another attack
and that the rest of Greece's people will
destroy each other if we do not take
them under our control.
 (a beat)
Oh, general, slander is of all crimes the
most terrible. In it, two men do
wrong, and one man has wrong done
to him. The slanderer does wrong
forasmuch as he abuses a man behind
his back, and the hearer forasmuch as
he believes what he has not searched
into thoroughly. The man slandered in
his absence suffers wrong at the hands
of both, for one brings against him a
false charge and the other thinks him
an evildoer.

Many find that last sentence offensive. There is a lot of mumbling.

ASSEMBLY
They are! . . . Remember Sardis?! . . .
Marathon! . . . Where were you?!

MARDONIUS
False charge? Is your memory
faltering!?

ARTABANUS
No. I remember everything. It's true.
The Athenians are guilty of
transgressions against us. I don't dispute
that. What I do take issue with,
however, is how you invoke the past to
prophesy future attacks, how you stir
the memories of your peers, prey upon
their old anger and, thus, make it new
again, how you would have us all
believe that it is necessary to strike this
enemy when, to you, Athens is nothing
but a convenient pretext to "save"
Greece from itself. But, above all this,
what disturbs me most is that you
would have our king march forth in
Persia's name to wage a war in yours.

GASPS abound. Xerxes leers forward. Mardonius is dumbfounded.

ARTABANUS
If you want to take up your arms, then
so be it. Actually, let us both stake
ourselves on the matter. How does that
sound? You choose out your men—take
with you whatever number of troops
you like—and then we'll lead forth our
armies to battle the Greeks together. If
things go well, as you say they will, let
me be put to death. But, if things fall
out as I prophesy, it's your head.

MARDONIUS
I will not be party to—

ARTABANUS
Should you refuse this wager, and still
resolve to march against Greece under
the empire's banner . . .
(MORE)

                    MARDONIUS(cont'd)
          (in Mardonius's face)
     I am sure that those whom you leave
     behind here will one day receive the sad
     tidings that Mardonius has brought a
     great tragedy upon the Persian people,
     and lies prey to dogs and birds
     somewhere in the land of the Athenians,
     or else in that of the Lacedaemonians—
     unless, indeed, you will have perished
     sooner on the way, experiencing for
     yourself the might of those men on
     whom you would induce the king to—

Xerxes rises from the throne, irate.

                    XERXES
     Enough!!!

A sly smile tugs at Mardonius's lips. Artabanus is in trouble.

                    XERXES
     Artabanus, you are my father's brother.
     That shall save you from receiving the
     due meed of your insolent words. One
     shame, however, I will lay upon you,
     coward and faint-hearted as you are, you
     shall not come with me to fight these
     Greeks, but shall be left behind to tarry
     with the women. Without your help, I
     will accomplish all of which I spoke.
          (a beat; to all)
     My father managed three last words
     before leaving me in his post, a simple,
     direct order. Remember. The
     Athenians . . . and I have. This assembly
     was not called to start a war. We have
     been at war with Athens since the day
     they decided to cross our borders. There
                    (MORE)

                    XERXES(cont'd)
is no power in the world greater than we,
yet they, this tiny, little polis on the edge
of Greece had the audacity to blanket
Sardis in a shroud of smoke. Only
madness could compel such a suicidal
mission and while the arsonists may have
been dealt with, the masterminds have
gone on freely all these years and you
would be a fool to believe that they have
since found their sanity. All reason is lost
when dealing with unreasonable men.
So, you see, retreat on both sides is
impossible and the choice lies between
doing and suffering injury. There is no
middle course.
          (a beat)
The day will come when another ashen
cloud will loom in the sky, and it shall be
called Athens, for let me not be thought
the son of Darius, or an Achaemenid, if I
do not take vengeance upon them!!

This receives another standing ovation.

We survey the audience again.

The court is more than pleased, applauding wildly.

                    COURT
          To the king! . . . To Xerxes!

The generals are up again, too.

Tigranes deliberately claps as he stares angrily at his father.

                    GENERALS
          To the ends of the earth! . . . We shall
          follow!

                    TIGRANES
              We will stand with you!

The nobles are so loud that their comments, for the most part, are indistinguishable.

We see Masistes peering over at Demaratus. The exiled Spartan is grinning so wildly that you would think he has just been renamed king.

                    DEMARATUS
              With Athens' downfall, the rest of
              Greece awaits!

Masistes regards Xerxes. Whether good or bad, he barely recognizes his friend.

EXT. SPARTA—ASSEMBLY—DAY

Spartan EPHORS and other POLITICIANS are exiting the building. Some stop to talk along the stoa, enjoying the view of the MENELAION and AMYKLAION—monuments to Menelaus and Helen—in the mountainous distance, as well as the ancient MYCENEAN PALACE.

INT. SPARTA—ASSEMBLY—DAY

Still lingering within the hall is LEONIDAS, one of the state's two kings. He is in his thirties, appealing to the eye, with dark features and the Spartans' trademark dreadlocks.

Keeping him company is his wife, GORGO, his nephew, PAUSANIAS, DIENECES, a Herculean built general, and Sparta's other king, CLEOMBROTUS, his brother.

A SPARTAN COURIER approaches as they nonchalantly talk. He holds within his arms two wooden tablets.

                  SPARTAN COURIER
              King Leonidas, Cleombrotus.

CLEOMBROTUS
(irritated)
What is it?

SPARTAN COURIER
I was told to put these directly into your hands.

LEONIDAS
Wood tablets?

The courier hands one to each king.

SPARTAN COURIER
I know it is peculiar, sir, but they must hold some importance. They were sent by Demaratus.

Pausanias is instantly intrigued. He peers over his father's shoulder to take a look.

PAUSANIAS
Isn't Demaratus in Persia?

DIENECES
He's not only with the Persians. He now is one.

PAUSANIAS
Could be worse. He could be an Athenian.

CLEOMBROTUS
(examining tablet)
Well, I see nothing. Leonidas?

LEONIDAS
No. Nothing but spilt wax.

Gorgo moves closer to her husband.

                    LEONIDAS
        Gorgo?

She begins to chip away at the wax with a fingernail.

                    GORGO
          There's something here. A word.

Cleombrotus abandons his tablet.

                    CLEOMBROTUS
        What is it?

                    LEONIDAS
                (looking up; confused)
        War.

INT. SUSA—APADANA—NIGHT

Artabanus and Tigranes stand in a corner of Susa's enormous audience hall. While the rest of the guests enjoy the ambience, the two are locked in an emotional argument, nearly sloshing their drinks on one another as they fight.

                    ARTABANUS
          Why won't you listen!?

                    TIGRANES
          Because everything you say is false.

                    ARTABANUS
          Tigranes, I can't stop this war, but I can
          ask that my son not be forced to fight
          it—

                    TIGRANES
          But that's just it. I'm not being forced.
          Only cowards would refuse to take up
          a sword for the empire.

ARTABANUS
We are not under threat! Hear me!
Hear me out, please.

He directs Tigranes to look up. Above a double-ramped rise reserved for the king, looms the hall's grand balcony. It is also accessible by two staircases, which, at the moment, are flanked by the king's guards. Xerxes, himself, stands atop the balcony, speaking with Masistes.

ARTABANUS
(referring to Masistes)
He's been named as one of the top six commanders.

TIGRANES
What? Masistes is not—

ARTABANUS
Masistes may not be much of a fighter himself, but he is well respected and a good strategist. As satrap of Bactria, he also has more power and influence than most. You should know that.

TIGRANES
This again, hmm?

ARTABANUS
You should have been satrap. You should have been the one to succeed me.

TIGRANES
What's done is done.

ARTABANUS
He will soon be returning to Bactria. If I can arrange it with Xerxes, you could go with him and stay there, get
(MORE)

ARTABANUS(cont'd)
reacquainted with the people. Then, when the time comes for Masistes to gather his troops and depart for the coast, he can simply hand control of the province over to you.

TIGRANES
Serve as satrap in his absence.

ARTABANUS
Yes, and should he not come back, the council will already have a strong leader there to take his place.

TIGRANES
Do you even hear yourself?!

ARTABANUS
He was able to take the post because war had pulled us away. Now here is an opportunity to set things right.

TIGRANES
No. What you mean is, here is an opportunity to run and hide.

ARTABANUS
Tigranes . . . you are such a light. Don't you know, if you were lost to me, my world would be plunged into darkness?

TIGRANES
I love you, father, but you must—

ARTABANUS
If you would only let me speak to Xerxes, I could ensure—

TIGRANES
Stop! I'm done speaking with you about this and should you suggest I turn my back on my men again, I shall finish speaking with you all together!

Artabanus is visibly pained by his words.

TIGRANES
I'm sorry. I didn't—

ARTABANUS
No, no. You're not a child. Own your words. Don't be ashamed of them. But, allow me one more question?

TIGRANES
(shamed)
What?

ARTABANUS
If this war claims you, how shall I ever reconcile such a senseless loss?

Tigranes cannot believe his father would say something he finds so dishonorable. He storms off.

Mardonius, smug, emerges from the crowd and stops beside Artabanus.

MARDONIUS
You could stand to be more like Tigranes.

ARTABANUS
Because he is more like you?

MARDONIUS
Whether you think it necessary or not, we will be going to war. It has been
(MORE)

MARDONIUS(cont'd)
decided. The time to protest ended
long ago. As a father, you should be
supporting your son—Tritan, too, and
as Persia's prime minister, our king.

Artabanus looks at Xerxes.

ARTABANUS
For these last six months, he has drawn
people here, entertained them night
after night, and all to make them
believe he is a force unstoppable.

Standing tall, he empties his drink and glares at Mardonius.

ARTABANUS
(continuing)
The campaign which he thinks will be
chronicled as the definition of greatness,
could prove to be remembered as
nothing more than an egocentric
folly . . . even the end of his reign, seeing
as though, just as my son, he insists on
going with the army, and, just as my son,
he is no more than flesh and bone.

MARDONIUS
Nothing is going to—

Artabanus briskly walks away.

MARDONIUS
(continuing)
—befall Xerxes.

Alone, Mardonius spies Darius. The prince is partaking in the delicious amenities, laughing, drinking and nearly losing his balance as his eyes wander over the women. The general's expression turns grim, for this is Xerxes' successor should anything happen.

ON ARTABANUS—weaving through the guests. A hand reaches out and grabs him by the shoulder. He stops and turns to see his oldest son.

> TRITAN
> Father—

Cruelly, Artabanus shakes his head and keeps going.

ATOP THE BALCONY

Xerxes still stands with Masistes, watching the amassed guests with great interest. From this height, the party looks like the eye of a churning storm.

> XERXES
> So, you leave for Bactria . . . ?

> MASISTES
> By the end of the week.

> XERXES
> It's been good seeing you again,
> Masistes. I know we weren't able to
> talk much during your stay, apart from
> the council meetings, but . . . .

> MASISTES
> With all the delegations, I'm surprised
> you have been able to spare a single
> moment to speak with me.

> XERXES
> It has been dizzying, hasn't it?

> MASISTES
> I don't think I have ever spoken or
> eaten as much in my entire life as I
> have since being summoned here . . .
> (MORE)

MASISTES (cont'd)
And all the wine. I have drunk enough to fill the entire Gulf of Kaldu. Good thing the day we embark for Greece is yet far off. If it were tomorrow, we'd be crawling, not marching. Well, at least I would.

Xerxes softly chuckles, but never moves his stare.

MASISTES
I shall hopefully be back to my old, handsome self by the time I reach Bactria, otherwise Suraz may not recognize me. Or maybe she will, but, even so, be reluctant to call me husband.

XERXES
Must be hard, being apart for so long.

MASISTES
It is. We've been exchanging messages, though. Her last included a request of you.

Xerxes tries his best to pretend he is not intrigued.

XERXES
(dryly)
What is it she's asked for?

MASISTES
That if I should indeed go with you, please bring me back, as well. Preferably, unharmed, all limbs still attached and in working order.

XERXES
Well, if she insists.

MASISTES
Oh, she does.

They both laugh, but the mood turns serious.

XERXES
It seems so close. We talk as if it is, yet there is still so much to be done.

MASISTES
You can count on me to do my part.

XERXES
I know. I have complete trust in you.
    (off silence)
Masistes?

MASISTES
I was just thinking . . . last time I took up arms with you, it was game.

Xerxes moves to respond, but looking past Masistes, he spots Amestris peering from behind one of the balcony's curtained "wings".

MASISTES
    (off Xerxes' look)
What is it?

XERXES
Who, you mean.

Masistes turns. She's gone.

MASISTES
I don't see anyone.

XERXES
She's shy, apparently.

MASISTES
Amestris?

XERXES
(nodding)
We'll speak again before you depart for Bactria?

MASISTES
I look forward to it.

XERXES
Good, my friend. Good.

MASISTES
Till then.

XERXES
Enjoy the feast.

MASISTES
Oh, I will.

Masistes heads for the stairs, casting one last wave before descending them to join the party.

Xerxes leans back against the railing and, with no more than a finger, signals Amestris to come out.

XERXES
Retiring for the night?

AMESTRIS
No, not yet.
(a beat)
I didn't interrupt an important discussion, did I?

XERXES
I wouldn't have ended it if that were
the case.

AMESTRIS
Masistes has been here awhile now.

XERXES
He's leaving by week's end.

Xerxes turns around and resumes watching the party. Amestris draws close beside him.

AMESTRIS
Were you disappointed?

XERXES
Of what?

AMESTRIS
That she did not come with him?

XERXES
You've been meaning to ask me that
since the assembly, haven't you?
      (off her nod)
What an absurd question.

AMESTRIS
Is it?

He playfully grabs her by the wrist, pulls her between himself and the railing, and leans close to her ear.

XERXES
      (pointing to the crowd)
Look at them, Amestris. They are all
here for me.

AMESTRIS
The empire's king.

                    XERXES
            To them, I'm more than that. I am the
            embodiment of it. How could anything
            bring me low when held so high?

She leans back against him and nuzzles closer.

                    AMESTRIS
            I once heard someone say, it is always
            the large buildings and tall trees that are
            struck by lightning.

                    XERXES
            Oh, there is storm brewing, but I, my
            dear vashishta, shall not be the one
            seeking shelter.
                                                CUT TO:

MONTAGE—WAR PREPARATIONS

                    THEMISTOCLES (V.O.)
            When reports came, stating the Persians
            were gathering their forces, eyes
            glimmered with dread.

—Cavalry, infantry and archers are gathered throughout the empire.

—Smiths work in forges, producing swords and armor.

—Builders construct boats.

—Women weave reeds.

—Horses and oxen are brought in by the hundreds.

                                            DISSOLVE TO:

MONTAGE—PREPARATIONS ABROAD

> THEMISTOCLES (V.O.)
> When I learned many of our fellow Greeks turned traitor, my own did, as well. They have pledged earth and water, declared fealty to Persia, even changed the very landscape of Mount Athos to suit King Xerxes' purposes and display his power. He's shown it in other ways, too.

—Persian couriers speak with Greek statesmen.

—Earth and water are offered to Persian representatives.

—Persian banners are placed on Grecian soil.

—Both Persian and Greek workers stand on ladders within a deep, wide trench as buckets of earth are passed up to them to empty. They are in the process of digging a canal through the isthmus of MOUNT ATHOS.

DISSOLVE TO:

MONTAGE—SECOND BABYLONIAN REVOLT

> THEMISTOCLES (V.O.)
> After the army departed for Sardis, a rebel named Shamas-eriba led a revolt in Babylon. He must have thought it an opportune time and, in the beginning, things must have, indeed, looked encouraging. To me, as well. I thought, perhaps, we would be spared war. Instead, what followed could be a glimpse into our own future. Babylon was besieged for months. Oh, but the walls did come down and once fallen, the revolt was crushed so quickly it may as well never have happened at all.
> (MORE)

                    THEMISTOCLES (V.O.)(cont'd)
                Shamas-eriba and his cabal were
                executed. Their lands were taken and
                bestowed to Persian nobles, and by the
                time Xerxes' men were done, even the
                very course of the Euphrates had been
                redirected by their hands, and he, their
                Great King, has become all the more
                revered by his people. Even our own
                oracles see him as more than a man.

—Outside the city, Persian troops tear down a section of the wall.

—Persian and Babylonian forces battle against REBELS in the streets.

—SHAMAS-ERIBA is executed.

                                    DISSOLVE TO:

INT. GREECE—ASSEMBLY OF THE CITY-STATES—DAY

We see that Themistocles is only one of hundreds of POLITICOS gathered within the council hall. They represent poleis from throughout Greece. Most are not impressed by the Athenian's harangue, or the Athenians themselves for that matter.

Many of Athens' statesmen are present. A new face is among them, too—CIMON, early thirties, classic in looks and confident in manner.

                    THEMISTOCLES
                We went to Delphi. They were not
                happy to see us. On the contrary, there
                are many who would be very pleased to
                see us run from Greece.
                    (quoting the oracle)
                Wretches, why ye sit here? Fly, fly to
                ends of creation, quitting your homes,
                and the crags which your city crowns
                        (MORE)

>   THEMISTOCLES(cont'd)
> with her circlet. Neither the head, nor the body is firm in its place, nor at the bottom, firm the feet, nor the hands; nor resteth the middle uninjured. All—all ruined and lost, since fire and impetuous Ares, speeding along in an Assyrian chariot hastens to destroy her.
>   (a beat)
> I could go on, but I'm confident you gather the meaning. We, as I'm sure you can understand, were not satisfied with this. We went yet again to the oracle, taking with us an olive branch, in hopes of hearing better news, and we were thus told of the wooden wall, which has since, oddly enough, caused division between us. What I believe—

>   POLITICO 1
> Who cares what you think?!
>   (pointing to Athenians)
> Or any of you? Athens brought this war upon us!

A group of men get up and leave.

>   POLITICO 2
> Makes little difference now. There isn't time to point the finger of blame.

Cimon stands up.

>   CIMON
> Agreed. All your arguments will come to nothing, as will you, if you cannot cease to make enemies among your Greek brothers.

ARISTIDES
You should all listen to Cimon. Here he now stands, prepared to defend the same people by whose orders he was imprisoned, the same people who he called his own.

THEMISTOCLES
Would you all rather keep your grudges or your lands? Because that is the simple choice it comes down to.

POLITICO 3
You would have us all believe the Persians seek to enslave Greece. Well, Themistocles, I happen to believe, and I am not alone, that Greece is already enslaved, tied down by the greed of its own people. Xerxes may be the hand that finally frees us.

The man gets up and walks out, as do others.

POLITICO 4
Speaking of . . . I find it ironic that Sparta, which has made slaves of so many, now talks of fighting for the sake of our nation's freedom.

There is a rumble of grim laughter.

POLITICO 4
They support your resistance, only because, once Athens is taken, what's to stop the Persians from continuing into the Peloponnese? Demaratus is laughing at them from afar. Who knew a Spartan could have such a keen sense
(MORE)

                    POLITICO 4(cont'd)
          of humor, sending them word the way
          he did.
                    (a beat)
          They've finally decided to seek counsel
          from the Pythia at Delphi. Like you,
          like us, they're looking for an answer.
          Perhaps she shall tell them something
          we do not yet know . . . or perhaps she
          will tell them what we already do . . .
          Greece is lost.

He gets up and, like the others, leaves.

EXT. DELPHI—NIGHT

The Doric edifices of Delphi are nestled against Mount Parnassus. The site seethes with anxiety. People are crammed along the its winding paths, bathed in the glow of firelight, their eyes sparked with fear.

EXT. DELPHI—TEMPLE OF APOLLO—NIGHT

Before the guard-lined stairs is a SPARTAN DELEGATION, led by Pausanias. Behind them, an immense crowd has formed. Every eye is set on the portico.

When a TEMPLE OFFICIAL appears, the mob rushes forward, trying to push past the Spartans and the guards. One BEWILDERED MAN finally succeeds, only to be tackled just before the entrance.

                    BEWILDERED MAN
               (as he is dragged away)
          What of Xerxes?!!

Undeterred by the chaos, the official signals for the Spartans to come inside.

INT. DELPHI—TEMPLE OF APOLLO—ADYTON—NIGHT

In a small, dark compartment, below the building, INTERPRETERS surround the entranced ORACLE—the Pythia. Draped in a chiton, a laurel branch held in one hand, a bowl in the other, she sits atop a three-legged stool which straddles a fissure running along the floor. From its depths, vapors rise. DISTORTED WHISPERS spill from her lips and ricochet against the walls as she breathes them deep.

Pausanias and the other Spartans approach the entrance, but are kept from crossing it, halted by both the interpreters and the sound of a GASP. The oracle's eyes suddenly open. From beneath her lashes, an unsettling stare is cast upon them. They freeze on the spot.

>   ORACLE
> Hear your fate, O dwellers in Sparta of
> the wide spaces. Either your famed,
> great town must be sacked by Perseus's
> sons, or, if that be not, the whole land
> of Lacedaemon shall mourn the death
> of a king of the house of Heracles, for
> not the strength of lions or of bulls
> shall hold him, strength against
> strength; for he has the power of Zeus,
> and will not be checked till one of
> these two he has consumed.

CUT TO:

MONTAGE—XERXES' NIGHTMARE

—Bridges are wiped out.

—Ships are tossed and broken against jagged rocks.

—On a battlefield, spears fly. Arrows darken the sky. Horses squeal.

—The sun is eclipsed.

—The sound of soldiers in excruciating pain filters through the strata. Men drop to their knees, no life coursing through their bodies.

—Lightning strikes the ground setting everything aflame.

—The sun resumes its place in the sky, shedding light on the carnage below.

CUT TO:

INT. ABYDOS—XERXES' WAR TENT—JUST BEFORE DAWN

SUMMER, 480 B.C.

Xerxes jolts out of bed. Sweat glistens on his brow. The surroundings of the war tent begin to register. Tapestries line the walls, carpets are spread out on the floor. Candles, melted down to mere nubs, are perched upon metal candelabras around the tent. Maps litter a nearby table.

EXT. ABYDOS—HELLESPONT—JUST BEFORE DAWN

The sun will soon crest over the horizon, but the stars are reluctant to fall. They hold fast to the receding cloak of night and so does the silence . . . so does Xerxes.

He stands alone, as if on a precipice, his cloak shuffling about him as a stiff morning wind passes by, surveying all that stretches below. Camp fires of the early risers can be seen dotting the shoreline and every surrounding plain for miles. The Hellespont itself is consumed with the fleet's ships.

While, for us, this sight alone is impressive, it is only a mere preview as to the true immensity of the army. Xerxes, however, knows exactly what it is he beholds, what lies beneath the dark and the sheer, palpable awe of it moves him to tears.

ARTABANUS (O.S.)
Xerxes?

Artabanus approaches and stands beside his nephew. He is taken aback by such a show of emotion.

                    ARTABANUS
What is this? Only a little while ago
you were congratulating yourself and,
now . . .
          (astonished)
Behold, you weep.

                    XERXES
There came upon me . . . a sudden
pity, when I thought of the shortness
of a man's life and considered that all
those I see before me, as strong and
numerous as they are . . . there will
come a day when only one is left. Then
he, too, shall draw his last breath and
there will be none. How will our deeds
speak of us when we can no longer bear
witness . . . ?

It is a rhetorical question. Xerxes reflects on it before finally turning to Artabanus, dry eyed.

                    XERXES
I want you to return to Susa after we've
crossed.

Peering back from whence he came, Artabanus can just make out the sight of his two sons, Tritan and Tigranes, walking across the campsite, torches in hand. He watches them regretfully.

                    XERXES
Artabanus?

                    ARTABANUS
Yes. After you've crossed.

                    XERXES
I know your concern has not waned.

ARTABANUS
You could still abandon this plan,
Xerxes. Once you traverse the
Hellespont, nothing is assured.

XERXES
Well . . . very few things in life are, but you cannot allow your life to be dictated by fear, for if you do, you will never achieve anything. Far better it is to have a stout heart always and suffer one's share of evils than to be ever worried of what may happen. Success, for the most part, attends to those who act boldly, not those who weigh everything and are slack to venture. You see how great a height the power of Persia has reached? Never would it have grown to this point if those who sat upon the throne before me had been as fearful as you, or had listened to councilors of a like-mind. It was by brave ventures that they extended their sway . . . for great empires can only be conquered by great risks.

EXT. HELLESPONT—MORNING

The Hellespont is congested by hundreds of battle and cargo ships. The crews of all are on deck and at attention. We recognize two of the admirals—Achaemenes, leading the EGYPTIAN CONTINGENT and Ariabignes, who commands the PHOENICIAN. At the head of her own vessels, is QUEEN ARTEMISIA of HALICARNASSUS, whose outward grace is matched by an inner strength.

Two separate lines of Persian boats, tethered together, span nearly a mile in length across the water. Planks and earth are leveled atop them. These are the 'roads' which the army will cross in their pursuit of the Greek mainland.

They are decorated for the occasion with myrtle boughs, wreathes of garlands, and frankincense burners.

Already upon one bridge are large ox drawn wagons, surrounded by their soon to be occupants, among them, Onomacritus. Their covers flap against the chilling wind. Behind, are half the INFANTRY DEFENSES, followed by the ROYAL GROOMS. The men hold the leads of ten Nesaean stallions.

The next in the procession holds the eyes of all.

Eight white horses stand four-by-four, tied by leather straps to the king's embossed, gold chariot. The animals are restless, pawing the ground and their breath clouds upon meeting the cool, morning breeze.

Xerxes, elaborately armored, stands upon the chariot, facing his army lined along the bank and its top six generals: Mardonius, Masistes, Megabyzus, Smerdomenes, Tritan, and Gergis.

One thousand of the legendary IMMORTALS carry spears with pommes of gold. One thousand HORSEMEN, led by Masistius, sit on powerful mounts. Another nine thousand Immortals, commanded by Hydarnes, hold spears with pommes of silver.

More is to be seen. Ten thousand additional members of the CAVALRY rein in their horses.

Hundreds of large mastiffs, the king's war dogs, pull against their leashes, eager to proceed. The second half of the infantry stand at attention behind.

The landscape is, simply put, a sea of men and whether on foot, horseback, chariot, or camel, every face is turned toward their supreme commander.

An attendant stands beside the king's chariot, holding a chalice and bowl, both made of gold. Xerxes reaches for the former, takes a drink, and lifts it skyward as he addresses the army.

> XERXES
> The fruits of labor bear the sweet taste
> of triumph.

Tipping the chalice, wine spills down into the water.

                    XERXES
        We have drunken ourselves on such
        rewards.

He throws the chalice into the Hellespont and reaches for the bowl. Between two hands, he holds it up for all to see.

                    XERXES
        We have feasted on them.

The bowl is sent to meet the same fate as the chalice. Xerxes reaches for the akinakes at his side. Its metal edge resonates against the scabbard as it is drawn out. The king masterfully twirls it before grasping the hilt with both hands. Ceremoniously, the weapon is raised above his head. The sun beams off of it, causing a blinding light to flicker like lightning.

                    XERXES
        By the sword, we shall reap them
        again!

Xerxes sends the akinakes hurling into the Hellespont. Colliding with the currents, water explodes around the weapon before consuming it.

Suddenly, foreboding shadows stretch across the landscape, causing many to look up. Eyes widen as the sky darkens. Many gasp in wonder. The sun grows small, its face blocked by the premature moon.

Beside the wagons, we see Onomacritus's jaw drop.

                ONOMACRITUS
          (to himself; in awe)
        'Twas fated.

Xerxes watches in disbelief. It is the eclipse from his dream.

Taking considerate steps, Onomacritus approaches.

>   XERXES
>   What does this signify?
>
>   ONOMACRITUS
>   Destiny smiles upon us, O Great King.
>
>   XERXES
>   Explain.
>
>   ONOMACRITUS
>   (to the army)
>   The moon is symbolic of Persia, consuming
>   the light of Apollo—of the Greeks. It
>   portents the eclipse of their dominion.

CHEERS rise from the troops. Swords are raised. The beginnings of a smile draw across Xerxes' face as his eyes reflect the eerie glow of the sky. A memory speaks.

>   DARIUS THE GREAT (V.O.)
>   A legend is nothing more than a story
>   born beneath the moon.
>
>   XERXES
>   (whispering)
>   Then let the tale begin.

Through the shroud of shadow, the army proceeds to march.

                                                       CUT TO:

MONTAGE—PERSIAN MARCH

—Xerxes' forces cross into the mainland.

—We see an elderly, HELLESPONTINE man, standing upon the outskirts of his town with a friend, watching as the army approaches. Beholding Xerxes, his eyes begin to gloss.

> HELLESPONTINE
> Why, O' Jove, in the form of a Persian
> man, and by the name of Xerxes, do
> you lead the race of mankind to the
> destruction of Greece?

—The Greek council of city-states, including Spartan delegates, is convened once more. By their body language, they have chosen to stand as one.

> POLITICOS
> To the alliance! . . . To Greece!

—Throughout the country, whether in a tavern, on the street, conducting business in stately halls, or working the fields, GRECIANS discuss the war.

> GRECIAN 1
> What's the news?

> GRECIAN 2
> Athens has managed a shaky alliance,
> but I doubt it will do them any good.

> GRECIAN 3
> What of the Spartans?

> GRECIAN 4
> Leonidas could only offer a few
> hundred troops.

> GRECIAN 5
> The Ephors promise to send more after
> their ceremonial rites are over.

—In Sparta, Leonidas speaks before the three-hundred SPARTANS which will accompany him to the mainland. Among them is Dieneces. Even for a small group, they all look formidable, donning their signature helmets, shields and cloaks.

> LEONIDAS
> We shall go forth to meet our enemy,
> not with a frightful heart, but a
> contented one, for we fight as Spartans
> and shall not die as slaves.

> SPARTANS
> To Sparta! . . . Down with Xerxes!

—The THRACIANS welcome Xerxes and his army, smiling and bowing before them as they march past.

> THRACIANS
> All hail Xerxes! . . . We pledge loyalty
> to you!

—Grecians.

> GRECIAN 6
> They may as well not even bother.

> GRECIAN 7
> Is there no hope?

> GRECIAN 8
> If you had seen what my own eyes
> beheld in Thrace—

> GRECIAN 9
> —in Macedonia, you would understand
> why the oracles utter Xerxes' name in
> the same breath as Zeus and Ares.

—The king of Macedonia, ALEXANDER, is taken before Xerxes. He kneels before him while his servants offer gifts.

> ALEXANDER
> Alexander of Macedonia, O Great King.

—Grecians.

> GRECIAN 10
> He really bowed?

> GRECIAN 11
> Kneeled.

—In SUSA, we see Haman and Artabanus.

> HAMAN
> So far, the king has encountered
> nothing but Greeks bearing gifts.

> ARTABANUS
> And soon, he will meet those bearing arms.

—We see Greek FIGHTERS preparing swords, shields and armor.

—At ARTEMISIUM, Themistocles boards a Spartan ship commanded by EURYBIADES. They clasp hands.

> THEMISTOCLES
> Admiral Eurybiades, you've come.

> EURYBIADES
> We Spartans keep our word.

> THEMISTOCLES
> The Persians are descending upon
> Greece utterly unopposed. They must
> be stopped.

—In SUSA Darius and Amestris talk.

> DARIUS
> Where are they now?

> AMESTRIS
> Thessaly.

—The Persian fleet stays close to the army as it continues along the coastline through THESSALY.

—Xerxes, his men, and the THESSALIAN KINGS watch their best riders race one another. The Persian horse, stronger and much more swift, easily wins.

—Grecians.

> GRECIAN 12
> We're at our wits' end while the army sent to decimate us is engaged not in warfare, but racing their horses in Thessaly for sport?!

> GRECIAN 13
> They were. They've since left.

> GRECIAN 14
> I doubt their next reception will be so warm or leisurely.

—Leonidas's men reach THERMOPYLAE, and meet with approximately nine-thousand other troops sent from throughout the country. Together, they work on strengthening the ancient Thermopylae wall and using the nearby marshes to flood the pass.

—In ATHENS, Cimon and Aristides watch as the Acropolis is fortified.

> ARISTIDES
> They grow ever closer with each day.

> CIMON
> Should they breach the hot gates, we have no other choice than to evacuate, for whatever the 'wooden wall' is, it will not keep the Persians out of Athens.

—Grecians.

> GRECIAN 15
> So many will perish.

> GRECIAN 16
> So many will be lost.

—PERSIAN SOLDIERS talk around their campfire.

> SOLDIER 1
> It is the way of war.

> SOLDIER 2
> We shall stay the course.

—In BACTRIA, Suraz sullenly talks to herself

> SURAZ
> Please, find your way back.

—Xerxes' top generals look to him quizzically as he reads a message handed to him by Mardonius.

> MARDONIUS
> We must first handle these resisters
> who have posted themselves right in
> our path.

> HYDARNES
> Where?

> XERXES
> In a place known as Thermopylae.

EXT. THERMOPYLAE—LEONIDAS'S CAMP—NIGHT

Greek war tents are set up near the pass of Thermopylae. Though their forces total nearly nine-thousand men, only a few hundred of the troops are seen, the majority being Spartans. They, along with soldiers from other contingents, watch the distant hillside where fiery lights glimmer in the sky over the lands of Skiathos and Euboea.

Dieneces walks through the campsite, past a group of allied soldiers sharpening their weaponry. One looks up at the Spartan as he goes and ominously calls out.

>   GRECIAN SOLDIER
> I heard the Persian archers are in such
> great number, that the whole sky shall
> be darkened by the multitude of their
> arrows.

>   DIENECES
> Take this as good news, for our battle
> shall then be fought in the shade.

Dieneces pats the fellow on the back and continues on to speak with Leonidas who stands before his own lodgings, observing the light show.

>   DIENECES
> King Leonidas?

>   LEONIDAS
> Themistocles and his armada sit at
> Artemisium, Xerxes' at Aphetae.

>   DIENECES
> Think they can hold them off?

>   LEONIDAS
> Whether on land or sea, one of us
> must.

Dieneces looks back at the campsite.

>   DIENECES
> Many of our allies are beginning to
> panic.

> LEONIDAS
> They can't afford to.

They return their attention to the night sky, but the sound of a horse trotting up pulls Leonidas from his ruminations. He turns to see a YOUNG COURIER dismount and trudge through the muddy soil of the camp to hand him a bound scroll.

Leonidas scrutinizes the seal which binds it shut. It is Xerxes' crest. The surrounding soldiers gather close, eager to know what has been sent.

Taking his time, Leonidas breaks the seal and unrolls the document. Scanning it over, he nods, denoting that he already knew what he would find written.

> DIENECES
> What is it, King Leonidas?

Looking up, he breathes out and clears his throat so that all can hear.

> LEONIDAS
> (reading)
> King Xerxes orders all to give up their
> arms, to depart unharmed to their
> native lands, and to be allies of the
> Persians; and to all Greeks who do this,
> he will give more and better lands than
> they now possess.

The troops mumble amongst themselves. Leonidas rolls the scroll up and dismissively hands it back to the scribe.

> LEONIDAS
> Depart to our native lands . . . Do we
> not already stand on Hellenic soil?

> GREEK SOLDIERS
> Yes! . . . These are our lands! . . . We
> will not flee!

Leonidas regards the troops, impressed by their steadfast resolve.

> LEONIDAS
> He wants our arms? Let him come and take them.

INT. TRACHINIA—XERXES' WAR TENT—NIGHT

Xerxes, Mardonius and Demaratus sit at a large table laden with plates of food.

> DEMARATUS
> Shall I speak honestly?

> XERXES
> Always.

> DEMARATUS
> Sparta doesn't merely have an army. It is one. Its people are brave warriors, raised by the sword, and not to be underestimated.

> XERXES
> They make up only a small faction of the Thermopylae forces.

> DEMARATUS
> Yes, but they're leading them, and with the pass there being so narrow, if it came to battle, only so many men could be engaged at once, yet a single Spartan—

> MARDONIUS
> —could be worth ten men, a hundred, Demaratus. It matters not.

DEMARATUS
As incomprehensible as it may sound, you could present them with the entire army, yet they still would not run. Nor will they ever accept the terms you offer.

XERXES
(sarcastic)
Oh?

DEMARATUS
In their minds, by doing so, they submit themselves to slavery.

XERXES
(scoffs)
Slavery?

DEMARATUS
They believe you've come, not with an open hand, but a yoke.

MARDONIUS
The way you're talking . . . if I didn't know better, Demaratus, I would think you were still loyal to Sparta.

DEMARATUS
My allegiance was severed the day they took my title. I'm merely speaking as someone who knows the Spartan ideology. They will fight to the last man.

MARDONIUS
And when that last falls, what is it that they will have accomplished? Nothing.

                    DEMARATUS
          It is a matter of principle to these men.

Xerxes rolls his eyes and takes a drink. Demaratus is upset that the matter is not being taken earnestly. Silence takes the scene, but lasts only briefly. A soldier enters the tent and bows before the king.

                     SOLDIER
          King Xerxes, the Spartan commander
          has issued his response.

Grabbing the message, Xerxes casts a sly grin at Demaratus. He is sure what he holds is the Spartan's resignation. Upon reading it, however, the king's smile twists into an enraged sneer.

                      XERXES
          May they learn, in time to come, to
          take what is offered them.

Xerxes crumples the letter as if crushing the Spartans themselves.

                                                        CUT TO:

MONTAGE—BEFORE THE BATTLE

—The Persian army marches south through sporadic dust storms.

—Approaching Thermopylae, scenery includes the Malian Gulf, Euboea across the straits, ramparts of the Pindus Mountains.

—The Asopus Gorge fissure rises up in the distance.

—At Thermopylae, between the forested mountainside and the sea, Leonidas surveys his troops.

EXT. THERMOPYLAE—PERSIAN COMMAND POST—DAY

Atop a prime vantage point, Xerxes sits on a throne surrounded by Mardonius, Masistes, Hydarnes, Onomacritus and Demaratus; scribes awaiting dictation and messengers on horseback. Behind the post, the king's thousand 'gold' ranked Immortals are at attention.

BELOW, the MEDIAN contingent stands at the head of the army, the mountainside on their right and the coast at their left. The Greek forces are primed south of Thermopylae's most narrow path. Its entrance, or 'gate', is a mere wagon's breadth wide.

MARDONIUS
They await your orders.

Xerxes' order is silently issued with a turn of hand.

Mardonius looks to one of the messengers and tips his head. The man rides off.

EXT. THERMOPYLAE—BATTLEGROUND—DAY

Leonidas waits with Dieneces and the troops. Sitting on horseback, he looks to the Persians warily. They are beginning to head their way.

LEONIDAS
Ready yourselves!

The Greeks take up their arms.

LEONIDAS
March!

Leonidas and Dieneces concernedly watch as the Spartan phalanx steadily marches forward to the rhythm of a FLUTE. Its simple melody is a macabre, eloquent prelude to battle, meant to heighten the anxiety of their opponents.

With each disconcerting note, the pace of the Persian forces quickens, till, at last, the Medes detach from the front and charge ahead, spears raised. Their YELLS resonate against the mountainside, drowning out the sound of the flute. Spears leveled, the Spartans brace for impact within the 'gate', holding tight formation behind their weighty shields. Like a tidal wave, the Medes roll along the coastline and crash upon their foes. Many of the king's soldiers are impaled. A cacophony of chaos rises.

CUT TO:

MONTAGE—THERMOPYLAE—THE BATTLE—DAY 1

—Xerxes, watching from the distant hillside, leaps from his throne, astonished by the Greeks' prowess.

—The Medes are pulled back.

—CISSIANS and SCYTHIAN TRIBESMEN, the next of the Persian contingent, approach. The latter launch an onslaught of WHISTLING arrows upon the Greeks.

—The Scyths and Cissians rush to meet their weakened foes and close combat begins.

—Inch by inch, the Greeks are beat back.

—Leonidas signals his troops to retreat.

—At the command post, Xerxes and the others watch perplexed as the Greek army begins to withdraw.

—The Persian forces break rank, running after the departing enemy.

—The Greeks turn about abruptly and seize upon the unorganized ranks of their pursuers. It is a frenzy, disorienting and brutal.

—The two armies continue to fight beneath a darkening sky.

—The pass grows congested with the bodies of both armies. Soldiers jump, run, and clamber over their lost compatriots as they struggle against one another with swords and spears.

EXT. THERMOPYLAE—PERSIAN COMMAND POST—DUSK

Xerxes looks to the sky as forceful currents of HOWLING WIND cause banners to nearly tear from their staffs. Lightning flashes. THUNDER BOOMS. Waves dash the shoreline.

The armies continue to duke it out, but the king appears to be in anguish, noting that many of his men are tiring.

Gritting his teeth, Xerxes stands.

>   XERXES
>   Pull them back.

EXT. THERMOPYLAE—BATTLEGROUND—DUSK

The Persian troops are signaled to fall back. Many are reluctant to disengage from combat, but follow the order. As they depart, the severity of the attack is revealed. Thousands of corpses litter the pass.

The Greek troops, though exhausted, CHEER their success. Leonidas does not appear to share their excitement, for he is well-aware that this was merely the first round.

                                                            CUT TO:

MONTAGE—THE STORM—NIGHT

—Lightning cracks through the ebony sky, striking a tree and splitting it in two.

—Persian soldiers race for cover

—Grecian tents sway in the wind.

—The waters of the Malian Gulf jut and rock furiously under the torrents of rain.

—From a command tent on the coast of Artemisium, Themistocles confers with Eurybiades as they peer beyond their shelter.

—Many of the fallen soldiers, both Persian and Greek, are pulled from the Thermopylae coastline and carried out to sea by the tide.

—Persian ships are jostled against nearby cliffs. Their crews scramble to draw away.

—Xerxes, completely alone, sits on his bed, legs sprawled out, staring straight ahead at nothing. Moments later, he closes his eyes.

CUT TO:

MONTAGE—THERMOPYLAE—THE BATTLE—DAY 2

—Xerxes opens his eyes as he sits on the hillside, surrounded by generals, scurrying attendants and debris from the storm.

—From their own post, Leonidas and Dieneces watch the Greek infantry hold the line against the Persians.

—Tiring Persian troops, unable to breach the passageway, are called back as the 'silver' ranked Immortals march concertedly toward the battle under Hydarnes' command.

—Xerxes anxiously sits up.

—Leonidas anxiously looks to Dieneces.

—The Immortals begin to force the Greeks back.

—Fresh Greek troops are sent in. The front rank reestablishes a tight, phalanx formation and, serving as a grinder, shred any who cross their line.

—Xerxes, for the third time, rises from his throne.

—The Immortals are signaled to pull back.

—The pass, consumed with broken arrows, swords, shredded wicker shields and the bodies of the fallen, is now silent.

INT. XERXES' WAR TENT—AFTERNOON

The sound of soldiers piling into camp echoes beyond Xerxes' quarters. He sits at the head of a table, staring at a map of the area and rubs his temples as if greatly pained.

The army's top six commanders, as well as Hydarnes and Demaratus, sit in uncomfortable silence, waiting to hear the thoughts of their brooding leader.

Finally, he breathes out.

> XERXES
> They fought valiantly.

> MARDONIUS
> Yes, our troops—

> XERXES
> The Greeks.

Xerxes rises from his chair and begins to pace around the table. All eyes are upon him.

> XERXES
> You were right, Demaratus. I should not have underestimated them.

Demaratus looks down, sorry that he was right.

> MARDONIUS
> After a night's rest, the troops will be refreshed and the fleet has repaired their ships since the storm. These are only setbacks.

> XERXES
> Walk amongst my soldiers and echo those words. See if they consider their losses so easily dismissed.

Stopping before his empty seat, Xerxes glares at Mardonius bemusedly and sits.

> MARDONIUS
> We will breach the Greek defenses. It is only a matter of time.

> XERXES
> (repeating; trying to reassure himself)
> Only a matter of time.

An Immortal enters the tent, drawing the eyes of all. By the man's haggard appearance, it is apparent that he participated in the battle.

> IMMORTAL
> (bowing)
> King Xerxes, I beg your pardons for interrupting, but there is a matter which may interest you.

> XERXES
> Your apology is not necessary. What is this matter?

Rising to stand tall, the soldier briefly tips his head to the gathered generals.

> IMMORTAL
> We found a man lurking beyond the perimeter. He claims to know of a path which bypasses the Greek forces.

Xerxes leans back in his chair, intrigued by the news.

> XERXES
> Where is he now?

> IMMORTAL
> Just outside your tent.

XERXES
Bring him here.

IMMORTAL
Yes, your highness.

Xerxes thoughtfully rubs his chin as the guard goes to fulfill the command. Skeptical, Masistes leans across the table.

MASISTES
What if this is a ruse? An attempt by the Greeks to draw us into a trap?

XERXES
Could be. Demaratus?

Demaratus shakes his head.

DEMARATUS
No, the Spartans would not concoct such a plan.

MASISTES
Can you be so sure?

Mardonius looks to the entrance of the tent expectantly.

MARDONIUS
I think we must consider all of our options.

The flaps of the tent are flung open. The Immortal enters, clutching EPHIALTES, a short, commonly dressed man in his thirties, around the arm. Xerxes further reclines in his chair as the two approach and stop to stand before him. Masistes suspiciously scans the guest over.

XERXES
Unhand him.

The Immortal does as ordered. Ephialtes, strangely confident, looks around the table.

> XERXES
> I am told you are in possession of
> information which could prove useful
> to me.

> EPHIALTES
> Yes, I am.

> MARDONIUS
> For a reward, no doubt.

> EPHIALTES
> (to Xerxes)
> As you see, I am not a man of great means.
> My family is all that I have. My presence
> here betrays them, but perhaps, I may make
> amends if I do not return empty handed.

Xerxes smirks, recognizing a truly greedy man when he sees one.

> XERXES
> What is your name?

> EPHIALTES
> Ephialtes.

> XERXES
> Well, Ephialtes, tell me what you
> know. If it is of use, then we will
> discuss the measure by which your
> family's shame will be eased. If not—
> (leaning forward)
> —their clemency will be the last of
> your worries.

Ephialtes shrinks at the insinuated threat.

EPHIALTES
(shakily)
I know your army has found considerable difficulty pushing past Leonidas's troops.

XERXES
Go on.

EPHIALTES
There is another way into the plain.

XERXES
(pointing to the map on the table)
Our map shows no such passage.

EPHIALTES
I wouldn't expect it to. It is a goat path which runs along the Kallindromos.

XERXES
(turning the map)
Show me.

Ephialtes gingerly extends an arm across the table to trace the path. All watch intently.

EPHIALTES
It starts at the Asopus, takes you along the ridge, ends here. There is a small group of Phocian soldiers stationed just before this plain, but they are no real threat.

Xerxes looks to his compatriots, the wheels of thought turning.

XERXES
(to the Immortal)
Take our new friend outside.

The soldier grabs Ephialtes around the arm. Frightened, he reluctantly backs up as he is drawn away.

> EPHIALTES
> King Xerxes?? Your highness?? What is
> to happen to me??

> XERXES
> (looking at the map)
> Fear not. No harm will come to you.

Ephialtes is lead out of the tent. Masistes watches as they exit.

> MASISTES
> Does he truly have no reason to worry?

> XERXES
> Ephialtes' work is not done.

> MASISTES
> When it is?

> XERXES
> He will be rewarded.

The generals intently regard Xerxes, curious to know his thoughts. Finally, he looks up from the map.

> XERXES
> The Immortals' numbers must be replenished. I want you all to go with General Hydarnes and select the most noble fighters from each of your contingents. They're to be promoted to the silver rank.

> HYDARNES
> Are you planning to—

                    XERXES
Send them in? Yes. Ephialtes will guide your troops across the Kallindromos tonight, and Mardonius will advance the infantry against the Greek frontline in the morning.

                    MARDONIUS
When the Immortals come down the path—

                    XERXES
Leonidas and his men will be crushed in between.

EXT. KALLINDROMOS RIDGE—NIGHT

The moon is full, the wind still. CRICKETS CHIRP. The PHOCIANS, a contingent of the Grecian army, comprised of a thousand men, are scattered along the trail's border.

The bulk of them are asleep, their armor and swords discarded nearby. Two men lazily stand guard at the entrance of the

Phocian post, picking at pieces of bread and cheese as they lean against a tree.

The crickets suddenly grow silent. In place of their melodies is the sound of RUSTLING LEAVES.

One of the men looks up at the rolling, forested landscape and nudges his friend's arm.

                    PHOCIAN 1
Did you hear that?

                    PHOCIAN 2
Hear what?

Phocian 1 steps away from the tree and waits for the noise to sound again. It doesn't. Phocian 2 quietly laughs at him.

> PHOCIAN 2
> Your mind is playing tricks on you.

> PHOCIAN 1
> (facing the guard)
> Must be the full moon.

> PHOCIAN 2
> Or boredom.

Phocian 2 chuckles again, but the amused look on his face turns to one of trepidation as a flock of birds takes to the sky. Their bodies dot the moon and, moments later, so do the bodies of something else. He drops his food.

> PHOCIAN 1
> (off guard's look)
> What is it?

> PHOCIAN 2
> (yelling to wake the others)
> The Persians!!!
> (running from the tree)
> They're here!! The Persians!!!

As his friend runs off, Phocian 1 turns around. His eyes grow wide with fear. Ascending the crest of the path and silhouetted against the moon are the Immortals.

INT. THERMOPYLAE—LEONIDAS'S WAR TENT—NIGHT

It is hours before sunrise, but there is a lot of noise emanating from the camp.

Leaders of the Greek contingents: THEGEAN, LOCRIAN, MANTINEAN, CORINTHEAN, THESPIAN, THEBAN, ORCHOMENEAN, and MYCENEAN, are gathered for an emergency meeting. Most are panicked, confrontationally standing in a semi-circle around Leonidas's conference table.

                    THEGEAN
               We must pull out now!

                    LOCRIAN
             There is nothing more to be done!

                    DIENECES
                    (mumbling)
               Cowardice.

                    THEGEAN
             Cowardice?! No, it is common sense!
             You Spartans and your supposed—

                    LEONIDAS
               That is enough!!

Leonidas is overwhelmed by their arguments. Flashing a distraught look at Dieneces, he raises his hands attempting to silence the fearful.

                    LEONIDAS
             We must hold up the Persian land
             forces for as long as possible!

                    MYCENEAN
             It will be a slaughter if we remain!
                    (attempting to rationalize)
             The report before you tells all. If we do
             not set out now, the Persians will
             surround us by morning.

The others angrily nod.

                    ORCHOMENEAN
             We knew there was a possibility that they
             would find the trail. We discussed what it
             would mean for our troops. Leonidas, I do
             not intend to watch my men be butchered
             just to delay Xerxes for a few hours!

THEGEAN
Neither do I!
(to the others)
Come, let us depart while there is still time.

Leonidas grits his teeth and furiously points toward the 'door'.

LEONIDAS
Go! Go on then!! But do not shed a tear when they take your lands!!

The Mycenean leans across the table as the others begin to pile out of the tent.

MYCENEAN
Tearful or not, at least our eyes shall behold a new day.

Backing up, he forlornly stares at Leonidas before turning to leave.

The room, greatly emptied, is silent as the Spartan king raises his hands to his face, attempting to rub the burning fury from his eyes. Drawing them away, he looks around and sets sights on the leaders of the Thespians and Thebans who, along with Dieneces, still remain.

LEONIDAS
(bitterly)
Are you not going to run, too?

THESPIAN
We swore to remain till the end. What do you want us to do?

DIENECES
Yes, what are your orders?

A melancholy smile pulls at Leonidas's lips.

> LEONIDAS
> As of now, there is only one.
> (a beat)
> Tell the troops to eat well, for tonight,
> we dine in Hades.

EXT. GREECE—ARTEMISIUM DOCKS—BEFORE DAWN

TRIERARCHS (captains of the Grecian fleet), soldiers and OARSMEN scuttle about beneath the light of the descending moon. Some work on their ships, others stand on the wooden docks discussing tactics.

Two such men, Themistocles and Eurybiades, look to the distant horizon of the sea. The water contentedly rolls, but their stares contradict the peacefulness of the scene—so does their armor.

> THEMISTOCLES
> Looks serene, does it not? One could
> easily be lulled into believing that the
> threat is over, that it was nothing more
> than a passing nightmare. But, beyond
> the horizon, reality comes for us.

> EURYBIADES
> Any word from King Leonidas?

> THEMISTOCLES
> Not since yesterday afternoon.

> EURYBIADES
> If there were any emergencies, I am
> sure we would have been alerted.

Crossing his arms, Themistocles turns to watch the trierarchs make their preparations. Though impressed by their stoicism, he does not look confident.

THEMISTOCLES
Eurybiades, I hope you are right.
If Xerxes' army takes Thermopylae, our
plans here are all for not.

CUT TO:

MONTAGE—PRELUDE TO BATTLE—LAND AND SEA—DAY 3

—The sun crests over the hills of Thermopylae.

—Birds fly over the sea, plunging into the water for fish.

—Smoke rises from extinguished Greek campfires.

—Soldiers, Persian and Greek, fasten armor.

—Ships, Persian and Greek, raise masts.

—Wrists, Xerxes' and Leonidas's, are cuffed.

—Water rushes against the hulls of onward ships.

—Royal hands, Xerxes' and Leonidas's, take up their weapons.

—Themistocles takes hold of the deck rail of his ship.

—Both land armies prepare to file in.

—Themistocles watches as Persian ships, led by the Egyptian contingent, under the command of Achaemenes, head toward his own.

—Flanked by body guards and with the thousand gold-ranked Immortals at his back, Xerxes stands upon his chariot, behind the bulk of the infantry. Mardonius, on horseback, waits for orders.

—Posted north of the narrow 'gate', where there is more room to fight, Leonidas looks sullenly to Dieneces and the Grecian troops, now dwindled to a few thousand. The two take their places at the front of the Spartan phalanx.

EXT. MALIAN GULF—DAY

Four-hundred Persian ships cut through the water. They approach in half-crescent formation. Each one carries a captain, thirty fighters, and nearly two-hundred oarsmen below deck.

Three-hundred Greek triremes wait for them in a tactical formation known as a 'kyklos': boats gathered in a circle, their rams facing their pursuers. Each ship carries a trierarch, fourteen fighters, and one-hundred-seventy oarsmen.

Themistocles stands on the deck of his own trireme, watching as the Egyptian contingent approaches with their bow and spearmen primed for battle. Surrounding the Athenian are his own warriors, armed in the same manner.

The oncoming ships reflecting in his eyes, Themistocles raises an arm.

      THEMISTOCLES
 Prepare—

               CUT TO:

EXT. THERMOPYLAE—BATTLE GROUND—GREEKS—DAY

Imminent danger continues to be reflected off of fearful eyes, but now, that threat is the Persian army as seen by Leonidas. The Spartan's arm is raised skyward, just like Themistocles', as he picks up the command where the Athenian left off.

      LEONIDAS
 —for—

               CUT TO:

EXT. THERMOPYLAE—BATTLE GROUND—PERSIANS—DAY

From atop the chariot, Xerxes looks toward the steadfast Greeks. Nonchalantly, he points forward and issues the order.

> XERXES
> —attack.

Mardonius tips his head, draws his sword and prompts his horse into a sprint as he rides to the front of the of the army. The soldiers mobilize behind the charge.

CUT TO:

MONTAGE—BATTLE—LAND AND SEA

—The hulls of Greek ships are rammed.

—The Greek and Persian armies collide.

—Arrows are let loose upon both fleets.

—Swords clash in a brilliant fusion of sparks.

—Fire briskets are launched at the sails of passing boats.

—Soldiers ferociously battle along the Thermopylae pass.

—Leonidas takes down a Persian.

—The sea reflects burning ships. Those not on fire are boarded. Crews engage in battle atop the decks. Many, of both sides, are thrown overboard.

—Themistocles ducks an arrow while watching a trireme take on water nearby.

—Mardonius, in the midst of battle, briefly peers back from whence he came to see that Xerxes' chariot is missing.

—Clouds block the sun.

EXT. THERMOPYLAE—PERSIAN COMMAND POST OUTSKIRTS—DAY

Standing atop a tree stump, Onomacritus grins at the sight of Persian soldiers ushering along dozens of Greek PRISONERS OF WAR.

> ONOMACRITUS
> You ignorant dogs! You mindless drones! You would put your necks on the line for Athens!? Its fate has already been sealed. It is doomed and because you would question the word of the Pythia, so are all of you!!

One of the prisoners, a Spartan, manages to break away from the group. He charges Onomacritus and grabs him by the robes.

> SPARTAN
> You traitor! Athens may be finished-

> ONOMACRITUS
> (struggling)
> By the looks of it, Sparta shall be, too. Remaining here was a foolish mistake on Leonidas's part, for, now, he will never leave!

The Spartan laughs.

> ONOMACRITUS
> You find this amusing?

> SPARTAN
> Oh, oracle monger, allow me to enlighten you—

Jerking Onomacritus forward, he whispers something in his ear.

> ONOMACRITUS
> No . . . I have to speak with the king.
> I—

Lifting a dagger from the folds of Onomacritus's garment, the Spartan pulls back and stabs him.

> SPARTAN
> You take that with you to Tartarus!

Onomacritus slides to the ground. The Spartan turns and is subsequently run through by a Persian soldier.

Masistes comes upon the scene. The young man waves him over.

> SOLDIER
> General!!! General Masistes!

> MASISTES
> (running)
> Onomacritus!?

Masistes drops to his knees beside Onomacritus. He is still breathing, though shallowly.

> MASISTES
> Onomacritus?

> ONOMACRITUS
> The king . . . must . . . not . . . Leo—

> MASISTES
> What? What is it!?

Helplessly, Masistes scans the area. Tigranes rides up.

                    TIGRANES
              General Masistes? What's happened?

                    MASISTES
                   He was attacked.

                   ONOMACRITUS
                    The king . . .

Not another word falls from Onomacritus's lips. He exhales one last breath instead.

Masistes rises to his feet.

                    MASISTES
              Find Xerxes. Hurry! Go! Now!

EXT. THERMOPYLAE—BATTLE GROUND—DAY

Grass and earth are uprooted beneath the tread of soldiers trying to maintain footing on the slick ground. Muscles bulge as combatants' swords grind against the pressure. Others, not locked in a stalemate, cut through their opponents with lightning fast twists and turns.

Though the majority of both troops fight on foot, a few tear up the ground on horseback. The animals stride through the disorienting melee as soldiers, reining them to and fro, level weapons at oncoming attackers.

Other men allow their mounts to guide the way, their hands already busy arming bows with arrows or launching spears.

One man in particular, races across the congested 'battlefield' on a stunning black stallion. Clutching a bow, he picks off man after man with arrows, intent on assisting fellow soldiers. No more bolts to fire, the bow is discarded and a sabre drawn. He continues on his way.

Elsewhere, a Spartan takes an arrow to the neck and falls at the feet of his leader. Leonidas, though briefly shocked, keeps his wits about him, bouncing a sword from hand to hand, anticipating another attack. None comes.

He dares a look back through the pass. Flashes of light flicker from behind the distant, southern tree-line. A look of utter dread crosses his face as he continues to stare.

Dieneces cuts down a Persian soldier just in time to see a stray arrow hurl through the sky. Nearly tripping on the body of a fellow compatriot, he lunges for his superior.

                    DEINECES
                Get down!

Tackling Leonidas to the ground, he almost takes the arrow himself, missing it by mere inches.

                    DIENECES
                (scrambling to stand)
            King Leonidas, are you alright?!

                    LEONIDAS
                  (getting up)
              For now.

                    DIENECES
              Sir?

Before Leonidas can explain, Greek soldiers of the Theban contingent stop fighting and begin to run. One such man hurries past, frantically signaling with raised hands to all he sees.

                    THEBAN
              Retreat!! Retreat!!!

                    DIENECES
            Stop running! Stand your ground!!

Though not in response to the order, the Theban does stop. The head of a spear rips through his chest. He falls face down, displaying the wooden shaft of the weapon extending from his back. Its base is made of gold.

                    DIENECES
                (gasping)
            Xerxes' Immortals.

Other Thebans continue to run as Dienices looks from the spear to where it came from—north.

                    DIENECES
            They were reported to come from the
            south!

Leonidas points south. Dieneces sees the tell-tale flashes of light set off by Hydarnes' troops.

                    LEONIDAS
            They are.

                    DIENECES
            Then—

                    LEONIDAS
                (pointing to the spear)
            Look at the base. It's gold. These are
            Xerxes' elite. They never—

Realization dawns.

                    LEONIDAS
                (under his breath; to himself)
            He's out here.

                    DIENECES
            Sir?

                    LEONIDAS
                (forceful)
            He's out here!!

Mind made up after an all too brief silent deliberation, Leonidas trades his short-sword for a discarded falchion sword found on the ground and starts off.

                    DIENECES
                Where are you going!?

                    LEONIDAS
                  To end this!

He bounds away and disappears into the abyss of battle before Dieneces' questioning look even has a chance to wane.

ON LEONIDAS—as he determinately struggles through the dense static of war, taking down any who challenge his next step. He is on a path of destruction, one which elevates the senses, raises the volume to a point where the slightest draw of BREATH HOARSELY RESONATES, to where tonality is hollowed, turning the sharpest CRIES into DULL ECHOES.

Leonidas continues on with ease, until spotting the elite Immortals. It is at that exact moment, that Xerxes himself, dressed as any other Persian soldier, wheels round on the Spartan, blocking his way and strike. Above their heads, their weapons collide in an array of sparks.

In this pose they remain, each scrutinizing the other, neither aware of who the other is.

                    LEONIDAS
                You're in my way, barbarian.

                    XERXES
                  And you . . . ?

Leonidas is surprised he understood.

                    LEONIDAS
                    Leonidas.

                    XERXES
                 You are in mine.

                    LEONIDAS
             Then it looks as though we're at an
             impasse, doesn't it?

                    XERXES
            It would appear so . . . but, then . . .

Xerxes forces their arms lower. Locked in a battle of wills, the two stare at each other from between crossed swords.

                    XERXES
            Things are not always as they seem.

Leonidas looks down at Xerxes' hands. He sees the king's signet ring. His eyes widen.

                    LEONIDAS
                     (shocked)
            Xerxes—

Breaking the stalemate, Xerxes pushes Leonidas away and lands a subsequent right hook to the jaw, sending the Spartan back a few steps.

                    XERXES
            It never had to come to this, you
            know?

                    LEONIDAS
            It did, and, now, a king must fall. I still
            hold hope that it may yet be you.

Composure regained, he charges. Xerxes twirls his sabre. Like before, the collision of steel results in a shatter of sparks as both block and initiate strike after strike.

Leonidas backs off, only to rush forward again a second later. Xerxes steps out of the way, but not before being sliced across the arm. This does not slow him down.

Adrenaline pumping, he turns and ducks another attack. Leonidas nearly stumbles from the force of his own, empty swing, allowing Xerxes to rise and spin behind him. Brutally, he kicks the Spartan across the back of a leg, sending him to his knees.

Standing behind Leonidas, Xerxes levels the sabre before his neck.

> **XERXES**
> Surrender!

Leonidas does not answer. Agitated by the silence, but keeping the weapon steady against his jugular, Xerxes walks around to face him.

> **XERXES**
> Surrender and I will grant you reprieve!

> **LEONIDAS**
> I was born a Spartan, and if it should
> be so—will die as one.

This statement causes Xerxes to momentarily drop his guard. Leonidas dips away from the sabre, rises to his feet and charges. Both kings meet each other head on again.

Between blinding flashes of steel, Xerxes' expression turns more and more savage. Then, just as before, Leonidas steps back only to lunge forward a moment later.

Going by instinct, Xerxes turns and plunges the sabre through his side as he runs past.

An expression of sheer shock emotes from Leonidas's face upon taking in the sight of the weapon buried between his ribs. He descends to the ground, the fall slowed by Xerxes himself.

Locking eyes with the king, Leonidas is confused, for he stares back—not with anger—but with empathy, as if to say, 'You put up a good fight, but now it is done.'

> **SPARTANS (O.S.)**
> Leonidas!! . . . No!! . . . Hurry!

A trio of Spartan soldiers, having witnessed the fall of their leader, come running.

Grimacing, Xerxes yanks the sabre from Leonidas's side in time to defend himself against one of the Spartans, who calls out to the other two.

SPARTAN 1
Go! Get him out of here!

They obey the order and proceed to drag Leonidas away. The remaining Spartan continues to cut and jab at Xerxes. The king manages to grab his wrist and run him through as Mardonius and Tigranes ride up. The latter leads the black stallion seen earlier.

TIGRANES
Your horse!

Xerxes sheathes his sabre, takes the reins and prepares to mount. A hand grabs his leg, stopping him. He looks down. At his feet is a YOUNG PERSIAN SOLDIER, mortally wounded.

YOUNG PERSIAN SOLDIER
Please, Great King—

The youth reaches for his hand. He moves to take it, but, their finger tips mere inches apart, the boy succumbs, his eyes still open and pleading. The sight grips Xerxes.

MARDONIUS (O.S.)
We have the Greeks surrounded!
We have to get you out of here!

Mardonius's urgent words break the hold.

Xerxes mounts and scans the scene. Persia's forces are rallying excellently. The remaining Greeks are being forced to pull back through the pass and it's as if he's idling in a giant game of chase.

MARDONIUS
You must go!

The horse, its eyes wide, swishes its tail, paws the ground and pulls against the reins as Xerxes spares one last look at the boy.

                    XERXES
                It won't be in vain.

Pulling his stare away, he prompts his horse into a sprint toward the command post. Mardonius and Tigranes follow closely behind, speeding across the ground, past scattered weapons and the fallen men who once wielded them.

EXT. MALIAN GULF—DAY

Bodies float atop the water amongst ship debris, flotsam and jetsam. Themistocles, battling a Persian soldier, barely manages to miss being gutted. He tackles the warrior against the rail of the boat and pushes him off into the sea.

Other boat commanders, unable to fend off their own intruders, jump ship and swim to other triremes which are departing from battle. Many ships are burning and beginning to go down. Skirting nearby one, Themistocles watches as Eurybiades and his crew leap to his deck to escape the fire.

                   EURYBIADES
             (yelling at Themistocles' crew)
           Turn about! Turn about now before we
           are all dead men!

Themistocles is not pleased by this usurp of authority and marches toward the frantic crew members.

                  THEMISTOCLES
              No! We are not retreating!

Eurybiades grabs Themistocles by the shoulders, forcing him back as he continues to rant.

        EURYBIADES   THEMISTOCLES
   Stop this insanity! Stop it now!   We are not retreating!

                  THEMISTOCLES
              You Spartans aren't supposed to
              retreat!!

                    EURYBIADES
                (shaking Themistocles)
            Look around you! We can not lose any
                more ships! Look!!

Themistocles does as ordered. Many of the Greek triremes are destroyed, abandoned, or already heading back toward Artemisium.

                    EURYBIADES
                  (calming down)
            Look . . .

Realizing the futility of continuing to fight a losing battle, Themistocles breathes out in frustration.

EXT. THERMOPYLAE—WAKE OF WAR—DAY

From the coastline battleground, through the narrow pass, and to the plain south of it, war has left its mark and silence is only interrupted by the maddening BUZZ of SWARMING FLIES.

At the edge of the plain, we see part of the ancient Thermopylae wall has been brought asunder.

EXT. THERMOPYLAE—HILLOCK—DAY

On the other side of the wall, the remaining Greek forces are surrounded by the Persians on a hillock. Dieneces waits defiantly, armed only with a broken sword. Fellow Spartans cradle the body of their, now, dead king.

Beyond the circumference of soldiers, Mardonius sits on horseback along side Xerxes. They are conferring. Finally, the general nods. An order has been issued. He rides up between the amassed Persians.

MARDONIUS
(to the Greeks)
Your bravery and skill has greatly impressed King Xerxes, but now it is time to exercise your intelligence and stand down. This battle is concluded.

DIENECES
No, it is not! Not as long as we breathe!

MARDONIUS
These lands are now our lands, to share as family—one empire under the rule of our Great King.

DIENECES
(pointing to Leonidas)
Impossible, for you see, our king is dead.

MARDONIUS
King—Xerxes—has no wish to punish you for your sentimental reluctance to let go of the past, but senseless defiance is another matter. If you will not be our allies, then you remain our enemies and will be dealt with accordingly.

The Spartans say nothing. Mardonius looks back at Xerxes. It is apparent that the king does not want to use force, but knows he must if they will not back down.

MARDONIUS
Do you concede or no?

The Greeks stand tall and prepare for the coming attack.

                          DIENECES
                  No.

Xerxes disappointedly sighs, turns his horse around and departs. Mardonius addresses the archers.

                          MARDONIUS
                  Finish it.

Dieneces and his men rush the Persians, but are stopped in their tracks as hundreds of arrows are let loose.

Masistes rides up alongside Xerxes, who is obviously saddened by what has resulted.

                          MASISTES
                  So, it is done . . .

                          XERXES
                      (looking back)
                  It is also a shame.

Both cross the plain, careful to go around fallen soldiers.

                          MASISTES
                  It was too great a risk to fight alongside
                  the army.

                          XERXES
                  I am their king.

                          MARDONIUS (O.S.)
                  You are king of an entire empire,
                  Xerxes. You must be kept safe for the
                  good of all your people.

Mardonius joins them.

                          XERXES
                  Yes, I know.

Mardonius takes a deep breath, unsure if what he wants to say is out of line. Exhaling, he decides to just speak his mind, though discreetly.

>MARDONIUS
> The prince is not yet—

>XERXES
> —capable of taking the throne?
> (a beat)
> This I know, as well.
> (to both)
> So . . . Onomacritus's last words?
> He warned you to come find me?

>MASISTES
> Desperately.

>XERXES
> What do you think it means . . . ?

>MARDONIUS
> Means?

>XERXES
> That a man so obsessed with the future did not see his own demise?

EXT. EUBOEA—PORT ARTEMISIUM—NIGHT

The inhabitants of Artemisium are panicked. COMMONERS: men, women, and children are packing their goods and preparing to evacuate to a safer location. Boats are stocked with grain, water barrels and other necessities.

Campfires dot the coastline beyond the docks. Members of the Greek fleet warm themselves by the firelight, eat dinner and watch as cattle are herded along the plains behind them. Still further back, fires burn across the landscape, sending dark clouds of smoke to coalesce with those of the sky.

Themistocles stands with Eurybiades within an open-ended tent situated beyond the hustle and bustle. With drinks in hand, they mournfully watch the goings-on.

> EURYBIADES
> It is a tragic day.

> THEMISTOCLES
> If we allow ourselves to be ruled by our emotions, then we might as well surrender now.

Eurybiades takes a swig of wine and leans against a support pole.

> EURYBIADES
> Perhaps we already have. Tonight alone, nearly the whole population of Euboea has uprooted itself. Hundreds of their cattle are or will be slaughtered, and by dawn, their bountiful fields will be nothing more than soot and ash.

> THEMISTOCLES
> Would you rather sacrifice them to the Persians? Allow them to draw sustenance and strength from the labors of our people?

The admiral's response comes in the form of a sigh. He takes another drink, trying to ease unsteady feelings.

A pause.

> THEMISTOCLES
> Leonidas's death—

> EURYBIADES
> —was prophesied.

He walks out of the tent and stares at waves as they break against the coast.

EXT. THERMOPYLAE COASTLINE—NIGHT

Waves also break against the coastline of Thermopylae. The moon shines above, causing the rolling surface to glitter. Though there are men all around, all is silent except for the water as it laps their lifeless bodies.

This sight is reflected in the eyes of one perched at a great height above on the overlooking cliffs. The surveyor's stare is steadfast, not once does he blink—not even when a fly lands upon his skin.

> ORACLE (V.O.)
> . . . or, if that be not, the whole land of Lacedaemon shall mourn the death of a king of the house of Heracles . . .

King Leonidas, his head severed from body and fixed on a pole, watches in death what he was sent to guard in life.

EXT. GREEK COASTLINE—JUST BEFORE DAWN

Stars, still peering through the waning night sky, dimly sparkle. A cool, morning breeze shuffles across the grassy plains, causing them to shimmer like water. Below, the Aegean Sea rolls, its waves crashing against the base of jutting cliffs.

> XERXES (V.O.)
> When King Darius named me successor, he entrusted me not only with the empire which flourished under his reign, but with dreams of one still greater. When I took the throne, I also took a vow—to embrace the legacy left in my hands, to preserve and further it. Look how far we have come.

A warm light begins to flicker from beyond the lush landscape. Birds sit on tree limbs, preparing to take to the sky.

>   XERXES (V.O.)
>   Through the lands of Thrace,
>   Macedonia and Thessaly, cities bowed
>   to our majesty, offered both tribute
>   and friendship. They knew what the
>   future held, what, I am told, their own
>   oracles had seen in the mist . . . us,
>   victorious.

EXT. THERMOPYLAE PASS—JUST BEFORE DAWN

The sky begins to take on the coalescing colors of magenta and blue. Shadows are slowly vanquished by the increasing light of the sun as it begins to crest the mountainside.

>   XERXES (V.O.)
>   Alas, not all heeded the portent; the
>   counsel not to fight it . . . disbelievers
>   on whose ears all warning fell deaf—
>   even mine—but they soon realized the
>   futility of standing in our way. Despite
>   the admirable attempt, they could not
>   stop what was destined to be—

Debris from destroyed boats washes up against Thermopylae's coastline. Discarded weapons, strewn across the ground, begin to reflect the sunlight. Scavenger birds circle the battlefield below.

EXT. VALLEY OF CEPHISSUS—DAWN

The sun peers through the peaks of Mount Parnassus. Picked up by the breeze, ash twirls and spins above the Cephissus River which winds through the valley.

>   XERXES (V.O.)
>   —nor could the regions of Phocis and
>   Boeotia, whose cities smoldered in
>   ruin.

EXT. ATTICA—PLAIN—DAWN

Tracks created by the wheels of wagons, the tread of boots, and the hooves of both horses and oxen, line the ground. The result of an army at march, they span a great breadth and contrast the surrounding long-stemmed grass which glistens with morning dew.

> XERXES (V.O.)
> Upon Attica's fall, my eyes welled with
> tears. Beyond the grassy plain which
> my own father would have crossed, sat
> a city he had never beheld, yet swore
> never to forget—Athens, and it was all
> but left for the taking.

The trail leads past Mount Parnes, and continues on toward the distant hillside where the city of Athens sits, the tops of its buildings barely in focus.

EXT. ATHENS—DAYBREAK

Units of the Persian Army stand quietly, listening to their king speak, their faces raised and reverent. The Agora, or 'gathering place', of Athens sprawls beyond the crowd. Beautiful, rich trees surround the troops and the increasing light of the sun causes brilliant flashes of light to reflect from their weaponry and adornments.

Xerxes stands atop the stony mount of the Areopagus, above the gathered crowd. His gold scaled armor also reflects the sun, but does so to such a degree, one would think he were glowing. With a commanding presence, he speaks to them, eyes bright with sincerity.

> XERXES
> Now, as I look upon you, my heart
> swells in gratitude, for by your
> strength, your courage and kinship, the
> will of Darius has been fulfilled.
> Honor has been restored. My promise
> has not been broken.

The king pauses and looks to the Acropolis above. Sunlight filters through the columns of its many, colossal buildings. It is a breathtaking sight.

>XERXES
>(pointing)
>The Acropolis—It was there that the Athenians conspired to raise forces against the empire. Even now, if you listen closely, you can hear their lingering whispers winding through the columns. They will be purged, for behold, the might of Persia has prevailed, and tonight—
>(a pause)
>—we shall light up the sky so all can see.

EXT. SALAMIS COASTLINE—NIGHT

Thousands of Greeks are gathered along the coast of Salamis, mournfully watching the Acropolis burn across the water. Billowing, dark clouds of smoke churn through the night sky. Though barely loud enough to register, the sounds of MUSIC and LAUGHTER emanate from the mainland, where the Persian army has set up camp.

On the harbor docks, beside Eurybiades' idle warship, the admiral, Cimon, Themistocles, and other Athenian statesmen stare at the sight.

>THEMISTOCLES
>While our people tremble in fear, he feasts on the spoils of war.
>(to statesmen)
>I told you all this day would come.

>STATEMAN 1
>You would gloat just to spite us, wouldn't you, Themistocles?

THEMISTOCLES
And you would cast fault upon others
only to conceal your own—

CIMON
(interrupting)
Athens has fallen to the barbarian, and
we brought low with it, yet you two?
You think yourselves fit to condescend?

THEMISTOCLES
You make it difficult to miss Aristides,
Cimon, when you sound so very much
like him. Where is he, by the way?

CIMON
Last I had heard, he was preparing to
leave Aegina and meet us here.
Whether plans have changed, I cannot
answer, for I haven't one.

Statesman 2 takes an uneasy step forward.

STATESMAN 2
We're all without answers, aren't we?

CIMON
We must not abandon hope.

STATESMAN 2
Is there any left to be found? Hasn't it
all been dashed beneath Xerxes' tread?
The army he commands . . . what's
been left in its wake to hold onto?
What? Greece has succumbed to a new
master and there is no one who can
bring him down.

                    EURYBIADES
          No. No, he hasn't everything.

                    STATESMAN 2
                      (to Eurybiades)
          Not yet. Your king has been reduced to
          a memory and, chances are, his brother
          shall soon be, as well.

                    EURYBIADES
          Cleombrotus—

                    THEMISTOCLES
                      (interrupts)
          Will do what? Keep Xerxes from the
          Peloponnese with his little Isthmus
          construct? They'll eventually breach it,
          just as they did at Thermopylae. Just as
          they did in Athens.
                      (a beat)
          No, my friends, if there is indeed a
          wall which shall save Greece, it isn't on
          land. Our fleet—

                    EURYBIADES
          Could not stop them either.

                    THEMISTOCLES
          Perhaps not on the open sea, but . . .

Eurybiades regards Themistocles with a raised brow. He can tell he has a
plan coming together. Statesman 1 can, too.

                    STATESMAN 1
          What?

                    THEMISTOCLES
                      (to statesman 2)
          You are right.
                         (MORE)

                    THEMISTOCLES(cont'd)
                        (to all)
                    There is not a man capable of defeating
                    Xerxes.

                    STATESMAN 1
                    Thank you, Themistocles, for that
                    astute obser—

                    THEMISTOCLES
                    The only one who can bring him
                    down is himself.

                    EURYBIADES
                    I am not sure I follow.

                    THEMISTOCLES
                        (thoughtfully)
                    He thinks he has won, so let him
                    continue to. When he grows too
                    confident, it will be his own ego that
                    trips him up.
                        (a pause)
                    Eurybiades, I think you ought to
                    gather the fleet commanders.

Eurybiades and the others are addled by Themistocles, who stares at the burning Acropolis with a smile on his face.

EXT. GREECE—PHALERUM—DAY

An enormous Persian battle ship sits in the harbor of Phalerum amongst hundreds of smaller boats. Soldiers stand at attention on the deck.

INSIDE THE SHIP

Sunlight pours through small portals, but the main source of illumination comes from candles set around the 'conference' room. Xerxes, the top commanders of both land and sea, as well as Demaratus and the regal Queen Artemisia, are seated at an impressively long table. Drinks, bowls of grapes, and other delicacies are sprawled out before them.

Xerxes sits at the head of the table, passing a few morsels of food to the mastiff at his side. Patting the animal on the back, he turns his attention to the group.

>   XERXES
> As I am sure you are well aware, since securing Athens, we have found ourselves at a cross-roads of sorts. To move on to the southern territories, we must take decisive action and soon. With the change in season and coming weather, bridging the coasts is no longer an option. This leaves us with the prospect of naval warfare—unless any of you see an alternative?

Admiral Ariabignes shrugs.

>   ARIABIGNES
> Truthfully, I do not. Pushing onward with the army, and enough ships to supply it, would entail leaving a contingent behind to impede pursuit. Considering the fleet has already lost a number of vessels, our numerical superiority would be lost.

>   MARDONIUS
> What do you suggest?

>   ARIABIGNES
> A large-scale assault in the Saronic Gulf would be to our greatest advantage. That is, if we can draw them out of the Salamis Channel.

Seated across the table, Achaemenes nods.

> **ACHAEMENES**
> I agree with Admiral Ariabignes. Now that the Greek fleet has been fortified with reserve ships, it will take a concerted effort by our own.

The gathered commanders echo the same thoughts.

> **COMMANDERS**
> Yes . . . Agreed . . .

Xerxes stares at Artemisia. She does not appear as enthusiastic as the others.

> **XERXES**
> Seems our lady is not as eager to concur. What are your thoughts, Queen Artemisia?

She is reticent to share, but his expectant look urges her on.

> **ARTEMISIA**
> Whatever you so choose, your highness, my support and ships are with you, but, in truth, I think a forced attack could potentially do more harm than good—

> **ACHAEMENES**
> What do you mean, 'more harm than good'? We must do something.

Xerxes raises a silencing hand.

> **XERXES**
> Let her speak, Achaemenes.
> (a beat; to Artemisia)
> Please, go on.

ARTEMISIA
With all due respect, King Xerxes, your primary goal has been won. The rest of Greece will easily fall to Persia— provided patience is maintained.

Artemisia looks around the table. The men's curiosity is obviously piqued. They wait for elaboration.

ARTEMISIA
I doubt your enemies stationed here would, themselves, initiate a fight. So, I suggest you keep your forces where they now are. Wait out the season. Unlike the Greeks, a shortage of supplies is not a concern for your army, as you now control both land and sea north of the Peloponnese. As time passes, so will their stocks and, more importantly, their resistance.

Mardonius is not convinced.

MARDONIUS
It is a good idea in theory, but—
    (to Xerxes)
The faster this campaign is wrapped up, the sooner the empire may welcome back its king.

XERXES
    (to himself)
Yes, there are matters there that must be tended to.

ARTEMISIA
I understand the urgency, but hastily made decisions oft times result in folly.

Artemisia's boldness prompts incredulous stares from the commanders. They obviously think she has committed an offense. Achaemenes, in particular, casts her a chastising stare, but she remains firm.

Xerxes earnestly ponders her words. They are reminiscent of the warning Artabanus issued on the floor of the assembly so long ago.

A tense moment passes, till the king tips his head to her, to the surprise of all.

>   **XERXES**
> My lady, Halicarnassus is fortunate to be
> guided by your hand, as are we to be offered
> it, but—I must agree with the others.
>   (to all)
> Time is of the essence and if we are to
> move on, we must eliminate any threat
> the Grecian fleet poses.
>
>   **DEMARATUS**
> Perhaps the Peloponnesians will
> abandon their cohorts. Up until your
> advance, relations between their lands
> and Athens were anything but cordial.
>
>   **ACHAEMENES**
> If they did detach, we could easily
> overtake them as they left the channel.

Xerxes thoughtfully leans back in his chair, considering the plan of action.

>   **ARIABIGNES**
> Pressure their alliance?
>
>   **XERXES**
> Sounds promising. If the tie that binds
> them is indeed unstable, let us see if we
> can sever it altogether.
>   (MORE)

                    XERXES(cont'd)
                (a beat; to generals)
            I want a large army corps to set out
            tonight to the Isthmus line. The
            Greeks must believe preparations are
            being made for an attack on the
            Peloponnese. This is sure to cause
            dissention among their ranks and could
            panic them into making a mistake.
            Now, as to the fleet . . .

EXT. GREECE—ELEUSIS ROAD—NIGHT

Along the wide earthy trail, a Persian army corps, comprised of nearly thirty-thousand soldiers, marches under the command of Megabyzus. Torches burn bright in hand while they SING SONGS of Persia's majesty at the tops of their lungs.

EXT. GREECE—SALAMIS—NIGHT

The Greeks stationed on the island of Salamis, some standing on rocking boats in the harbors, others on the coast itself, watch the Persian torchlight trail across the mainland. Fearful onlookers begin to argue, but their words are drowned out by the SINGING soldiers.

INT. GREECE—SALAMIS—WAREHOUSE—NIGHT

Gathered within a warehouse on the coast of Salamis, an audience is being held with a small, select group of Athenian statesmen and leaders of the Greek navy contingents—PELOPONNESIAN, AEGINETAN, MEGAREAN. Many sit on crates, among stock-piled food, water barrels, and other rations. Others, such as Cimon and Eurybiades, lean against support beams. At the center of attention, pacing upon the tiny patch of floor not cluttered with goods, is Themistocles.

> THEMISTOCLES
> While I had held an unrealistic hope that the Persians would be stopped early in their tracks, I take a modicum of comfort knowing that we took the right measures years ago and increased our fleet, for now it comes down to beating them on the water.

A commander scoffs from the sidelines.

> COMMANDER 1 (O.S.)
> Like at Artemisium?

> THEMISTOCLES
> Now that the reserves are gathered, we may stand a chance.

> COMMANDER 1
> Chance of prolonging what is sure to be another loss. Why don't you save your optimism for those still too daft to know it's baseless!

Statesman 1 stands before Themistocles can respond.

> STATESMAN 1
> Even with the Peloponnesian League we simply cannot overpower them.

> THEMISTOCLES
> Yes, I am aware of this. We can not stand up to them unless more evenly matched and that means drawing them into combat where their numbers are no longer an advantage.

Many of the commanders look cynically around the room. Most of them are tired, resentful. They see no hope in the situation and it shows.

One of these men, the young, quick-tempered, ADMIRAL ADEIMANTUS of Corinth, rises from his seat.

>ADEIMANTUS
>Whatever it is that you are scheming,
>you may as well forget.
>>(to all)
>Our efforts should be concentrated at
>the Isthmus.

Eurybiades shifts his weight onto another foot. He appears extremely weary, as if he has not slept for a week.

>EURYBIADES
>Themistocles, if you are insinuating we fight
>here at Salamis, you have lost what was left
>of your sanity. A defeat in these waters would
>result in complete entrapment.

>ADEIMANTUS
>Exactly! Better we sail to the Isthmus
>where we can defend and find comfort
>with our own people.

>PELOPONNESIAN COMMANDERS
>Yes! . . . I agree! . . . The Isthmus!

Themistocles is clearly on the verge of erupting.

>THEMISTOCLES
>Fine, fight at the Isthmus, but as
>pointed out earlier, it would mean
>taking to battle in the open sea where
>the Persian fleet has the upper hand.

>EURYBIADES
>Themisto—

THEMISTOCLES
Yes, draw them to the Isthmus and watch
as the rest of their army follows suit.
They do work in tandem, you realize.
Watch the land forces descend upon the
Peloponnese—knowing you led them
there. Watch—knowing your work is
done, for there is no reason left to fight.

This chastising prompts an uproar of anger from the Peloponnesians. Many rise from their crates, incoherently refuting Themistocles' brazen sarcasm.

Eurybiades takes the floor, trying to bring a sense of order back to the conference.

EURYBIADES
Themistocles, that is enough!! Instead
of using your time on the floor
mocking your fellow Greeks, why
don't you elaborate on this plan you
seem to think will work so well?

STATESMAN 1
Yes, why don't you explain it to us?

Themistocles looks around, finding himself surrounded by skepticism, but, brushing past Eurybiades, he resumes his pacing.

THEMISTOCLES
The Persian troops rely on their fleet
for transport of reinforcements, rations
and other necessities. I repeat: They
work—in—tandem. Now, if we can
manage to render enough of their ships
immobile, sufficiently upset their
supply chain, there is no way such a
large army can be supported. They'll be
forced to cut their numbers.

EURYBIADES
Continue . . .

THEMISTOCLES
At the Isthmus, we would only be able to slow them down—at best. No, they must be lured into narrow waters where their size will work against them.

EURYBIADES
But, again, if we were to lose—

THEMISTOCLES
(interrupting)
We will most assuredly lose if we sail toward Corinth. At least here we stand a chance. We can preserve what is left of our lands and defend the Peloponnese without drawing the Persians near it.

Eurybiades and Cimon are somewhat impressed.

ADEIMANTUS
That is all well and good, but you seem to forget one, rather important, component to your grand plan. Why would they engage us in battle here? They know, the same as we, that it would be risky.

COMMANDER 1
Yes, how do you know they won't merely bottle us in, keep us from reaching fresh supplies, thereby starving us all?

STATESMAN 2
They make a good argument, Themistocles.

THEMISTOCLES
With autumn soon approaching, Xerxes will, undoubtedly, want to make sure that all is in order so that they may continue their conquest before the change of season. What better way to ensure this than neutralizing our fleet as soon as possible?
(a beat)
Now that he has had reprisal on Athens, he probably thinks he can do no wrong and will not tarry when such an opportunity presents itself.

STATESMAN 1
Is this where your 'only Xerxes can defeat Xerxes' statement begins to make some sort of sense?

THEMISTOCLES
(nodding)
How does one ensnare a wolf?
(a pause; looking around)
He presents it with what it thinks to be an easy meal.

COMMANDER 1
Why are we even considering this ludicrous plan?! Themistocles is a man with no land left to stand on and, now, he expects us to abandon ours!

Themistocles confronts the commander, fed up with the impetuous attitude.

THEMISTOCLES
I will tell you why!! If you do decide to defend the Isthmus, you will do so without Athens' ships.

A rumbling of worried whispers is emitted from the crowd.

      EURYBIADES
   You would leave us to fend—

      THEMISTOCLES
   That is right! Either you do as I
   suggest, or go it alone!
     (a beat)
   The choice is yours!

INT. GREECE—PHALERUM—XERXES' WAR TENT—PREDAWN

Tossing and turning upon his bed, Xerxes is in the throes of what appears to be a foreboding nightmare.

Mardonius urgently enters the tent with a message in hand.

      MARDONIUS
   Xerxes!

He reaches for his arm to stir him awake.

      MARDONIUS
   Xerxes!

Xerxes jolts up, eyes wide. It takes him a few moments to focus.

      XERXES
   Mardonius? What is it?

      MARDONIUS
   Something that may ease your mind.

He hands the message to him. Xerxes opens it and as he reads his brows raise in surprise.

      XERXES
   Interesting . . .

                              MARDONIUS
                            To say the least!

With his eyes fixed on the note, Xerxes rises and pours a cup of water at the
bedside stand.

                               XERXES
                          Organize a meeting.

Mardonius tips his head and quickly leaves. Alone, Xerxes, drink in hand,
walks over to the conference table and slowly sits, still regarding the message
intently.

INT. GREECE—PHALERUM—XERXES' WAR TENT—DAY

The letter remaining firmly in his grasp, Xerxes sits at the head of the table,
but no longer alone. Now in attendance are Mardonius, Masistes, Hydarnes,
Demaratus, and Artemisia, as well as admirals Ariabignes and Achaemenes.
Maps and drinks are set out before all.

                             DEMARATUS
                        Seems plausible enough. As I told you
                        before, there is no love lost between
                        the Peloponnesians and the people of
                        Athens.

                              HYDARNES
                          But to do this to them?

                             ARTEMISIA
                         It is cause for suspicion.

                              MASISTES
                            Yes, it is.

Xerxes takes in their commentary with little more than a nod in response.
Masistes is mildly concerned by his friend's unease. Mardonius, on the other
hand, is more than a bit excited.

MARDONIUS
Not really. Couple the friction between
their contingents along with the fact
that Athens is a lost cause, and the
message this 'Themistocles' has sent the
king is not so hard to believe.

XERXES
Ariabignes, have you seen anything to
suggest the validity of this claim? Is the
Greek fleet really primed to withdraw?

Ariabignes considers the question and gradually begins to nod.

ARIABIGNES
They did not make their routine
rounds yesterday. This could support
what was written. They may, indeed,
be demoralized and preparing to pull
out.

MARDONIUS
If you ask me, sending troops to the
Isthmus line has worked better than
expected. Once we destroy their fleet,
there is nothing left for the remaining
regions to do other than surrender.

Xerxes scratches his head, still not completely convinced. Holding up the message, he begins to read aloud.

XERXES
(reading)
With our commanders at each others'
throats, it is apparent that there is no
hope left to be found. The
Peloponnesians are intent on
abandoning us just before dawn in an
(MORE)

XERXES(cont'd)
effort to join their land forces. Move to
strike them down, and you will find
support from Athens' fleet, as our
contempt for them is now greater than any.

Putting the letter down, Xerxes leans back and taps his fingers atop the table, looking to the others expectantly.

MARDONIUS
Again, I am inclined to believe this to be true.

ACHAEMENES
As am I. Your highness, if we are to
make use of this information we must
act quickly.

XERXES
(to Ariabignes)
Your thoughts?

ARIABIGNES
The choice is ultimately up to you, but
taking everything into consideration, I
think we would be remiss to do nothing.

Xerxes leans forward, scanning a map of the area.

HYDARNES
I would also suggest stationing troops
along the coast.

MARDONIUS
As would I.
(whispering; to Xerxes)
Think of it—you already cast a shadow
to rival King Darius's and, now, you are
poised to bring all of Greece under you
in one glorious battle.

Xerxes digests the general's words. He stands and traces a finger along the map of the suggested 'battlefield'. It stops on what appears to be an island at the southern mouth of the Salamis Channel. The name "Psyttaleia" is written across it.

As he begins to talk, the actual scene comes to life, coalescing with the map itself.

>   XERXES (V.O.)
> The Phoenician and Ionian squadrons
> are to take up posts on either side of
> this island.

Phoenician ships, under the command of Admiral Ariabignes, settle on the right side of the island of Psyttaleia. Ionians are poised on its left side.

>   ARIABIGNES (V.O.)
> Understood.

>   MARDONIUS (V.O.)
> Psyttaleia . . . we should station soldiers
> there, too.

From a few of the Phoenician and Ionian ships, planks are lowered onto the island. Land soldiers begin to descend them.

>   HYDARNES (V.O.)
> How many do you suggest?

>   MARDONIUS (V.O.)
> Three or four hundred should suffice.

>   XERXES (V.O.)
> Do it.

On the map, he points to the name "Saronic Gulf", just south of the island. Artemisia's ships patrol the water.

>   XERXES (V.O.)
> Queen Artemisia, your fleet would be
> best positioned behind the charge, here
> in the Saronic. Agreed?

                    ARTEMISIA (V.O.)
            Agreed.

                    ACHAEMENES (V.O.)
            And mine?

Xerxes draws his finger northwest of the Salamis Channel to where the name "Megara Channel" is boldly written.

The map and the actual location still overlapping one another, we see the Egyptian fleet in the Megara, blocking entry from the Salamis Channel.

                    XERXES (V.O.)
            You, Achaemenes, will station the
            Egyptians here in the Megara Channel.

                    ACHAEMENES (V.O.)
            To attack from the north?

                    XERXES (V.O.)
            No, to block escape.

Xerxes rubs his finger back and forth along the letters which spell out the name "Salamis Channel".

EXT. GREECE—SALAMIS COAST—NIGHT

The coast of Salamis itself is quiet. Themistocles, standing beside the water's edge, smiles as he regards a note. Aristides approaches, clearly distressed.

                    THEMISTOCLES
            So, Aristides, you've arrived.

                    ARISTIDES
            I barely slipped through. The Persians . . .
                    (a beat)
            They have us surrounded.

To Aristides' shock, Themistocles looks pleased.

EXT. GREECE—MOUNT AEGALEUS—DAWN

SEPTEMBER 23, 480 B.C.

The sky, just now beginning to take on the light of the cresting sun, is clear. A gentle, southern breeze shuffles the grass. The Salamis Channel pleasantly flows and, on the coastline at the base of the mount, Persian soldiers stand like sport spectators awaiting a match.

Upon a throne of gold, strategically placed on a plateau of the mountain, Xerxes sits and surveys the scene with Masistes at his side—from his ships stationed about the area, to the serene channel itself. Though he keeps his thoughts well guarded under a stoic façade, there are subtle indications that he is agitated.

Messengers on horseback and attendants stand at attention behind, while Demaratus, Hydarnes, and Mardonius watch beneath the foliage of a nearby tree.

                HYDARNES
        They have yet to make a move.

               MARDONIUS
        We mustn't dismiss what we have been
        told on basis of tardiness. Patience,
        Hydarnes, patience.

ON XERXES, MASISTES

                 XERXES
           (under his breath)
        Patience.

Xerxes taps his fingers atop the arm of the throne, drawing a concerned look from his friend.

                MASISTES
      Xerxes?

XERXES
Hmm?

MASISTES
Might I ask a favor of you?
  (off look)
When this is over, be sure to get some sleep.

XERXES
  (jokingly)
Are you saying I look tired, Masistes?

MASISTES
Very much so.

Masistes' reply catches Xerxes off guard, but he knows he's right.

XERXES
I don't believe I have slept through a single night since leaving Abydos.

MASISTES
I understand the campaign demands a lot of you, but you must get your rest. Drink a tonic if you must, but whatever thoughts keep you—

XERXES
They're more like . . . like visions . . . Yet try as might, I cannot see them. They always slip away before the dawn. I thought, after taking Athens, they would be satisfied to reveal themselves to me, but . . .

MASISTES
They persist.

XERXES
As does this feeling they leave behind.
I'm not saying it's bad, or good, it's
just—
  (tapping head)
there—
  (tapping chest)
—here.

MARDONIUS (O.S.)
Look!

Xerxes and Masistes turn their attention to Mardonius, who rushes past them and points toward Salamis' northern coast.

Ships stationed there are beginning to pull out. Sails bearing the crest of Corinth are run up their masts and beckon the wind.

MARDONIUS
The Corinthians are hoisting their sails!

General Hydarnes joins Mardonius, eyes wide as he, too, now sees a sight worth celebrating over. Peloponnesian ships are pulling out of another of Salamis' harbors—one blocked by the island of Pharmakoussae. Rounding it and heading north, the ships are revealed, directly passing the king's vantage point.

HYDARNES
There, too! More ships are departing!

Mardonius beams as Xerxes stands to witness the sight. Placing a hand upon the king's shoulder, he points to the departing fleet and gloats.

MARDONIUS
You see! Your reservations were for
nothing!! They are leaving! Greece is
nearly—

>XERXES
>Ours!

Demaratus turns to the king as more ships, this time Athenian, pull from the harbor, apparently chasing after those ahead.

>DEMARATUS
>The Athenians! They are in pursuit!

There is a buzz of sheer excitement, not only from the gathered authorities, but the attendants and messengers, as well.

Below, on the coastline, members of the Persian army CHEER. Their JOYOUS CRIES resound, compelling Xerxes to wildly grin.

A NAVAL MESSENGER, sitting on horseback, realizes that, with all the elation, an order has yet to be made. Taking a breath, he attempts to get Xerxes' attention.

>NAVAL MESSENGER
>Pardon me, your highness?

Turning, a smile still gracing his face, Xerxes looks up as if he cannot fathom what he wants.

>NAVAL MESSENGER
>Your . . . orders?

Xerxes and his friends chuckle.

>XERXES
>My orders . . .

The king looks to the channel, eyes lighted by the promise of success, and sits back down upon his throne.

>XERXES
>Advance against the enemy.

EXT. ARIABIGNES' SHIP DECK

At the head of the Phoenician fleet, stationed along the right side of Pysttaleia Island, Admiral Ariabignes stands atop the deck of his ship, eyes set on the main coastline, where a banner is being waved. Turning to his crew, he raises a hand and shouts down to the oarsmen.

> ARIABIGNES
> Forward!

A STACCATO BEAT is DRUMMED from beneath, setting the pace for their advance. CHEERS of support echo from the stationed guards on the island.

EXT. ARTEMISIA'S SHIP DECK

Atop her own deck and in complete battle regalia, Queen Artemisia stares ahead, watching the Phoenician contingent draw away.

> ARTEMISIA
> (to crew)
> Ready yourselves.

CUT TO:

MONTAGE—MOVING IN FOR ATTACK—MORNING

—Persian contingents, Ionian on the left, Phoenician on the right, pull through the straits on either side of Pysttaleia Island and advance into the Salamis Channel.

—Ships from Halicarnassus, led by Artemisia's, follow suit.

—Those atop Mount Aegaleus watch expectantly.

—Corinthian and other Peloponnesian ships continue their way north up the channel with the Athenians pursuing them.

—Aboard one of the Corinthian triremes, Admiral Adeimantus peers south to gauge how much time they have.

—On his own ship, Eurybiades turns to look south, as well, taking in the sight of the advancing Athenian fleet.

—Themistocles, aboard the lead Athenian trireme, stares at the Greeks ahead with a sinister, closed-mouthed smile.

EXT. MOUNT AEGALEUS

Observing from his throne, Xerxes reclines in his seat with a drink, grinning from ear to ear. It is a grin matched upon the faces of each of his surrounding friends.

All watch as the northbound Greek contingents—nearly two-hundred-fifty ships all together—sail into the widest part of the channel, seventy abreast. Chasing them down, the majority of the Persian fleet now passes by the island of Pharmakoussae.

> MARDONIUS
> It is, surely, a beautiful morning.

> XERXES
> (raising his drink)
> A new day.

> HYDARNES
> Look how fast they flee!

> MARDONIUS
> It is only a matter of time now.

Cup poised at his lips, Xerxes freezes upon hearing this line and suddenly does not look too content. The expression turns to one of suspended shock as he sets eyes on the Athenian ships. Their oars are now idle, no longer are they in pursuit of the retreating fleets.

> MASISTES
> What are they doing?

Xerxes rises to his feet.

                        XERXES
            A trap.

Horrified by what he now realizes, the drink slips from his hand.

                        XERXES
            It is a trap!

EXT. IONIAN SHIP DECK

Nearing the Island of Pharmakoussae, Persian ships both ahead and behind his own, an IONIAN COMMANDER looks warily at the water. It gushes from the left flank. The wind picks up. He turns to his crew. Something is amiss. Then, just as this unsettling feeling sinks in, a HORN is sounded from beyond. Its call is met with resounding CHEERS.

The commander redirects his attentions to the island, where, from the narrow strait between it and Salamis, the Aeginetan and Megarian contingents finally reveal themselves. Their bronze rams take on the gleam of the sun as they furiously cut through the water. Upon their decks, men raise bows and spears.

The Ionian commander, frantic with fear, looks to his astonished crew.

                    IONIAN COMMANDER
            Get down!!!

A barrage of spears and arrows are sent skyward, ripping through both ships and men.

EXT. EURYBIADES' SHIP DECK

Looking south to the Athenians, Eurybiades sees a banner climb the mast of their lead trireme.

                        EURYBIADES
                        (to crew)
            Prepare to turn about!

EXT. THEMISTOCLES' SHIP DECK

While his crew continues to hoist their banner, Themistocles takes in the sight of the ships ahead of him with an enigmatic smile plastered across his face.

> THEMISTOCLES (V.O.)
> We went yet again to the oracle, taking with us an olive branch, in hopes of hearing better news, and we were thus told . . .

His own ship begins to turn about. He closes his eyes.

> THEMISTOCLES
> (quoting the oracle)
> When the foe shall have taken whatever the limit Of Cecrops holds within it, and all which divine Cithaeron shelters, then far-seeing Jove grants this to the prayers of Athene.
> (takes hold of the rail)
> Safe shall the wooden wall continue for thee and thy children. Wait not the tramp of the horse, nor the footmen mightily moving over the land, but turn your back to the foe and retire ye.

EXT. MOUNT AEGALEUS

Unable to stop what has been set in motion, Xerxes can do nothing but watch and hope for the best.

> THEMISTOCLES (O.S.)
> Yet shall a day arrive when ye shall meet him in battle.

EXT. THEMISTOCLES' SHIP DECK

Ship completely turned about, Themistocles opens his eyes and beholds the sight of the rest of the Athenian fleet, ready to do battle.

THEMISTOCLES
And it has come.

FADE TO BLACK.

Courtesy of the Oriental Institute of the University of Chicago

EXT. ATTICA—TOPOGRAPHY—DAY

Like a bird, we sweep across green plains, the emptied outskirts of Athens, and above the capital itself, where Persian-allied soldiers, not citizens, occupy the streets.

Continuing . . . over the acropolis, where toppled statues and columns rest in pieces amongst the gutted, charred remains of its stately buildings.

Onward . . . across another serene field, a small wood, dipping back and forth through a canopy of green . . .

Climbing . . . the silent peak of Mount Aegaleus, over it, and down its opposite side—taking-in just a glimpse of the anxious Persian command post situated upon its plateau . . .

Beholding . . . chaos, for what now stretches before us is a panorama of the Salamis Channel, the present 'battleground' in the Greco-Persian war.

EXT. SALAMIS CHANNEL—BATTLE—DAY

The majority of the Persian fleet is bottled in the middle of the channel. The Megarians and Aeginetans force them further north, where the bulk of the Greek fleet is now barreling (southward) toward them.

Ships not blocked in this horrific trap, continue to push forward, but, as they ram the enemy triremes stern-side, it only causes a domino effect, knocking them in turn into the very crews they are trying to assist.

EXT. MOUNT AEGALEUS—DAY

Enraged, Xerxes paces along the edge of the mount. Masistes, concerned for him, approaches Mardonius, Demaratus, and Hydarnes, who are in the midst of discussing the present situation.

                    DEMARATUS
          It's like a noose. Can nothing be done?
          Can they not be called back??

                    HYDARNES
         There is no way out. Either they face
         the enemy before them or crush the
         allied ships behind.

                    MARDONIUS
         All we can do is wait and watch.

                    MASISTES
         You say that so coldly.

                    MARDONIUS
         I can only speak of fact, not feeling.
         The two in war cannot coexist.

Mardonius turns his sights on Xerxes.

                    XERXES
              (mumbling to himself)
         Come on. Come on. Free yourselves.
         Fight.

EXT. ARIABIGNES' SHIP DECK—DAY

A southbound Greek ship heads for Ariabignes'. The admiral calls back to his men.

                    ARIABIGNES
         Archers—Spearmen—

The soldiers ready their weapons. Ariabignes raises a hand, awaiting the right moment to strike.

                    ARIABIGNES
         Hold . . . Hold . . .

The enemy ship draws near enough for the admiral's liking. He drops his hand.

                    ARIABIGNES
         Attack!!!

Arrows and spears are volleyed back and forth across the water as the Greek trireme is rowed, head on, into Ariabignes' ship, impaling the hull. The crews of both boats lose footing upon impact. The admiral himself is pinned to a rail by an enemy spear which has run through his scaled cuirass. Quickly, he unbuckles himself, leaving the armor behind.

>ARIABIGNES
>(stumbling to his feet)
>Take the ship!!!

Drawing a sword, he prompts his men to do the same and leads them on an assault. They leap onto the enemy deck.

>CUT TO:

MONTAGE—THE BATTLE CONTINUES—DAY

—Men fight upon the decks of rocking ships with swords, axes and spears.

—Boats burn in the distance, their oarsmen trapped inside.

—Commoners flood the coast of Salamis, watching their allies defend them.

—Debris and bodies skirt between colliding forces.

—Some Persian ships attempt to pull out, only to back into members of their own forces, which are still trying to advance.

—Many run aground boats, both Greek and Persian, are abandoned by their crews. The soldiers duke it out on the various coastlines of the Salamis Channel.

EXT. PHOENICIAN SHIP DECK—DAY

One of the Phoenician commanders, realizing his ship is in the path of oncoming Greeks, looks around anxiously. Spotting a familiar body floating in the water, the fear intensifies. One of his soldiers approaches.

> PHOENICIAN 1
> What is it, sir?

The commander brushes past the soldier and runs along the deck, grabbing various members of the crew.

> PHOENICIAN COMMANDER
> Turn—turn about!! Retreat!!

A banner is hastily hoisted up the mast. The oarsmen below subdue backing water and attempt to turn about, but only manage to run themselves broadside into one of their own ships.

EXT. MOUNT AEGALEUS—DAY

Xerxes sits amidst the commanders, incredulous. Mardonius can scarcely believe the sight below, either.

> MARDONIUS
> They are exposing the center forces–

> XERXES
> —putting the entire fleet in jeopardy.

> CUT TO:

PHOENICIAN RETREAT—DAY

—Disorganized and crashing into their own, Phoenician ships begin to retreat, leaving a gap through the right side of the channel.

—Many men, losing footing as their boats are turned about, fall into the water, only to be plowed by oncoming Greek triremes. Some of the Greeks bash the drowning soldiers over the head with their oars as they pass by.

—Artemisia's ship barely manages to swerve out of the way of an oncoming, fleeing Phoenician. She spots something (which we do not see) in the water and signals for help from one of her crew.

—The Greeks continue to pursue the Phoenicians, causing a great many of them to run aground.

EXT. THEMISTOCLES' SHIP DECK—DAY

Themistocles joins the chorus of his cheering crew as the Persian ship they pursue runs aground a few hundred yards ahead.

Peering to a ship at his right, he spots Eurybiades.

> THEMISTOCLES
> (shouting across the water)
> Nice day for hunting, is it not?!

The Spartan admiral cracks a grin.

EXT. SALAMIS CHANNEL—DAY

The disastrous retreat continues, but the steadfast Ionian contingent continues to hold the left side of the channel, valiantly fighting their oppressors. Now that the center line is all but gone, many of these ships disengage from their posts to supplement their forces.

Triremes barrel in on them. Dozens of ships are boarded. Crews battle. Men, of both fleets, fall lifelessly into the congested water below.

One of the Ionian ships charges an Athenian, brutally crushing its hull, causing it to sink. No sooner do they accomplish this feat, than they, too, are rammed. As their boat begins to go down, the Ionian crew, armed with javelins, send their attackers to a watery grave and take their vessel.

EXT. MOUNT AEGALEUS—AFTERNOON

The command post remains in a state of alarm. While Xerxes stares at the Salamis Channel, completely consumed with the remains of both destroyed ships and soldiers, he furiously shakes.

The Ionian fleet is now in disarray, attempting a futile stand off with the Greek forces. Many ships, abandoned and breaking up against coastline cliffs, are on fire. The light of their burning masts reflects against the water.

On the surrounding, flat coastlines of the channel, Persian and Greek crews, having made it to shore, fight to the death amongst washed up bodies.

The king, from this height, is witness to it all. He stands, walks to the edge of the plateau, and continues to anxiously survey the scene.

Mardonius approaches.

>   MARDONIUS
> If we are to salvage what is left of this battle, you must send your fastest messenger to Achaemenes. Tell the Egyptian squadron to advance.

No answer.

>   MARDONIUS
>   (placing a hand on Xerxes' shoulder)
> We must—

Xerxes jerks from his grasp and turns on the general.

>   XERXES
> No! I will not order them to their deaths! Open your eyes! There is nothing left to salvage! This—this is the beginning of the end.

Nearly knocking Mardonius to the ground, he storms off.

EXT. MEGARA CHANNEL—ACHAEMENES' SHIP DECK—ONSET OF SUNSET

Billowing clouds languish above the distant countryside and islands sprawled before the Egyptian squadron. Though barely bright enough to see, lit arrows, used like flares, are shot into the sky in rapid succession. It is a signal that the admiral has dreaded. Achaemenes grips the rail of his ship, teetering slightly as he turns away to look upon his crew.

                      ACHAEMENES
                Set sail for Phalerum.

EXT. SALAMIS CHANNEL—ADEIMANTUS' SHIP DECK

Adeimantus, arms crossed at his chest, looks toward the Megara Channel. What he sees inspires an expressed relief.

                      ADEIMANTUS
                The Egyptians are pulling out.

                      CORINTHIAN SOLDIER
                So, our work here is done.

                      ADEIMANTUS
                Here? Yes. Altogether? No.
                    (facing him)
                Prepare the squadron to join the others.
                This battle is not yet over, though, by
                all appearances, it soon will be.

EXT. QUEEN ARTEMISIA'S SHIP DECK

Unrelentingly pursued by an Athenian ship, Artemisia, along with her men, fire off arrows. Though obviously worn from battle, her armor no longer cast with the sheen of invincibility, the queen remains undeterred. With grace and fluidity she proceeds like a masterful musician strumming a harp. Her rhythm never falters, not even as she issues orders to the oarsmen below.

                      ARTEMISIA
                They are nearly upon us. Pick up the
                pace!!

With an expert hand she launches two arrows at once. Both find a mark. Two Athenians fall from their trireme, through the rolling oars of it, and into the water. This, however, does not curtail their shipmates' pursuit. They prepare to return fire.

ARTEMISIA
Eyes up, men!

An onslaught of weapons—arrows, spears, javelins—are fired. HOLLOW THUDS beat against the ship as it's impaled. One of the queen's soldiers is also struck. The man falls atop her.

Nails digging into the deck, Artemisia attempts to drag her way free. While doing so, she happens to set sights toward the bow of the ship. Her mouth drops. One of their own allies is before them and they are about to collide.

ARTEMISIA
Bear right!!! Bear right!!!

A crewmember reaches for the rail, preparing for impact.

HALICARNASSIAN
It's too late! We're going to crash!

They plow into the smaller vessel. Planks GROAN and SNAP as its hull is ruptured. Water begins to fill the gaping hole.

Artemisia's ship, having lost little of its momentum, continues on, for the most part, unscathed. The queen, however, is overcome with guilt as she watches the other crew abandon their sinking boat.

CUT TO:

MONTAGE—MASS RETREAT—SUNSET

—What is left of the Persian fleet, heads south as fast as possible. With broken oars, sprung planks, and panicking crews, they hastily cut through the water, which is consumed with wreckage and bodies, the Greeks still on their tails.

—Mid-channel, their ships idle alongside one another on Salamis' shore, Themistocles and Eurybiades share a congratulatory salute as the rest of their forces press on.

—The Persian soldiers stationed on the Island of Pysttaleia watch, clearly frantic, as their retreating allies bypass them. Instead of their compatriots stopping to gather them up, Athenian triremes, led by Aristides and Cimon, begin to come ashore, armed warriors leaping from their decks.

—Beyond the disorienting sights of the Salamis Channel, the SHRILL CRIES of those being massacred resound.

EXT. MOUNT AEGALEUS—DUSK

Silence has overtaken the command post. Commanders, servants and scribes stand in cliques, no one daring to utter a word, but every eye focused ahead, where, slumped upon the throne, Xerxes stares at the channel with a deadpan expression.

Rising the height of the slope, Artemisia and a few of her crewmen approach. They carry a body.

The first to notice their presence are the compliant attendants. They WHISPER among their inner circle. These LOW MUMBLINGS call the attention of Mardonius. The general watches, still with idle tongue, as the Queen of Halicarnassus leads the way to Xerxes.

Though not a word beckons the king to look, he turns. Upon seeing the body, he mournfully averts his stare.

                    ARTEMISIA
          I know you held Ariabignes in high
          esteem. We fought to bring him back
          so that he may be properly—

Realizing that Xerxes is of no mind to handle this now, Artemisia whispers to her crew.

                    ARTEMISIA
          The attendants will see to the body.

Nodding, they depart. Artemisia sympathetically kneels beside the throne.

> ARTEMISIA
> If it had been possible, I would have
> brought them all back to you.

Artemisia puts a hand on his knee. The threat of tears burning his eyes, the great king squeezes them tightly shut before shaking the feeling away.

The naval messenger rides up, dismounts, and approaches Xerxes. Mardonius follows suit. Artemisia stands.

> XERXES
> (reluctantly looks up)
> Dare I hope you bring better news?

Regretfully, the man lowers his head and hands Xerxes a report.

> NAVAL MESSENGER
> The numbers are rough estimates. We
> expect a more thorough account to be
> much . . . higher.

Reading the account, Xerxes pales. The document slips from his grasp—as if he can no longer hold it up.

Mardonius, curious, picks the report up off the ground and reads.

Looking upon the channel, Xerxes beholds the burning wreckage, upturned hulls and corpses bobbing in the water. From across the way, on the shores of Salamis, the sounds of celebration are swept up on the breeze and dissonantly ring in his ears.

Drawing his hands to his face, he lowers his head.

EXT. SALAMIS COASTLINE—MORNING

Smoke rises from burnt out funeral pyres lined along the coast. Boats bob in the water, their crew members busily working on repairs. Other wreckage debris, as well as bodies, still consume the channel.

INT. SALAMIS—WAREHOUSE—MORNING

The Greek fleet commanders are gathered once more among the wares within the building. Though they are much more at ease than they were during their last meeting, the mood remains earnest.

>EURYBIADES
>We must not grow too confident. While it is true that their fleet is greatly diminished, they could very well be rallying for another attack as we speak.

>CIMON
>Agreed, but I do think we managed to send a message.

>THEMISTOCLES
>Not only to the Persians, Cimon, but our own people, as well. I see the gleam of hope in their eyes. If we tread with caution, this whole ordeal may soon come to an end.

>ARISTIDES
>The question is—what can we expect them to do next?

EXT. ATHENS—ACROPOLIS—DAY

Through a downpour of ash, we see Mardonius standing in the midst the acropolis's ruins. He is uncharacteristically anxious, his eyes set on the shadowy figure crouched at the top of debris littered stairs. Expending a shaky breath, he ascends the steps, but stops before taking the last.

>MARDONIUS
>I see that you grieve, but you shouldn't take what befell us at Salamis so greatly to heart.

We now see Xerxes, still crouched, his hands enveloped with soot. Dusting them off, he rises and leans against a fallen column. A twisted smile tugs at his lips.

> XERXES
> Is that so, Mardonius?

> MARDONIUS
> It is. Duplicity has won them little.

> XERXES
> But presumption has cost us much!
> Only a third of the fleet remains.

> MARDONIUS
> Our hopes hang not altogether on the fate of a few planks, but on our brave steeds and horsemen. While you stand here, master of all you see, your enemies remain cast away on that island and will not venture—not one of them—to come ashore to contend with our land army. They are at your mercy, not you at theirs so, for now, I say, think nothing more of them.

> XERXES
> To consider what instead?

> MARDONIUS
> The Peloponnese.
>   (off Xerxes' skeptical look)
> No matter what has happened, our original plan to force the Greeks' alliance was—still is—sound.

> XERXES
> But their fleet . . . .

MARDONIUS
Is a meager remnant without Athens' ships. There was an underlying truth to be found in the lie sent to us. They care only for what is no longer theirs and will not set sail in support of their convenient, new friends.

XERXES
(quietly)
So familiar this sounds, yet how different it is.

MARDONIUS
If you so please, we may attack at once—

XERXES
No. No, Mardonius—

MARDONIUS
Or if you would rather wait awhile, that, too, is in our power, only do not be disheartened. The Greeks will be brought to account for this and for their former injuries—

XERXES
We embarked on this campaign with numerous intentions, not foes. It is interesting . . . how a war against so few has become a war against so many.

MARDONIUS
A war we will win.

XERXES
But, I don't know that it is one worth pursuing . . . at least not now.

Bypassing Mardonius, he descends a few steps and takes in the scope of the destruction which surrounds them.

> XERXES
> (continuing)
> You can offer no assurances about the enemy fleet and, in its present state, ours cannot be deployed for battle without compromising our defenses.

Mardonius squares his jaw and sits down.

> MARDONIUS
> They could target the bridges.

Xerxes turns.

> XERXES
> Just as Artabanus warned.

> MARDONIUS
> So we wait—

> XERXES
> Winter is soon on its way and after this last debacle in Babylon, keeping my back turned on the region till spring's thaw . . . .

He trails off at a loss. Mardonius stands.

> MARDONIUS
> My counsel is this, if you'll hear it?

Xerxes nods. Mardonius begins, sounding more and more desperate as he continues.

                    MARDONIUS
Go if you must, but do not let these
people make a laughing-stock of the
Persian name. All you swore to do has
been done. Our dominion is increased
and Athens has fallen, but despite your
success, and despite the fact that it was
our foreign allies they faced at Salamis,
they will twist the facts. They will claim
to have defeated our army, they will
boast of forcing us to retreat, and in
doing so, quite possibly inspire the
surrounding cities to revolt. As quickly as
it was won, all we've accomplished, all
we fought for, could be lost. Persia's sons
are without fault. Let it remain so. If you
are so minded, depart home, and take
with you the bulk of the army, but first
allow me to choose my own troops.

                    XERXES
Mardonius . . .

                    MARDONIUS
You kept your word to the empire. I
must keep mine. Let me bring the
whole of Greece beneath your sway.

INT. XERXES' WAR TENT—NIGHT

Concluding a meeting with the army's top six generals, among them Hydarnes, Xerxes looks up from the conference table.

Gingerly entering the tent is Artemisia.

                    XERXES
               (to men)
          Dismissed.

Held by Mardonius's intrigued stare, Artemisa remains fixed in place as he and the rest of the men file around her and into the night.

Rising from his chair, Xerxes redirects her attentions and motions for her to join him in the 'nook', where a cart topped with assorted food and drink has been set out between two lounges.

          XERXES
        (taking a seat)
    Queen Artemisia. Please, sit.

She settles in and he silently offers her to take something to eat.

         ARTEMISIA
       (shakes head)
    Thank you.

Xerxes reclines further into the cushions. A considerate pause follows.

          XERXES
    Mardonius wishes to stay and attack the
    Peloponnese come spring. My land
    forces, and in particular my Persians, he
    says, are all the more eager to prove
    themselves after the . . . fleet's late
    misfortune. He therefore exhorts me to
    either stay and oversee matters personally,
    or to let him choose out a number of my
    troops to command himself.
       (uneasily shifts; a beat)
    You wisely counseled me to decline the
    sea-fight. Now, advise me in this
    matter? Tell me, Artemisia, which
    course I ought to take?

         ARTEMISIA
    O king, it is a difficult question you
    ask me. Nevertheless . . . as your affairs
          (MORE)

ARTEMISIA(cont'd)
now stand, it seems to me it would be best for you to return home. You have gained the purpose of your expedition. You have burnt Athens. As for Mardonius, if he prefers to remain and continue, by all means, leave him behind with the troops he desires. If his design succeeds, thine is the conquest.

XERXES
If Mardonius fails?

ARTEMISIA
It matters nothing. The Greeks will have gained a poor triumph, a victory over one of your servants.

Xerxes solemnly sits up and twists his ring.

ARTEMISIA
So long as you are safe and your house flourishes, we can suffer no great loss, but they? They will be left in a state of constant alarm, knowing the scales of peace and war may at any time be tipped by Persia's hand.

He gets up and slowly walks behind the lounge, dragging a hand along it as he goes. At its end is the statue of a woman—the wife of Odysseus, Penelope. Xerxes stands before her observantly.

XERXES
Beautiful, isn't she? But such sadness.

By her melancholy expression, Artemisia recognizes the piece. She stands and approaches.

ARTEMISIA
She longs for her love to return.

                    XERXES
          From where?

                  ARTEMISIA
          Battle.
               (a beat; stops beside Xerxes)
          One waged far across the sea.

EXT. PERSIAN ARMY CAMPSITE—NIGHT

ON THE OUTSKIRTS

Leaning against a tree, Masistes stares off into the distance, a finger pressed to his lips. He clearly misses his wife.

Just a few yards away, the campsite is buzzing. Talk circles the fires, accented by the sounds of dinner being served.

Tritan sits atop a fallen tree trunk, staring agitatedly at Mardonius afar. The general speaks with a small group of soldiers, Hydarnes and Masistius among them.

                 ARTABANUS (V.O.)
          . . . those whom you leave behind here
          will one day receive the sad tidings that
          Mardonius has brought a great tragedy
          upon the Persian people, and lies prey
          to dogs and birds somewhere in the
          land of the Athenians, or else in that of
          the Lacedaemonians—unless, indeed,
          you will have perished sooner on the
          way, experiencing for yourself the
          might of those men on whom you
          would induce the king to—

                    TRITAN
          Stop! Stop it.

> TIGRANES (O.S.)
> Stop what?

Tigranes appears, rations in hand, and takes a seat.

> TRITAN
> Tigranes.

> TIGRANES
> Tritan?

> TRITAN
> Oh, it's—no, I'm fine.

> TIGRANES
> I know you and the others were summoned earlier. Has something happened? Has the king issued new orders?

> TRITAN
> No. Not yet.

> TIGRANES
> Then—

> TRITAN
> I just—I was just thinking of father. That confrontation he had with Mardonius in front of the assembly—you remember?

> TIGRANES
> Yes, though I would rather not.

> TRITAN
> (increasing resentment)
> He was so sure of himself. The way he talked—as if he could see . . . So there
> (MORE)

                    TRITAN(cont'd)
were a few more obstacles than
anticipated. Still, we overcame them.
We reached our destination. But, you
know, you could take father on a grand
trip; he could be entertained by kings
like Alexander, the Aleuadae in
Thessaly; see Boeotia, Thebes, Attica—
you could let the man run laps around
the acropolis, Tigranes, and yet, even
presented with all this, all we have earned,
he would not concede our success.
          (a beat)
When he hears of the fleet . . . I can
hear him now: 'Warned you, didn't I?'

                    TIGRANES
It's not so simple.

                    TRITAN
No, it's not, but he doesn't—
          (realization)
He doesn't even understand his own
son, so why believe he could
understand something as complicated
as this? Why? Why even bother
worrying over—

Tritan stops short as Tigranes looks up. Mardonius is approaching. The young man tips his head as the general he holds in high esteem passes by.

                    TIGRANES
General.

                    MARDONIUS
Tigranes. Tritan.

Tritan manages a weary nod. Mardonius continues on. Tigranes returns his attention back to his brother.

                    TIGRANES
            So, what were going to say? You're
            worrying over . . . what?

Tritan ponders the question, takes another look at the departing Mardonius, and finally shakes his head.

                    TRITAN
            Nothing. I'm worrying over absolutely
            nothing.

ON MARDONIUS, reaching the outskirts of the camp.

He sees Masistes, still beneath the tree, quietly talking with one of Xerxes' messengers.

The conversation is soon ended and Mardonius watches with piqued interest as Masistes follows the messenger in the direction of the king's war tent.

INT. XERXES' WAR TENT—NIGHT

Xerxes is sprawled atop the lounge, his head propped by a pillow, one hand draped atop a bent knee, the other holding a drink, his eyes fixed on the statue of Penelope.

                    MASISTES (O.S.)
            Xerxes?

He raises his drink in signal.

                    XERXES
            Here.

Masistes walks up. The sight of his friend prompts a raised brow.

                    MASISTES
            Are you?

XERXES
Mostly. Sit.

MASISTES
(pointing to the food cart)
May I?

XERXES
Of course.

Masistes pours himself a drink and takes a seat on the other lounge.

MASISTES
So . . . Artemisia—

XERXES
Will be returning to Halicarnassus.

MASISTES
Then you've decided?

Xerxes sits up and nods.

XERXES
I can't remain occupied with one country when I have so many others to mind. We took what we came for. We've come far . . . and I'm granting Mardonius's request to go further.

MASISTES
With the troops of his choice?

XERXES
Yes, and that is what I wanted to speak with you about.

MASISTES
Well, you know I'm prepared to do my—

> XERXES
> You're exempt.

> MASISTES
> What?

> XERXES
> You are exempt. Should Mardonius ask, you are under no obligation to serve.

> MASISTES
> If I decide to?

> XERXES
> What?

> MASISTES
> If Mardonius is to build an army, then I believe he should be trusted and allowed to do so freely.

> XERXES
> Even if it means you stay here indefinitely? Think of your family, Masistes—
>   (glancing at the statue)
> —your wife.

> MASISTES
> What? Are you worried that if anything should happen to me, you'll have her to contend with?

Masistes laughs. Xerxes remains grim.

> MASISTES
>   (serious)
> I know you're troubled. Even a little . . . disillusioned?

XERXES
Is that a question or a statement?

MASISTES
Perhaps a bit of both. Xerxes, I have known you since we were children, but I could have met you a short time ago and it would still be plain to see that something is amiss.

XERXES
(incredulous)
Well, after the other day—

MASISTES
It was noticeable before then. I saw a glimpse of it, ever-sobriefly, at Thermopylae. It resurfaced at Salamis and has yet to wane.

XERXES
'It'. 'It' what?

MASISTES
The look of a man who's woken from a stupor.

Offended, Xerxes stands and begins to pace around the room.

XERXES
Masistes, you are my friend, but consider your thoughts before you utter them.

MASISTES
It is out of friendship that I do dare to speak. Xerxes, I was there the day this campaign was announced. I saw how
(MORE)

MASISTES(cont'd)
confident, how unshakable you were.
Now, it is as if you're at war with your
own self. Remember, you told me, before
the battle began, of being exhausted by
persistent visions? Perhaps they go on
unsatisfied because you refuse to accept
that they were not and cannot be fulfilled
as your mind's eye beheld them.

XERXES
But, Masistes, in the beginning, it was
as brilliant as I had—it was as if all the
stories which fed my imagination as a
child were only referred to as myth,
because no one had seen to making them
come true and, for a time, I thought—
You saw.

Xerxes sits down.

XERXES
We marched into Greece and city after
city fell to us with no more than a
whisper of our arrival. It was . . . what I
had hoped for. Still, I knew better than
to believe it would all be so easy. I knew
there would be resistance, but—You
know I tried to spare them. I wanted to.
I wanted them to understand my—our
purpose, to be our friends.
 (a beat)
I will never be able to put into words
what it feels like when a nation kneels
before you . . . or how great the price is
to make them do it.

MASISTES
I know it is steep.

XERXES
But once we took Athens . . .

He becomes transfixed by the flicker of a nearby candle.

XERXES
I stood in the cast of that ocher light, was warmed by it, not just on the outside, but within, because I could see through the destruction . . . a new beginning.
　　(returning attention on Masistes)
We're raised on stories of mighty kings, courageous heroes; of war and triumph. They are the fantasies of youth, but can so easily become the nightmares of men.

He grows silent.

MASISTES
Xerxes?

XERXES
It was just like one: the chaos, the ships afire—such a different kind of fire—the screams of trapped men burning to death above the water . . . and those of soldiers being dragged below it . . .
　　(a beat)
. . . and all the while, the 'mighty king' watching from his throne.

MASISTES
Xerxes, you could do nothing—

XERXES
(rises to his feet)
Nothing!!! I could do nothing . . .

MASISTES
And that is a feeling so unfamiliar to you.

XERXES
(briefly glances at the statue)
Not entirely. My hands have been tied before. Salamis, however—

MASISTES
It was awful. I know. I was there and the thoughts that must have come to mind—

XERXES
I will tell you the most disturbing of all.
   (a beat)
As those men—loyal men—were slaughtered in front of me, I knew it was all for lie—a lie I chose to believe—

MASISTES
No, you were cautious about that message. We were all consulted. So, they set a trap. We sailed into it—but our fate was not sealed upon doing so. Who knows what would have happened had that Phoenician not taken it upon himself to signal a premature retreat?

XERXES
(macabre)
He might still have his head.

MASISTES
The point is, what's done is done.

XERXES
I know, but if I had it to do over—

MASISTES
Time is not tangible. It cannot be slowed, reversed, remolded, and you can not turn to the past without turning away from the present.

XERXES
Presently, Mardonius has it right. We allow them the opportunity, and our enemies spin their lies yet again, and then we do revisit the past, for they'll tout the battle of Salamis as a testament to their bravery and as a symbol of defiance—just as they did with Sardis.

MASISTES
They may try to stir a revolt.

XERXES
(nods)
Potentially, everything the army accomplished would be undone. All those who believed—with such conviction—that they fought for a noble cause that they died for it, would have done so in vain. I will not betray their sacrifice.

Xerxes sighs and draws his hands to his face.

XERXES
If only patience had been exercised I would be returning to Persia contented.

MASISTES
If you wish to honor the fallen, then you must. Remain strong in both body and mind so that the empire which they died for may do the same.

Masistes grabs his cup off the table and stands. With characteristic showmanship, he raises it and grins, despite spilling some water on himself.

> MASISTES
> You have been consumed with war for so long, that your first order of business upon returning home should be rediscovering peace. Feel the breeze on your skin, the warmth of the sun. Take a deep breath and fill your lungs till they grow so tight you think them ready to burst. Eat and drink until you can no longer stand. Find your wife and keep her occupied till neither can she.

Xerxes' eyes widen and he cannot help but shudder with suppressed laughter.

> XERXES
> I think you have turned mad.

> MASISTES
> Not I, though you surely will if you do not allow yourself these simple pleasures. Spend time with your family.

> XERXES
> You're part of that, you know? My family. Won't you return to Persia, too?

> MASISTES
> Only Mardonius knows the answer to that.

> XERXES
> But, as I told you, should he ask—

                    MASISTES
            I can't say no.
                (jokingly)
            Everyone knows there is no
            replacement for me.

                    XERXES
            Exactly. Listen, we will talk on it more
            tomorrow. For now, get your rest.

EXT. PERSIAN ARMY CAMPSITE—OUTSKIRTS—NIGHT

Masistes is heading back to the campsite. The pace of his walk suddenly slows before he stops altogether. We do not yet see what he does—someone standing beneath the tree he stood under earlier.

                    MASISTES
            I know you're anxious for an answer. You
            needn't wait any longer. Congratulations,
            general, you have your army.

The sound of BARKING DOGS emanates from beyond.

Now, we turn our attention . . .

A startled bird takes flight from its tree-limb perch, shaking loose leaves free. They gracefully descend upon a grinning Mardonius, his eyes glinting.

INT. XERXES' WAR TENT—NIGHT

Xerxes stares at the flickering candle, draws his fingers through its flame, and snuffs it out.

EXT. SALAMIS COASTLINE—MORNING

Though the coastline is already coated in a few days' worth of soot, smoke rises from yet more burnt out funeral pyres. Boats bob in the water, their crew members busily working on repairs, but all work is suddenly brought to a halt as a YOUNG ATHENIAN runs past, a message in hand.

> YOUNG ATHENIAN
> Strategos! Strategos!! The Persian fleet!
> They've withdrawn! Strategos!

EXT. AEGEAN SEA—DAY

Flying above the water, we see the island of Andros, where the Grecian fleet is in the midst of docking.

EXT. ANDROS—HARBOR—DAY

The Grecian fleet commanders are gathered together along the dock.

> CIMON
> Eurybiades?

Themistocles brushes past Cimon and approaches Eurybiades, hands questioningly up.

> THEMISTOCLES
> Why were we signaled to dock?

> CIMON
> Yes, why?

> ADEIMANTUS
> We should continue on to the
> Hellespont, take control of it.

> EURYBIADES
> If they are withdrawing from Greece, it's
> more than likely that what you suggest
> has been anticipated and guarded against.

                    ADEIMANTUS
          Well, if we can't take control of the
          waterway, then we do all we can to
          disrupt it.

                    EURYBIADES
          That is the last thing we want to do!

                    ADEIMANTUS
          What do you mean? This could be our
          chance to—

Aristides steps forward.

                    ARISTIDES
          Listen to Eurybiades. You trap them
          here and, just like a cornered animal,
          they will cut down anyone foolish
          enough to get in their way.

Themistocles slowly begins to nod his head, reaching the same conclusion. He takes command of the scene.

                    THEMISTOCLES
          Aristides is right.
              (a beat)
          Xerxes will, no doubt, ride into Persia,
          entreating all to look upon his majesty,
          but the sooner we are free of them, the
          better.

EXT. SUSA—PROCESSIONAL WAY—DAY

MONTHS LATER

The entire population of Susa is gathered. Each side-street is crowded, each alley, every rooftop. Soldiers march through the capital, their armor gleaming against the sunlight. Cavalry members lead the way, carrying banners and raising their swords in salute. Following them, one-thousand of the Immortals, led by General Hydarnes, march with their spears poised toward the sky.

The next in procession is Xerxes' chariot, flanked by guards. Marching close behind are the rest of the Immortals and the infantry.

The people of Susa seethe with excitement, shouting Xerxes' name and ululating. Lotus flowers are thrown from the rooftops in such bulk that they carpet the ground below.

While the atmosphere is one of sheer joy, Xerxes looks absolutely despondent as he is drawn through the street. Every cry of his name falls on deaf ears. Accosted by memories of the war, all he can hear are cries of agony, all he can see are faces twisted in pain. Time and time again, he attempts to shake the delusions, half-heartedly raising the golden scepter in acknowledgement of his people.

This whole ordeal comes across as surreal. Nobody, not one single citizen, recognizes that Xerxes is in a state of distress. No, they continue to honor their king, blissfully unaware that something is wrong.

More and more flowers cascade around Xerxes, brushing his face, lulling his eyes closed. The sight is symbolic. Here the king is, consumed with gruesome memories, and he is being showered with beauty—with the very flower which represents royalty.

Dizzied, he reaches out to steady himself against the side of the chariot and, upon opening his eyes, a look of relief, as well as apprehension, is expressed. Rising up in the distance is the citadel.

EXT. SUSA—TERRACE

The court stands in wait along with others with ties to the palace. At the forefront are Artabanus, Haman, Amestris,

Artaxerxes (now three) and Darius (now twenty). All sights are on Xerxes, who draws near, his chariot shining so brightly that it looks as though he rides on a cloud of fire.

                    ARTABANUS (O.S.)
                    (subtly sarcastic)
                 Our great king has returned.

INT. SUSA—PALACE PORTICO—DAY

In a corner nook, a musician STRUMS a tar. Artaxerxes plays with his nanny, as Amestris is already occupied. Stretched atop a bounty of pillows, she watches the scene before her, amused—

Leaning against a pillar, drink in hand, Xerxes struggles to keep focus as members of the court babble.

                    HAMAN
            Tales of your tremendous success have
            spilled from the lips of every man,
            woman and child.

                    ADMATHA
            Your highness should have seen Susa
            when news of Athens' downfall reached
            us. People poured out into the streets,
            sang and danced.

                    MERES
            Myrtle boughs—strewn everywhere—
            and so much incense was burned that, for
            weeks, every breath you took was
            perfumed.

                    CARSHENA
            You would have thought everyone had
            lost their minds, the way they carried
            on.

                    ARTABANUS
                    (under his breath)
            Lost their minds, indeed.

SHETHAR
Though, nothing has brought them as much joy as beholding their triumphant king, safely returned.

XERXES
I'm heartened.

MERES
Indeed, for as much as they delighted in good news, when word came of the Greeks' treachery, so sore was their dismay, that they all, with one accord, rent their garments and cried aloud, and wept and wailed without stint—less on account of the damage done to the ships, than owing to the alarm which they felt about your safety.

MARSENA
Their trouble did not cease till you yourself, by your arrival, put an end to their fears.

DARIUS
The entire account of Sala— Salamis? . . . is baffling to me.

Awkward silence.

Xerxes idly traces the rim of his cup.

Trying to end the uncomfortable quiet, Haman turns to Hydarnes.

HAMAN
So, general, Mardonius is in Thessaly now? Is that right?

HYDARNES
Yes, wintering with the troops he selected.

DARIUS
I still don't understand why so many men were withdrawn or why some were chosen to remain over others.

ARTABANUS
(to himself)
Among them my sons.

DARIUS
(to Hydarnes)
You being here make sense. Your place is with the king, but of the six top generals, only three remain in command. Why?

This information rouses Amestris's suspicions.

XERXES
(irritated)
Darius—

Artabanus is also annoyed and tries his best to keep calm.

ARTABANUS
Allow me—O' king?
(off nod)
Prince Darius, there is more than one answer to your question. The number of troops allotted to Mardonius is in good measure to the number of ships left to accommodate them. Besides, you couldn't expect your father to leave all the empire's men behind to wage Mardonius's war when they best serve her here.

Xerxes is none too pleased with Artabanus's sardonic tone. He takes a drink and looks away, locking eyes with Artaxerxes. The young boy pries himself away from the nanny, goes to his father and clutches his hand. For the first time since returning to Persia, a genuine smile crosses the king's face.

> DARIUS
> Doing what? The provinces are
> without incident.

> SHETHAR
> We must remain mindful of Babylon.

> DARIUS
> I sincerely doubt they'll—

Memucan spots the touching sight of the king and his child. Artaxerxes is fixated on Xerxes' royal signet.

> MEMUCAN
> (interrupting)
> Looks as though young Artaxerxes
> desires the king's ring.

The men turn their attention to the boy, smile and softly laugh. Darius is not impressed, however. The prince reaches over and roughly ruffles his brother's hair. Artaxerxes swats at his hand.

> DARIUS
> Too bad he was born second in line.
> (to Artaxerxes)
> Is that not right, you little monster?

Xerxes is not humored by Darius's teasing. Artaxerxes looks like he's about to make a retaliatory scene. Amestris frowns.

> AMESTRIS
> My pardons, dear husband.

She gets up, pulls the boy away, and signals for the nanny.

                    AMESTRIS
            He is tired. Come on. Here.

As soon as the woman reaches them, the boy is handed off.

Amestris turns to Xerxes.

                    AMESTRIS
            Know that I am so pleased to have you
            back where you belong.
                    (she kisses the king's ring)
            Again, my pardons.
                    (turning to the nanny)
            Come.

                    NANNY
            Yes, my queen.

Xerxes watches them leave, now feeling more alone than ever.

                    DARIUS (O.S.)
            Well, as I was saying . . .

INT. SUSA—XERXES' CHAMBERS—NIGHT

Exhausted, Xerxes crosses the room to get some rest, but stops at the sight of Amestris's gown heaped on the floor. He looks to the bed and, kneeling atop it is his wife, draped in an exquisite robe fit for an emperor.

                    AMESTRIS
            Do you like it?

He is more than a little intrigued and slowly approaches her.

                    XERXES
            It's extraordinary. Is it a gift?

AMESTRIS
Fashioned just for the king.

XERXES
(leaning in for a kiss)
And to whom does he owe his thanks?

AMESTRIS
(lips a hair's breadth away)
Why, the seamstress, of course.

XERXES
Not the queen?

AMESTRIS
To thank her is to thank them both,
for they are one in the same.

XERXES
You? Made this?

AMESTRIS
Mm-hmm, all by myself. It helped to
keep my mind off of . . .

She trails off, reluctant to show any vulnerability.

AMESTRIS
So, you really like it?

He clasps her shoulders and, raking his eyes hungrily over her, nods.

XERXES
Very much.

AMESTRIS
What are you waiting for? Try it on.

They draw together for a kiss as his hands trail down and into the folds of the robe to peel it away.

She pulls him on the bed with her, but her touch and kiss is uncharacteristically gentle. He stops and searches her eyes.

> XERXES
> Is something wrong?

To us, it is plain to see that she has sincerely missed her husband. He, on the other hand, cannot recognize it. She prefers it that way, and the role of seductress is resumed.

> AMESTRIS
> No. Not a thing.

She draws him back down.

LATER . . .

Amestris appears to be sound asleep in Xerxes' bed. He, however, stands at the doors to his room, speaking with a SCRIBE.

> XERXES
> As I understand it, she's been waiting for him there and will continue to for the foreseeable future. I want a subtle eye kept on her. If there are any problems with her house, servants—if she requires anything, even a talent, send word of it to me.

> SCRIBE
> Is that all, your highness?

> XERXES
> For now.

> SCRIBE
> Your orders shall be on their way to Sardis before dawn.

> XERXES
> Good. Dismissed.

Xerxes closes the door, returns to the bed, and sits. Amestris's eyes snap open.

> AMESTRIS
> You would do nearly anything for her, wouldn't you?

She angrily rolls over and sits up.

> XERXES
> You were listening?

> AMESTRIS
> Says the man keeping watch over another's wife?!

> XERXES
> It is the least I can do. Masistes is like a brother to me and, right now, he is stationed on the Ionian coast ensuring that the peace is kept.

Amestris throws her gown on and gets up.

> AMESTRIS
> (rueful laugh)
> How convenient.

> XERXES
> (shocked at what she's implying)
> What?

> AMESTRIS
> Oh, come now. As much you may desire peace, well, should it be lost and he with it, you would find a way to console yourself . . . and his sorrowful widow.

He confronts her.

XERXES
Because you don't mean that, I will forgive that it passed your lips at all.

AMESTRIS
Oh, yes I do. Never will I forget your ridiculous letter, those saccharine sentiments. It is pathetic, really, that after all these years, all her denials, you still lust for that peasant. Is it because she has never let you conquer her completely? That her heart was not enough?

Amestris turns away.

XERXES
(reaching for her)
Do not turn your back on me.

AMESTRIS
Do not touch me!

She spins on him. The glossiness of her eyes is shocking.

AMESTRIS
I had so many opportunities to tell poor, clueless Masistes what kind of friend you truly are, but I kept my silence for one reason. I wasn't prepared to humiliate myself. I've told you before, intrigues with the harem—they mean nothing to me, but that you would so passionately pursue this one woman? You can not expect me to be so complacent.

Xerxes softens.

XERXES
Amestris . . .

He pulls her into his embrace.

> AMESTRIS
> I meant what I told you earlier. I did miss you, but now? Do you know what my fantasy is?

> XERXES
> Tell me.

She draws her lips close to his ear.

> AMESTRIS
> That you had never come back.

EXT. SUSA—PALACE GARDEN—SUNSET

The great week-long banquet detailed in the Book of Esther has reached its last day.

MUSIC, HEARTY LAUGHTER, and INCOHERENT TALK resonate throughout the garden.

The royal wine is in abundance and the WINE STEWARDS are kept busy. From goblets of gold, each uniquely adorned, the citadel's men, from the least to the greatest, drink their fill.

Xerxes, thoroughly and joyfully drunk, sits upon a golden couch in the company of nobles and members of his court.

> PARTYGOER 1
> So, he says to the man, 'Listen, you may take back the gold, take back the silver, and I shall even pay you a thousand talents more, if you will just, please, take back your daughter, too!'

Laughter abounds, but the men are soon struck silent (and paranoid) by an outburst of FEMININE GIGGLES emanating from beyond.

PARTYGOER 2
What do you suppose that's about?

PARTYGOER 1
Us?

A beat.

PARTYGOER 1   PARTYGOER 2
Nah!   Nah!

The men make a ruckus again.

Artabanus stands on the periphery of the group, watching.

ARTABANUS
Oh, how it would seem that the days
of war were over.

Back on the group . . . Xerxes spots Hydarnes walking by with a few guards, surveying the goings-on. The king waves him over.

XERXES
General. Yes, you, Hydarnes. Come here.

Hydarnes makes his way to Xerxes and tips his head.

HYDARNES
Yes, my king?

XERXES
At ease, general. Sit.

He instructs the nearest attendant to get Hydarnes a drink.

PARTYGOER 1
General Hydarnes, it's good to see you.
How are things? Are you happy to be
back in Susa?

HYDARNES
Thank you. Of course, yes. I've missed my family a great deal.

PARTYGOER 3
They say a man never realizes the wealth he possesses until he's been parted from it.

Hydarnes nods.

HAMAN
(to Hydarnes)
So, tell us a story.

HYDARNES
Story?

HAMAN
About Greece. I'm sure you have many. Tell us about—

The general notes Xerxes' sudden discomfort.

HYDARNES
Actually, I would be more interested to know what you were all laughing about.

PARTYGOER 2
He was telling us of an arranged marriage gone wrong.

PARTYGOER 1
Indeed. Pretty girl, but no prize.

PARTYGOER 2
And yours is?

PARTYGOER 1
Which one?

The men share another laugh.

PARTYGOER 1
You know what I have discovered?

HAMAN
No, but I'm sure you'll tell us?

PARTYGOER 1
If there is anything that means more to a woman than a declaration of your love, it is a declaration of their beauty. Because, believe me, when you get the lot of them together, they may be pleasant to one another, but really, they're eyeing each other up like there's some contest afoot. You tell your wife that there is no other more lovely than she and—

PARTYGOER 2
This could easily turn into a real contest over whose wife is the most beautiful.

XERXES
No need. The winner has already been crowned.

Xerxes signals for an attendant.

CUT TO:

INT. SUSA—PALACE—WOMEN'S BANQUET HALL—DAY

Seven male chamberlains enter the party. The leader, MEHUMAN, carries the queen's royal crown atop a pillow. The sight draws the coal-lined eyes of her guests.

Amestris rises from her lounge, analytically watching as the men stop before her and kneel. Though all sights are set on them, they speak discreetly.

> AMESTRIS
> What is this about?

> MEHUMAN
> The king has summoned you to join him in the garden. He wishes you to wear your royal crown.

> AMESTRIS
> Why?

> MEHUMAN
> To display your beauty before the people and nobles.

> AMESTRIS
> Really . . . ? Tell me, Mehuman, do you think I'm beautiful?

> MEHUMAN
> Beyond words, my queen.

Tracing the jeweled crown with her fingertips, she sadly smiles.

> AMESTRIS
> If only I could believe he thought me beyond compare.

EXT. SUSA—PALACE GARDEN—DAY

We see, in slow motion, Xerxes laughing with his guests. He looks up and sees Mehuman coming. The king locks eyes with him, questioningly. The chamberlain begins to shake his head 'no'. Xerxes' expression darkens.

INT. SUSA—PALACE—HALLWAY—DAY

Fueled by a burning fury, Xerxes paces back and forth.

> XERXES
> I try to make amends with her and this is what she does?! To think I felt regret for—no, the only thing I regret now is affording her the opportunity to—

The king's court advisors file into the hallway.

> XERXES
> It is an affront! No one defies the king! No one!

> MEMUCAN
> Of course not, your highness. It is unacceptable. A crime by law!

Xerxes abruptly stops.

> XERXES
> (to himself)
> A crime . . .
> (to Memucan)
> According to law, what must be done to the queen?

Memucan and the others do not know what has happened and wait for elaboration.

> XERXES
> She has not obeyed my command that the eunuchs have taken to her.

Now realization dawns.

> MEMUCAN
> The queen has done wrong, not only against the king, but also against all the nobles and the peoples of all the provinces of which you rule. For her conduct will become known to all the women, and so they will despise their husbands and say, 'King Xerxes commanded the queen to be brought before him, but she would not come.' This very day the Persian and Median women of the nobility who have heard about the queen's conduct will respond to all the king's nobles in the same way. There will be no end of disrespect and discord. Therefore, if it pleases the king, let him issue a royal decree and let it be written in the laws of Persia and Media, which cannot be repealed, that she is never again to enter the presence of King Xerxes. Also let the king give her royal position to someone else who is better than she.

Xerxes earnestly considers his words.

EXT. SARDIS—MARKET—DAY

Though the weather is chilly, the market is abuzz. From produce to textiles, the street-wise MERCHANTS peddle their wares.

Along with a few attendants, Suraz meanders along, scanning the goods. Though she is, for the most part, serene, every now and then, she looks over her shoulder. She senses she is being watched, but her composure would infer that it is something to which she has become reluctantly accustomed.

Finally, she stops before a booth overflowing with an array of spectacular fabrics and begins to sift through them while the proprietors, an elderly MOTHER and pregnant DAUGHTER team, gossip.

                    DAUGHTER
            (disbelief)
No!

                    MOTHER
Yes!

                    DAUGHTER
No!

                    MOTHER
Yes!

                    DAUGHTER
Truly, mother?

                    MOTHER
Sounds unbelievable, yet it is fact.
Amira saw the decree herself!

The girl glances over her shoulder at her FATHER and her HUSBAND, a comical-looking fellow, who are out of earshot, working another stand. The former ends what appears to be a pleasant talk with a pat on the shoulder and joins the women.

                    MOTHER
Husband.

                      FATHER
Wife.
            (a beat; concerned)
Daughter?

Their daughter rubs her belly and looks at her own husband again. He sets sights upon her, too, and goofily motions for her to join him.

> DAUGHTER
> (to herself; wincing)
> Husband.

> FATHER
> What's wrong with you?

She turns to her parents and gulps.

> DAUGHTER
> I could have been a contender!

The girl gets up and grudgingly goes to her husband, leaving her father bewildered. He turns to his wife.

> FATHER
> What was that about? A contender for what?

> MOTHER
> You haven't heard? The queen has been deposed and, now, a search has been decreed!

Suraz stops going through the merchandise. She cannot believe what she is hearing.

> FATHER
> A search?

> MOTHER
> Commissioners are being appointed in every province of the empire to seek out beautiful, young virgins for the king! From what I hear, they are to be taken to Susa, undergo a years worth of beautification rites and, then, he intends to pick one of the lot and name her Persia's new queen!

A sly grin draws across his face and he begins to laugh.

> MOTHER
> What?

> FATHER
> What can I say? It is good to be king!

She playfully shakes her head.

> MOTHER
> I also heard that he'll be staying here in the meantime.

> FATHER
> Makes sense. We're just between Greece and Babylon; good place to keep an eye on both. When do you think he'll come?

> MOTHER
> Rumor has it he has already left.

Suraz sets her sights on the distant ACROPOLIS, sitting prestigiously atop a spur of MOUNT TMOLUS. She takes a shaky step back, intending to leave.

Attentions are suddenly turned on her.

> MOTHER
> (to Suraz)
> There's more!

> SURAZ
> I'm sorry?

> MOTHER
> If you didn't find what you were looking for—

> SURAZ
> Oh. Um, perhaps another day. Thank you.

She departs.

EXT. SARDIS—RESIDENTIAL AREA—ALLEYWAY

In the midst of the alley, Suraz stops and waves her attendants on.

> SURAZ
> Go on inside. I will be there in a moment.

They go. She nervously looks down.

> SURAZ
> I know you're there and I know who sent you. You may soon be reporting to him face to face, and when you do, please, pass along a message for me? You tell your master that, while I appreciate the sentiment, I am in no need of such attention. I am in no need of anything.

She holds her head up high and leaves.

EXT. SARDIS—PALACE STOA—DAY

Standing over a small table, Xerxes writes a letter, intermittently glancing up from the scroll to scan the sprawling city of Sardis.

A messenger approaches. Xerxes spares him a brief look.

> XERXES
> Did you see her?

SARDIS MESSENGER
Yes, majesty.

XERXES
And did she read the message?

SARDIS MESSENGER
She did.

XERXES
Her answer?

SARDIS MESSENGER
The same as yesterday.

XERXES
As yesterday, the day before that, the week . . . same as the day I arrived. Such consistency.
    (a beat)
Go on.

SARDIS MESSENGER
Sir?

XERXES
At least report it as if it's new.

SARDIS MESSENGER
Um, well, the lady thanks the king for his most gracious invitation to carry out her stay in Sardis within the palace gate, but she is more than satisfied with her current arrangements, humble as they may be in comparison and—

XERXES
She wants for nothing.

> SARDIS MESSENGER
> So she says.

> XERXES
> So she says, indeed.

Xerxes finally puts down the writing reed and stands tall.

> XERXES
> Alright, then. I need to speak with
> Hydarnes. Go, fetch him.

The messenger bows and leaves. Xerxes glances at the city again.

> XERXES
> Nothing? No, I know exactly what
> you want, Suraz.

He re-reads his letter and, satisfied, marks it with the signet ring.

EXT. SUSA—PALACE BALCONY—DAY

From her perch, Amestris can see a crowd of young women gathered within the citadel. She frowns. Darius appears and puts a hand on her shoulder.

> DARIUS
> Why do you continue to do this to
> yourself? Why don't you—

> AMESTRIS
> Do you know how disappointed I was
> with you, Darius? When my title was
> taken, I thought, surely, my son would
> stand up for me. Alas, your care is
> limited to your own—

He moves to defend himself, but she raises a hand.

                        AMESTRIS
                    (continuing)
                —but, it's alright, the feeling of
                abandonment has passed, because I
                know now. This punishment . . . it's
                only temporary.

She turns around.

                        AMESTRIS
                I heard news today. It gave me hope.

                        DARIUS
                That . . . ?

                        AMESTRIS
                That your father is yet too scrupulous to just
                take what he wants. That, perhaps, he truly
                does want to keep the peace, as it were.

Darius furrows a brow.

                        DARIUS
                Mother? What are you talking about?

                        AMESTRIS
                You know when they drew back to
                Thessaly for the winter, the Athenians
                were allowed to return to their city?

                        DARIUS
                Yes, so?

                        AMESTRIS
                While Mardonius is eager to expel them
                once again, seems Xerxes is not so anxious to
                unleash his forces and has, instead, ordered
                the good general to issue a proposal.

DARIUS
                To the Athenians?

                    AMESTRIS
                Yes.

                    DARIUS
                Himself?

                    AMESTRIS
                No. An ambassador is to be sent.
                Alexander of Macedonia.

                    DARIUS
                Well, as interesting as this all is, what
                does it have to do with you?

                    AMESTRIS
                Well, if the terms are accepted, battle
                will be avoided. That would make
                everyone happy, no? The troops would
                eventually return. Families would be
                reunited . . . husbands and wives.
                Witnessing such joy may be the thing
                to inspire within your father a change
                of heart, or, at least, a change in
                wedding plans.

EXT. ATHENS—AREOPAGUS—DAY

Set against the backdrop of a city and acropolis in a state of repair, Alexander and his MACEDONIAN ENTOURAGE hold the attention of the Athenians.

At the forefront of the audience, we see Themistocles,

Aristides, and Cimon. Also present and watching skeptically from the sidelines, are members of a LACEDAEMONIAN EMBASSY.

Alexander holds up a letter.

> ALEXANDER
> O men of Athens, these be the words of Mardonius.
> (reading)
> The king has sent a message to me, saying all the trespasses which the Athenians have committed against him . . .

Alexander's voice begins to coalesce with Mardonius's.

ALEXANDER	MARDONIUS (V.O.)
. . . he freely forgives. Now then . . .	. . . he freely forgives. Now then . . .

Scanning the crowd, it is only Mardonius's voice we hear.

> MARDONIUS (V.O.)
> He has empowered me to restore to you your territory, let you choose for yourselves whatever lands you like besides, and let you dwell therein as a free people. Likewise, all which was destroyed, we shall rebuild, if on these terms you will consent to enter into a league with Persia. Such are the orders which I have received, and which I must obey . . . unless there is a hindrance on your part. So, now I say to you, why would you be so mad as to levy war against the king, whom you cannot possibly overcome, or even resist? You have seen the multitude and the bravery of the host of Xerxes. You know, also, how large a power remains with me in your land.
> (MORE)

> MARDONIUS (V.O.)(cont'd)
> Suppose you do get the better of us, and defeat this army—a thing which you will not, if you are wise, entertain the least hope of actually succeeding in—what follows then but a contest with a still greater force? Do not, because you would fain match yourselves with the king, consent to lose your country and live in constant danger. Rather, agree to make peace— which you can now do without any tarnish to your honor since the king invites you to it.

Once again, the voices of the two men begin to coalesce.

> MARDONIUS (V.O.)
> Continue free, and make an alliance with us, without or deceit.

> ALEXANDER (O.S.)
> Continue free, and make an alliance with us, without fraud fraud or deceit.

Alexander lowers the letter and looks upon the crowd.

> ALEXANDER
> These are the words, O Athenians, which Mardonius had bid me speak to you. For my own part, I will say nothing of the good will I bear your nation, since you have not now for the first time become acquainted with it, but . . . I will add my entreaties also, and implore you to give ear to Mardonius, for I see clearly that it is impossible for you to go on forever contending against Xerxes. If it were, I would not have come here the bearer
> (MORE)

ALEXANDER(cont'd)
of such a message. But the king's
power surpasses that of man and his
arm reaches far. If you do not hasten to
conclude a peace when such fair terms
are offered you, I tremble to think of
what you will have to endure—you,
who of all the allies, lie most directly in
the path of danger, whose land will
always be the chief battleground of the
contending powers, and who will
therefore have to constantly suffer
alone. Hearken then, I beseech you, to
Mardonius! Surely, it is no small
matter that the Great King chooses you
out from all the rest of the Greeks to
offer you forgiveness of the wrongs
you have done to him and to propose
himself as your friend and ally!

The Lacedaemonians, worried by the crowd's whispers, 'stage crash' before Alexander can go on.

LACEDAEMONIAN
We are sent here by the
Lacedaemonians to entreat you not to
do the unheard of by agreeing to these
terms offered you by the barbarian!
Such conduct on the part of any Greek
is both unjust and dishonorable, but in
you, it would be worse than in others,
for many reasons. It was you who
kindled this war in the first place—our
wishes were in no way considered—
now the entire fate of Greece is
involved in it! Besides, is it not an
intolerable thing that you Athenians,
known, until now, as a nation to which
(MORE)

                    LACEDAEMONIAN(cont'd)
           many men owed their freedom, should
           now become the means of bringing all
           other Greeks into slavery? We do feel
           for the heavy calamities which press on
           you—the loss of your harvest these
           two years, and the ruin in which your
           houses have lain for so long a time. We
           offer you, therefore, on the part of the
           Lacedaemonians and the allies,
           sustenance for your women and for the
           unwarlike portion of your households,
           so long as the war endures. Be not
           seduced by Alexander the Macedonian,
           who softens the rough words of
           Mardonius. He does as is natural for
           him to do—a tyrant himself, he helps
           forward a tyrant's cause. But you
           Athenians, if you truly are wise, will
           resist it, for you know with barbarians
           there is neither faith nor truth.

The reaction from the audience is imperceptible.

EXT. ATHENS—AREOPAGUS—LATER

Time has passed for deliberation. It is now Aristides commanding the audience's attention.

                    ARISTIDES
           We know the power of the Persian is
           many times greater than our own. We
           did not need to have that cast in our
           teeth. Nevertheless, not all the gold
           that the whole earth contains, not the
           fairest and most fertile of all lands,
           would bribe us to take part and help
                       (MORE)

                    ARISTIDES(cont'd)
          them to enslave our countrymen.
          Could we turn our backs on our
          common brotherhood, our common
          language, the altars and the sacrifices of
          which we all partake, the common
          character which we bear? Were we to
          betray all these . . .
                    (shakes head; a beat; to Alexander)
          Alexander, you are a guest and friend to
          this nation, but coming here on behalf of
          our enemy is something we counsel you
          not to do again. Go now, and take with
          you this message to Mardonius: So long
          as the sun keeps its present course, we
          shall never make an alliance with Xerxes.

INT. THESSALY—MARDONIUS'S WINTER HEADQUARTERS—NIGHT

Alexander stands before Mardonius's desk. The general's posture is one of humored confidence, a 'tsk-tsk' smile plays upon his lips.

                    MARDONIUS
          So they choose to deal with me . . .

EXT. ATHENS—CITY—DAY

SUMMER 479 B.C.

The Athenians are desperately fleeing the city.

EXT. SPARTA—CITY—DAY

The Spartans are celebrating the Hyacinthian holiday.

> ARISTIDES (O.S.)
> When Alexander conveyed Xerxes' offer, as generous as it was, we resisted it. We turned it down, for how could we allow fear to get the better of us and surrender, when you, our dear, Greek brethren so nobly swore to stand united?

INT. SPARTA—COUNCIL HALL—DELIBERATION ROOM—DAY

Aristides, accompanied by a few Athenian compatriots, heatedly addresses several, seated Spartan Ephors.

> ARISTIDES
> Well, brothers, where was your kinship—your army—when Mardonius's passed through Boeotia!? Where is it now that he is just outside Attica?! You called upon us to remain true to our bonds, yet here you all are, in the midst of festival, while Athens is in the midst of evacuation! If I were a cynical man, I would argue that your overtures were issued that day out of despair, rather than loyalty to your fellow Greek—despair that your wall across the Isthmus was not yet completed and, now that it is, why should you bother to cross it in defense of us?

The stubborn Ephors show no signs of concession.

> ARISTIDES
> Where is your king?

No answer. Desperate, he slams his fist down on the table.

> ARISTIDES
> Where is he?!

The Ephors are not intimidated. One of them stands and goes eye to eye with the Aristides.

> EPHOR 1
> Cleombrotus is dead.

> ARISTIDES
> What? When?

> EPHOR 1
> Shortly after returning from the Isthmus.

> ARISTIDES
> Who has succeeded him?

> EPHOR 1
> The son of Leonidas.

The Ephor looks out a window. The Athenians peer out, as well.

We see what they do: Gorgo and LEONIDAS'S SON, who is a small boy, sitting together on a bench beneath the stoa.

> ARISTIDES
> A child? Sparta has been left to a child?

> PAUSANIAS (O.S.)
> No. It has been left to me.

> EPHOR 1
> Pausanias.

Aristides turns to find power-hungry Pausanias nonchalantly leaning against the wall.

> PAUSANIAS
> I'm serving as regent in his stead.

> ARISTIDES
> Well, your highness, I offer my congratulations and a regretful warning . . .

He approaches. Pausanias stands tall.

> ARISTIDES
> If Sparta does not make good its promised offer, we may be forced to reconsider Persia's.

> CUT TO:

MONTAGE—THE SIGNALS GO UP—NIGHT

—On the coastline of Cape Mycale, Masistes and Tigranes set sights on the fiery lights which climb the sky above the islands of the Aegean. Masistes motions for Tigranes to go.

—A Persian archer lets a burning arrow fly. A beat later, he sees another, in response, go up in the distance—then another, further than the last, and so on.

—The streets of Sardis come to life as more and more people take to them, watching the signal fires go up, each one closer than the last.

—Nervously pulling a cloak around her, Suraz steps out into the night and spots an archer atop a nearby tower sending his own signal arrow up.

EXT. SARDIS—PALACE PORTICO—NIGHT

The 'fireworks' reflect in Xerxes' eyes. Hydarnes joins the king.

> XERXES
> Mardonius has retaken Athens.

EXT. ATHENS—CITY—OVERVIEW—DAY

The Persians are absolutely everywhere.

> MARDONIUS (V.O.)
> So . . . ?

CUT TO:

EXT. SALAMIS—COASTLINE—DAY

Once again, the coastal harbors, and many of the ships docked within them, are flooded with absconded, heartbroken Athenians.

The sight of a strange ship approaching raises suspicion.

Atop its deck stands a Hellespontine Greek, Persia's latest ambassador to Athens.

> AMBASSADOR (V.O.)
> I did as you instructed. I went before them and relayed your message—let them know that they might yet forge an alliance.

> MARDONIUS (V.O.)
> But?

CUT TO:

EXT. SALAMIS—SECLUDED COURTYARD—DAY

Athens' councilmen are imposingly lined around the perimeter. At the center of attention is the ambassador. It looks as though he might be lynched at any time. Still, he speaks animatedly, as if begging them to just hear the matter out.

> AMBASSADOR (V.O.)
> But, for the most part, none of them cared to listen—except one man.

Athenian 2 goes to the ambassador, takes and scans the message, and admonishes the others to consider it.

> AMBASSADOR (V.O.)
> He suggested the king's proposal be put before the people.

> MARDONIUS (V.O.)
> And how did the others respond?

We see one of the men pick up a rock. Themistocles witnesses this, too, and is immediately alarmed.

> AMBASSADOR (V.O.)
> They stoned him to death.

The rock is hurled at Athenian 2. He dodges it, but another is soon thrown, then another and another.

> MARDONIUS (V.O.)
> What?

CUT TO:

EXT. SALAMIS—RESIDENTIAL AREA—NIGHT

An out-of-control mob fills a narrow street.

> AMBASSADOR (V.O.)
> As well as his wife and children.

Aristides, newly arrived and out-of-the-loop, rushes toward the melee to see what is going on. He is shocked by what he finds.

The crowd is intent on stoning ATHENIAN 2's WIFE and CHILDREN.

Themistocles is tangled in the mess, doing everything short of throwing himself in front of the rocks, but is powerless to stop the madness.

Appalled and shaken, Themistocles CRIES OUT.

CUT TO:

INT. ATHENS—BOULEUTERION—DAY

Mardonius, Tritan, Masistius, Demaratus and Alexander informally sit around the battle-scarred council-hall, which, by the looks of things, was being slowly restored until the Athenians' recent evacuation.

Standing before them all, the ambassador is obviously upset.

> AMBASSADOR
> Why they let me go unharmed—

> ARTABAZUS (O.S.)
> General Mardonius.

Mardonius sees Artabazus beneath the damaged door jamb. He motions for him to come forward.

> MARDONIUS
> Artabazus?

Artabazus remains discreet and, passing by the ambassador, climbs up a few bench-rows to talk directly to Mardonius.

> MARDONIUS
> What is it?

> ARTABAZUS
> A messenger has just arrived from the Peloponnese. The Spartans are on the march.

> MARDONIUS
> That so?
> (off nod)
> Do we know how many?

ARTABAZUS
Well, including a separate Lacedaemon contingent, six-thousand.

Mardonius laughs.

ARTABAZUS
Along with some thirty to forty thousand helots.

MARDONIUS
(serious)
What?

ARTABAZUS
And those are only initial figures. The number is sure to grow as they continue north to the mainland.

MARDONIUS
Yes, it is. Well, that's that, then.

Mardonius gets up and points to the ambassador.

MARDONIUS
(to Artabazus, but loud enough for all to hear)
He just returned from Salamis. The Athenians turned on one of their own for simply suggesting that our proposal be put forward for review.

AMBASSADOR
Never have I beheld such a scene and I hope never to do so again. You . . . you don't intend on sending me back, do you, general?

                    MARDONIUS
                (stepping down to the floor)
            When they initially refused us, I was
            not surprised. Such stubbornness was
            to be expected.

He stops beside an Athenian bust and lazily props an arm atop it.

                    MARDONIUS
                (continuing)
            I thought, however, that realizing their
            time was borrowed would compel
            them to bargain for more, but, now, it
            is clear. Their minds are set.
                (looks at the bust and smirks)
            If they want nothing from us, well
            then, that is exactly what they shall
            have.

With that, Mardonius draws his hand down the face of the bust and pushes, sending the likeness and its attached pedestal to the floor.

                                            CUT TO:

MONTAGE—PERSIAN/GREEKS

—The Persian army rampages through ATHENS, leveling its walls and buildings to the ground, setting it afire.

—In the Greek city of MEGARA, General Masistius leads the cavalry in an attack against ONE-THOUSAND LACEDAEMON TROOPS, destroying them utterly and ravaging the land.

—Pausanias's army prepares to strike camp and cross the ISTHMUS.

—The Persian army marches into the friendly territory of THEBES.

—The Persians construct a rampart along the ASOPUS, between ERYTHRAE and PLATAEA.

—Like a man left behind, Themistocles watches from atop his ship deck as EIGHT-THOUSAND ATHENIAN HOPLITES, led by Aristides, disembark to the mainland.

—In ELEUSIS, the Athenian forces, along with thousands of other Greeks, join Pausanias's army, becoming one with it.

EXT. GREECE—THEBAN ESTATE—NIGHT

ATTAGINUS, a wealthy citizen, hosts a magnificent feast for Mardonius, fifty of the noblest Persians and fifty Thebans. The dinner has long been finished, the drinking long-since begun.

Attaginus himself talks with a GREEK GUEST.

> ATTAGINUS
> Well, he quit Athens as soon as he
> heard of the gathering army.

> GREEK GUEST
> I hear there's not much left of it.

> ATTAGINUS
> All cast to the ground and set afire. The
> Megarid, too. That's where those
> thousand Lacedaemonians had gone in
> advance of Pausanias's army.

> GREEK GUEST
> So, why, exactly, did the Persians
> decide to turn course and camp here?

> ATTAGINUS
> These lands are better suited for
> cavalry. Friendlier, too.

> **GREEK GUEST**
> Friendly enough to yield all of Thebes' trees to them.

> **ATTAGINUS**
> Yes, for their rampart. I know.

Another Grecian guest walks past, saluting with his drink.

> **GREEK GUEST 2**
> Excellent banquet, Attaginus!

> **ATTAGINUS**
> (raising his own cup)
> Thank you, good sir.

The man continues on his way.

> **GREEK GUEST**
> So, who's leading the Athenians? Themistocles?

> **ATTAGINUS**
> No, no. Themistocles' star has dwindled it seems.

> **GREEK GUEST**
> Really? Since when? Wasn't that long ago that he was being esteemed not only by Athens, but by the Spartans, too. Didn't they award the man a crown and chariot?

> **ATTAGINUS**
> And a sense of superiority, too, which quickly became tiresome. No, weren't you aware that Aristides won the people's election?

The guest shakes his head.

GREEK GUEST
So. he's in command of their troops?

ATTAGINUS
Yes, and they're on their way here.

GREEK GUEST
How many men do you think?

ATTAGINUS
Just of Athens?

GREEK GUEST
The whole force.

ATTAGINUS
That I don't know . . .

Sitting across the way is a terribly DEPRESSED PERSIAN soldier. Attaginus is moderately unnerved by the sight.

ATTAGINUS
. . . but I tell you what, it must be enough to elicit serious concern.

We now move to the couch upon which the Persian sits, drunk and troubled. THERSANDER, a Greek seated beside him, unintentionally stares.

DEPRESSED PERSIAN
What city are you from?

The Persian sits back and looks at him. Thersander is surprised.

THERSANDER
Uh, um, Orchomenus. My name is Thersander.
    (a pause)
Um, you seem terribly upset, might you share why?

DEPRESSED PERSIAN
Well, Thersander of Orchomenus, since you've eaten with me at one table, poured drink from one pitcher, why not share my troubles, too? You might then escape them. See these Persians here feasting?

THERSANDER
Yes?

DEPRESSED PERSIAN
And did you see the army encamped over by the riverside?

THERSANDER
It cannot be missed.

The Persian slightly smiles, but tears line his eyes.

DEPRESSED PERSIAN
Yet, in a little while, of all this number, only a few will survive.

THERSANDER
If you feel this so strongly, then why not speak to Mardonius and those next in rank?

Thersander sees Mardonius afar, enjoying the party as if without a care.

DEPRESSED PERSIAN
Dear friend, they don't believe the warnings, however true. Many of us Persians know our danger, but we are constrained by necessity to do as our leader commands us.
    (a beat)
Truly it is the sorest of all human ills, to abound in knowledge and, yet, have no power over action.

The soldier drinks and we pan up to see Tritan standing behind the couch, troubled by what he has just heard.

EXT. GREECE—ERYTHRAE—SUNSET

The Greek army has stopped for a brief rest. Pausanias gets water from a well. Aristides joins him.

> ARISTIDES
> So, has a decision been reached?

The Spartan nods as he drinks.

> ARISTIDES
> Well?

> PAUSANIAS
> (points to the well)
> Yes, this is a well.

Aristides, though patient, is not amused.

> ARISTIDES
> Where, Pausanias, have we decided to establish camp?

> PAUSANIAS
> The foothills of Cithaeron.

EXT. GREECE—MOUNT CITHAERON—NIGHT

Rolling clouds keep the moon's glow from falling definitively. Light and dark alternate as the Greek army, now comprised of one-hundred-ten-thousand men, deploys along the slopes.

EXT. GREECE—PERSIAN FORTRESS—DAY

Masistius determinedly walks through camp, eyes set on three CAVALIERS who are at the mercy of the general's crazed horse. Though tethered to a post, it rears and kicks.

Another cavalier stands on the sidelines, watching helplessly with the animal's gear at his feet.

>MASISTIUS
>I told you to have him ready.

>CAVALIER 1
>Yes, General Masistius, but, as you can see . . .

>CAVALIER 2
>As unpredictable as this Grecian weather.

Masistius motions for the others to get out of his way.

>MASISTIUS
>Careful! Get back! Watch the kicking!

The general approaches the horse.

>MASISTIUS
>Easy, boy. Shh. Calm down.

It does just that, simply by the sound of Masistius's steady voice. He takes hold of it.

>MASISTIUS
>There now. That's it.

The others watch in awe.

>MASISTIUS
>Such perception. So attune to the human heart. He was merely dancing to the beat of yours. Go on now, the others are nearly finished.

                    CAVALIER 1
                 Yes, general.

The men go.

                    MASISTIUS
                    (to horse)
                 And you—save your legs.

                    TRITAN (O.S.)
                 For what, Masistius?

Masistius gathers his gear and tends to his horse.

                    MASISTIUS
                 Didn't Mardonius inform you of—

                    TRITAN
                 Of the Greeks on Cithaeron? Yes, but
                 no word of any move against them.

                    MASISTIUS
                 It's not so much a move . . .

                    TRITAN
                 As it is . . . ?

The cavalry commander finishes his work and we now see his horse beautifully arrayed in gold. He mounts and prepares to start off.

                    MASISTIUS
                 A welcoming.
                                                    CUT TO:

EXT. GREECE—CITHAERON FOOTHILLS—MEGARIAN POST—DAY

A few thousand Megarians, held up behind the bunker-esque hills, are under brutal assault by the cavalry.

Masistius marshals the lines. Scythian, Boeotian, Median and Persian contingents cycle in attack, assailing the Grecian body with an array of arrows and spears. Each charge leaves the desperate foot soldiers scrambling.

A small window of time presents itself when the Boeotian cavalry forces reel round to change lines. It is an opportunity which the MEGARIAN GENERAL uses to reorder the ranks of his own regiment.

Leaving the majority of his men below, he advances the front lines to crest the hilltops, so as to keep the cavalry from riding up so close again.

>   MEGARIAN GENERAL
> Together! Hurry! Tight formation! On
> their approach, get low, get your shields
> up!
>   (to nearby soldier)
> They ride up closer and closer with
> each charge. We cannot hold for much
> longer. If those replacements do not
> arrive soon, they leave us no other
> option. We'll have to abandon the
> post.

We now switch to Masistius's post as the Boeotian contingent returns. He signals the next to proceed.

>   MASISTIUS
> Scythians!

The Scythian standard is raised and off they go!

Masistius's horse paws the ground.

>   MASISTIUS
> Hold on just a little longer. You'll be
> on the wind soon enough.

ON THE MEGARIANS

MEGARIAN GENERAL
They're coming. They're coming! Get
down and, as much as your feet may
beg you, do not move!

The Greeks descend under their shields and we with them. Crouched beneath this disquieting canopy, the senses are piqued; the anxiety near unbearable. Breath quickens as the OMINOUS RUMBLE of oncoming attack grows louder and louder with each passing second . . .

Suddenly, it stops.

MEGARIAN GENERAL
Do not move.

The dreadful WHISTLING of hundreds of arrows pierces the silence. They pelt the shields like a hailstorm.

The sound is maddening. One of the Megarians flinches, allowing an opening. An arrow slips through, he falls and a gap is created. Defenses are weakened and the fissure further widens.

MEGARIAN GENERAL
No! Stay together! Together!!

The Megarians work quickly to close the gap, but this shuffle is not completed in time to ward off another barrage of arrows. While numerous soldiers drop where they stand, many more stumble down the hillside and onto the plain.

Those that still breathe are desperate to rejoin their forces, but the sight of the oncoming Scythians freezes many men in their tracks.

MEGARIAN GENERAL
(to the fallen)
Get up! Get up!!

Some soldiers, overcoming their nerves, heed the order and dash up the hill.

Few actually make it, either stopped short by an arrow or trampled beneath the charge.

There is little time for the distraught Megarians on the high ground to mourn their peers. The Scythians are not wheeling back around—they are sprinting toward them.

>   MEGARIAN GENERAL
>   (aghast)
>   They're not stopping. Swords!!
>   Shields!!

He barely has time to extricate his own sword from its scabbard before the Scythians collide with the front line. The horsemen dominate the scene, winding through and around the Megarians, forcing a great many of them to the plain below.

ON MASISTIUS

The time has come.

>   MASISTIUS
>   Attack!!!!

The Persian standard is raised. Masistius leads the charge, intent on mowing down the growing number of Megarians descending onto the plain.

ON THE PLAIN MEGARIANS

They're horrified by the sight of the Persians racing to meet them. With the Scythians still working upon their kinsmen on the high ground, there is nowhere to run and nothing to do but fight. They gather to stand united, ready their weapons, and wait.

Their ranks, however, are once again disorganized as more men, with the Scythians hot on their heels, are chased down the high ground.

The Megarians are trapped. They are the eye of a storm, one which closes in and circles them, its lightning flashing in the form of steel.

The Megarian general, battle worn, is dizzied by the sight. He and his troops look like lambs to the slaughter.

The Persians and Scythians let their weapons fly. Scores of trapped Greeks drop, some to dodge the bolts, some from being struck by one.

The cavalry whirlwind unwinds and both contingents ride back to their posts, WHOOPING it up all the way.

The Megarians on the plain (those who can), get back up and hastily return to their lines upon the high ground.

>   MEGARIAN GENERAL
>   (rejoining the ranks)
>   They toy with us like animals!

Watching the Persians return to their post, the Megarian general debates using this window of opportunity to call for a retreat. He turns to address his men, but is dumbstruck by what he sees. A contingent of three-hundred Athenian hoplites, ready to do battle, march through the Megarian ranks. The general is not at all impressed, nor are his subordinates.

>   MEGARIAN SOLDIER 1
>   That's all they've sent?? That's—

>   MEGARIAN SOLDIER 2
>   We're finished.

>   MEGARIAN GENERAL
>   Yes, we are finished—because we are
>   leaving!

Before he can muster a step, the Athenian general, OLYMPIODORUS, motions for him to stay put.

OLYMPIODORUS
(approaching)
My name is Olympiodorus, and you are not going anywhere.

MEGARIAN GENERAL
Who's going to stop us? You and this meager lot? Pausanias and Aristides must think themselves better than we. Apparently, to them, we're expendable. Well, they are not our masters and we are not their slaves!

OLYMPIODORUS
If you would kindly be quiet, then—

Looking past the fuming Megarian, Olympiodorus abruptly quiets.

MEGARIAN GENERAL
If no others will come, no more shall we stay!!

OLYMPIODORUS
(ignoring Megarian; to hoplites)
To your lines!

The Megarian turns around as the hoplites rush past him to get into formation along the high ground.

The Persian-allied Medes are coming.

MEGARIAN SOLDIER 1
General? Do we stay or go?

A beat as the remaining, surrounding soldiers look at him expectantly.

Their answer finally comes in the form of action. The general directs his troops to line up behind their shields.

The Medes let their weapons fly. It is another agonizing assault, but the Athenians and Megarians bear it together.

ON MASISTIUS

He watches the Medes return from their offensive. Their commander, cavalier 1, rides up and flanks the general.

                    CAVALIER 1
    The others—

                    MASISTIUS
Yes?

                    CAVALIER 1
    They're Athenians.

                    MASISTIUS
    How many, you think?

                    CAVALIER 1
    Few hundred.

Digesting the info, the general cues the next contingent.

                    MASISTIUS
    Boeotians!

The Boeotian standard goes up and they ride off. Masistius's eyes narrow, calculatingly.

                    MASISTIUS
    Scythians!

Signalled, they depart. The doubling of forces prompts a quizzical look from the cavalier.

                    CAVALIER 1
    Sir?

                    MASISTIUS
            Thought we might pick up the pace.

BACK ON MEGARIANS/ATHENIANS

They are under fire by the Boeotians. A few arrows manage to slip through their defenses and, as before, a gap is created. With the Boeotarchs' turn at an end, the Scythians seize upon the Greek ranks, repeating their last go-round and chasing numbers of them onto the plain.

The Scythians sweep through these men, striking them with swords and spears, before continuing on their way.

Both the Megarian general and Olympiodorus are with the Greeks forced from the high-ground. The former finds one of his top-ranking soldiers among the casualties and, mentally snapping, charges the Athenian with his sword.

                MEGARIAN GENERAL
            This is your fault!! This is—

Olympiodorus aggressively blocks the Megarian's strike with his shield, knocking the incensed man to the ground.

                    OLYMPIODORUS
            What's wrong with you?!

                    MEGARIAN GENERAL
                  (laughing to himself)
            Three-hundred men. They send us
            three-hundred men.

                    OLYMPIODORUS
            Calm down!!!

                    MEGARIAN GENERAL
                  (sits up; yelling)
            Calm down?!!

> OLYMPIODORUS
> Yes! The only ones who are to blame
> for this are them!

Olympiodorus points across the plain. Both he and the Megarian set their sights there, too. Their eyes simultaneously widen.

The Persians are coming.

> OLYMPIODORUS
> (offering a helping hand)
> Get up! Get up, I say!!

The Megarian rises and the two generals, as well as dozens of their soldiers, race for the high-ground.

Masistius leads the charge determinedly and, one-by-one, the Grecian stragglers are picked-off.

> MEGARIAN GENERAL
> (desperately running)
> No! Oh, no!

A HORN sounds from beyond the hills.

Though only a few yards away from the Greek front line, Olympiodorus grabs the Megarian's arm.

> MEGARIAN GENERAL
> What are you doing?!

> OLYMPIODORUS
> (yelling to the Greeks ahead)
> Get down!!!

They do as ordered.

MEGARIAN GENERAL
What are you doing!?!
> (turning toward the oncoming Persians)

They'll trample us all!

Frustrated, Olympiodorus kicks the Megarian's legs out from under him before throwing himself to the ground, too.

He does so just in time, for a bleak shadow passes over them as the Persian cavalry, only feet away, is showered by thousands of arrows.

THE ENTIRE BODY of the GREEK ARMY'S ARCHERS crests the highground.

The Persians are unprepared for such an attack and wheel around, disarranged.

In the chaos, Masistius's horse is struck in the flank and rears. The general unceremoniously falls to the ground and is left behind, directly in front of the Greek line, unbeknownst to his own troops.

One of the Athenians seizes Masistius's horse, while others encircle the Persian with their spears before he can stand.

ON THE CAVALRY

Returned to their post, the cavaliers realize their leader is not among them.

CAVALIER 1
Where is Masistius!?

ON THE GREEKS

Olympiodorus and the Megarian general go to see who the hoplites surround. The latter points to Masistius's uniform.

                    MEGARIAN GENERAL
                  He's their commander.

Olympiodorus directs the Athenians to attack. They do, attempting to spear Masistius to the ground. He courageously struggles with sword and limbs and, to their wonder, remains unharmed.

ON THE CAVALRY

Cavalier 1 has assumed the role of leader. Poised to lead the charge, he raises his sword.

                        CAVALIER 1
                         Attack!!!!

The cry to battle is heeded. An array of weapons are drawn and readied as the Persians, Medes, Scythians and Boeotians take off sprinting.

ON THE GREEKS/MASISTIUS

Masistius hears the RUMBLE of the approaching cavalry—so do his captors. They look up and are terribly shaken by the sight of the amassed cavalry heading straight for them.

                       OLYMPIODORUS
                         (to a soldier)
                  Hurry!! Send for the infantry!!

The soldier runs off.

Masistius's horse suddenly raises a ruckus, rearing and kicking at anyone in close proximity; creating an opportunity for its master to fight back.

                       OLYMPIODORUS
                   Get that beast out of here!

With Olympiodorus and the others momentarily distracted, Masistius attempts to rise and fight.

> OLYMPIODORUS
> (returning attention to Masistius)
> Watch out!

The hoplites are fast to respond and seize upon Masistius. A spearhead tears his scarlet tunic, revealing gold-scaled body armor underneath. The general's secret to surviving the Athenians' attack thus far is exposed and he is promptly stabbed through the eye.

Everything goes to black.

EXT. GREECE—CITHAERON FOOTHILLS—NIGHT

Upon the highest ground Cithaeron offers, Pausanias and Aristides stare out into the night. Their expressions are strikingly different. While the Spartan looks greatly emboldened, Aristides is grim.

Though unseen, Greek troops are heard CELEBRATING nearby, but there is something else which echoes in the dark, something unsettling—the sound of MOURNING.

Aristides briefly closes his eyes.

> ARISTIDES
> They vent their grief in such loud cries.
> All Boeotia resounds with the clamor.

> PAUSANIAS
> Mm-hmm. What a sight they must make, too. Our scouts say they began shearing the hair off their own heads and the manes off their war horses upon returning to camp. Speaking of camp, we should discuss moving ours.

> ARISTIDES
> Quit the high ground?

                    PAUSANIAS
          Yes, and go nearer to Plataea where the
          water supply is better.

Aristides simply bobs his head.

                    PAUSANIAS
          Why are you in such a sorry mood? We
          took a great prize today—not easily
          won, by the way. Those cavalrymen
          were relentless.

                    ARISTIDES
          He was their general.

We now pan down to lower ground, where Masistius's defiant horse is being forced to pull a cart holding the body of its master before the Greek ranks.

EXT. GREECE—BOEOTIA—ASOPUS—DAY

The Persian and Greek armies are encamped opposite of one another, with only the Asopus River separating them.

INT. GREECE—PERSIAN FORTRESS—MARDONIUS'S TENT—DAY

Sunlight flickers across the table and atop the downcast, shorn head of the general. He looks up from his work, runs a hand across a beard of stubble, and sits back to address Demaratus, who stands in the folds of the tent's entrance.

                    MARDONIUS
          So, Demaratus, what has your friend
          seen?

                    DEMARATUS
          He has come to tell you himself.

                    MARDONIUS
                Send him in.

Demaratus peers back outside.

                    DEMARATUS
                Hegesistratus.

His call is answered by peculiar footfall—a normal STEP, a THUD, normal STEP, THUD . . .

Demaratus backs up and we see a sandaled foot step into the tent, followed by wooden one.

The shadow of HEGESISTRATUS falls upon Mardonius.

                    MARDONIUS
                Well, soothsayer?

Though wild in appearance, Hegesistratus is a shrewd man, and eyes a chest of gold sitting on the floor.

                    MARDONIUS
                After.

                    HEGESISTRATUS
                Should I tell you news contrary to your wishes?

                    MARDONIUS
                I will believe you to be a fake, but still thank you for the joke. Now, talk.

                    HEGESISTRATUS
                Triumph and defeat, they are undecided.

                    MARDONIUS
                    (snickering)
                Oh, undecided.

                    HEGESISTRATUS
Undecided, but dictated.

                    MARDONIUS
By what? Whom?

                    HEGESISTRATUS
You. You and Pausanias of Sparta.

                    MARDONIUS
Go on . . .

                    HEGESISTRATUS
It comes down to this, Persian.
Whosoever initiates attack and leads
their troops across the river divide,
leads them to ruin.

EXT. GREECE—PERSIAN FORTRESS—DAY

Days have passed, evidenced by Mardonius's hair growth. He and Artabazus walk through the bustling camp.

                    MARDONIUS
Three days ago, the cavalry intercepted
a body of Greeks on route to deliver
provisions from the Peloponnese. It
was a generous bounty, hundreds of
sumpter-beasts and so forth, and its
loss has surely been damaging . . .

                    ARTABAZUS
But?

                    MARDONIUS
We cannot wait forever for them to
lose their resolve and begin this battle.
                        (MORE)

MARDONIUS(cont'd)
We have advanced as far as Asopus itself,
but they will not cross it and, meanwhile,
their numbers continue to grow!

ARTABAZUS
I know you're impatient to settle this
war, but I strongly feel—

MARDONIUS
(bringing himself and Artabazus to a halt)
What, Artabazus?!

Mardonius is startled by his own outburst. He looks around, hoping no one took notice.

MARDONIUS
You think there's another way?

ARTABAZUS
I don't know, but I do think we ought
to see if there is. Why do we not break
up our respective quarters as soon as
possible and withdraw to Thebes? The
city is fortified, there's abundant stores
of corn for ourselves and animals—

MARDONIUS
No.

ARTABAZUS
We simply sit quiet and perhaps the
war might be brought to an end this
way—Our riches are plentiful, both in
gold and silver, both coined and
uncoined. We distribute them among
the Greeks, especially their leaders,
and in short time, they'll offer their
concessions—

                    MARDONIUS
            No!! They had their chance. They
            refused. No more! No. More.

Mardonius storms off.

EXT. GREECE—GREEK CAMP—ATHENIAN POST—NIGHT

Shrouded in darkness, an ATHENIAN WATCHMAN leads Aristides and a few other generals to the post's outskirts.

                    WATCHMAN
            The horseman would not say a word,
            except that he wished to speak with you.

They reach the post's edge, where the other watchmen wait, weapons leveled at the CLOAKED HORSEMAN before them.

                    ARISTIDES
            Well, here we are. Now, who are you
            and what do you want?

                    CLOAKED HORSEMAN
            Men of Athens, that which I am about
            to say I trust to your honor; and I
            charge you to keep it secret from all
            excepting Pausanias, if you would not
            bring me to destruction.

Aristides shares a look with his peers before turning to the watchmen.

                    ARISTIDES
            Stand down.

They are dismissed.

                    ARISTIDES
            Alright, then, what—

CLOAKED HORSEMAN
Had I not greatly at heart the common welfare of Greece, I would not have come to tell you; but I am myself a Greek by descent, and I would not willingly see Greece exchange freedom for slavery. Know then that Mardonius and his army cannot obtain favorable omens; had it not been for this, they would have fought with you long ago. Now, however, they have determined to let the victims pass unheeded, and, as soon as day dawns, to engage in battle. Mardonius, I imagine, is worried that if he delays, your forces will further increase in number. Make ready then to receive him.

ARISTIDES
If this proves to be false?

CLOAKED HORSEMAN
Then simply stay where you are, for his provisions will not hold out many more days.

He turns his horse around and begins to leave.

ARISTIDES
Stop! Wait! You tell us all this and want nothing in return?

CLOAKED HORSEMAN
(stops horse)
If you prosper in this war, forget not to do something for my freedom.

ARISTIDES
Tell us who you are.

The man pulls down his hood and turns his mount to face them. The Athenians are taken aback.

> ALEXANDER
> I am Alexander of Macedon.

EXT. GREECE—GREEK CAMP—SPARTAN POST—NIGHT

Aristides and the other Athenian generals hold audience with Pausanias. He fretfully paces before them.

> PAUSANIAS
> So, we're agreed?

> ARISTIDES
> We were going to suggest it ourselves.

> PAUSANIAS
> It simply makes sense. You are the only ones with experience against these men. Well, the only ones still breathing, anyway. There's not a Spartan among us who has ever fought a Persian—oh, but we are quite familiar with the Boeotians and Thessalians—the traitors.

> ARISTIDES
> So, we're going to switch—

> PAUSANIAS
> Yes—yes, Aristides.

Pausanias abruptly stops infront of him.

> PAUSANIAS
> You Athenians will take the right wing, we the left.

EXT. GREECE—PERSIAN FORTRESS—MARDONIUS'S TENT—NIGHT

Standing over his desk, Mardonius scans a map with the army's two top-ranking cavaliers and Demaratus.

>   DEMARATUS
>   Apart from the river, this fount is the
>   only other source.

>   MARDONIUS
>   (to cavaliers)
>   Manageable?

>   CAVALIER 1
>   Yes, general.

>   CAVALIER 2
>   Absolutely.

Tritan enters. Mardonius looks up.

>   MARDONIUS
>   What is it?

>   TRITAN
>   The Spartans—they've pulled back
>   from their post and it looks as though
>   the Athenians are taking their place.

Mardonius turns to the shadowy sitting area and shares a knowing look with the man standing there—Alexander.

EXT. GREECE—THE FRONT LINES—DAY

From above, we behold the sight of the Persians filing in opposite the Spartans. They are two fierce armies, separated only by a gentle stream.

PAUSANIAS (O.S.)
We take to the left, they switch to their right.

EXT. GREECE—THE FRONT LINES—SPARTAN POST—DAY

Pausanias stands before his troops, who have now returned to the right wing. He is frustrated beyond belief, glaring across the Asopus at the Persians.

PAUSANIAS
We go back, they follow suit!

He turns to find two Spartans escorting a mounted HERALD.

PAUSANIAS
Now, what's this?

HERALD
I come on behalf of General Mardonius.

PAUSANIAS
(to Spartans)
It's alright.

They let the herald's horse go.

PAUSANIAS
(to herald)
On Mardonius's behalf . . . that's too bad. No offense, but I am rather disappointed he didn't see fit to come himself. He must know he's welcome to grace us with his presence, any time.

HERALD
(sarcastic)
Oh, yes. Everyone, in fact, knows he is welcome to go where and do whatever he pleases.

Pausanias is bristled by the response, but keeps his cool.

> PAUSANIAS
> So, are you here to relay his warm regards?

> HERALD
> That, and a message.

The herald pulls a letter from his robes and prepares to read.

> PAUSANIAS
> How exciting.
> (prompting)
> Please.

> HERALD
> (loud enough for the front line to hear)
> Spartans! In these parts, the men say you are the bravest of mankind and admire you because you never turn your backs in flight nor quit your ranks, but always stand firm, and either die at your posts or else destroy your adversaries. But in all this which they say concerning you—there is not one word of truth; for now have we seen you, before battle was even joined, flying and leaving your posts, wishing the Athenians to make the first trial of our arms. Surely, these are not the deeds of brave men. Much do we find ourselves deceived; for we believed the reports of you that reached our ears, and expected that you would send a herald with a challenge to us, proposing to fight by yourselves against our division of native Persians. We, for our part, were
> (MORE)

> HERALD(cont'd)
> ready to have agreed to this; but you have made no such offer. No, rather, you seem to shrink from meeting us. So, as no challenge of this kind comes from you to us—behold—we send a challenge to you. Now, why don't you, on the part of the Greeks, as you are thought to be the bravest of all, and we on the part of the 'barbarians', fight a battle with equal numbers on both sides, and whichever side wins—let them win it for their whole army.

Pausanias glowers.

EXT. GREECE—FRONT LINES—PERSIAN POST

In the company of Tritan, and flanked by the two cavaliers, Mardonius sits atop his own horse before the Persian ranks, listening to the returned herald's report.

> HERALD
> They wouldn't even spare a breath in response.
>
> MARDONIUS
> (entertained)
> Shame.
> (to cavaliers)
> Take care of it.

CUT TO:

MONTAGE—GREEKS EMBATTLED

—Mardonius leads his infantry away.

—The Greeks watch suspiciously.

—As the foot soldiers continue to draw back, the cavalry, appearing from nowhere, charge.

—The Greeks, from the right wing to the left, are under an unexpected attack by the horsemen.

—Day is overtaken by night.

—The worn Greeks file into camp.

EXT. GREECE—GREEK CAMP—NIGHT

The injured are being tended to.

We see one soldier, head wrapped, skin glistening with sweat, weakly reach out to the men who have just put him down on the ground.

> INJURED SOLDIER
> Wa—water. Please.

> ASSISTING SOLDIER 1
> (picks up water-skin; grimacing)
> It's empty and those savages won't let anyone within sight of the river.

> ASSISTING SOLDIER 2
> Why don't you go down to the spring, get your skin refilled—

> ASSISTING SOLDIER 1
> I thought the Spartans were controlling it.

> ASSISTING SOLDIER 2
> They're not going to refuse you water. They didn't refuse me. In fact, there, take mine, too.

He nods to another injured soldier, presumably asleep, holding his waterskin. The other assistant goes to get it.

                    ASSISTING SOLDIER 2
          I didn't even get a drop. He drank the
          whole thing.

                    ASSISTING SOLDIER 1
            (standing over the soldier; perplexed)
          What were his injuries?

                    ASSISTING SOLDIER 2
          Nothing serious. Broken leg. Why?
          Don't tell me he's passed out.

                    ASSISTING SOLDIER 1
          No.
            (turns; holding waterskin)
          He's dead.

INT. GREECE—GREEK CAMP—SPARTAN POST—NIGHT

Pausanias stands before the gathered Greek generals.

                    PAUSANIAS
          They distracted us—choked and
          spoiled the spring. We can't get to the
          river. The provisions we brought with
          us are gone, and they've seen to it that
          no more can get through. There's no
          other choice. At the second watch of
          the night, we abandon camp.

INT. GREECE—PERSIAN FORTRESS—MARDONIUS'S TENT—PRE-DAWN

All, except for the sound of CRICKETS, is serenely quiet. For the first time, we see Mardonius out of uniform, wearing a simple robe. He sits at his desk, re-reading two letters he has written.

A messenger enters.

>MESSENGER
>General?

Mardonius is preoccupied, looking back and forth between the two sheets.

>MESSENGER
>Sir? You have reports to be sent?

Mardonius finally settles on the first page and hastily seals it before handing it off.

>MARDONIUS
>Here.

>MESSENGER
>Just the one?

>MARDONIUS
>(scanning the other letter over)
>This isn't finished.

>CAVALIER 2 (O.S.)
>General Mardonius!! General Mardonius!!

He gets up from his seat just as the cavalier enters.

>CAVALIER 2
>General—

>MARDONIUS
>What? What is it?

> CAVALIER 2
> The Greeks have deserted camp.
> They're on the move, heading for
> Plataea.

> MARDONIUS
> (to messenger)
> Send word to Artabazus, tell him to
> gather his troops and advance to meet us.
> (to cavalier)
> As for you, go—get Tritan and the
> others.

Mardonius spares another brief look at the letter on the desk and, with a determined bob of the head, goes to get ready.

We now focus on the letter itself. Its words spring to life.

> MARDONIUS (V.O.)
> History points two fingers. One
> admonishing us to remember it, the
> other demanding we make it.

CUT TO:

EXT. GREECE—BATTLE OF PLATAEA—SEQUENCE

BEFORE THE ASOPUS

Beneath the receding dark of night, an army looks to the east, awaiting the rising sun. It is a force of over one-hundred-twenty-thousand men, a coalition of nations, drawn up standard by standard.

> MARDONIUS (V.O.)
> It is written, that while it is a great
> thing to win an empire, it is a still
> greater thing to preserve it after it has
> been won.

At the head of the army . . . of the Persian troops who lead them . . . of their frontline of a thousand-mounted Immortals . . . is the man who controls them all.

Mardonius sits atop a white, Niscean charger, bedecked in gold armor, just before the bank of the Asopus where the water runs shallow.

He knows that this is the defining moment of his life.

> MARDONIUS (V.O.)
> Our forebears knew that it took self-control, temperance and unflagging care to keep a kingdom—

We see the cresting sun ignite in his eyes.

> MARDONIUS (V.O.)
> —that the perpetuity of valor is only assured when one devotes themselves to it to the end.

Mardonius draws his sword, sounds the BATTLE CRY and commands his horse into the stream. The water explodes beneath its tread.

THE PLATAEAN PLAIN

We see contingents of the Greek army, led by the Athenian hoplites, marching toward Plataea.

> MARDONIUS (V.O.)
> They also knew, that the more a man has, the more people will envy him, and plot against him, and become his enemies.

Aristides signals them to halt, however, sensing something amiss. He turns to see the Persian-allied Theban and Boeotian cavalries spill into the plain.

THE SKIRTS OF MOUNT CITHAERON

We see the rest of the Greek army, led by the Spartans, traveling close to the foothills. Like Aristides, Pausanias is compelled to look back at the mountain ridge they have only recently passed.

> MARDONIUS (V.O.)
> But those who resent our ascension,
> resent what they do not understand.

The Scythians crest the top—

> MARDONIUS (V.O.)
> They fail to consider that all we
> possess, we also mind—that our
> blessings are also our burden, which we
> gratefully bear . . .

—as do the Medes—

> MARDONIUS (V.O.)
> . . . for it is only by the noble pursuit
> of the right and the just, of unity,
> that we have risen to such towering
> heights.

—between them, the Persian cavaliers.

They pour into the plain and race to block the Greeks' retreat.

The Persian archers descend the ridge, sprinting on foot. Within bow range of the Grecian forces, they pitch their shields before them and fire volley after volley of arrows.

The Greeks form up behind their own shields, but now trapped between the cavalry and archers, they take on numerous casualties.

> MARDONIUS (V.O.)
> These people see our virtues and
> thereby recognize their faults.

The TEGEANS, one of the Grecian contingents, cannot stand still for long. Desperate, they charge the archers.

The first few lines of Persian bowmen, seeing this, pick up their shields and prepare to defend, while their peers continue to fire over their heads, taking down scores of oncoming soldiers.

> MARDONIUS (V.O.)
> Their shaken confidence is manifested
> as defiant spite.

Pausanias takes up his spear and, leveling it toward the archers, signals the Spartans to attack. Keeping a well ordered phalanx formation, they make their approach.

The Persian shield wall is forcefully slammed. A ferocious struggle ensues as the Spartans try to breach it.

> MARDONIUS (V.O.)
> They seek to reduce us to their level,
> rather than work to aspire to ours.

ON THE PLATAEAN PLAIN

Aristides, Olympiodorus and the other Greeks with them are surrounded by the Boeotian and Theban horsemen. Drawing their weapons, they prepare to engage.

> MARDONIUS (V.O.)
> Alas, our foes are both malcontent and
> inconsolable.

ON THE SKIRTS OF CITHAERON

The Persian shield wall finally falls away. Still firing upon the Spartans, the bowmen pedal back, left and right.

The center is left open for another force to advance into.

> MARDONIUS (V.O.)
> They believe that we cannot enjoy the
> sun without forcing them into the dark.

The sight of it leaves embattled Pausanias aghast.

> MARDONIUS (V.O.)
> Yet, when we open our arms and
> beckon them to join us, they
> petulantly refuse—

The Persian infantry, led by Mardonius and the thousand Immortals, charges between the archer wings, then expands to confront the Greek line.

> MARDONIUS (V.O.)
> —believing, also, that to be held in our
> embrace is to be smothered by it.

The Persians swarm the Greeks, with hundreds of war dogs following behind.

Order, formation, strategy—they all are forgotten as the bewildering frenzy of war takes over—the sheer madness of it.

> MARDONIUS (V.O.)
> No, our enemies would rather see their
> country in chaos than concede that we have
> the power to change the world because we,
> of all men, are the best to rule it.

We see glimpses of Tritan, Pausanias and various others, including Mardonius himself, who weaves through the masses, cutting man—after man—after man—down. There is nothing but a primal rage flashing in the general's eyes.

> MARDONIUS (V.O.)
> We fight for the cause of good, so,
> how can those who oppose us be
> thought anything other than evil?

ON THE PLATAEAN PLAIN

The scene is just as crazed, perhaps even more so, as every man who falls, whether a Persian-allied Boeotian or Athenian hoplite, is Greek.

> MARDONIUS (V.O.)
> Their muse is discord.

We see Aristides, well aware of this truth, as he locks weapons and regretful stares with the soldier before him.

> MARDONIUS (V.O.)
> The kind that pits brother against—

ON THE SKIRTS OF CITHAERON

Locked against one another, just as Aristides and his nemesis, just as regretfully too, is Tritan and a Spartan who uncannily looks like Tigranes.

The irony is striking and, in this brief moment, we realize that Greek against Greek or Persian against Greek, man is man. Therefore, it still means brother against—

> MARDONIUS (V.O.)
> (continuing)
> —brother—

Tritan remains transfixed by the resemblance to his brother. He even mouths Tigranes' name perplexedly, but the crossed swords soon slip, demanding reality be accepted and forcing the men to make a move.

> MARDONIUS (V.O.)
> (continuing)
> —meaning nothing but misery for both.

Both soldiers strike at once, but it is Tritan who 'succeeds'.

> MARDONIUS (V.O.)
> We cannot allow these men to prevail.

There is little time to celebrate, to mourn, to feel anything, as he is confronted by another Spartan. The fight goes on . . .

It is LATER . . .

The afternoon sun intensely burns and the Persians continue to beat back the Greeks. It appears that Mardonius's triumph is within reach.

> MARDONIUS (V.O.)
> Silence can be shattered by a single
> voice . . .

The Spartans are forced further and further back.

> MARDONIUS (V.O.)
> . . . a foundation compromised by a
> single fissure . . .

ON THE PLATAEAN PLAIN

The Greeks there are not faring much better. Casualties are mounting. We see the Megarian general among them.

> MARDONIUS (V.O.)
> We must tear these men down and
> bury them so deep that their cries can
> never be heard again.

On another part of the field, Olympiodorus takes an arrow and falls to his knees.

ON THE SKIRTS OF CITHAERON

We are enveloped in the battle, as though part of it.

> MARDONIUS (V.O.)
> This is the way of history.

We see men brought down by dogs—

> MARDONIUS (V.O.)
> This is how nations are born . . .

—by swords and spears—

> MARDONIUS (V.O.)
> . . . how they rise . . .

—trampled under foot—

> MARDONIUS (V.O.)
> . . . how they fall . . .

—under horses—

> MARDONIUS (V.O.)
> . . . how they are built anew.

It is not two armies battling for supremacy that we are witnessing, but rather, the falling away of humanity.

> MARDONIUS (V.O.)
> This is how peace is attained.

Mardonius and the Immortals continue to press the Spartans.

> MARDONIUS (V.O.)
> We are the architects; the sword is our hammer.

Mardonius spots Pausanias and, deducing from his armor that he is the Spartan commander, pursues him, tearing down anyone who gets in his way.

> MARDONIUS (V.O.)
> We are the guardians, and this is our cause.

Pausanias sees the general coming and is taken aback.

Mardonius is unstoppable, seemingly undefeatable.

> MARDONIUS (V.O.)
> That is why this mission, though it has not been without loss, and even though there will be more before we may count it complete, is worth it. That is why it is justified, why it shall resonate—because what we do here, we do not for ourselves, but for all mankind. By bringing this nation into the fold, we grow one step closer to an empire without borders—a world without dissent.

Pausanias is frozen.

> MARDONIUS (V.O.)
> It is the profound desire to see this realized that compels me and the confidence of success in which I find solace on the darkest of days. I knew what I was asking for when I petitioned an army and what responsibilities were placed upon my shoulders when it was granted me. I know this, as well. I will conquer Greece—

Mardonius twirls his sword and prepares to take the Spartan's head off.

> MARDONIUS (V.O.)
> —for it is either victory—

We see the sunlight ricochet off the sword and spark in Pausanias's widened eyes.

> MARDONIUS (V.O.)
> (as if unwilling to finish the sentence)
> —or else a glorious . . .

Inches away from his intended prey, Mardonius pulls his horse up.

Appearing confused and winded, he draws a hand to his temple and finds that he has been wounded. He looks to Pausanias, finding only an expressed incredulity. He looks to his right and there stands an anxious Spartan, his arm still extended from having thrown a weapon.

The Greeks' stares do not linger. The Persian forces continue their push, passing right by their own general, completely unaware that he is no longer with them.

Mardonius's brow furrows. He buckles forward and clutches the neck of his horse before slowly sliding off. Upon the ground, a few feet away from his writhing body, is the shocking weapon which has brought him down . . . a mere rock.

With each passing second, he grows more numb to the pain, till he ceases to struggle against it at all. He turns his head and, though he knows he is not long for the world, smiles contentedly at what he beholds through welling eyes.

The Persians are winning the war.

Mardonius is satisfied and, as if rewarding himself with a nap, turns his head the other way. Right before his face, so close that his breath clouds upon it, is a Greek shield, held up in the earth.

The general's eyes narrow. He sees something reflected in it—a precariously leaning pole topped with the Persian standard (the golden "eagle"). Any comfort this offers, though, is forgotten as something else comes into sight.

It is initially indiscernible; the shield's surface distorts it. Mardonius narrows his eyes again. It gets bigger and bigger, till he suddenly realizes what it is—a vulture.

The bird swoops down on him, but is not allowed time to settle in, for a war dog trots up. It is forced to take flight and we go with it, now seeing that, while the battle is far from over, it has already taken a toll and the great Mardonius, left behind, is just one man among a graveyard of many.

>HYDARNES (V.O.)
>The tide turned then.

The bird's giant shadow passes over Tritan as he takes down an opponent. He looks to the sky and observes the scavenger as it circles back.

Through the dense tumult of battle, he sees Mardonius's horse and instantly knows the general is no more.

>HYDARNES(V.O.)
>So long as Mardonius led the fight, the
>army was indestructible, irrepressible.

Tritan is not the only one aware of this. He turns and sees the somber Persian whose words he overheard at Attaginus's party. The two share a silent, mournful moment, but it is cut terribly short.

>HYDARNES (V.O.)
>They followed him into battle, never
>expecting he would not be there to lead
>them through it.

The young Persian, seeing a Greek approach Tritan, pushes him out of the way and falls upon the sword himself.

Tritan is horrified to the point of distraction.

>HYDARNES (V.O.)
>And without him, they had no hope of
>finding their way out.

He drops his weapon, then falls to his knees, eyes wide—he, as well as we, never saw the other Greek coming. A sandaled foot is brought upon his shoulder and the sword tip protruding through his chest is drawn back.

Tritan slumps to the ground.

It is as if Mardonius was the first in a line of many dominoes, because now everything falls apart. The Persians, which had, for so long, dominated this battle, are now without a leader and, as such, are panicked.

The Spartans regroup under the command of a reenergized Pausanias and, preying upon the Persians' confusion, force them to flee.

> HYDARNES (V.O.)
> Many were struck down by the Greeks
> on their retreat.

The Greek pursuit, however, is curtailed as the Scythian, Median, and Persian cavaliers attempt to hold them back.

> HYDARNES (V.O.)
> Had it not been for the cavalry putting
> themselves between the infantry and
> their pursuers, they would have never
> made it to the rampart in time to rally
> for the oncoming assault.

IN THE PERSIAN FORTRESS

The panic has yet to wane, but the soldiers work through it, gathering arrows and other weaponry, as well as fortifying the gates and walls.

> HYDARNES (V.O.)
> Perhaps it would have been better that way.

We simply see what Hydarnes describes.

> HYDARNES (V.O.)
> The Spartans were the first to tempt
> the walls. The archers held them off.
> Scores fell by their arrows.
> (MORE)

                    HYDARNES (V.O.)(cont'd)
                    (a pause for direction)
              The Athenians soon joined them and
              the struggle went on . . .
                    (a pause for direction)
              . . . but, eventually, the fortifications
              were breached and the Greeks . . .
                    (a pause for direction)
              . . . they looted the camp and
              slaughtered them all, whether soldier or
              not, whether man or woman.

                    MAN (V.O.)
              Where was Artabazus through all this?

THEBAN COUNTRYSIDE

We see Artabazus, obviously torn and distressed, leading his troops on a paranoid march back to friendly territory.

                    HYDARNES (V.O.)
              He and his forces never made it to
              battle. They had advanced too late.
              Mardonius's were already in retreat.
              Some may think he was a coward for
              not following the others back to the
              rampart, but I believe, had he done so,
              it would have only resulted in the
              deaths of forty-thousand more men.

Traveling in their company is Demaratus and Alexander.

They, too, are troubled.

ON THE IONIAN COAST

We see the remaining ships of the Persian fleet being followed by hundreds of Greek triremes.

                    HYDARNES (V.O.)
           Before the sun set, news of our defeat
           at Plataea had reached across the
           Aegean. The emboldened Greeks sent
           their fleet against our ships on the
           Ionian coast and forced them to
           disembark on the shoreline of Mycale.

ON THE SHORE OF MYCALE

We, again, see what Hydarnes describes.

                    HYDARNES (V.O.)
           The crewmen drew up along the beach,
           pitched their shields in the sand, and waited.
                    (a pause for direction)
           The Athenians were the first to land and
           advance. Their initial attacks were repelled
           by archery fire and by the time they forced
           hand-to-hand combat, they had already
           taken on many casualties. Our men were
           still outnumbered, though, and aware that
           the Spartans were lurking.
                    (a pause for direction)
           They pulled back in hopes of finding refuge
           within the local garrison and the soldiers
           stationed there—some sixty-thousand men.

                    MAN (V.O.)
           What happened?

IN THE GARRISON

Masistes and a few guards stand atop a tall platform, watching intently as the hunted Persian crewmen, still firing weapons at the relentless Athenians, draw near.

                    HYDARNES(V.O.)
           The gates were opened to them.

Below, the garrison soldiers stand ready to defend the fortress as the gates to it are pulled back.

> HYDARNES (V.O.)
> The crewmen rushed in—

The men pour into the compound.

> HYDARNES (V.O)
> —but, then, the Greeks did, too.

Before the gates can be closed, the Athenians force their way through.

Masistes's guards, to his surprise, suddenly grab and remove him from the scene.

Warfare ensues.

> HYDARNES (V.O.)
> The battle waxed fierce and we may
> have very well claimed victory . . .

Empire-allied Ionians enter the fortress, led by a Persian soldier, and are signaled to join the battle against the Athenians.

> HYDARNES (V.O.)
> . . . had the Ionians not betrayed us.

They turn on their commander and, instead, join the Athenians against the Persians.

> HYDARNES (V.O.)
> When the Spartans finally arrived, the
> ranks were dispersed in hopes of
> sparing the lot.

The Spartans file into the fortress. While some Persians continue to fight, others are evacuated over the walls.

                    HYDARNES (V.O.)
               A small remnant remained behind as
               they fled to the hills. Among them, a
               young general named Tigranes.

We see Tigranes on the frontline of this terrible battle. He holds his own, like a one-man army, and fends off the mob.

                    HYDARNES (V.O.)
               May his father be proud, he fought to
               the bitter end, sacrificing himself to
               ensure their escape.

The idealistic general and his men are surrounded and, in the end, overcome.

                                        CUT TO:

EXT. SARDIS—CITADEL—PORTICO—DAY

Hydarnes and a wealthy-looking Persian stand on the portico, watching the rain fall as they talk.

                    HYDARNES
               It was not in vain, even if . . .

                    MAN
               Even if . . . ?

                    HYDARNES
               Even if all of them are not yet
               accounted for. So many . . . so many
               are still missing.

                    MAN
               Do you think they're—

                    HYDARNES
          I don't know. We've sent scouts, but, at this
          point, there is little reason to remain—

Hydarnes attention is drawn away. He sees a guard running toward him.

                    HYDARNES
               (moving the man out of his way)
          Excuse me.

INT. SARDIS—PALACE—XERXES' QUARTERS—DAY

The drizzle continues to fall, DRIP, DRIP, DRIPPING off the balcony overhang.

Xerxes is overtaken with depression. Lying on his side upon the bed, he stares straight ahead, mesmerized by the curling, sheer curtains. The expression on his face is one of despondency, of hopelessness, and it would seem he has only taken to bed because his body is tired, for he refuses to even blink, dreading the prospect of falling asleep.

Even the RUCKUS which suddenly erupts beyond his door fails to stir him from his trance.

                    HYDARNES (O.S.)
               King Xerxes!! Your highness!

INT. SARDIS—SURAZ'S QUARTERS—DAY

Suraz is the mirror image of Xerxes, lying atop her own bed, her expression just as removed as his own—despite the KNOCKING at her door.

                    CHAMBERLAIN (O.S.)
               My lady! My lady!

INT. SARDIS—SURAZ'S FOYER—DAY

Xerxes' messenger and a guard stand just inside the door.

Escorted by her chamberlain, an emotionally exhausted Suraz enters the room.

> SURAZ
> I have been expecting you. So, go on.
> Tell me.

> SARDIS MESSENGER
> You are to come with us to—

> SURAZ
> No! No! You say it, now!
> (off silence)
> What's the matter? Just say it.

The messenger approaches and attempts to calm her down.

> SARDIS MESSENGER
> My lady, all I know is that I am to
> bring you—

> SURAZ
> So, he wants to tell me himself? Is that
> it? You are going to bring me before
> him and he is going to look me in the
> eye and tell me—

He tries to take hold of her.

> SURAZ
> No!! I don't want to hear it from him!

> SARDIS MESSENGER
> You need to calm yourself—

She beats against his chest with her fists.

> SURAZ
> Then stop pretending!! Stop pretending—

> SARDIS MESSENGER
> I tell you, I'm not!

> SURAZ
> Liar! Liar! You know just as well as I!!
> You know. You know he's dead!!

She breaks down in his arms, sobbing.

> SURAZ
> You know he's dead.
> (whispering)
> My husband is dead.

INT. SARDIS—PALACE—PORTICO—DAY

The sky has cleared.

Suraz enters. She has tried to maintain a steely façade, but, setting eyes upon the back of the man before her, it begins to crack. She swallows the ache and shakily breathes out.

The dark figure turns. Suraz's tears flow.

> SURAZ
> (inaudible)
> M-Masistes?
> (a beat)
> Masistes?

He nods and opens his arms to her.

> MASISTES
> Yes. Yes, Suraz, yes.

She throws herself into his embrace.

                    SURAZ
          You've come back to me. You've come
          back.

AROUND THE CORNER

Leaning against the wall, listening, but not daring a look, is Xerxes.

It is surely a bittersweet moment.

INT. SARDIS—PALACE—STUDY—SUNSET

Masistes, as animated a speaker as ever, sits across from Xerxes at his desk.

                   MASISTES
          I never lost hope. I knew we would be
          found. I knew you would do all in
          your power to bring us home.

The sour expression on Xerxes' face, like he got a whiff of something pungent, quiets Masistes.

Brows raised questioningly, he quickly draws his nose to his arm for a scent-check and, finding all well on that front, looks to his friend again.

                   MASISTES
                   (earnestly)
          What is it?

                    XERXES
                   (shaking head)
          You . . . thanking me.

                    MASISTES
     They told me the truth, Xerxes—when
     we were lost in those mountains—
     about the orders. Initially, I didn't
     know what was going on. When they
     grabbed me and wouldn't let go, no
     matter how loud I yelled or how hard I
     struggled, I admit, I was frightened. I
     mean, for the briefest moment, I
     couldn't help but think they turned on
     me, which was, of course, absurd
     because—

Masistes' body language finishes the sentence, joking, "it's me for crying out loud!"

                    MASISTES
                    (serious)
     But, um . . . No, they confirmed what
     I realized once the panic subsided. They
     took me away because you had ordered
     them to do so should any conflict arise.

Xerxes silence is affirmation enough.

                    MASISTES
     I was angry at first, to be honest . . .
     that I was forced to abandon my
     men . . . then guilty that I had been
     spared . . . even more so to be relieved
     that I had been. But, I must tell you,
     Xerxes, when I saw my wife again . . .
                    (a beat)
     I lament that Tigranes and those other,
     courageous soldiers are no longer here,
     but I would be lying if I told you I'm
     not overcome with joy that I am.
                    (a beat)
                    (MORE)

MASISTES(cont'd)
You saved my life. You kept your word.
       (raising hands)
All limbs, all attached and um, after
last night, I can affirm . . .
       (hushed)
. . . all in working order.

Xerxes feigns a flicker of a smile—too much info.

MASISTES
I am so sorry about Mardonius. I
know you must be devastated.

XERXES
Before we split the army up, two
envoys from Sparta sought audience
with me.

MASISTES
What did they want?

XERXES
Atonement for, what they called, the
murder of their king.

MASISTES
Leonidas.

Xerxes nods.

MASISTES
Well, what did you say?

XERXES
I laughed in their faces and told them
all the justice they deserved they would
get—from Mardonius.
       (MORE)

XERXES (cont'd)
(looks away; a beat)
Everyone blames him for what happened . . .
for losing the battle, the territory, the
Aegean . . . for everything short of the rain.

MASISTES
(self-consciously)
He did command the troops.

XERXES
But only because I allowed it. Had he been
successful, these same people who now
decry him, who claim that all culpability
for the loss died on the battlefield with
him, would credit me with the triumph,
because I let him seek it out.

Xerxes does not offer Masistes a chance to answer that question. He gets up and goes to the window.

XERXES
I sent my condolences to Artabanus.
Both sons, gone—
(snaps fingers)
—just like that.

MASISTES
How is he taking it?

XERXES
They say, when he was told the news,
he simply nodded his head, like he
knew, and, then, he went about his
business as if it were any other day.

MASISTES
Perhaps because he cannot let their
defeat be his own?

XERXES
I know what you are inferring, but, Masistes, in this case, I don't believe he carries on so much as a means to honor them, but rather, to forget . . .
    (a beat)
I don't—I don't know. I could be wrong.

MASISTES
What of Artabazus?

XERXES
He and his troops should reach Sardis within the month.

MASISTES
Do you plan to stay here—

XERXES
No. I'm leaving for Susa.

MASISTES
When?

XERXES
Tomorrow.

MASISTES
So soon??

XERXES
I was prepared to stay here so long as we were at war. The war's over, Masistes.

Xerxes returns to his seat. Masistes shifts in his own as he prepares to broach a new subject.

MASISTES
So, Susa . . .

XERXES
What?

MASISTES
Amestris?

XERXES
You've heard.

MASISTES
About all your awaiting lovelies? Yes, indeed.

XERXES
(almost apologetic)
I know how it looks. I wanted to punish her . . . and so I did, and it's done. The decree is irreversible.

MASISTES
You can't—

XERXES
Even if I wanted to.

MASISTES
So you're going to do it then? Choose a new bride?

XERXES
If anyone should be selecting a bride, it's my son.

MASISTES
How is Darius?

XERXES
Twenty years of age and none the more responsible.

MASISTES
(musing, not suggesting)
Artaynta is also twenty.

This piques Xerxes' interest.

XERXES
Your daughter.

MASISTES
She's been in Bactria all this time, now.

XERXES
So you plan to return right away?

MASISTES
Well, as you stated, the war is over. As soon as the house here is closed, there's no reason to—

XERXES
I thought you might join me in Susa— you, your wife . . . and daughter. You could send for her while settling your arrangements here, and converge at the capital.

Masistes tilts his head, wondering where this is leading.

MASISTES

Xerxes?

XERXES
Masistes . . . you know that I have always considered you family. Why don't we, together, put the past behind us and look to the future by making it official?

EXT. GREECE—ATHENIAN ESTATE—NIGHT

The Athenians decadently celebrate the return of their war heroes. Guests are gathered around the esteemed, including Aristides.

Pausanias is also present and draws more than a few stares.

Torchlight beams of off the rings on his fingers as he speaks to a small crowd. Though modest compared to the accessories of other guests, they are an oddity on a Spartan.

> PAUSANIAS
> You should have seen it. Gold lounges, goblets, bracelets—even their weapons are adorned with it—chest after chest brimming with coins . . . I could not help but wonder aloud, what absolute greed must possess a man who already enjoys wealth such as this to rob us of our penury?

Sitting on the edge of a nearby, large, marble planter are a trio of wealthy Athenians, each with a drink in hand and an eye on Pausanias.

> ATHENIAN GUEST 1
> Look at him. You don't think all this attention has gone to his head, do you?

> ATHENIAN GUEST 2
> No, not at all. Pausanias is as Spartan as they come.

> ATHENIAN GUEST 3
> So true, so true. He's only being polite by repeating the same story over and over again. There are a few guests left who have not yet heard it more than once.

> ATHENIAN GUEST 2
> The gold rings?

                    ATHENIAN GUEST 3
Gifts.

                    ATHENIAN GUEST 1
To himself.

The only guest not enjoying the party, Themistocles, stops beside the planter to observe the goings-on. He does not intend to eavesdrop on the on-going conversation, but cannot help but do so—with a cynical ear.

                    ATHENIAN GUEST 2
Shame what happened to Leonidas.

                    ATHENIAN 1
                    (nods)
To be disgraced the way he was by
those animals.

                    ATHENIAN 3
You think that was monstrous? Did
you hear what Xerxes did before they
crossed the Hellespont?

                    ATHENIAN 1
No, tell us.

                    ATHENIAN 3
Well, there is a friend of mine in
Thessaly whose cousin is married to a
Hellespontine girl. Now, she still has
family in the area, and they heard from
a friend of theirs that, before the
Persians began their march, a loyal
subject to the king, who was greatly
esteemed by him—or so the poor man
thought—issued a simple request. You
see, every one of his sons was in the
service of the army and he was rightly
                    (MORE)

ATHENIAN 3(cont'd)
concerned that all could be lost in the war. So, he entreated the king to allow his eldest to remain behind so that he might take care of the family estate.

He stops to take a long, long drink.

ATHENIAN 1
(impatiently)
Well, go on, will you?

ATHENIAN 3
Alright, alright. Where was I?

ATHENIAN 2
Eldest son, family estate.

ATHENIAN 3
Ah, yes. So, he asks this, believing Xerxes to be a fair and generous man, but he was incensed. He screamed that he himself was going to war and who did this man think he was to put the worth of his son above him.

ATHENIAN 2
All those soldiers and he couldn't find it in him to let one boy remain behind!?

ATHENIAN 3
That's it, though. He released the man and all his sons from duty, save for the one he loved the most—the eldest.

ATHENIAN 1
That's your story?

ATHENIAN 3
Xerxes then had the young man severed in two, each half placed on either side of the bridge, and it is between them that the army marched across the Hellespont.

ATHENIAN 2
You're serious?!

ATHENIAN 3
I told it to you exactly as my friend told it to me.

Themistocles has heard enough.

THEMISTOCLES
Yes, your friend, who we all know is a reliable source because . . . ?

ATHENIAN 1
Themistocles.

ATHENIAN 3
You almost sound offended.

THEMISTOCLES
What can I say? Lies and hypocrisies insult me.

ATHENIAN 3
My apologies. I didn't realize you and Xerxes were such good friends.

THEMISTOCLES
Oh, stop it! This war has barely been concluded, yet, already, nearly every thing about it has been distorted. Why it happened, how it was met, how it was won. All of it . . . exaggerations, lies and half-truths.

The Athenians cannot believe what they are hearing.

ATHENIAN 1
That is you, Themistocles? Isn't it?

THEMISTOCLES
Do you know there are people who are claiming that Leonidas's three-hundred Spartans alone held off a million soldiers at Thermopylae? Never mind that this million man figure is nothing but a figment of the imagination. Never mind that there were thousands of Greeks, from all over the country, who boldly stood against the enemy.

ATHENIAN 3
Many of them ran and there may as well have been two million men in that army, Themistocles, for all the damage done. What does it matter, anyway—

THEMISTOCLES
It matters!! It matters because you tell a man he can fly, then you better be prepared to catch him when he falls. It matters because you cannot expect anyone to differentiate between you and the so-called animals when—when—

ATHENIAN 1
When what?

THEMISTOCLES
You believe Leonidas was disgraced?

ATHENIAN 1
Themistocles, they took his body like a trophy—

THEMISTOCLES
A trophy? Interesting. I was just listening to a man over there go on about the Persian general they carted before the ranks of the army and how it boosted morale.

The surrounding guests, including those of honor, halt all conversation.

ATHENIAN 1
That's different—

THEMISTOCLES
Why? Because the corpse was kept intact? You talk of Xerxes' cruelty and even if every word were true, even if he is the monster you all must believe he is, what he is not, is an excuse.

ATHENIAN 3
You're really bitter, aren't you, Themistocles? Feeling underappreciated? It probably tears you up inside that your time has passed.

THEMISTOCLES
No. What tears me up inside is that I defended 'people' like you—

ATHENIAN 3
Like us?

THEMISTOCLES
—who would lynch a man because he wished to exhaust all options before being resigned to war.

ATHENIAN 1
Yours was one of the loudest cries forbidding any more talk of that proposal—

> THEMISTOCLES
> —who would drag his wife and
> children into the street, take a rock in
> each hand and revel in each throw—
> and you presume to talk of animals?
> You believe yourselves so civilized?!

Aristides places a hand on Themistocles shoulder.

> ARISTIDES
> Themistocles.

> THEMISTOCLES
> I'm sorry. Am I making a scene? I
> should know better, shouldn't I? Those
> are only acceptable when done in the
> company of a mob.
> (raising his cup)
> Enjoy the celebration. I, myself, haven't
> the stomach for it.

Themistocles pushes through the guests, strides past an amused Pausanias and disappears into the night.

INT. SUSA—XERXES' THRONE ROOM—NIGHT

Torches flicker brightly, shedding a warm glow on stately columns, ornate decor, and an audience of nobles, officials and guards. They stand in observant silence, every eye set on the open doors to the room—including those of an enthroned Xerxes and his unenthused son, Darius, who stands beside him.

Shadowed figures cross the threshold of the room, revealing themselves to be BACTRIAN SERVANTS. They walk in formal procession between the audience, each holding a gift for the king.

Jars of frankincense, flowers, and jewel encrusted boxes are some of the tokens of appreciation they carry. They offer them with respect, kneel, then filter back to the walls, leaving the path open for the guests of honor.

Masistes enters the room. Xerxes subtley edges forward. Standing beside his friend is Suraz. This is the first time he has seen her in years and he cannot help but stare as she is led toward him on the arm of her husband.

Since this is not a casual reception, the proceedings are handled with great orchestration. Masistes stops before Xerxes, slightly bows and 'blows a kiss'.

Suraz, meanwhile, keeps her head down. The tension between she and Xerxes is palpable and it is with great hesitation that she dares to glance up from her feet.

Though he conceals his feelings well, her presence briefly distracts him.

>   MASISTES
> Allow me the great honor of presenting
> my daughter, Artaynta.

Xerxes returns his attention to the matter at hand. The bride-to-be is brought before him and her servant girl, ZOSTRA, unveils her.

Darius is, unexpectedly, pleased.

Xerxes is also taken by surprise. He regards her with a youthful curiosity as she bows.

>   ARTAYNTA
> Great King.

She looks up and they lock eyes. There is something behind Artaynta's stare contrary to her innocent, sweet-natured appearance.

>   MASISTES
> Through this union, may our houses
> prosper.

INT. SUSA—ARTAYNTA'S GUEST QUARTERS—NIGHT

The quarters are, essentially, the ancient Persian version of a posh, room-for-two at a luxury hotel. Fabric is draped along the walls and gently curls with the night's breeze. Pillows litter two parallel beds.

Artaynta sits on a chair before an elaborately etched table. Upon it, a superfluous amount of beauty accoutrements are sprawled. The young attendant girl, Zostra, brushes her hair as the soon-to-be princess giggles.

> ARTAYNTA
> Is he not handsome?

> ZOSTRA
> Yes, he is quite attractive.

> ARTAYNTA
> Oh, the thoughts that came to mind upon seeing him.

> ZOSTRA
> Thoughts one keeps silent?

> ARTAYNTA
> Only the modest. Merely being in his presence was enough to cause a tremble to stir.

> ZOSTRA
> It lingers I see. Hold still.

> ARTAYNTA
> I cannot seem to help myself, Zostra. I tell you, it felt like my body had been set aflame from his stare alone.

> ZOSTRA
> A fire you would not mind being stoked.

> ARTAYNTA
> (laughing)
> My, my. Where ever did you learn to speak so crassly?

                    ZOSTRA
          In all earnestness, it sounds as though
          you are pleased with this arrangement.
          The prince appeared to be, as well.

Artaynta considerately bites her lip. Suddenly, she spins in her seat and clutches Zostra's hand.

                    ARTAYNTA
          We are like sisters, you and I, and I know
          you would never betray my confidence.

                    ZOSTRA
          Of course not. What is this about?

Zostra kneels beside the chair. The two look like conspirators.

                    ARTAYNTA
          It is not Darius I speak of.

                    ZOSTRA
          Then who?

                    ARTAYNTA
          Xerxes.

                    ZOSTRA
          The king?!

                    ARTAYNTA
          Shh!

                    ZOSTRA
          I'm sorry. Artaynta—

                    ARTAYNTA
              (rising from her chair)
          I know, I know. You are going to tell
          me I am crazed for even thinking it.

ZOSTRA
You are to marry his son by month's end. Not to mention, the queen—

ARTAYNTA
—has been stripped of her title and a new one has yet to be named.

Like the besotted young girl she is, Artaynta leans against the wall and looks dreamily ahead.

ARTAYNTA
You cannot tell me you didn't feel it earlier.

ZOSTRA
What?

ARTAYNTA
That presence—the same that comes on a storm, causes your skin to tingle, teeth to ring, hands to shake . . . that seduces you to stand against the wind when instinct tells you to run for shelter.

ZOSTRA
You do know what this 'presence' is?

Artaynta flashes a coy smile.

ARTAYNTA
An unabated power.

ZOSTRA
Yes, and it is that which you are drawn to—nothing more. I admit, it can be awe-inspiring. The man can shape destinies at will, but to think you
(MORE)

> ZOSTRA(cont'd)
> might, in some way, influence his is a
> dangerous thought to entertain. All one
> need do is watch moths dare the
> candlelight to see why.

With a roll of the eyes, Artaynta confrontationally approaches her friend, arms crossed, jaw locked. The servant is onto her mistress, though, quite aware that the miffed expression is mock anger. Confirming this, Artaynta cracks a grin as she tugs at a lock of Zostra's hair and sits back down.

> ARTAYNTA
> (sarcastic)
> How insightful. Can you prognosticate too?

> ZOSTRA
> (resumes brushing)
> I can clearly see your future. It is with
> Darius and, eventually, it will be he
> who is king. Forget this fantasy of—

> ARTAYNTA
> I won't speak of it again.

> ZOSTRA
> Good.

Zostra continues to comb Artaynta's tresses, oblivious to the sly smile playing upon her lips.

INT. SUSA—XERXES' QUARTERS—MORNING

Xerxes wakes from a troubled slumber, as if expecting someone to be standing over him.

He sits up, disoriented initially, but the growing awareness that he has, yet again, been assaulted by indiscernible images leads to frustration. He throws off the covers and gets up.

EXT. SUSA—CITY—MORNING

People scuttle about, bartering and commiserating. Cattle are herded through the city. Merchants carry baskets of wheat and other goods.

INT. SUSA—XERXES' QUARTERS—MORNING

A table, situated before the balcony, offers a view of the distant, bustling streets. In the company of Haman, who has rolled documents in front of him and scribes standing at his side, Xerxes picks at breakfast.

> HAMAN
> It is ridiculous.

Xerxes absentmindedly nods and turns to look, not at the city, but at—

THE TERRACE COURTYARD BELOW.

Walking across it are Masistes, his family, and their attendants.

It is initially the sight of Suraz that draws Xerxes' attention, but, a blink later, it is her daughter, Artaynta, that he admires. It appears he's unaware that he's indulging his fascination. His bellicose guest takes no notice, either.

> HAMAN (O.S.)
> (continuing)
> Making an official arrangement with your son is just as, if not more, binding than with anyone else, and if you are willing to betray your own family, then those you do business with are right to assume you are an unscrupulous liar. That is essentially what I told him, but I think he still has no intention of amending the situation.

Xerxes blinks and looks at Haman.

XERXES
What are you rattling on about?

HAMAN
My neighbor. He promised his son ten
horses and did not honor the agreement.

XERXES
Ah.

HAMAN
Did you rest soundly, your highness?
You seem distant.

XERXES
There is much on my mind, Haman.
  (a beat)
How is Artabanus this morning?

HAMAN
As stern and steadfast as he is everyday.
Did you want to speak with him?

XERXES
No. Not this early.

HAMAN
Yes, well . . .
  (stands)
I did not intend to squander your time.
I only meant to bring these documents
to you for approval.

XERXES
Fine, fine. As soon as I finish here, I
will see to them.

Haman bows and departs with the scribes. Slowly, Xerxes rises from the table and leans against a pillar near the balcony. Shadow conceals him from the waist up as he searches the courtyard. Again, he spots Artaynta in—

THE COURTYARD

While her father, mother and their attendants continue their walk, Artaynta stops. As if she knows she is being watched, the girl looks up at Xerxes' palace and sets sights on his shadowed figure above.

Realizing her daughter is no longer beside her, Suraz turns to find Artaynta steps behind, transfixed by something. She follows her stare and, discovering it is a 'who' the young woman is so taken with, directs her to rejoin the group.

> SURAZ
> Come. We mustn't fall behind.

Artaynta reluctantly continues on. Her mother, however, lingers a moment longer, stealing one more look.

> AMESTRIS (O.S.)
> You're just aching to go to him, aren't you? Right into his waiting, open arms.

INT. SUSA—AMESTRIS' QUARTERS—DAY

Peering out her balcony, Amestris witnesses the silent connection between Suraz below and her estranged husband across the way.

> AMESTRIS
> I will not be so easily deposed. I am the
> mother of his heir, and I refuse to be
> cast aside all for the want of—
>   (can't bear to say her name; shakes head)
> I have remained patient all this time,
> hoping that his resentment of me
> might slip away, but, instead, he's
> remained obsessed with what I will
> never let him have. Never.

INT. SUSA—MASISTES' GUEST QUARTERS—NIGHT

The decorative rim of a gold basin causes candlelight to converge like an ethereal mist above the water—and the reflection it holds. The image is that of a melancholy face, a woman examining her countenance for something, anything that might indicate where her youth has gone. Fingers trace the lines of her delicate brows and weary eyes, then descend to her frowning mouth. She bows her head in resignation. Though, in reality, Suraz is still as beautiful as she has always been, she sees nothing but an old crone staring back at her from the depths of the bowl.

Wearing a simple nightgown, she leans against the dresser the basin sits upon, her arms sprawled on either side of it for support. She is alone. The bed behind her is empty, the sheets yet to be pulled back, the day's robe sprawled messily atop it.

With a defeated sigh, she makes herself look into the basin again. Trembling fingers glide over the water.

> SURAZ
> You've come apart, woman, having lost
> your youth on the outside . . . trapped
> by it within.

Disgusted with herself, she submerges her hand, effectively 'shattering' her reflection. She hears the DOOR OPEN, but stays silent, unflinching, doing nothing but watching the liquid bob back and forth. It isn't till a set of arms wrap around her waist, and a chin settles upon her shoulder that she moves, leaning back into the embrace.

> SURAZ
> So much has changed, Masistes.

Masistes holds her tighter and nuzzles her ear. He can't see the look of sheer despair on her face. She's on the verge of tears.

> MASISTES
> Not all things.

SURAZ
(apologetic)
I know.

MASISTES
I know it's hard to let go, but she'll be fine.

SURAZ
Artaynta.

Suraz can't help but emit a half-hearted laugh. If only he knew what she was really talking about. Gingerly, she wipes her eyes. Masistes places a quick kiss atop her shoulder and goes to take a seat on the bed.

MASISTES
She is so much like you.

SURAZ
Better that she weren't.

MASISTES
Nonsense. Why do you say such a thing?

SURAZ
Masistes, have I been enough for you all these years?

In the midst of fumbling with his sandals, he looks up to regard the back of her head, his brow furrowed in confusion.

MASISTES
Suraz?

SURAZ
Have I made you happy?

                        MASISTES
            Made me happy? Made me happy?
            You—you are my happiness, my
            treasure.

She turns around, a forced smile and a tear upon her face.

                        SURAZ
            Small fortune.

                        MASISTES
            No, the greatest.
                    (patting the bed)
            Come here. Sit. Let me tell you a little
            story. You may wonder what it has to
            do with you, but bear with me.

Suraz goes to her husband and is once again enveloped in his hold. She takes comfort in this, not only for the gesture itself, but because he can't see what's clearly on display.

Normally quite stoic, she is vulnerable to the shame she feels—the same shame she's kept hidden for years.

                        MASISTES
            First, an astonishing secret. Believe it or
            not, I used to be so envious of Xerxes.

She tenses.

                        MASISTES
            I know what you're thinking: 'But,
            Masistes, my darling, my joy, why were
            you jealous when you were so obviously
            graced with better looks and wit?'

Her husband's humor puts her at ease.

MASISTES
Yes, that's true, but he . . . he had everything and anything a boy could want. Sure, I wasn't exactly poor, but to be an heir to destiny—not merely by birthright—but because it is—yours—to claim. I once jested that, even had Xerxes been born sheperd's son, he would have found his way to the palace.

SURAZ
Or would have brought the court to the field.

MASISTES
Yes. It seemed all he had to do was be and time would take care of the rest. Of course, I was wrong, naive, but it wasn't till years later that I realized it.

SURAZ
What happened?

MASISTES
A great deal. Poor Xerxes was so smitten with some young girl. I always tried to pry her identity out of him. He never did tell. I suppose she was the only thing he had to himself—the only secret in a life of scrutiny. He did tell me he wanted to marry her, though, and planned to express this desire to his father. I remember I urged him to go, if only to finally end the mystery. So, off he went, so sure of the future . . . but, the moment he entered the throne room, all that changed, as did he. Holding audience with King Darius were General Otanes and his daughter—

> SURAZ
> Amestris.

> MASISTES
> And despite everything, to please his father, he married her. That day I realized, for all the wealth and power he possessed, he was never really free. Suffice it to say, my envy vanished, because, put in the same situation, I could never make the sacrifice he did. Not if it meant losing you.

> SURAZ
> Masistes . . .

She turns around in his arms and raises a hand to his lips to protest what is, to her, a compliment of which she is not worthy. Masistes, however, will not be silenced. He takes her hand in one of his own, cradles her face with the other, and beseeches her to meet his stare, to see herself in his eyes.

> MASISTES
> You see?

She can see what she means to him and it's too much to bear. Kissing the side of his face, she pulls him to her and quietly weeps upon his shoulder.

> SURAZ
> I do love you.

> MASISTES
> I know you do. I know.

Masistes chuckles as he holds his wife close. She clutches him tightly, her eyes brimming with more tears.

INT. SUSA—PALACE CORRIDOR—DAY

Artaynta and Zostra are walking through the hallway. Suddenly, the former grabs her attendant and backs them both against the wall just a few feet from the ornate opening which leads to the portico.

> ZOSTRA
> What is it?

> ARTAYNTA
> Quiet.

She peeks around the corner to the—

OUTDOOR COVERED WALKWAY

Shadows roll across Xerxes, Hydarnes, trailing guards and attendants as they briskly walk between the palace and a secluded atrium. They are desperately attempting to keep up with their king's brisk pace.

> HYDARNES
> We've increased the number of troops along the border.

> XERXES
> Do the magistrates feel it is sufficient?

> HYDARNES
> More than.

> XERXES
> Good. I expect to be notified the moment they think otherwise.

Aggravated by the sounds of those following behind him, Xerxes abruptly stops and turns to Hydarnes. The rest of the group slides to a sheepish halt behind him. Bemused by the sight, Xerxes gestures the general closer.

> XERXES
> On the domestic front, Hydarnes, there is a minor issue to be settled.

                    HYDARNES
Yes?

                    XERXES
          (referring to the entourage)
     Everywhere I go, a great shadow
     follows me. I would like for it to stop.

                    HYDARNES
     They are for your own safety.

                    XERXES
     From what? What threat lies in my
     own house?

                    HYDARNES
     None of which I am aware, but up until
     recently, we were a nation at war and, as
     king, your security is of the utmost
     importance. The Greeks could employ—

                    XERXES
Assassins?

                    HYDARNES
     Yes, sir.

A most incredulous smirk, bordering on unruly, draws across Xerxes' face. He clasps the general's shoulder with startling speed, prompting the burly man to slightly retract in reflex.

                    XERXES
     If you think that I'd let my days be dictated
     by fear, then you are mistaken. So, unless I
     deem accompaniment appropriate, no one
     is to follow me. Is that understood?
          (off nod)
     Excellent. Now, if you will see to what
     we discussed.

                    HYDARNES
                (bows; to entourage)
            Come away.

The general motions for the guards and attendants to follow him, leaving Xerxes behind.

Meanwhile, in the—

PALACE CORRIDOR

Artaynta and Zostra continue to stealthily watch as General Hydarnes leads the group away. Once gone, Artaynta sets her sights on Xerxes. This, she thinks, is her opportunity.

                    ARTAYNTA
            Zostra, go back to our room.

                    ZOSTRA
            You are not considering—

                    ARTAYNTA
            Perhaps I am. Now go.

                    ZOSTRA
            We have had a discussion about this.

                    ARTAYNTA
            Yes, and you didn't want to hear any
            more about it, correct? Go on. Good
            bye.

Not at all content leaving her alone, Zostra hesitates. Artaynta is none too pleased, and with a look that could kill, shoos her away once more. The demand is finally adhered to, leaving the would-be princess alone to regain her poise.

OUTSIDE ON THE WALKWAY

Xerxes takes in the sight of the atrium. Its serene beauty starkly contrasts his brooding visage. A bitter smirk creeps across his lips, as he is well aware of this. He also knows someone is watching him. He exasperatedly huffs.

                XERXES
        I ordered you all to leave me be.

He turns to find no one there. Calculatingly, he approaches the entrance and casually leans on its frame.

                XERXES
        Who is there?

To his surprise, Artaynta steps out of the shadows. Just as easily as she emerges from the dark and steps into the light, so does her persona. It's been transformed from scheming tease, to demure innocent. There is much sexual tension between them. Both are cognizant of the pull they have to each other.

                ARTAYNTA
        I ask for your pardons, your highness. I
        was told I could view the gardens and
        had been on my way to do so when I
        heard you and the general. I didn't
        intend to eavesdrop.

                XERXES
        Why were you hiding?

                ARTAYNTA
        After you expressed your desire to be
        alone, I didn't want to intrude. I was
        about to leave when your guards passed
        by and I froze. I don't know what came
        over me.

                XERXES
        Guards are meant to be imposing. Is
        no one escorting you?

                    ARTAYNTA
          My attendant girl had been with me.

                    XERXES
          Then why is she no longer?

                    ARTAYNTA
          I—I sent her away—on an errand.

                    XERXES
          Will she return soon?

                    ARTAYNTA
          I can not say for certain how long it
          might take.

                    XERXES
          You wanted to see the gardens?

                    ARTAYNTA
          Yes, if I may?

                    XERXES
          Then come. There's time enough to
          show you at least the one.

Xerxes stands tall and extends a hand. Shakily, Artaynta takes it. He leads her down a set of steps and into the atrium.

EXT. SUSA—SECLUDED ATRIUM—DAY

Beneath a canopy of foliage, Xerxes and Artaynta walk through the inner garden.

                    ARTAYNTA
          It is so lovely.

XERXES
Yes, it is.
> (a beat)

So, do you miss Bactria?

ARTAYNTA
No. Not a bit. But, for all these years, I have missed Susa.

XERXES
So, I take it you weren't averse to the journey?

ARTAYNTA
No. It felt like a homecoming. When I finally saw the city rise up from the plain, never have I felt such a sense of—of—I'm sorry. I cannot seem to find the right word.

XERXES
Don't apologize. I know what you speak of and I, too, am without a name for it.

ARTAYNTA
I believe the only one who has missed Susa more than I is my mother. Strange to say that, considering she resisted every opportunity to visit.

XERXES
She did? And why is that?

ARTAYNTA
Only because, I think, she feared her love of the city might be rekindled and she wouldn't want to leave again.

                    XERXES
               Oh?

                    ARTAYNTA
               It nearly broke her heart when we left
               for Bactria.
                    (a beat)
               Whatever the cause, she had no choice
               but to come this time.

                    XERXES
               Yes, the arrangement.

                    ARTAYNTA
               It is a privilege. I hope you—and Prince
               Darius—were not disappointed with
               me.

                    XERXES
               Far from it.

                    ARTAYNTA
               Truly?

Artaynta stops and shyly looks down, causing a lock of hair to fall in her face. Xerxes, gentleman that he is, takes it upon himself to gently push it back.

                    XERXES
               You possess all the attributes a man
               could hope for in a wife, and one
               which I have not seen in so very long.
                    (off her confused look)
               There, in your eyes—a glimmer—a
               simple, hopeful glimmer. You would
               be surprised how rare it is to find.

He turns away and plucks a blossom.

      XERXES
      (continuing)
  Lately, I think it would be easier to
  find one of these in the desert.

Offering it to her, their hands touch.

      ARTAYNTA
  It is a wonder.

      XERXES
  What is?

Their eyes meet.

      ARTAYNTA
  That the king, even brandishing a
  flower, can cause the knees to shake.

Xerxes draws away.

      ARTAYNTA
  If I have spoken too boldly—

      XERXES
  No. No, you have done nothing to offend.

      ARTAYNTA
  But I have done something.

Concerned, Artaynta takes a step closer to him, but he halts her approach by placing a hand on her shoulder.

      XERXES
  My son is a fortunate man.

He lets go of her and forces a smile. The two start off again, walking in silence till reaching the garden's clearing.

> XERXES
> I enjoyed our walk, but I must leave
> you now.

> ARTAYNTA
> I understand. May I stay here a little
> while longer?

> XERXES
> As long as you like.

He slowly backs away, turns and heads for the palace. Artaynta remains and it's clear that she's pleased with herself. Her eyes aglow, she lazily twirls the flower across her lips.

Little does she know that someone is watching her from above.

EXT. WOODS—DAY

A heavy mist parts between the steady tread of horses. Hunting game, Darius, trailed closely by guards, rides through the forested area, looking expectantly around as he goes. Xerxes and Masistes follow at a moderate distance behind. Sunlight, streaming through crooked branches, causes flickers of light to play off of them. A stream flows along the embankment they are traversing. For the most part, all is quiet—except for themselves.

> MASISTES
> I must admit, I was beginning to think
> you had reconsidered and were avoiding
> me.

> XERXES
> (bringing his horse to a halt)
> No, that was not the case.

Masistes stops along side him and wistfully smiles.

MASISTES
I know. That was only a passing thought. I realized very soon after taking up the post in Bactria that there is barely enough time in a day to find a moment for one's self—so many demand attention. It is an amazing thing that you can even make time to sleep, Xerxes.

XERXES
Not that I make use of it.

MASISTES
If it is because of any lingering doubts you may have about what happened in Greece—

XERXES
It is a myriad of issues and before you question them, my friend, know that I would rather they be left to rest for now.

MASISTES
I understand. There are many, better things to discuss—such as the coming wedding.

XERXES
It's nearly upon us.

MASISTES
Good thing, too. I cannot leave matters to the council and magistrate much longer. Wonderful coincidence that your birth's celebration is but a few days after.

XERXES
Must you remind me?

MASISTES
Yes, because it is the only day of the year that king's court and loved ones may ask what they will of him and he must grant their request.

XERXES
Within reason.

MASISTES
May be necessary to reevaluate my gift.

The two share a chuckle.

MASISTES
Honestly though, there's really not a single thing I can think of.

XERXES
Really?

MASISTES
Really. Oh, except perhaps a monument! Yes, yes, one in my striking likeness. That—that would be tremendous!

XERXES
Why only a monument? Why not an entire city dedicated to your prestige? Better yet, a satrapy.

MASISTES
Oooh, I can see it now. We change the name of Bactria to Masistesstan!

They both try to suppress laughter. After all, they are on a hunting excursion. Masistes nods ahead toward Darius.

> MASISTES
> Though their encounters have been
> limited, your son seems to have
> captured my daughter's heart.

> XERXES
> Truth be told?

> MASISTES
> Oh, yes. Artaynta floats around as
> though still slumbering, her nose
> buried in a flower he gave her—despite
> the fact that it has since dried out—and
> I think she may be growing deaf. It
> takes considerable repetition to get her
> attention. Has Darius mentioned
> anything to you? Does he look forward
> to the wedding?

The sound of RUSTLING LEAVES, prompted by departing birds, draws Xerxes' attention away. The prey they're hunting is obviously close. He looks ahead to find his son and the rest of the group are lining up between the trees and bushes.

> XERXES
> I believe your answers will have to
> wait.

> MASISTES
> You're right—look.

Masistes points down the embankment to the brush lining the far side of the stream. A herd of deer emerges and, though suspicious of their surroundings, begin to cross the water.

Darius readies his bow, as do those around him. Xerxes watches with a growing sense of anxiety. He can barely stand the anticipation of what is to come.

The prince signals the guards with a tip of the head. ARROWS WHISTLE as they travel, igniting panic, and deer after deer falls. The assault is quick to conclude, as the rest of the herd retreats. Only one remains in the open and with life yet left in it: the buck.

Darius lowers his weapon, frustrated that he cannot zero in on it, and waves.

> DARIUS
> Father! Father! It's heading your way!

Xerxes forces himself to look. Sure enough, the deer is barreling wildly downstream. Mortally wounded, he runs more on reflex than in hopes of escape.

Quickly, Xerxes draws his bow. Lining the target up, there is a moment of hesitation, a flicker of regret in his eyes. Composure is hard to regain, but he finally lets the arrow fly. It rips right through the buck's chest and sends it headlong into the water.

> MASISTES
> Good thing your mark was on. Had it
> reached cover, it would have suffered.

Xerxes remains silent, shaken by what he has done. Darius gallops up to the two.

> DARIUS
> Excellently done, father. Father? Are
> you alright?

> MASISTES
> Xerxes?

> XERXES
> (curtly)
> I'm fine.

Masistes and Darius share a 'no, you're not' look. An awkward silence follows, during which Xerxes looks up. Through the flittering leaves, he sees dark clouds gathering.

>   XERXES
>   There is a storm approaching.

>   DARIUS
>   What an unusual change in weather. I
>   never saw it coming.

>   MASISTES
>   Neither did I.

>   XERXES
>   Darius, tell the men to gather the
>   carcasses. If we are to beat the rain, we
>   must leave now.

>   DARIUS
>   Yes, by the looks of it we haven't much
>   time.

Darius, eyes on the sky, turns his mount about and gallops back to the guards.

Masistes stares at the amassing tempest, as well, and thoughtfully rubs his brow. THUNDER RUMBLES in the distance, prompting his horse to anxiously side-step.

>   MASISTES
>   Steady . . .

>   XERXES
>   Careful, Masistes.

>   MASISTES
>   Steady . . .

Regaining control, he resumes his 'storm' watching. Xerxes does the same.

                        MASISTES
              You know, they say the worst, most
              destructive storms are those that come
              without warning.

The two sit in silent observance as guards cautiously navigate their horses down the steep slope to the stream below, the length of their cloaks beginning to curl against the wind, the surrounding leaves and flora madly shuffling . . . darkness closing in.

INT. SUSA—ARTAYNTA'S GUEST QUARTERS—NIGHT

Sitting in the window, Artaynta stares out into the dark. THUNDER RUMBLES and lightning flashes. Zostra sits by, diligently working on mixing powders and oils to produce makeup. The DOOR OPENS and Artaynta turns to see Suraz enter.

                        ARTAYNTA
              Do you think they were caught in the
              storm, mother?

                        SURAZ
              I do not know. Zostra?

                        ZOSTRA
              Yes, my lady?

                        SURAZ
              Would you please excuse us?

                        ZOSTRA
              Yes, of course.

Zostra carefully puts a mixing bowl down and goes. Once gone, Suraz slowly walks across the room and stops at the sight of a dried up flower lying on the table.

ARTAYNTA
What is the matter?

SURAZ
I had come to ask you that very question.

ARTAYNTA
I do not understand.

SURAZ
And I think that may be the answer. You do not understand.

Artaynta rises to her feet, perplexed.

ARTAYNTA
Perhaps I could if you would be less cryptic, mother, and explain what it is I—

SURAZ
It is not 'what', but 'who'. I am not as blind as you might think. I know what thoughts lurk behind your eyes.

ARTAYNTA
Whatever it is you think you see—

SURAZ
I know what I saw, what I have been witness to since we came here.

ARTAYNTA
Where is this coming from? Where? You have barely spoken more than three words to me since we arrived here and now this?

SURAZ
Don't be coy with me. I wanted to talk about this before now, but you have been keen to make yourself scarce as of late and, as I'm sure you must know, discussing your indiscretion in front of your father wouldn't have been in your best interest.

ARTAYNTA
Indiscretion? I have done nothing.

SURAZ
Yet.

ARTAYNTA
You've come here to chastise me for an offense that has not even been committed. Why are you—

Interrupting, Suraz picks the flower up from the table and admonishes her daughter to look at it. Artaynta is visibly angered that her mother has dared to touch it.

SURAZ
I saw you in the garden with him, Artaynta! I saw you. I saw you with Xerxes.

She softens, and strokes her daughter's hair. It is a false calm, however. Her hand shakes, her voice wavers, and the look upon her face is one of desperation.

SURAZ
(continued)
Artaynta, please, listen to me. You will soon be princess and, one day, queen of all Persia. Please, do not be so eager to settle for the title of concubine— because that is all you could ever hope to be to him.

Artaynta, consumed with defiance, bats her mother's hand away and bolts out the door. Helplessly, Suraz closes her eyes and balls her hands into fists, consequently crushing the flower.

                    SURAZ
                  (continuing)
            That's all you could ever be.

EXT. SUSA—PALACE—COVERED WALKWAY—NIGHT

Standing on the steps which lead to the atrium is Artaynta, her head lowered in shame. Leaves whip in the wind, glimmering sporadically as dense, foreboding clouds roll across the moon.

Chilled by the weather, she shudders and decides to go inside before the rain starts to fall, but the moment she turns, lightning sparks in the sky, illuminating the dark figure of Xerxes standing behind her. She gasps.

                    XERXES
            Easy. I did not mean to startle you. You
            shouldn't be out here. The rain will fall
            soon.

                    ARTAYNTA
            I know. I shouldn't be here at all.

                    XERXES
            What do you mean?

                    ARTAYNTA
            Nothing. I forget myself.

Shakily, Artaynta heads for the palace. Xerxes, unaccustomed to such dismissal, promptly grabs her arm.

                    XERXES
            No. Wait. Explain.

ARTAYNTA
May I please just go?

XERXES
No. Now tell me, what is wrong?

ARTAYNTA
This. This is. It is shameful of me, I know . . .

XERXES
Artaynta?

The clouds open up and rain starts to beat down upon both of them. Artaynta's hair begins to cling to her face, her simple robe to her body. She looks cold, lost and lonely, and despite being king, so does he.

ARTAYNTA
I told you, that day in the garden, that when I saw Susa again, I felt something . . . a sense that I could not put a word to? I lied. All along, I knew what it was, its name.

XERXES
Then speak it.

ARTAYNTA
Belonging . . . a sense of belonging.

XERXES
Why be shameful of this? After you are married, you will be—

ARTAYNTA
It was not when setting eyes on the city that I felt it.

XERXES
No?

> ARTAYNTA
> No.

The storm whirls about, as if wrapping an invisible rope around the pair, drawing them closer together. Artaynta hesitantly pushes a lock of wet hair behind his ear and this one simple gesture is enough to entreat Xerxes to submit to his desire. Taking her hand, he kisses the palm of it before pulling her against him to kiss her lips instead.

Just when things start to heat up, he shows signs of regret and backs away.

> XERXES
> No. You're right. This cannot happen.
> It cannot.

Instead of retreating to the palace, Xerxes heads off into the dark of night leaving, Artaynta greatly dismayed and soaked to the bone.

Moments later, Zostra steps out onto the walkway and, spotting Artaynta, hastily retrieves her from the weather.

> ZOSTRA
> What has happened? Is it only the rain,
> or do you shed tears?

> ARTAYNTA
> I am a fool. I—I—I must go amend
> what I have done. I must beg the king
> to forgive me.

> ZOSTRA
> Slow down. What crime did you
> commit?

> ARTAYNTA
> I stole a kiss.

> ZOSTRA
> Oh, Artaynta. Why?

                    ARTAYNTA
            I must go find him. I must tell him I
            am sorry.

Zostra keeps her from going, much to Artaynta's frustration.

                    ZOSTRA
            No. Do not—

                    ARTAYNTA
            Let go of me!

                    ZOSTRA
            No! Begging the king for your pardons
            may only serve to make the situation
            worse. Trust me, Artaynta. It is better
            to let it go. Trust me.

                    ARTAYNTA
            You must not speak a word of this to
            anyone.

Zostra pulls Artaynta into a hug and rocks her.

                    ZOSTRA
            I won't. I won't.

INT. SUSA—XERXES' QUARTERS—NIGHT

While the storm's intensity grows, Xerxes lies silently atop his bed. On an adjacent nightstand, a waning candle burns, its light licking the smooth surface of a small, translucent flask that he holds before his eyes. The thick, milky content within lazily rocks back and forth, drawing up the darker, powder-like matter at the bottom. In widening swirls, the elements gradually coalesce.

This liquid is not a means to an end, but a concoction known as the "drink of the immortals". (Depending on potency, it offers an array of results; from a sense of ease and affording one a good night's rest, to producing feelings of euphoria, lust and even megalomaniacal delusions of grandeur. It is also utilized by magis as a hallucinogen.)

Gingerly, Xerxes pulls out the stopper and raises the flask to his lips. It sits there, poised to be tipped as he himself freezes. Does he want to numb himself this way? Is guilt, regret and anger built so great within him that he now fears to face it? The answer, he finds, is no.

Sitting up, he reluctantly pours the potion into the depths of a basin. It disperses upon hitting the water. Curling trails billow and cloud, and what was once clear, is no longer.

EXT. SUSA—NIGHT

The storm continues. Rain pounds the distant landscape, the city and the capital complex. The garden is further ravaged by the wind. Guards stay dry, posted beneath the covered stoas of the palace.

INT. SUSA—ARTAYNTA'S GUEST QUARTERS—NIGHT

A bolt of LIGHTNING sears the sky and rouses Artaynta. Finding Zostra still fast asleep, she takes the opportunity to escape.

INT. SUSA—PALACE CORRIDOR—NIGHT

Artaynta approaches the entrance to Xerxes' room. THUNDER continues to boom and she is as nervous as can be. Standing in front one of the doors, she sees it is already ajar and extends a trembling hand to open it further.

     XERXES (O.S.)
  No . . .

She freezes.

     XERXES (O.S.)
  Forgive me . . . Please . . .

INT. SUSA—XERXES' QUARTERS—NIGHT

LIGHTNING CRACKLES in the sky again, flooding the room with a brief explosion of light. Xerxes writhes on the bed.

> XERXES
> No!

INSIDE XERXES' NIGHTMARE

Unlike the previous ones, this dream is not a mere flash of random images. At least, not at first.

Xerxes stands, facing a fruitful, lush plain, upon which, Darius the Great is enthroned. He directs his son to turn around.

> DARIUS THE GREAT
> Is this what defines you? Consumes you? Is this what will blind you?

Xerxes turns and the dichotomy is made clear. He now stands on a barren plain—barren, except for the thousands of soldiers' bodies strewn across it.

> XERXES
> No! This is not how it's supposed to be!

Artabanus appears beside him.

> ARTABANUS
> But this is what I warned would happen, yet you would not listen and, now, my sons are dead.

Amestris wraps her arms around Xerxes' neck.

> AMESTRIS
> All the dreams that had to die for your one. Is it so surprising that you be left—

                        XERXES
                —with only nightmares.

                        DARIUS THE GREAT (O.S.)
                No, my son.

Amestris and Artabanus disappear as Xerxes, bewildered, turns back to his father, only to find thousands of gawking, crying MOURNERS instead. They wear sackcloths, ash and rent their garments; EVERY TEAR SHED RESONATES upon the ground.

                        MOURNERS
                What did we do? Why?? Xerxes! Please!

Xerxes covers his ears and looks to the sky. There is an eclipse. It begins to storm. Converging streams of rain and tears rise in level, deluging the bodies on the barren plain, burying them beneath the currents.

Suddenly, Xerxes is on his back on what is now a riverbank. Lotus flowers begin to fall. He turns his head to face the water. Something appears to be rising from its depths. A small funnel starts to build and is soon breached.

A MYSTERIOUS WOMAN emerges and the sun resumes its place, backlighting her and keeping her identity concealed.

Xerxes, essentially paralyzed, looks up as she comes to stand beside him. Whether friend or foe, he knows not. He sees only a shadowed figure looming above him. She begins to lean down and, upon doing so, a brief flutter of light dances off a necklace she wears. He is perplexed by it as we . . .

WAKE UP

Xerxes opens his eyes in unison with a loud CRASH of LIGHTNING, which briefly illuminates Artaynta's figure standing beside his bed. He, however, has no idea it's her.

Paranoid from the nightmare, he pulls a dagger from beneath his pillow, roughly grabs and flips her onto the sheets. With one arm pinned above her head and a weapon leveled against her throat, she GASPS in fear.

LIGHTNING CRASHES again, revealing Artaynta to Xerxes. Shocked and horrified by what he has almost done, he quickly releases her, puts the dagger down and sits on the edge of the bed, where he grasps his head in pain.

Artaynta may still be shaken, but he appears even more so and it is from this vulnerability that she pulls the strength to make her move. He raises his head as she slides beside him. His disturbed expression sporadically flickers into sight and she grows all the more bold.

Cupping his face, she draws close and, innocently plants a kiss upon it. A second follows suit, though, then a third, and a fourth. Languidly, she works her way from one side to the other, till their hesitant lips meet. This is the moment, the edge, the brink . . . and though they know they should, they don't step back from it. Together they embark upon what is to be a passionate, erotic interlude.

This is not just sex. It is a catharsis.

Xerxes is fighting the thoughts running rampant in his head, trying to distract himself with her embrace; trying to drown out terrible sounds with those intensifying the heat. All the while, LIGHTNING still flashes. THUNDER still roars.

LATER

When it is finally over, the torrential RAIN has eased to a steady, even beat. For now, the worst of the storm has passed. Xerxes collapses on her, eyes closed, a single tear rolling down his face.

INT. SUSA—BANQUET HALL—NIGHT

A hundred or so guests, including Artabanus and Haman, recline around their designated tables, drinking wine and sharing stories. Servants scuttle about with pitchers and platters while guards, under the command of General Hydarnes, stand at attention around the hall.

At the royals' table, tension abounds, at least for the king. He is alone in his predicament. Masistes has eyes only for the feast sprawled before him.

Darius is too occupied playing the role of the respectful groom-to-be—when he's really mentally undressing Artaynta. Meanwhile, the superficial smile on Xerxes' face does nothing to deflect the looks of suspicion and helplessness that prod him from Suraz and her daughter.

Anxiously, Xerxes takes a drink and unintentionally sets the cup down too hard. Masistes looks up, a piece of bread pinched between the fingers of one hand, the other reaching for a cloth. He spots Darius staring intently at Artaynta and, popping the food into his mouth, grins as he wipes his hands.

      MASISTES
   So, are you ready for tomorrow?

Xerxes takes another drink.

      DARIUS
   It can't come soon enough.
    (breaking his stare)
   I must confess, Masistes, when my
   father told me of the betrothal, I was
   mightily distressed.

      XERXES
   Darius.

      DARIUS
   All I mean is, and take no offense, but
   I had no idea of what to expect. Years
   had passed, after all, but, once I saw
   your daughter, my apprehension
   disappeared.

      MASISTES
   Relieved that she takes after her mother
   and not her father, you mean?

Darius laughs. Xerxes drinks. Masistes prepares to say more, but the music suddenly halts. All attentions are directed to a YOUNG NOBLEMAN standing in the audience with a raised drink.

               YOUNG NOBLEMAN
      The house of Jur wishes to express our
      congratulations to the Royal Family on
      Prince Darius's coming wedding. May
      you enjoy a happy and plentiful union,
      and by it, may the line of our Great
      King be continued forevermore!

The guests echo the speaker as they all rise and salute Xerxes and Darius. Only Artabanus, seated at a corner table, watches unmoved. No one notices him.

LATER

Food taken away, the atmosphere is one of excitement. MUSIC is played at an intense pace, dominated by powerful DRUM BEATS. At the center of the floor, Darius and Artaynta are propped upon the shoulders of guests, the former laughing and smiling. Others follow the pair, CLAPPING in time with the instrumental, including an extremely inebriated Masistes and reserved Suraz.

Yet more guests, hand in hand, dance in a large circle around the tumult. Concertedly, they step back, forth and sideways in colloquial, choreographed moves.

At the royal table, Xerxes is alone, peering over the edge of his cup at the proceedings. He is increasingly dizzied by the sight and abruptly gets up to leave.

Gathered in a corner with other officials, Artabanus sees this. From the crowd, Suraz does, too, but the witness who follows suit is Hydarnes.

EXT. SUSA—BANQUET HALL—STOA

Moonlight and shadow take turns revealing and shrouding Xerxes as he continues along the columned walkway. Hydarnes runs after him.

                  HYDARNES
            King Xerxes! Please, wait!

          XERXES
        (stopping)
What?

Catching up to him, Hydarnes realizes how drunk he really is.

        HYDARNES
You should not be unaccompanied.

         XERXES
General, I thank you for your concern,
but I don't care for company.

        HYDARNES
Fine, but let me escort you to the palace first.

         XERXES
I wasn't intending to leave. I only wanted
a moment's peace. So, you may go.

        HYDARNES
With all due respect, I am reluctant to
leave you by yourself while . . .

He offers a slight tip of the head toward the cup. Xerxes raises it.

         XERXES
I'm drunk? Perhaps a little.

        HYDARNES
Then you must understand that—

Xerxes takes a drink, hands the empty cup to Hydarnes, and moves to lean against the rail to stare off into the night.

         XERXES
General, I will rejoin you all after I
clear my head—now, go.

Frustrated, Hydarnes does the only thing he can. He backs off.

                    HYDARNES
          As you command, but, if you do not
          return shortly, I will be back.

Xerxes, anxious to get him to leave, nods and waves him off.

A few moments of silence pass after he disappears, but soon, FOOTSTEPS are heard.

Xerxes turns to find Suraz heading towards him.

The anticipation of speaking with him, as well as the prospect of being caught together, makes each step an effort. She looks back over her shoulder, making sure no one is behind her, and is slightly comforted by the unwavering sounds of the PARTY spilling into the dark.

                    SURAZ
          Xerxes?

                    XERXES
          Well, is this not familiar . . .

She stops where the pale blue rays of the moon can't reach her and leans against one of the columns a few feet away from him.

                    SURAZ
          Xerxes, I must speak with you. We
          haven't much time.

This prompts an indignant smirk from him. It's as if the very word "time" is something he bitterly feels powerless against, but something he remains defiant of none-the-less.

                    XERXES
          Time. It always comes down to that,
          doesn't it? "We haven't much time." "In
                    (MORE)

XERXES(cont'd)
time, you'll see." "Just give it time."
"It's only a matter of time." But then,
what isn't? Everything is changed and
more than not distorted by it. Like
fragments of memory that no longer
fit together . . . like us, I suppose.

SURAZ
What's past is past.

XERXES
So I'm told.

SURAZ
But, Xerxes, if you . . . if you ever
cared for me—

XERXES
Cared?! I wanted to love you.

SURAZ
But you couldn't. I know. I think I
always knew . . . even before
Amestris . . . But, I didn't come here to
talk about—

Too late. This tiny detour to the past has taken Suraz's intended conversation off course. Xerxes is insulted. There is no question that he feels guilt for the affair with Artaynta, that a part of him wonders whether or not Suraz knows, but he is also drunk. For him, deluded by alcohol, it's easier to be the accuser before he's made the defendant. He closes in on her.

XERXES
No! You're wrong. I could have.
Amestris or no, Masistes or no, I could
have kept you and you knew that, but
you married him anyway! My closest
friend! For what, Suraz? Why?

SURAZ
Xerxes—

XERXES
To punish me??

SURAZ
No—

XERXES
Spite me?

SURAZ
No—

XERXES
Then why? What other reason could there possibly be? What? What??

SURAZ
To save myself from being bound!

That confession is like a slap to Xerxes' face. Suraz's eyes well with tears.

SURAZ
I know you could have 'kept' me and, if I hadn't married, you would have. You would have had me resign myself to a life of being known only as one of the king's many women—to a life of waiting . . . of having to wait ever-so-patiently for my turn to come to even speak with you . . . of being confined like some bird in a gilded cage and left to wonder if you'll call upon me this night or the next or the one after that, a month from then, a year. That's not love. That's possession. It was too great a price to pay to be with you.

XERXES
Must be infuriating then . . . to be
enjoying a life absent of my presence,
of what-ifs, and these bonds you
feared . . . only to discover that I could
still control you, summon you here,
make you come to me.

SURAZ
(softly)
Is that what you've done? At first, I
thought so. I did, and yes, I was
furious, but no more with you than
with myself because . . . I wanted to
come. I wanted to see you.
(increasingly emotional)
My mother used to say that wars made
heroes of men and widows of women.
The most terrible—terrible—thoughts
left me restless each and every night
that my husband was not by my side.
They were my only company in those
dark hours—like an uninvited guest
you feel obligated to entertain—who
asks questions they have no right to
ask. What if they don't come back?
What if both can't? What if you had to
choose which one . . .
(she shakes the thought away; a beat)
When I heard you had returned—that
you were safe—I wanted so badly to
see for myself, but every time that
messenger came to my door, it was as if
he was demanding me to answer that
final question, and I would not
condemn my husband. If he were
lost . . . I thought he was—when they
came for me—and that you would be
(MORE)

SURAZ(cont'd)
the one to tell me that even one,
forgotten, conflicted whisper was
enough to throw him to the wind; a
good and decent man who loved me—

XERXES
(as if finally accepting)
—and whom you love.

She nods.

SURAZ
When I saw him, it was like an absolution
and an opportunity to say good-bye.
(a beat)
If any good came from you returning
from battle while he remained, it was
that he never had to question whether or
not all my thoughts were with him. Had
it been the reverse, how would he have
ever been able to believe that the ache in
my heart was merely that of a subject
longing for the return of their king?
(a beat)
No . . . When he reached for me, I felt
that the dark had finally lifted, and
while I wanted to see you, it was
enough to know you were there . . . at
least, I thought so. I thought I could
walk away, that you would, once again,
let me. Instead, you finally did what I
had come to believe you would never
do—you left me no excuses . . . and I
realized I have been waiting, after all.
(a beat)
(MORE)

                    SURAZ(cont'd)
            You beckoned. I came and, for the
            briefest moment, it was as if the years
            were only a day. There you were, still
            so imposing, so sharp even beheld in a
            blur, but where we once spoke without
            speaking at all, I found silence and it
            was my . . .
                (she can hardly bear to go on)
            Xerxes, I beg you, please do not seek
            Artaynta's attentions. Let her find
            happiness with Darius.

Xerxes, moved by Suraz's speech, is caught off guard with this.

                    SURAZ
            The way you look at her . . .

                    XERXES
            You believe is the way I once looked at
            you?

Though the question lends nothing in the way of being an admission of guilt to Suraz, they lock stares. She still doesn't know, perhaps because she doesn't want to. If she truly did, she would be able to see the remorse in his eyes, but she can't see past the sting of her own.

They stand in silence till Artabanus approaches. Suraz quickly wipes her tears away and flashes a smile.

                    SURAZ
            Prime minister.

With a condescending smirk, Artabanus tips his head.

                    ARTABANUS
            Evening.

                    SURAZ
Thank you, King Xerxes, for hearing
my request. It means so very much to
myself and my family. It truly is going
to be a beautiful wedding.

Suraz bows and leaves. Xerxes, paying no mind to Artabanus, watches her go.

                    ARTABANUS
I did not mean to bring your
conversation to a premature end.

                    XERXES
There was nothing more to be
discussed.
        (a beat; turning to him)
It was good of you to come tonight,
Artabanus.

                    ARTABANUS
You didn't think I would?

                    XERXES
No.

                    ARTABANUS
I didn't think I would either, but I am
well pleased that I changed my mind.

Artabanus is on to something.

EXT/INT. SUSA—XERXES' QUARTERS—NIGHT

Xerxes sits on a lounge on the balcony. The city's sprawling houses and buildings beam coolly under the moon in the distance. The colossal structures of the citadel itself are also aglow, magnificently defined against the night, seemingly conscious, and reveling in it.

From here, he could see it all, but not an inch holds his interest. Xerxes' eyes are set on the robe Amestris made for him. He draws his thumb back and forth across it, deep in thought. She told him that she had missed him. Perhaps this was genuine. Perhaps she, like Suraz, was waiting, too.

Hearing a DOOR to the room being OPENED and CLOSED, he is pulled from his ruminations, but does not turn. He knows who it is. He's been expecting her.

Wrapping her arms around his neck, Artaynta hasn't a clue anything is wrong. She sees before her such a stunning sight that all else is in the periphery.

> ARTAYNTA
> You know, people would pay fortunes
> to stand here for just one moment—to
> see the center of which the rest of the
> world revolves like this.

Artaynta, perplexed by his silence, tilts her head to find what he's so taken with. Seeing the garment, she reaches for a corner of it to admire.

> ARTAYNTA
> It's beautiful. Whose work?

> XERXES
> My—Amestris's.

Abruptly, the material is pulled from her grasp as he folds it up and stands.

> ARTAYNTA
> Oh.

Xerxes, head low, proceeds back into the room. She follows him, her smile gone, her confidence sinking.

> ARTAYNTA
> It is unusual that she took it upon
> herself to make it.

He goes to an old, opened chest sitting in the corner of the room. This is one of many chests, but certainly, the least grand and the least used. The items inside appear to be miscellaneous articles of clothing, most of which are gathered in bundles, never worn.

> XERXES
> Yes, I know.

Putting the robe in the trunk, he closes it—not realizing that a piece of the fabric is hanging out—and goes to sit on the bed. Wearily, he rubs his face. He's reluctant to look at her.

> XERXES
> Artaynta . . .

> ARTAYNTA
> (approaching the bed)
> Why do I gather the sense that I was summoned here to be told something I do not want to hear?

Finally, he looks up at her.

> XERXES
> Because you were.

Artaynta kneels on the floor before him, grasps his hands and tries to search his face for an explanation.

> ARTAYNTA
> Why? Why? What I have done? Whatever it is, I will do—

> XERXES
> It is what I have done . . . the way I used you so that I might be free of myself for a time.

> ARTAYNTA
> Used me?

XERXES
Like some potent tonic, you offered an
escape and I took it—

ARTAYNTA
Is that all I am to you?

Xerxes doesn't answer. Blinking away the sting of her eyes, she draws herself up, nearly upon his lap, and gently tries to make him face her.

ARTAYNTA
I could be so much more than that. So
much more. I know I could.

She leans in, her lips a hair's breadth away.

ARTAYNTA
I can be whatever you want.

She engages a kiss. Despite himself, he reciprocates and pulls her closer. The moment is brief, though, as his conscience will not allow it to continue.

XERXES
No. No, Artaynta, you can't. This has
to stop.

Xerxes gets up and turns his back to her.

XERXES
I regret that I took advantage of you.

ARTAYNTA
But you didn't.

XERXES
You must have not heard me before.

ARTAYNTA
Because it was not you speaking.

Artaynta approaches him, but he still will not face her.

> XERXES
> Listen now. You will not come to me
> again, nor I to you. Do you
> understand?

> ARTAYNTA
> No. What am I to do? Go on to marry
> Darius as if there's nothing between us?

> XERXES
> Yes, because, as of now, there isn't . . .
> there can't be. Darius will never know
> that there ever was.

> ARTAYNTA
> While I will always remember . . .

Xerxes turns and meets her stare. What he sees is that the very thing that originally lured him to her isn't there anymore—that glimmer of hopefulness. He thinks he's to blame for taking from her what he found so special and, consequently, says something he's not accustomed to saying—consciously anyway.

> XERXES
> I'm sorry . . .

Xerxes storms back to the balcony. Artaynta watches helplessly, mouthing the word 'no' as he goes. At a loss, she stumbles back into the chest. Feeling the robe beneath her hand, she eyes it covetously, decides to take it and runs out of the room.

INT. SUSA—XERXES' THRONE ROOM—DAY

Darius and Artaynta kneel on a blanket covered with an array of spice jars, small boxes of precious jewels and metals, and burning caskets of frankincense. An OFFICIANT, dressed in ceremonial robes, looms over their bowed heads.

Atop his throne, Xerxes watches the proceedings. Artaxerxes and his nanny sit beside him.

Regarding the wedding couple, Suraz, Masistes, and the mob of onlooking guests beyond them, Xerxes finds it all too much to take in. He sets sights on his young child and flashes him a brief flicker of a smile, one which disappears as he looks to the nanny and feels the absence of his wife.

CUT TO:

MONTAGE—PRELUDE TO REVENGE

—In the prince's chambers, Darius kisses Artaynta's neck, oblivious to her deadpan expression.

—Standing on his balcony, Xerxes stares across the courtyard at his wife's quarters, transfixed by her silhouette.

—Amestris opens her door to an attendant and is handed a message. She is intrigued by what she reads.

—Morning. Workers scuttle about the complex, preparing for the king's birthday.

—Guests climb the steps to the capital.

—The entire complex is packed. Servants pass through the crowds with trays of drinks.

—Xerxes sits in the throne room, surrounded court advisors. The room is brimming with diplomats and other officials. One by one, they approach the king and kneel as they issue their requests.

INT. SUSA—PALACE CORRIDOR—AFTERNOON

Amestris, flanked by attendants and personal guards, walks pristinely down the corridor. Artaynta, in the company of Zostra, rounds the corner and nearly collides with her.

ARTAYNTA
Pardon my clumsiness.

Wearing an elaborately stitched cloak, the young princess thinks herself well concealed. To Amestris's shock, however, a small piece of fabric is peeking out from beneath it—a piece of Xerxes' robe.

AMESTRIS
If I hadn't been distracted, I would have seen you coming.

ARTAYNTA
Well, if you will excuse me—

Amestris grabs her.

AMESTRIS
Must you go so soon?
(off silence)
Strange, isn't it? We haven't even been properly introduced, yet you are already married to my son. So sorry I missed the ceremony, but, as you must know, it was beyond my control.

ARTAYNTA
You need not explain.

AMESTRIS
Yes, I—I can see that.

ARTAYNTA
I really must be on my way.

AMESTRIS
The celebration is soon to begin. I regret that I am unable to attend. I always loved Tykta.

ARTAYNTA
I'm sorry.

AMESTRIS
Oh, don't be. It isn't your fault.

Suraz, Masistes and their entourage come up behind Artaynta. Amestris shifts her glare to Suraz.

MASISTES
Amestris.

AMESTRIS
(warmly)
Masistes.

MASISTES
This is an unexpected surprise.

AMESTRIS
Yes, it is.

MASISTES
May I say, you look exquisite.

AMESTRIS
Thank you. I was just about to say the same of your lovely daughter. She has most certainly taken after your wife.

SURAZ
You flatter me.

AMESTRIS
It is the—least—I can do. If not for you, I doubt Artaynta would have become the woman she is today.
(MORE)

AMESTRIS(cont'd)
(a beat)
So, are you on your way to the terrace to for the procession?

MASISTES
Yes, that is where we were off to.

AMESTRIS
Very good.

An awkward silence falls upon the group.

AMESTRIS
Oh, I am in no need of your pity. I may be excluded from attending, but, in a gracious and, perhaps, conciliatory gesture, the king has invited me to ask for a gift.
(she holds up a folded document)
I was on my way to pass along my request when I crossed paths with the princess and it is so fortuitous that I did.

MASISTES
Oh?

AMESTRIS
Yes, because I realized I was too hasty in deciding what to ask for and had we not stopped to talk, well, it would be too late to revise this—speaking of late—I don't want to keep you all, so . . . enjoy the festivities and, again, don't worry about me. Thanks to the rules of the day, one of my most fervent wishes will finally come true.

Before Masistes can get a single word out, Amestris snaps her fingers and she and her entourage continue on. He turns to his daughter, but she is primed to go, too.

                ARTAYNTA
       My husband is waiting for me.

She grabs Zostra by the hand and bolts, leaving her confused parents behind.

INT. SUSA—MAIN HALL—AFTERNOON

Artaynta slowly unties and removes her cloak as she and Zostra move to sit on one of the wall-length benches, which line the hall. The princess stares at the guarded doors to the throne room in nervous anticipation.

Moments later, they are opened.

Numerous nobles and officials exit into the hall, followed by the king's council and, behind them, Artaxerxes, whose nanny leads him to the bench to sit. Artaynta offers him a shy smile.

The next to exit is a jovial Darius, surrounded by a group of friends. Artaynta stands and waits to be noticed, not by her husband, but by Xerxes, who files into the hall with his guards.

Artaxerxes slips from his nanny's grasp.

                NANNY
       No, child.

              ARTAXERXES
       Father!

Xerxes turns to see his youngest racing to meet him, but, in so doing, he also sees where he's run from, and the sight of Artaynta wearing the robe Amestris fashioned takes him aback.

She and he stare at each other across the bustling room. Her look is one of defiance, his disbelief. The connection is only severed when Artaxerxes clutches his father's hand.

The nanny apologetically comes to get him.

>   NANNY
>   I'm so sorry, your highness.

>   XERXES
>   No, it's . . . alright.

Meanwhile, Darius, still among his friends, is approached by an attendant, who promptly whispers in his ear.

>   DARIUS
>   Right now?

The attendant nods.

>   DARIUS
>   Very well, then.

He begins to make his way through the crowd with the attendant. Like an afterthought, he locates Artaynta and acknowledges her with a simple tip of the head.

>   DARIUS
>   (to the attendant)
>   Tell my wife to wait for me here.

He continues on alone.

INT. SUSA—PALACE CORRIDOR—AFTERNOON

Darius walks along, looking expectantly down branching hallways.

>   DARIUS
>   Hello?
>   (a beat)
>   Hello?

                    AMESTRIS (O.S.)
    Darius.

He stops. Amestris steps out of the shadows.

                    AMESTRIS
             My son.

                    DARIUS
             Mother? What do you want?

                    AMESTRIS
             To speak with you—

                    DARIUS
             This isn't really the best time.

                    AMESTRIS
             Actually, it's rather quite perfect.

                    DARIUS
             But they're about to begin.

                    AMESTRIS
             Then you will just have to be late.

Like a grounded adolescent, Darius crosses his arms and scuffs the floor with his sandal.

                    DARIUS
             Fine. What is this about?

                    AMESTRIS
             Something that those who would
             make fools of us can no longer cover—
             the truth.

INT. SUSA—MAIN HALL—AFTERNOON

Xerxes' sights are back on Artaynta. Artaxerxes tugs his robes.

ARTAXERXES
When do you go?

XERXES
Soon.
 (turning to son and nanny)
In fact, why don't you two go to the terrace, where you'll best be able to see?

ARTAXERXES
Yes, father.
 (to nanny)
Come on. Lets go.

The nanny tries to bow, but with Artaxerxes pulling her along, it looks more like she's tripping.

Xerxes considers confronting Artaynta, but, before he can take a step, Artabanus approaches and hands him a sealed message.

XERXES
Artabanus. So, you've changed your mind.
 (opening the message)
I was hoping you would. For all your sacrifices, you deserve to be rewarded.

ARTABANUS
Actually, this is not my petition.

Xerxes stops short of reading.

XERXES
No?

ARTABANUS
It is the one you've been waiting for.

XERXES
Amestris's?

ARTABANUS
Yes.

XERXES
This should be interesting.

Xerxes debates whether to read it or not. He opts to delay doing so, at least for a moment.

XERXES
Artabanus, should you decide there is something you want, do not hesitate to tell me.

ARTABANUS
I mean no disrespect, my king, but what I want is not in your power to bestow.

Xerxes knows just what he means and the silence between them is deafening. He returns his attention to the message and reopens it, but is appalled by what he reads.

ARTABANUS
Xerxes?

XERXES
(to himself)
She's gone mad. Why would she—

He looks up from the letter to Artaynta and begins to put two and two together, but before he can decide what should be done about it, a guard signals Artabanus from across the room.

ARTABANUS
(to Xerxes)
It's time to begin.

Xerxes turns to Artabanus—back to Artaynta—back to the letter.

ARTABANUS
Are you alright? Has this upset you?

XERXES
That was her intention.

ARTABANUS
(pointing to the letter)
May I—

XERXES
As you just stated, it's time to begin.

He spares one more glance at Artaynta.

XERXES
Let's be on our way.

Xerxes crushes the letter.

CUT TO:

MONTAGE—REVENGE IN SLOW MOTION

—We see an overview of the city. People are packed in the streets and on rooftops. We also note that "Hadassah's" familiar rooftop is unoccupied.

—In the jam packed citadel, every courtyard and every building, whether part of the ministerial or palace complexes, is brimming with guests.

—Crammed along the railing of the harem's portico, we see numerous girls. One, however, remains undefined in the background.

—In the palace's emptied main hall, Darius comes up behind Artaynta and swings her around to face him. Gripping her tightly, he whispers in her ear. She slumps to the floor. He mouths an obscenity and, gesturing, demands she leave. Zostra assists her up and they go.

—Outside, the gathered take notice as the Immortals, led by Hydarnes, descend the palace portico and line the courtyard below.

—Standing on one of the palace balconies beside Artaxerxes and his nanny are Masistes and Suraz. A messenger approaches the latter and urges her to come with him. Offering Masistes a reassuring pat on the arm, Suraz does just that.

—Walking two-by-two, the king's court appears and, splitting off left and right, lines the palace steps.

—Suraz walks with the messenger down one of the palace's hallways.

—Xerxes is carried upon a sedan through the passageway leading outside.

—Suraz knocks on a door, but there is no answer.

—As Xerxes crosses the palace threshold, he looks up and sees Artaxerxes, but is greatly troubled as he realizes Masistes is without his wife.

—Confused, Suraz turns around, only to be roughly pushed back against the door, her eyes wide with fear. She SCREAMS-

—simultaneously as MUSIC and CHEERING herald Xerxes' arrival atop the palace steps.

—Alone in her room, Amestris closes her eyes and smiles.

EXT. SUSA—CITY/CITADEL—NIGHT

Porters busily make rounds distributing bread, fabrics, jewelry and coins to the masses.

INT. SUSA—APADANA—NIGHT

Attendants filter throughout the hall with platters of food and drink. The guests are preoccupied, paying no notice as Masistes is escorted to the grand stairs by Hydarnes.

At the base of them, the general directs him to proceed alone. A curious wrinkle stretches across Masistes' brow, one that deepens upon seeing Xerxes impatiently waiting for him above.

> MASISTES
> (climbing the steps)
> Xerxes? What's wrong? Oh no, is it my Tykta gift? Yes, I thought about it and, in hindsight, it wasn't the best idea, but I was just thinking of the monument, ah, thing, and then, well, I thought, you know, a marble bust would be—

Masistes, having reached the final step, is caught off guard by his friend's dire expression.

> MASISTES
> You do know I wasn't being serious? See, I truly could not think of anything—

Xerxes grabs him by the shoulder and leads him into a—

PRIVATE HALL

Once secluded, he lets go of Masistes, but the urgent look on his face remains.

> XERXES
> Where is your wife?

> MASISTES
> Suraz was called away a little while ago. Why?

> XERXES
> When exactly?

> MASISTES
> Just before the procession. What's this all about—

XERXES
By who?

Xerxes takes hold of him again.

XERXES
By who, Masistes?! By who!?

MASISTES
Artaynta. Artaynta.

MASISTES
She wasn't feeling well and so she sent a messenger for Suraz to return—

XERXES
Are you certain it was your daughter?!

MASISTES
Who else would request her?

XERXES
Amestris!

MASISTES
What? I don't follow—

DARIUS (O.S.)
Perhaps I can help you understand.

Darius enters, seething with anger, and slowly walks toward them.

DARIUS
My father, the Great Xerxes; loyal to his people, his court, his family; a paragon of wisdom, strength, and courage; a man of integrity, of honor. I have been raised on this rhetoric, encouraged to repeat it, and repeat it I did. Why wouldn't I? Like a good, obedient subject I believed it all to be true . . . but no longer.

MASISTES
You cannot speak to your father—

DARIUS
What I now know is of interest to you, as well. So, I suggest you be quiet, Masistes.

MASISTES
Why you—

DARIUS
Mother told me all. He has wanted your wife since before you were married, and when he could not have her, he took your daughter instead.
  (to Xerxes)
Go on. Tell him. Tell your friend what you have done, how you betrayed him.

Xerxes is speechless.

MASISTES
You expect me to believe these preposterous lies?

DARIUS
Isn't his silence proof enough?

MASISTES
Xerxes? Xerxes, the whole thing is ridiculous, isn't it? Isn't it?

DARIUS
It is the truth.

MASISTES
  (to Darius)
Never!
   (MORE)

MASISTES(cont'd)
(turning to Xerxes)
You would never betray our friendship in such a way. You would never do something so . . . you wouldn't. You wouldn't. He's lying, right? Tell me these are lies. Xerxes? Tell me your son is lying. Tell me!

The desperation on Masistes' face as he pleads is palpable, but Xerxes is unable to dispel the accusations. He is silenced by guilt. Seconds go by and, with each, Masistes' rage grows.

MASISTES
I'd call you a stranger if not for the fact that I know your name . . . and it is 'enemy'.

He storms off.

XERXES
Masistes!

Xerxes starts after him, but Darius is not satisfied. He grabs his father by the shoulder, whipping him around. Xerxes, in reflex, forcefully swipes his hand away.

DARIUS
We're not finished!

XERXES
Get out of my way!

DARIUS
My marriage is done, so do not expect to carry on your affair. When I become king, I will find a bride worthy of—

XERXES
Of you? Of a child who refuses to grow up and takes everything for granted?

                    DARIUS
          Unlike you—who just 'takes'.

                    XERXES
          You're right, Darius. I have made many
          mistakes in my life and, before I reach
          the end of it, I'm sure to make more,
          but leaving you as king in my wake
          will—not—be one of them.

Xerxes brushes past Darius, leaving the boy devastated.

INT. SUSA—MASISTES' GUEST QUARTERS—NIGHT

A shadow eerily rises and falls against the door. Painful MOANING is heard.

FOOTSTEPS ECHO down the hall beyond, growing louder with each bounding stride.

                    MASISTES (O.S.)
          Suraz?! Suraz?!

The door is flung open so hard that it slams against the inner wall.

                    MASISTES
                    (continuing)
          Suraz?!

Upon setting sights on what is before him, Masistes is overcome with wave after wave of nausea. He grips the door frame to steady himself, cuffing his mouth with his free hand.

                    ARTAYNTA (O.S.)
          Father? Father?!

Artaynta runs up with Zostra and clutches her father by the shoulders, but the moment she sees the cause of his sorrow, she SCREAMS and turns to her friend.

                    MASISTES
               (gasping)
         Get our guards. This will not go
         unpunished. I will make him pay.

Atop the bed, Suraz is strewn and still throatily moaning. She has been horribly disfigured—her ears, eyes, nose, tongue and breasts have all been cut off.

INT. SUSA—MASISTES' GUEST QUARTERS—LATER

Hydarnes stands silently by as Xerxes stares, open-mouthed at the sight before him. The room is in total disarray and indicates that whatever has befallen his friends was of a nightmarish nature.

Xerxes is so transfixed by the calamitous surroundings that he barely notices as Artabanus and Haman approach.

                    ARTABANUS
         He has gone to raise forces against you.

Though this falls deaf on the king's ears, Hydarnes turns.

                    HYDARNES
         How do you know?

                    ARTABANUS
         Because, Masistes was heard ranting
         and raving as he fled from the palace.

                    HAMAN
         He will return to Bactria to incite a
         revolt, your majesty.

                    ARTABANUS
         Yes, he has to be stopped.

Xerxes is at a loss.

                    HYDARNES
          I know he is your friend, but I agree. We
          can seize Masistes without harm coming
          to him, but he cannot be allowed to leave.

Still, Xerxes fails to respond.

                    ARTABANUS
          He is obviously in distress and of no
          mind to issue the order. As prime
          minister, the decision now falls to me.
          So, general, you stay with him and I
          will see to it that the threat is
          sufficiently eliminated.
                                                    CUT TO:

MONTAGE

—Masistes' caravan, flanked by guards, crosses a plain.

—Horses tear up the ground.

—In his carriage, Masistes, cradling a veiled Suraz on his lap, looks up.

—Bows and spears are leveled.

—Artaynta raises her head from Zostra's shoulder.

—Masistes' guards turn their horses around and ready for attack.

—Weapons are let loose upon the entourage.

EXT. PLAIN—NIGHT

The stars do not shine, but what light the moon provides shows the scattered bodies of Masistes' guards. The caravan is idle. The last carriage's flap is open. A hand lifelessly hangs out of it—Masistes'.

EXT. SUSA—XERXES' QUARTERS—BALCONY—NIGHT

TORCHES SPIT and CRACKLE. The light emitted from them flickers violently across Xerxes' glossy eyes.

He stares across the courtyard at Amestris's quarters.

> XERXES
> You probably believe you taught me a great lesson in justice tonight. But you've really only served to remind me of one I learned as a child . . .

This is not the temper we expect of Xerxes. The suppression of it is more unsettling than if it were unleashed.

> CUT TO:

INT. SUSA—PALACE TREASURY—NIGHT

Among statues, flasks, and artwork of all mediums, we see a column nearly three feet tall.

> XERXES (V.O.)
> (continuing)
> I was here, in Susa. My father was showing me all sorts of old artifacts . . . statues tablets, tapestries. Among them was an ancient inscribed column, a stela, bearing a code of laws written well over a millennia ago by the Sumerian king, Hammurabi. You see, Hammurabi spoke of justice, too . . .
>
> CUT TO:

INT. SUSA—AMESTRIS'S QUARTERS—NIGHT

Sitting at her vanity, Amestris admires herself in the mirror.

                    XERXES (V.O.)
                    (continuing)
            . . . of crimes being punished in equal
            measure. He believed . . .
                    (as she traces her brows)
            . . . in an eye for an eye . . .
                    (as she traces her lips)
            . . . a tooth for a tooth . . .

In the mirror's reflection, she sees the door to her room thrown open.

                    XERXES (V.O.)
            . . . a life for a life.

Guards pour inside.

                    XERXES (V.O.)
            I wouldn't dare execute the mother of
            my children—is that what you're
            thinking?
                    (as they seize her)
            You are no kind of mother. But it's
            true, I wouldn't.
                                        CUT TO:

INT/EXT. SUSA—XERXES' QUARTERS—NIGHT

Xerxes, still on the balcony, speaks as if in a trance.

                    XERXES
            I have always known there was evil in
            this world, though, only tonight did I
            realize how much of it is in you . . .
            but, so long as you breathe, it is
            limited to the extent of your reach, and
            that is about to be drastically
            shortened.

He turns around and proceeds into his room as we see, in the background, below in the courtyard, Amestris being taken from the premises.

> AMESTRIS
> (struggling)
> No!! Let go of me!! No!! Xerxes!

Despite her pleas, he keeps walking.

> AMESTRIS (O.S.)
> No!! You can't do this! You can't banish me!

Xerxes sits on his bed. A candle flickers beside it on the nightstand.

> XERXES
> You're finished.

One sharp breath and we . . .

FADE TO BLACK

Courtesy of the Oriental Institute of the University of Chicago

FADE IN:

INT. SUSA—PALACE STUDY—DAY

JANUARY 478 B.C.

Sunlight spills into the room through an open passage which leads to a small courtyard. Artaxerxes, going on four years old, sits on the floor, head propped atop his gathered knees, gazing up at his seated TUTOR.

What shadows do linger envelop Xerxes, who works at his desk.

> TUTOR
> (reading from a scroll)
> . . . all the peoples and nations and
> men of every language dreaded and
> feared him.

Xerxes glances up.

> TUTOR
> Those the king wanted to put to death,
> he put to death; those he wanted to
> spare, he spared; those he wanted to
> promote, he promoted; and those he
> wanted to humble, he humbled.

Attempting to redirect his attentions on the documents before him, Xerxes picks one up. As the tutor goes on, however, he simply cannot concentrate.

> TUTOR
> But when his heart became arrogant
> and hardened with pride, he was
> deposed of his royal throne and stripped
> of his glory.

Feeling self-conscious and overwhelmed, Xerxes gets up and goes outside.

EXT. SUSA—STUDY COURTYARD—CONTINUING

The tutor's voice stalks the king. He is clearly disturbed.

> TUTOR (O.S.)
> (continuing)
> He was driven away from people and
> given the mind of an animal; he lived
> with the wild donkeys and ate grass
> like cattle; and his body was drenched
> with the dew of heaven . . .

From above, we see that a bordering hedgerow separates this courtyard from yet another and, just as Xerxes walks along the brush, drawing his hand along the leaves as he goes, there is a woman, who we will come to know as ESTHER, on the other side doing the same.

Neither is initially aware of the other. It is not until both stop that they get the feeling they are not alone. Xerxes turns to the hedge and peers through the leafy cover. He sees only the dark of her hair through the miniscule 'peep hole' until she, too, turns, bringing them, literally, eye to eye.

Though hers is tearful, it widens in surprise.

> ATTENDANT (O.S.)
> King Xerxes—

Looking to the attendant, Xerxes raises finger.

> XERXES
> Just a moment.

He peers back through the hedge, but it is too late. She is gone, leaving Xerxes wondering if she was ever there at all.

EXT. SUSA—DAY

Escorted by attendants, a large caravan rolls through the city.

INSIDE ONE OF THE CARRIAGES

Darius rests his head against the interior. He is an emotional wreck, scowling and clenching his hands. Amestris, lounging across from him, thoughtfully regards her son.

>DARIUS
>What?

>AMESTRIS
>I still can't believe you're here, with me.

>DARIUS
>You're my mother and he threw you to the streets without so much a coin for comfort. Did you really expect that I would stay with him and leave you to be a beggar?

>AMESTRIS
>Yes.

>DARIUS
>I left of my own accord—

>AMESTRIS
>—because you had no reason to stay.

Darius shifts uncomfortably in his seat.

>DARIUS
>So, he plans to remain in Susa. With all that has happened, it is surprising he hasn't run to Parsa to escape . . . escape . . .

>AMESTRIS
>Scrutiny?

DARIUS
Yes, scrutiny.

AMESTRIS
Oh, Darius, your father—

DARIUS
My betrayer.

AMESTRIS
He is greatly beloved and feared. So, it would be woefully naïve to believe that this foray, as scandalous as it may be, will spark anything more than idle gossip.

DARIUS
It isn't fair.

AMESTRIS
No, it isn't. We, the wronged, are instead considered the unworthy and, eventually, we will not be considered at all.
　　(a beat)
He's going through with it, you know.

DARIUS
What are you talking about?

AMESTRIS
With what he and his council put into motion last winter—replacing me.

DARIUS
You can't be serious.

AMESTRIS
What better way to turn attention
from what has happened than to give
the people something to look forward
to—and the ascension of a new queen?
They're probably already anticipating
the celebration.

DARIUS
You honestly expect there's anything
left of a heart beating in that chest of
his?

AMESTRIS
(somber; alluding to her own marriage)
What does love matter? All he needs is
a pretty head to carry the crown.

DARIUS
How do you know this to be true,
anyway?

AMESTRIS
What can I say, my son? I'm
resourceful.

DARIUS
And he's being watched.

AMESTRIS
Undoubtedly, by more than a few. I'm
told he has been working tirelessly
during the day . . . and keeping
company with one new girl after
another at night.

DARIUS
Drowning his sorrows.

AMESTRIS
Perhaps he will sink right along with
them.

INT. SUSA—XERXES' QUARTERS—NIGHT

Xerxes is asleep with a woman at his side. He rolls over and we realize that he has been using the 'drink of the immortals', as there is a small bottle, half empty, in the palm of his hand.

INSIDE XERXES' NIGHTMARE—THROUGH THE MOURNER'S EYES

Beneath an eclipse, thousands of crying mourners are dressed in sackcloth and covered in ash. Their tears spill to the earth, run together and rise as a river. A small funnel starts to build and is soon breached. A mysterious woman emerges, seen only from the back. The sun resumes its place as we . . .

WAKE UP IN:

INT. SUSA—CITY—MORDECAI'S ROOM—DAWN

It is not Xerxes who is rattled awake by this intense dream, but an older man, who we do not recognize—MORDECAI.

EXT. SUSA—CITADEL—DAY

With a satchel slung across his shoulder, Mordecai makes his way to the ministerial quarter, but his sights are set on an edifice far past his destination—the harem.

EXT/INT. SUSA—TREASURY—CONTINUING

Keeping to himself, Mordecai passes by a group of his peers talking on the steps and enters the building. Once inside, though, he appears to be more interested in their on-going conversation than he let on. He stops within the hall to rifle through the contents of his satchel as he listens in.

> TREASURER 1
> . . . well, that's Haman for you. He believes they are responsible for every woe.
>
> TREASURER 2
> Tension has been rife in that region for as long as I can remember.
>
> TREASURER 1
> True . . .
> (changing subject)
> Achaemenes sent word, I hear. The Egyptians have resumed quarry excavations.
>
> TREASURER 3
> It would seem things are slowly returning to normal, hmm?
>
> TREASURER 2
> Well, the Greeks remain a concern, but yes, I would say so. As much as they can, anyway. A new satrap has been appointed in Bactria—can't recall his name, but he was on the council there and popular with the people.
>
> TREASURER 1
> (quietly)
> Either of you believe the rumors, you know, about Masistes and—

>   TREASURER 3
>   I don't even care to speculate.
>
>   TREASURER 2
>   Yes, I would rather speculate on this
>   marriage business.

This topic appeals to everyone, including the concealed Mordecai. Treasurer 1, with the inside scoop, waves the men closer.

>   TREASURER 1
>   They're allowed to take whatever they
>   want from the harem before going to
>   see him.
>
>   TREASURER 2
>   That so?
>
>   TREASURER 1
>   So, it is. With so many girls vying for
>   his favor, one must leave an
>   impression.
>
>   TREASURER 2
>   What a way to find a bride!
>
>   TREASURER 3
>   I don't know. If you were him,
>   wouldn't you constantly be wondering
>   if they were competing for you or the
>   crown—
>
>   TREASURER 2
>   Absolutely . . . not!
>
>   TREASURER 1
>   Can't fathom I would be thinking
>   much of anything for that matter.

                              TREASURER 2
                          Ah, to be king.

                           TREASURER 4 (O.S.)
                       Ah, to be an underling futilely
                       attempting to put off work.

A newly arrived treasurer pats '2' on the back and bounds up the steps. The others reluctantly follow. Mordecai closes his satchel and goes before they see him.

INT. SUSA—ARTAXERXES' ROOM—NIGHT

Xerxes sits in the dark, watching his child peacefully sleep. It is a sight which inspires both thanks and envy.

Gently sweeping Artaxerxes' hair back, he wistfully smiles.

                                XERXES
                        I wonder what your dreams are like.
                        Maybe you'll share them with me. I
                        seem to have lost sight of mine.

He plants a kiss atop his son's head and goes.

INT. SUSA—HAREM—GREAT ROOM—NIGHT

Curtains, gossip and MUSIC flow in what is the ancient world's answer to a modern-day luxury spa. Dozens of girls lounge around while attendants see to their every whim and carry out beautification rites.

Numerous doors, spaced apart by urns and small palms, line the walls. Each leads to a separate chamber.

One of these rooms, however, set apart from the rest, is accessed by double doors.

EGEUS, the man in charge of the harem, heads for this master chamber. In his hands is a necklace; a simple gold chain and bauble.

INT. SUSA—HAREM—ESTHER'S QUARTERS—CONTINUING

In a room fit for a queen, seven female attendants busily work. While two open the doors for Egeus to enter, the others are clustered around Esther, who we see only glimpses of as they apply oil of myrrh to her skin, comb her hair, line her eyes in coal, and stain her lips.

Through an open balcony, the citadel courtyard below and the sprawling city beyond can be seen. The view is momentarily blocked as Egeus comes up behind Esther to slip on the necklace. The clasp is secured and the bauble is guided by her own hand to rest against her chest.

A tear falls and rolls across her fingers.

Egeus moves and we see the courtyard again.

Mordecai stands there.

INT. SUSA—HAREM—GREAT ROOM—NIGHT

The doors to Esther's chamber open. She is led out and, though she remains obfuscated from our view, her competition is silenced and transfixed by the sight of her as she crosses the room.

INT. SUSA—XERXES' QUARTERS—NIGHT

A KNOCK raps at the doors. Xerxes, standing at a table with a flask of wine, turns.

> XERXES
> Enter.

Egeus and Esther, keeping her head tightly bowed, step into the room.

> XERXES
> So, is this she; the one you're so fond
> of, Egeus?

                        EGEUS
            She is.

                        XERXES
            Leave us.

The harem-keeper, perhaps wrestling with his own feelings for Esther, goes. The moment the doors close behind him, the tension heightens.

                        XERXES
            I have been waiting for you.

Xerxes pours himself a drink and, like a panther stalking its prey, moves toward her. He is obviously already buzzed from alcohol, and she begins to shake.

                        XERXES
                    (circling her)
            Do you tremble for fear?

                        ESTHER
                    (nearly inaudible)
            No.

                        XERXES
            It can't be for surprise, can it? You've
            been here for a year.

He stops behind her and, drawing his hand along her jaw, attempts to lull her head back for a kiss.

                        XERXES
            You knew this day would come.

She breaks free of the spell he is trying to cast and resumes her downcast posture.

                        ESTHER
            I did, O king.

Xerxes finds her all the more intriguing. He traces the side of her face, her neckline, her shoulder . . .

> XERXES
> Ah, but that's it, isn't it? To wake and work and sleep—to breathe—for one day, and then that day finally comes, and then it goes, and you find yourself left unprepared for the next. You don't know what's to become of you—but be comforted. You're in like company, because neither do I. So, why not simply be in the moment . . .

He moves around her, his finger following the line of her collar bone, the necklace—

> XERXES
> (continuing)
> . . . in this touch . . .
> (drawing her chin up)
> . . . this breath . . .
> (leaning in; closing his eyes)
> . . . this kiss.

Their lips chastely meet. A tear slides down Esther's face. Feeling it, Xerxes pulls away and, for the first time, seriously regards her.

> ESTHER
> Your highness?

> XERXES
> What do they call you?

> ESTHER
> Esther.

> XERXES
> Esther.

Another tear falls, trailing dark.

> XERXES
> Now you cry? For what reason?

He wipes it away and shows her.

> XERXES
> For innocence?

He turns to the table, sets his drink down and, grabbing a cloth, moves to a basin—pausing only momentarily at the sight of his reflection in the water.

> XERXES
> It's fleeting.

He dips the cloth in, wrings it out, and hands it to her. She gingerly takes it and begins to clean up as he returns to his drink.

> XERXES
> Or is it for your mother? Your father?

> ESTHER
> I am an orphan.

Xerxes apologetically lowers his head—he feels like an orphan too. He turns, meaning to say something, but stops before getting a single word out.

With her make-up removed, Esther looks familiar.

He immediately sets his goblet down and gently raises her face to search her eyes. Esther stands quite still, unsure of his intentions.

> XERXES
> (whispering)
> You . . . ?

Her breath falls heavy upon his touch.

XERXES
It was you.

ESTHER
I'm sorry?

He finally lets her go.

XERXES
Through the hedgerow.

ESTHER
(to herself)
That was you.
    (she realizes what he must be thinking)
I wasn't spy—

XERXES
No, I know. But you were crying then, as you cry now. Did you ever stop or is this a continuance?

ESTHER
I'm not weak.

She meets his stare.

XERXES
I believe you.

Though he does not know why.

XERXES
What do you know of me?

ESTHER
What do I know?

XERXES
Yes.

She composes herself, as if she has been prepared for this exact question.

ESTHER
(reciting)
You are Xerxes, king of kings; king of lands containing many men; son of Darius and of Atossa, daughter of the great Cyrus. You are a commander, a conqueror and a guardian—

XERXES
You know me not.

ESTHER
Perhaps not the man beneath the crown, but—

He abruptly turns from her.

XERXES
(to himself)
Why is it that I feel as though you do?

To Esther's shock, he begins to get ready for bed. All she can do is stand in place, frozen, and avert her stare as he slips off his robe, leaving only the 'libas' trousers beneath, and proceeds to remove his gold adornments.

XERXES
What would please you, Esther? Riches? A title? Authority?

To her own surprise, she is quick to answer.

ESTHER
Purpose.

                              XERXES
                    You think you have yet to find yours?
                    You think it's something you can
                    recognize? What if yours is passing you
                    by this very moment, because you're
                    here with me?

Finished, he leans against one of the bed's posts. Esther nervously lifts her gaze from the floor and, taking in the sight of him, sees the battle scar on his arm. Struck by this sign of his mortality, her anxiety wanes.

                              ESTHER
                    Is it not possible, O' king, that purpose
                    is not always for us to find—that,
                    sometimes, we are the ones to be
                    found?

Realizing what she's looking at, Xerxes is suddenly discomfited. He tries to subtly cover the scar up by crossing his arms and placing his hand over it.

                              XERXES
                    Perhaps . . . You're free—to return to
                    your quarters, or stay here. The
                    decision is yours to make.

She stares at him a moment longer, before shifting her gaze to the door.

LATER

All of the candles have been extinguished. Esther stares off into the night, reclined upon the king's lounge. He lies upon his bed, turning the bottle of tonic over and over in his hand. He finally decides to open it and take a sip, but, just inches from his lips, he stops.

The sight of Esther, bathed in starlight, captivates him.

We pan up to the moon, which gradually becomes the sun . . .

MORNING has come . . .

Xerxes wakes from the first night of serene slumber he has had since before the war. He sits up, marveling at this simple success, before remembering he is not alone.

Like a real-life masterpiece, Esther remains in a silent, dreamy repose on the lounge. The rays of morning gently kiss her upturned face. A great shadow rises to meet them, then falls away—that of Xerxes. Crouching beside her, he curiously looks on, convinced there is more to her than meets the eye.

INT. SUSA—COUNCIL HALL—DAY

Seated around a table, Haman, Artabanus and Xerxes' advisors regard him questioningly as he leafs through the numerous business proposals in front of him.

> SHETHAR
> So, your decision is final, then?

> XERXES
> Why not?

The old men share a befuddled look.

> XERXES
> Amestris was Otanes' daughter, one of the most dignified men I have ever known, yet she was more spoiled by his status than nurtured by his influence. I don't care to find another like her and besides, if everyone is as eager for me to take a wife as you and the others say, then they should not care where she came from.

> HAMAN
> As long as she is of our people.

> XERXES
> Correct.

Xerxes' attention is drawn away as General Hydarnes enters.

> MERES
> I suppose it would eliminate the possibility of anyone citing favoritism, as she has no father to favor, but still—

> XERXES
> But nothing. Listen, I have more important things to concern myself with than this.

Hydarnes stops beside his chair and hands him a message.

> HYDARNES
> This just came for you.

> XERXES
> From?

> HYDARNES
> Artabazus.

Xerxes eagerly opens and reads the letter, but is dismayed by what it says.

> XERXES
> The general has it on good authority that the Greeks are planning to make a move against us. No specifics.

Artabanus is not surprised.

> XERXES
> We'll increase the number of troops along the border.

ARTABANUS
That's really all we can do, isn't it?

SHETHAR
Yes, that and go about our affairs as normal. The citizens look to us to determine how they should to react to such news.

ARTABANUS
Yes, why worry them over something beyond their control?

Xerxes picks up on Artabanus's disdain and considers retorting, but Hydarnes interrupts.

HYDARNES
I recommend more guards be assigned to you.
(off Xerxes' grudging look)
Your highness—such an ambiguous threat could mean anything, including assa—

Xerxes abruptly gets up.

XERXES
Understood. Do as you see fit and I shall do the same, for myself and my people.

Casting a pointed look at Artabanus, he leaves.

EXT. ATHENS—ARGOS—DAY

While reconstruction efforts continue throughout the city, and despite the chilly, winter weather, the market buzzes with business.

Aristides and Cimon navigate through the crowds.

CIMON
I still can't believe it.

ARISTIDES
I am no admirer of the man, either,
Cimon, but so it is.

CIMON
Entrusting Pausanius with command
over our forces—

THEMISTOCLES (O.S.)
Did you think you would ever see the day?

Themistocles, architectural prints in hand, joins them.

CIMON
Themistocles.

THEMISTOCLES
The Persians, I hear, are aware there's
something afoot.

ARISTIDES
They may still have their informants,
but they know no details.

THEMISTOCLES
So, the league's plan?

ARISTIDES
It hasn't changed.

THEMISTOCLES
And it is about to be set into motion,
isn't it, Aristides?

ARISTIDES
No, Themistocles. It already has been.

EXT. SUSA—HAREM—FRONT COURTYARD—DAY

Esther heads for a lone, corner bench against one of the hedgerow enclosures, and takes a seat. Watching the other girls talk in cliques, she feels like an outsider looking in—she's not the only one. Through the leaves, she, too, is being watched.

Sensing this, she stiffens.

> MORDECAI (O.S.)
> Beautiful day, isn't it?

> ESTHER
> A beautiful day, it is.

> MORDECAI (O.S.)
> We haven't much time, do we?

> ESTHER
> Not long at all.

ON THE OTHER SIDE OF THE HEDGEROW

—we see Mordecai standing between it and a tree-line.

> ESTHER (O.S.)
> I have missed you.

Mordecai warmly grins.

> MORDECAI
> And I you, but you must understand why I keep my distance. If anyone were to suspect—

ON ESTHER

> ESTHER
> I know . . .

> MORDECAI (O.S.)
> So, tell me, how are things?

> ESTHER
> Well . . . I suppose. I mean, I have not
> a want. Anything I could ask for is
> granted me, but—

> MORDECAI (O.S.)
> But?

> ESTHER
> I did as you told me. I continue to. No
> one knows, but with each passing day . . .
> How is it possible that you can scarcely
> recognize your own self, who you've
> been all your life, and yet, in the eyes
> of strangers, never feel so bare?

> MORDECAI (O.S.)
> You mustn't doubt or lose yourself, but
> believe. You must believe you're there
> for a reason.

She absorbs these words of encouragement, but her response is cut short.

SHAASHGAZ, the eunuch in whose care the women are in, stands atop the harem steps, motioning for everyone to come in.

> ESTHER
> I have to go.

> MORDECAI (O.S.)
> Be strong. You are not alone.

She looks to the sky, takes a breath, and leaves to join the others.

ON THE HAREM STEPS

Shaashgaz continues to usher the girls in, but stops Esther from joining them.

> SHAASHGAZ
> You are coming with me.

ON THE OTHER SIDE OF THE HEDGEROW

Mordecai slips from behind the tree-line, back onto the—

WALKWAY

—and manages to do so unnoticed—passing right by Haman, who spares a glance at the harem as he speaks to his entourage.

> HAMAN
> (on the go)
> They'll be tightening security
> throughout the citadel.

This does not go unheard by Mordecai.

INT. SUSA—MAIN HALL—SUNSET

Shaashgaz and Esther enter, and their presence is immediately seized upon by Artabanus and the king's court advisors. They watch with great interest as Shaashgaz prods her to continue through the opened doors into the—

THRONE ROOM

To Esther's dismay, he does not follow her in, leaving her to present herself. Hesitantly, she proceeds, wringing her hands all the way, following the sound of what are, initially, low, indiscernible whispers—those of Xerxes and Artaxerxes.

The boy stands before his enthroned father, while his nanny does her best impersonation of someone trying to mind their own business.

> XERXES
> Perhaps when you grow this high.

He puts his hand about a foot above Artaxerxes' head. The child looks up at it and grouses.

> ARTAXERXES
> But that could take forever.

Xerxes inwardly laughs, but the rumble is quieted upon seeing Esther approaching. Distracted by her presence, he absentmindedly pats his son's shoulder.

> XERXES
> Time you get your dinner.
> (to nanny)
> Escort him.

She bows and reaches for Artaxerxes' hand. The two pass by Esther, who fondly smiles at the boy as he looks up at her. Her eyes continue to follow him till both he and his nanny exit the room.

> ESTHER
> The prince?

> XERXES
> Yes. Artaxerxes.

> ESTHER
> He is a fine boy.

> XERXES
> That is a title he is eager to lose.

> ESTHER
> Oh?

XERXES
He cannot grow soon enough for his liking, and here I am, envious of his youth . . . his innocence . . . the fact that his responsibilities are limited to learning his lessons and minding instruction.

Xerxes realizes he has been speaking much too casually with Esther, and his expression turns matter-of-fact.

XERXES
I summoned you here for a reason.
    (a beat)
You intrigue me, Esther, but that's to be expected.

ESTHER
It is?

XERXES
I know next to nothing about you. Then again, we rarely, really know anyone completely, do we? Not even our own selves.
    (mirthful; more to himself than to her)
Certainly keeps life interesting, though, I must say, I'm tired of being surprised. If your own instincts can betray you, well, anyone can. So, I do hope they prove to be right in this matter.
    (a beat)
When I asked you before—what would please you—what did you answer?

ESTHER
Purpose, your highness.

> XERXES
> This whole idea of taking another wife was not my own, but here we are, and, beyond the obvious, for one inexplicable reason or another, I'm drawn to you—more so than any of the others. Therefore, I am prepared to crown you as my queen.

She is stunned.

> XERXES
> So, what do you say, Esther? Have you been found?

Indeed, she begins to believe that there is a reason for all of this. Still, demure by nature, her epiphany translates quietly.

> ESTHER
> O king, I have no desire to hide.

> XERXES
> (to himself)
> Nor do I.

CUT TO:

INT. SUSA—THE HAREM—NIGHT

Esther walks through the harem to its large, open balcony. As she goes, her eyes scan the surrounding women. They stare as well, some bitterly, for this is the girl who was chosen over them as queen—but, when one of them begins to bow, another does the same, then another and another . . .

> ESTHER (V.O.)
> May I ask?

She makes it to the balcony and, once on it, stares out at the city of Susa sprawled beyond the walls of the citadel.

CUT TO:

EXT. SUSA—XERXES' QUARTERS—BALCONY—DAY

Xerxes stands on the balcony, looking at the distant harem building. He also scans the courtyard below. It is abuzz with porters delivering baskets of food and barrels of wine for the wedding.

                    XERXES (V.O.)
        Ask . . . ?

CUT TO:

INT. SUSA—HAREM—ESTHER'S QUARTERS—NIGHT

Esther stands atop a small chest as an attendant works on her wedding gown. Jewels are fastened to it, sparkling brilliantly against the pulsating candlelight.

                    ESTHER (V.O.)
        What do you want?

CUT TO:

INT. SUSA—PALACE—THRONE ROOM—NIGHT

Hundreds of candles flicker playfully. Many guests are gathered, though their faces remain shadowed.

                    XERXES (V.O.)
        What do I wish for?

                    ESTHER (V.O.)
        Not your court, or people—

                    XERXES (V.O.)
        But I alone?

On an elaborate tapestry, Xerxes is kneeling, his head bowed. Like Darius's wedding to Artaynta, jars of spices and boxes of jewels and gold are set out before him. Baskets of frankincense burn on every corner.

                    ESTHER (V.O.)
            Yes.

Esther steps onto the tapestry. She descends to her knees on his left, and her necklace ricochets the candles' light. Xerxes looks at her curiously, as if experiencing deja vu.

                    XERXES (V.O.)
            All I can do is share in theirs.
                                            DISSOLVE TO:

INT. SUSA—THRONE ROOM—LATER

Still kneeling, but now face to face beneath a sheer fabric canopy, which is held aloft by attendants, Esther and Xerxes lock eyes as he places the royal crown atop her head.

                    ESTHER (V.O.)
            Then might you also share another of mine?

They raise their right hands against one another other.

                    XERXES (V.O.)
            Which would be?

The OFFICIANT carefully binds their wrists together with cloth.

                    ESTHER (V.O.)
            To simply be happy.
                                            CUT TO:

EXT. SUSA—CITADEL—PALACE STEPS

The newly wed king and queen are brought before the ecstatic masses and, for once, Xerxes allows himself to enjoy the moment.

                                            CUT TO:

INT. SUSA—XERXES' QUARTERS—NIGHT

In an abstract whirlwind of gentle touches and kisses, candle and moonlight, clothes fall to the floor, man and wife into one another.

CUT TO:

EXT. SUSA—APADANA ENTRANCE—NIGHT

While the sounds of celebration swell throughout the citadel, Artabanus, though a bit drunk, is in no mood to take part. Peering over the rim of his cup, he leans against the wall in a disgruntled huff and glares back and forth from those passing by to the posted guards before him. Haman soon appears, eyes bright with drink, and staggeringly approaches.

                    HAMAN
        What a night!

                    ARTABANUS
        Hmm.

                    HAMAN
        But, I must say, you look completely
        miserable.

                    ARTABANUS
        Oh? I didn't realize it was recognizable
        through this delusional haze you all
        seem to be under.

                    HAMAN
        What's wrong with you, Artabanus?

                    ARTABANUS
        The fact that you even ask . . .

Artabanus swigs his drink. There is a brief interlude of silence, which is broken by rushed FOOTSTEPS beating against the steps.

                    MESSENGER (O.S.)
        The king!

Artabanus tries to get a look at who's causing the ruckus, but the messenger is blocked by the vigilant guards.

                    GUARD
            Halt!

                    MESSENGER (O.S.)
            You must let me by! I have urgent news
            for the king!

Curious, Artabanus sets his drink down and parts through the guards. Haman follows, also intrigued.

                    ARTABANUS
            What has happened?

                    MESSENGER
            I must see the king immediately.

                    HAMAN
            Impossible. He has just been wed and
            both he and his bride retired some
            hours ago.

                    MESSENGER
            Regardless, it is imperative that—

                    ARTABANUS
            Silence! Whatever news it is you bring,
            I will tend to.

                    MESSENGER
            I cannot—

                    ARTABANUS
            I am second to the king, so, yes, you
            can.

The messenger glances wildly around, seeking confirmation from the surrounding guards. They nod. Hesitantly, the young man passes a letter over. Artabanus promptly opens it, flashing him an 'it's about time' look, before reading the document. He subsequently bounds away, leaving a confused Haman behind.

INT. SUSA—XERXES' QUARTERS—NIGHT

Pulling a robe around her, Esther climbs back onto the bed and draws close to her sleeping husband.

> ESTHER
> If only things could be different.

She reaches into her robe and uncovers . . . her necklace, admiring it briefly before letting it dangle.

Xerxes wakes to his own, distorted reflection cast in the bobble and reaches for it, just as—

> GUARD 2 (O.S.)
> I am sorry, prime minister, but you cannot—

> HYDARNES (O.S.)
> What is going on?

> ARTABANUS (O.S.)
> Tell this man to stand down!

> GUARD 3 (O.S.)
> The king has explicitly ordered that he is not to be disturbed—

> ARTABANUS (O.S.)
> Oh he is about to be disturbed alright!

> HYDARNES (O.S.)
> Artabanus!

The doors to the bedchamber fly open, slamming harshly against the inner walls. Artabanus, the guards, and Hydarnes all spill into the room. Xerxes rises to his feet, not at all amused by the intrusion.

> XERXES
> What do you think you are doing?!

> ARTABANUS
> I am so sorry to interrupt, but I bring word of the Greeks.

Xerxes turns to one of the guards.

> XERXES
> Escort the queen to her quarters.

The guard tips his head and, as Esther is led away, she and Xerxes share one last look.

The doors close.

> XERXES
> What has happened??

> ARTABANUS
> (smiling)
> We know what they're intending to do.

Artabanus holds up the message. Xerxes yanks it from his hand.

> ARTABANUS
> (continuing; cruelly)
> Unfortunately, for us, there's nothing to be done about it.

Scanning the report over, Xerxes' expression darkens.

> HYDARNES
> Your highness?

ARTABANUS
Can't you see he's busy, general?
Though, if you wish to know what it
says, I shall tell you. The Greeks have
besieged the island of Cyprus and
targeted Byzantium.
      (a beat)
But, let us do as we have been, and see
only the good, rather than the bad, in
these turn of events.

Artabanus's flippancy comes as a shock. The reserved, though often sardonic, demeanor he is known for has been shed thanks to a little too much wine.

XERXES
(incredulous)
The good?

ARTABANUS
What are they taking from us? Only
what was once taken from them.
Could be worse. Cyprus and
Byzantium they're like . . . a lady's
earrings—accessories—expensive ones,
granted, but more palatable to lose
than a limb—figuratively speaking.

HYDARNES
What of our garrisons, Artabanus?

ARTABANUS
What's to worry over? In a war—
pardon me—after a war in which so
many were lost, who will miss these
men? Especially when, by all
appearances, they've been forgotten for
some time now. Nameless, faceless, not
like, oh,
(MORE)

ARTABANUS(cont'd)
someone such as our king's good friend
Masistes. No, when he met his
lamentable end, the people took
notice . . . well, for a day or two
anyway . . . and that was not even at
the hands of the Greeks.

XERXES
No, it wasn't, was it . . .

ARTABANUS
He couldn't be permitted to return to
Bactria. He and his house, your own,
too, to a certain extent, regrettable
casualties, but would you rather have
seen your affair become the impetus to
plunge us into civil war?

Xerxes is just astounded by Artabanus's brazenness. He cannot even find the words to respond. He instead turns and, rage brewing, steadies himself against the wall.

ARTABANUS
No, I didn't think so—not after
Greece. I told you what would happen.
I warned you, but, no, you just
couldn't resist throwing a rock into the
hornets' nest.
    (shakes head)
Every man has a weakness, but yours?

He takes a few steps towards his nephew.

ARTABANUS
Yours is your deluded sense of self
importance; your insincere nobility.
What good is remorse when you were
warned you would suffer it?

He moves closer.

> ARTABANUS
> You really are your own worst foe, contending with your own shadow every step you take.

> XERXES
> Well, aren't you observant.

> ARTABANUS
> Though, I will admit to being wrong on, at least, one count.

> XERXES
> Oh? Do tell.

> ARTABANUS
> I originally opposed your war because I believed it all for the sake of hegemony. No, no, I was wrong. I had my words crossed. It wasn't for hegemony. It was for hubris.
> (a beat)
> Oh, you thought yourself invincible, but not anymore, do you? Too bad it's too late for my son—my sons—and, despite all your power, you can't bring them back.

> XERXES
> No . . . but I can arrange for you to meet them.

Suddenly, Xerxes spins around and grabs Artabanus roughly by his robes. Like an unstoppable force, he pushes him onto the balcony, backing him up against its railing as if planning to push him over it. Hydarnes and the guard rush onto the balcony as well, but keep their distance.

HYDARNES
Your highness!

XERXES
This is none of your concern,
general!

Artabanus struggles against Xerxes' constricting grasp to no avail.

ARTABANUS
You would murder your own uncle?

XERXES
I have tolerated your arrogance
because you are my father's brother,
but make no mistake, you are nothing
to me!!

ARTABANUS
Because I tell you the truth? Because I
would dash your mask to pieces?!

XERXES
Because you insult their memory by
seeing no worth to their sacrifice.

ARTABANUS
Like you? Using them to prop yourself
up for all the world to see—

XERXES
You shut your mouth!

ARTABANUS
—desperate to immortalize yourself?
You got what you wanted and what
irony it is that your name will forever
be linked to—

              XERXES
    Shut—your—mouth, or I will silence
    it for you!

             ARTABANUS
    What is one more body, right? Oh,
    your father would be so pleased.

Xerxes is on the verge of doing away with Artabanus for good, but, at the last minute, he grabs him by the robes again and flings him back into the room. He lands painfully on the floor.

The doors open. Haman and a group of guards pile in and are taken aback by what they see.

Xerxes is on a rampage. Artabanus scurries backward, trying to gather himself to stand.

              XERXES
        Get up! Get up!!

He does not get up quick enough for Xerxes' liking. The king grabs and draws him up himself, but he remains defiant.

             ARTABANUS
    Behold, the indomitable Xerxes!

Artabanus offers a smirk in further provocation, which is expediently backhanded off his face. He falls to the ground once more.

Xerxes is seething. Hands clenching, he grits his teeth.

              XERXES
     Get him out of my sight. Now!

Two of the guards quickly rush to Artabanus and scoop him up. Dazed, he lifts his head and chuckles as he is taken away—just as the king's advisors arrive late to the scene.

They look to Xerxes for answers, but they are offered none.

XERXES
What are you all leering at?! What?!

He marches right through everyone, spins beneath the door frame and raises a finger. The look he casts is enough to strike fear into the hearts of all.

XERXES
I am spent and from this moment on,
I will be compensated by any fool who
dares to tax me more. Anyone that
comes to me without having been
summoned—be prepared to pay—
with your life.

Xerxes storms away, leaving the gathered dumbfounded.

INT. SUSA—THRONE ROOM—NIGHT

A door GROANS open. Firelight, cast from the hall, cuts through the dark and stretches to the empty throne. HAPHAZARD STEPS SCUFF the floor.

With his shoulder firm against the cool stone, Xerxes uses the wall to guide his way. It appears a temporary madness has come over him. Through mussed locks, his wild eyes wax fierce. He reaches into his askew robe to retrieve a bottle and backs flush up against the wall.

XERXES
The drink of the immortals . . .

He pulls the stopper and holds the bottle up, revealing that only a little remains.

XERXES
The nectar to numb your nightmares
or refill the well of dreams; the
transcendent—the way to be freed of
sleep's paralysis to discern your visions
in wake.

He downs the contents, closes his eyes and savors the taste. Prying himself from the wall, he skulks forward in a drunken waltz.

>   XERXES
>   What would those be? Hmm?

Catching himself against a pillar, he reopens his eyes and anger takes over.

>   XERXES
>   Can you not hear me!?

The words echo. He lets go of his anchor and proceeds into the abyss of his mania.

>   XERXES
>   I have heard you! You, who issue your
>   challenges and riddles only when night
>   has taken its hold and left me
>   defenseless! Oh, but I am not
>   defenseless now. My eyes, they are open,
>   and you will find no glint of fear—

We hear the DOOR SLAM SHUT.

The dissimilated sounds of lapsing memories encircle him; the BATTLE CRIES of MAN and BEAST. Enraptured by the cacophony, he throws his head back.

>   XERXES
>   You think this rings dissonant in my
>   head? It has been my lullaby for so
>   long now, that I have found its
>   rhythm. Go on, let the measure rise!

But it grows silent. Xerxes opens his eyes.

>   XERXES
>   Where are you? Why are you silent
>   now, father? Did I shame you so
>   (MORE)

> XERXES(cont'd)
> unforgivably? Am I not still your favorite son? I did all you wanted. I avenged your name. Do you abandon me now because I dared hope to eclipse it?!

Fire baskets about the room ignite. Xerxes remains unfazed.

> XERXES
> I resisted going to war, in part, because I believed I could do just that.

As Xerxes passes the various bas-reliefs on the wall, they subtly move.

> XERXES
> Did you see my legions? Did you? I raised an army unlike any to come before it; an awe-inspiring multitude of nations, all at my command. Did you see the way they revered me? Did you hear them pledge their undying loyalty to me? They testified to what even our enemies could not refute—that, of all men, I alone am the exalted—I, alone, reign supreme!

The adamant force of his words nearly causes him to stumble.

> XERXES
> Those dogs knew that, with one order, I could annihilate them all.

He laughs and leans against another pillar.

> XERXES
> Which only enforces how insane they were—are—that they would rather die than make peace with me.

A dizzy spell washes over him as he begins to notice the hallucinations.

> XERXES
> But, no, I tempered myself and destroyed only those whom it was necessary to destroy to keep my word to you. Did you witness it . . . that brilliant, emblazoned sunset?

The fire baskets burn all the more bright. Waves of heat trail before Xerxes' eyes.

> XERXES
> That was supposed to be the beginning, not the end . . . but what reason was there to spend a blink of time on those so undeserving of my attention? If they were, no fluke of a setback would have stopped me—certainly not the loss of a fleet. If I so wished, I could take the cedars of Lebanon and build thousands more. But not for them—ingrates—who would choose battling one another for scraps over sitting civilized at my feast. No, they weren't ready. They couldn't see past our differences to appreciate our commonalities. They are men of no vision, firm set in their ignorance, and how do you shape what's not malleable? Though, I do wonder, what crime did we commit against them to earn their ire? That we wished to right the unprovoked wrong perpetrated against us? That we wanted to purge them of the corrupt so the just could flourish—so they could learn from us—be one with us??

He gradually lets go of the pillar and continues on to the throne.

                    XERXES
            Why did they resist? Doubt? Doubt
            that we knew better than they? You
            would think the prosperity our empire
            would be proof enough of our
            mandate to rule. I had no desire to
            make slaves of them, but brothers.
                    (he scoffs)
            What do they know of kinship? Their
            nation was war torn before I even turned an
            eye in their direction. How despotic of me
            to want to mend it, unify them, and how
            ironic that that goal has been realized—
                    (laughing)
            —though not at all as I expected.

He stops.

                    XERXES
            No, they have, at last, found a
            common cause—

A vacant expression comes upon him. The bottle falls from his hand and SHATTERS on the floor.

                    XERXES
            —their hatred of us.

He covers his face and shudders . . . but not due to tears. No, when his hands slide away, we find he's smiling.

Xerxes proceeds up the steps.

                    XERXES
            But, I console myself in the knowledge
            that all things borne of hate cannot
            stand for long. No, eventually, they'll
            turn on themselves again, like the self-
            destructive heathens they are.

He takes the throne and lazily drapes himself across it.

>   XERXES
>   Won't they Mardonius?

Looking back to the floor, he sees a cloaked figure step out from the shadows. Though this person's head is obscured by a hood, we see enough of their downcast face to recognize it is Mardonius.

>   XERXES
>   Poor Mardonius—such ambition.
>   What a tragedy it is that your patience
>   was not in step with your conviction.
>   Though, neither was mine, was it?

Mardonius begins to shake his head 'no', but Xerxes sits up.

>   XERXES
>   No! I am not in your court to judge.
>   You are in mine. I will not be sentenced
>   by you or anyone! I have already bore
>   my share of guilt and I will bear no
>   more. Why should I? Because that's
>   what a good man would do; assume
>   responsibility for his mistakes? But
>   they're not all mine, are they? Are they!?

A cloaked Suraz steps out from the shadows and stands beside Mardonius.

>   XERXES
>   Like you, Suraz. Why should I lament
>   your loss? Your ruin is your own fault.
>   You would be here now, safe and
>   bound by side if not for your
>   selfishness—your false love. Had it
>   truly been genuine, you would never
>   have run. You built your house on a lie
>   and—that—is why it came crashing
>   down!!

A cloaked Masistes joins his wife.

> XERXES
> And, Masistes, my pitiful friend, is it my fault you were too blind to see? It isn't as if there weren't enough clues. I dropped enough them—spiteful, I know, but, I must admit, it was amusing. The more you proved your devotion to me, the more I resented you—as if I owed you anything. You took more than you could ever repay!

A cloaked Artaynta steps forward and joins her parents.

> XERXES
> And while I'm confessing, who knows, maybe I didn't try hard enough to resist your lovely daughter when she threw herself at me. Maybe I didn't really try at all.

He throws a leg across the arm of the throne and reclines.

> XERXES
> I refuse to shed a tear for any of you.

A cloaked Amestris appears.

> XERXES
> Amestris? What empathy have I for you? All that mattered was your title and stripping you of it? Oh, that was as sweet for me as venting your wrath upon Suraz must have been for you. Though, at least, unlike her, you fought for what you wanted.

A cloaked Darius joins his mother. A sentimental grin crosses Xerxes' face.

> XERXES
> Darius—perhaps I did fail you. Perhaps I was too busy proving myself to be a worthy son, that I couldn't be a proper father. But then, it is also possible that you were too spoiled and lazy to notice anyway . . .

Xerxes stands up.

> XERXES
> But I am a father to many now, aren't I? And they love me, don't they? Enough to die for me—by the thousands—

The throne room begins to fall away as thousands of cloaked figures appear . . .

> XERXES
> —tens of thousands—

They multiply, all around.

> XERXES
> —too many to count. So, how dare I now concede that . . .
>   (a beat; to everyone)
> I have not been your champion.

Xerxes' eyes well.

> XERXES
> I have been your villain.

A tear falls and he watches its descent, only to find that he now stands upon a mound of bodies. Raising accusatory fingers, the ambiguous hooded persons pass through the familiar and begin to close in around him.

He shows no fear—only resignation.

> XERXES
> May you forgive me.

They consume him.

> XERXES (O.S.)
> It wasn't supposed to be this way. It wasn't supposed to be—Stop! Stop this! If you don't, I can! I can stop this all now!

The black tide rolls back, revealing Xerxes, alone in the dark, kneeling before the steps to the throne, holding a dagger.

> XERXES
> Why did you leave me the way you did, father? With your vengeance and no time to mourn . . . How could I allow myself to feel for anyone what I had not allowed time to feel for you?

He tightens his hold on the dagger.

> XERXES
> So, I shall mourn for you now—for you all.

Bringing the razor-sharp edge to his throat, he takes hold of a lock of hair and cuts it away.

EXT. SUSA—CITADEL—DAY

A group of young women are escorted through the main square of the ministerial sector and up the guarded steps to the royal quarter.

Mordecai, sitting upon one of the flanking stairway terraces, issues little more than a glance as he goes about his business, looking over facts and figures.

The on duty officers admire the girls as they go by. Two in particular, THERESH and BIGTHAN, use the distraction to talk—in a foreign language known as Tarshish (Old Turkish).

>THERESH
>(subtitled)
>I am scheduled to stand watch in the
>palace day after tomorrow.

>BIGTHAN
>(subtitled)
>So, we do it then.

Mordecai looks up from his work. He both understands and is interested in what they are saying, but whether this is because he is in league with them or not is left for us to wonder.

>THERESH
>(subtitled)
>I am still not convinced.

>BIGTHAN
>(subtitled)
>Theresh, he is offering a fortune
>enough to last a lifetime and all for one
>moment's work.

Theresh nervously rubs his forehead.

>THERESH
>(subtitled)
>How do you know he can be
>trusted? You do not even know his
>name.

BIGTHAN
                    (subtitled)
Because he has already delivered half of
what he's promised. All you have to do
to earn your share is turn your head
and let me pass.

                    THERESH
                    (subtitled)
And what if by turning my head, I
then find my neck in a twist?

                    BIGTHAN
                    (subtitled)
You won't. By the time the body is
found, we will be well away.

                    THERESH
                    (subtitled)
What if you fail, Bigthan?? Xerxes
rarely sleeps and when he does, it is not
well. If you wake him, it is more than
likely that the only body found will be
yours.

                    BIGTHAN
                    (subtitled)
Then I will have to be quick about it,
won't I?

With all the girls through the gate; the distraction over, the two abruptly end their conversation.

Taking his time, Mordecai collects his things and prepares to enter the gate himself.

EXT. SUSA—HAREM—FRONT COURTYARD—DAY

Esther sits on the steps to the building, surrounded by attendants, a parasol leveled above her royal head.

Below, a SINGER stands before the rest of the king's women. She is an older lady, but the beauty of her voice is enough to cast her as a graceful enchantress.

With her arms stretched out and face raised to the sky, she sings of a lost love. Each bar prompts eyes to glisten, most of all Esther's, who absentmindedly draws a thumb along the bobble of her necklace.

With a breathtaking crescendo, the singer lowers her head. The audience exuberantly CLAPS. Esther wipes a tear away and spots Mordecai passing by the harem gates.

While we can tell he is somewhat taken aback by her prestigious transformation, it is with careful subtlety that he signals her to speak with him, before continuing on his way.

EXT. SUSA—HAREM—FRONT COURTYARD—LATER

While the other women join their usual cliques, Persia's new queen is off on her own.

Seated on the corner bench, Esther anxiously gazes into a cup, waiting for her attendant to finish filling it. Finally, the brim is reached, and she does not hesitate to wave the girl away.

> ESTHER
> Thank you. You are excused.

The girl bows and goes. Through the hedgerow, Mordecai observes this with much interest.

The shot cuts back and forth between them as they speak.

> ESTHER
> (cup close to her lips)
> I can't speak long.

> MORDECAI
> (firm)
> I know.

Esther tilts her head.

> ESTHER
> By your own words, we are to keep
> distance between us.

Mordecai spies the fine trinkets she drips with, the metallic-like threading lining her chiton and the perfect curls of her hair. He barely recognizes her.

> MORDECAI
> Yes, I did, but remember, Hadassah—

Her coal-lined eyes close upon hearing her true name.

> MORDECAI
> (continuing)
> —in keeping hidden the truth of who
> you are, do not bury it so deep that
> you yourself forget.

She is undoubtedly hurt.

> ESTHER
> I never would.

> MORDECAI
> Are you so certain? You had nothing to
> lose before.

> ESTHER
> Yes, I did.

He knows she speaks of him.

ESTHER
Uncle, I thought you wanted this for me.

MORDECAI
I did—I do.

ESTHER
I admit, it is not a hardship to play my role, but know that you are more prized to me than any of this.

MORDECAI
Oh, my dear girl . . . I regret my presumptions. You are the same, gentle creature you have always been. I did not come here to be critical.

ESTHER
What did you want to speak of?

MORDECAI
There are men plotting to assassinate the king.

Shocked, Esther can barely stop herself from turning to the hedgerow.

ESTHER
You must inform his security right away!

MORDECAI
I cannot.

ESTHER
Why??

MORDECAI
Because it was from two of his guards that I overheard the scheme.

ESTHER
Were you seen? Do they suspect you know?

MORDECAI
I was sitting in the king's gate, so yes, they saw me, but whether or not they think me a threat . . . I do not know. They spoke in a foreign tongue— which I happened to recognize.

ESTHER
What are we to do?

MORDECAI
Sights may be set on me, so I have been minding my steps well. There is no way of telling how rooted the conspiracy is.
    (a beat)
Hadassah, you must get word to your husband.

ESTHER
But the decree.

MORDECAI
You are his wife, surely you would be greeted—

ESTHER
He has not called on me since we were wed . . .

She sadly traces the rim of her cup.

ESTHER
Though, this man, Hathach, who has been assigned to me, says—
    (a beat; revelation)
Hathach.

> MORDECAI
> What of him?

> ESTHER
> He reports to the king daily.

> MORDECAI
> Yet you think he would do you harm if you personally went to him?

> ESTHER
> Any favor he may have for me could be wasted if I were to deny his order. Before a single word could breach my lips—I suppose I lack the courage.
> > (a pause)
> I will write a letter for Hathach to deliver. He is an honest man, one I trust implicitly.

> MORDECAI
> Then make haste and, Hadassah?

> ESTHER
> Yes?

> MORDECAI
> You know not what strengths you possess.

INT. SUSA—XERXES' BEDROOM—NIGHT

The room is trashed. Documents litter the floor, tapestries hang precariously from the walls, and the sheets of the bed are tightly twisted, telling of a restless night of tossing and turning.

Away from the clutter, Xerxes, whose hair is now short, sits within the frame of the balcony, somberly staring out into the night. This is a self-imposed exile and, though he does not speak, his lips move in silent reprimand.

A KNOCK sounds from beyond the doors.

                XERXES
        Hathach?

              HATHACH (O.S.)
        Yes, your highness.

                XERXES
        Enter.

HATHACH does so, but Xerxes remains still.

                XERXES
        Do you believe in dreams?

                HATHACH
        My king?

                XERXES
        Do you think they're all symbolic?
        That they only exist to portent what is
        to come, what could be . . . what you
        let pass by?

                HATHACH
        I know not. They are a mystery. Would
        you like me to send word for a mage—

Xerxes suddenly sets his sights on him.

                XERXES
        What of Esther? Has she asked to see
        me?

Hathach shakes his head.

                    XERXES
                Of course not.

                    HATHACH
                Perhaps if she knew you wished to see her—

                    XERXES
                But I don't.

Hathach knows he means, "Not like this."

                    HATHACH
                Well, ah, the queen has asked that I
                bring this to you.

He holds out a message. Xerxes, surprised, sits up and hesitantly takes it from him.

                    HATHACH
                    (continuing)
                Could be telling of her thoughts, and who
                better to report them than herself, right?

Xerxes is entranced by the letter and runs a finger along the seal.

                    XERXES
                    (detached)
                Right. Dismissed.

Hathach goes.

Xerxes clearly misses his new bride, for he stares at the letter for quite some time. He wonders if she has written lovely musings or terrible regrets. Finally, he breaks the wax crest.

Upon first reading, Xerxes is completely bewildered. He rises to his feet and scans it over again, making sure he understood it correctly. Confusion is then taken over by fury.

EXT. SUSA—OUTSKIRTS—NIGHT

Theresh and Bigthan dangle from a gallows. The ropes on which they are stretched unnervingly CREAK as their bodies sway back and forth in the night's breeze.

INT. SUSA—THRONE ROOM—NIGHT

Xerxes is slumped in his throne, rubbing his temples. Hydarnes stands before him with Haman.

          XERXES
  Is it done?

         HYDARNES
  It is. Do you want us to cut them
  down come morning?

          XERXES
  No. Let them swing for as long as the
  rope holds.

          HAMAN
  It was not a plan of their own devise,
  but whoever was the mastermind hasn't
  a name.

          XERXES
  Thoughts?

          HAMAN
    (hesitant)
  There are some still embittered over
  Masistes' death.

          XERXES
  He was admired by many.

         HYDARNES
  It is feasible that the Greeks bought
  these men off . . .

XERXES
But . . . ?

HYDARNES
The truth is, it could be anyone.

XERXES
Even Artabanus?

HYDARNES
There is nothing to implicate him, but perhaps.

HAMAN
Despite what transpired between the two of you, I do not believe him capable of doing such a thing. He is faithful to the empire above all else and would not leave it bereft of its king—especially with no heir capable to succeed.

XERXES
As Artaxerxes is just a child.

HAMAN
My point exactly.

Xerxes has heard enough. He sits up.

XERXES
Hydarnes, go and see to it that this message is heard loud and clear. Should there be any more traitors among us, they will be found out and, when they are, they will not be granted the same leniency as these two enjoyed.

The general tips his head and leaves. Xerxes slumps back down into his seat.

> XERXES
> I suppose I was prophetic in a way. I thought myself a reflection of the empire. So, it is fitting that it should turn on me, as I have turned on myself.

> HAMAN
> No, with all due respect, you are wrong. This was a treacherous—but isolated—assassination attempt, not an uprising. The allegiance of the kingdom has not faltered.

> XERXES
> Nor has yours—ever.

> HAMAN
> And it never will, my king.

> XERXES
> May your word be kept, Haman. May it always be kept.
>   (a beat)
> General Artabazus has sent word to me. It seems one of our informants has been approached by the Spartan, Pausanias.

> HAMAN
> But isn't he the—

> XERXES
> The head of the Greek army, yes.

> HAMAN
> What does he want?

XERXES
My friendship . . . and to that end, he is letting our men go free under the guise of an escape. Apparently, Pausanias has grown weary of the austere. He shares our view—sees Greece as a faithful subject nation, with himself appointed satrap.

HAMAN
Do you believe him?

XERXES
Hydarnes has asked me the same question. The answer is, I don't know, but this was sent along as a symbolic gesture of sorts.

Xerxes pulls out a letter. By the look of it, it has not had the smoothest journey from desk to hand.

XERXES
(extending it to Haman)
Go on.

Haman takes it and begins to read, but only a few lines in, finds himself confused.

HAMAN
These are not his words.

XERXES
No, they're Mardonius's.
(a beat)
I am going to go away for awhile, Haman.

HAMAN
Of course, if you wish to proceed with this—

Xerxes holds up a hand.

> XERXES
> I am in no hurry to. I am, however, in need of a change of scenery.

> HAMAN
> I understand.

> XERXES
> We'll see if you do.

By the look on Xerxes' face, we see he is considering Haman for something important.

INT. SUSA—HAREM—FRONT COURTYARD—DAY

Walking with Hathach, Esther stares through the harem gates as porters pass by with crates and other parcels.

> ESTHER
> For how long?

> HATHACH
> He did not say, but . . .

They both stop.

> ESTHER
> Hathach?

> HATHACH
> You may assume that he will be absent for some time.

> ESTHER
> Another day for which to wait.

                          HATHACH
            My queen?

                          ESTHER
            The day he returns.

They continue their walk.

                          ESTHER
            So, in whose charge is Susa being left?

                          HATHACH
            Our newly appointed prime minister.
                                                      CUT TO:

EXT. SUSA—CITADEL—DAY

We see Haman, followed by his own personal attendants and ensigns, exit the gate to the royal quarter and stop to stand atop the stairs.

The mulling officials below halt their affairs.

He descends the steps and the guards on duty bow; entering and passing through the main square, the officials do, too—revealing the one man who does not—Mordecai.

INT. SUSA—HAMAN'S ESTATE—GREAT ROOM—NIGHT

Tonight, Persia's new prime minister is entertaining a few rich ASSOCIATES and his TEN SONS:

PARSHANDATHA, DALPHON, ASPATHA, PORATHA, ADALIA, ARIDATHA, PARMASHTA, ARISAI, ARIDAI, and VAIZATHA.

The surroundings would suggest they are a well off, established family, but, compared to the prodigious aesthetics found in the palace, these are humble.

A decorative carpet, topped with pillows, serves as their 'table'. An assortment of goods are sprawled before them, and while they indulge their hunger for food and talk, ZERESH, Haman's wife, makes her rounds refilling drinks.

>   ASSOCIATE 1
>   Well, congratulations, Haman—to you
>   and your sons.
>
>   ASSOCIATE 2
>   May many good things come of it.
>
>   HAMAN
>   For us all.
>
>   DALPHON
>   Indeed, father.
>
>   ASSOCIATE 3
>   So, let's see if I have this right?

He begins to point around the room, naming off Haman's sons.

>   ASSOCIATE 3
>   Dalphon, Parshandatha, Aspatha,
>   Poratha, Adalia, ah, um . . .
>
>   ARIDATHA
>   Aridatha.
>
>   ASSOCIATE 3
>   Aridatha, yes.
>
>   ARIDATHA
>   (points to brother next to him)
>   Parmashta.
>
>   ASSOCIATE 3
>   (getting back into the groove)
>   Ah, yes, thank you. Parmashta,
>   Arisai, Aridai, and, finally . . .
>   finally . . .

                    VAISATHA
Vaizatha.

                    ASSOCIATE 3
Vaizatha. See, it isn't so hard to remember.

                    HAMAN
                    (laughing)
Yes, it is. Truly, I have a hard time remembering them all myself.

                    DALPHON
Be advised, if ever at a loss, we all answer to 'you there'.

                    ASSOCIATE 3
Noted.

                    HAMAN
Zeresh?

                    ZERESH
Yes, husband?

He holds up his cup.

                    ZERESH
Of course.

She musters her way over to him and refills his cup.

                    ASSOCIATE 1
So, are you content with ten, or had you hoped for more?

Horrified by the thought, Zeresh nearly spills the wine.

                    ZERESH
                    (to herself)
Dear me, no.

> HAMAN
>
> Zeresh?
>
> ZERESH
>
> Yes?

He motions for her to put the pitcher down and sit. She does.

> HAMAN
> (to associate 1)
> I'm quite satisfied with my sons—

Unbeknownst to his guests, Zeresh hits him on the back.

> HAMAN
> —and my wife.

She offers a gracious smile.

> ASSOCIATE 2
> And now you're prime minister.
>
> HAMAN
> Life is excellent, gentlemen. Though, that isn't to say it couldn't be better— for everyone.
>
> ASSOCIATE 1
> Yes, we've been so focused on this war with Greece all these years and then for it to end the way it did . . .
>
> ASSOCIATE 2
> No one was prepared.
>
> ASSOCIATE 1
> No, because in the beginning, everything panned out as anticipated. We were welcomed into the country, Athens was crushed . . .

HAMAN
I think it really came down to Mardonius—when he fell, the army did.

ASSOCIATE 3
You think if he had lived we would have won?

HAMAN
It's certainly possible. They say we were winning until he was struck down. You know what disturbs me most, though?

ASSOCIATE 2
What's that?

HAMAN
Mycale. Now, our garrison there was taken for one reason, and it wasn't the Athenians or the Spartans—it was those traitorous Ionians. Think about it. They turned on them like savages.

ASSOCIATE 1
Well, it wasn't so shocking.

HAMAN
No, it wasn't. They aren't one of us and that is why it was so easy for them to pledge their swords to us one moment, only to then cut our throats with them the next. That's why . . .

ASSOCIATE 1
Haman?

HAMAN
Well, I just think, in our pursuit of unity, we've begun to lose our own identity. Look at Susa for example—all these Jews. They should have all gone back to where they came from when Cyrus freed them. Instead, they've migrated throughout the provinces—peddling their wares, stealing patron and profit from the domestic businessmen. Oh, and this intermarrying? Even Judea is suffering for it.

ASSOCIATE 2
Really?

DELPHON
Oh yes. During the captivity, or whatever they care to call it—the Jews left behind began marrying outside their race. That's where these Samaritans came from.

ASSOCIATE 2
I did not know that.

PARSHANDATHA
Yes, and ever since their release, the returned Jews have been complaining about them and every other sect that moved into the region during their absence.

HAMAN
Yet the Jews who remain here, because they're too good to go home and
(MORE)

                    HAMAN (cont'd)
            associate with these halfbreeds and
            foreign tribes, expect us to accept them
            cutting in to our affairs, our
            provisions—as if they are entitled? They
            want acceptance, but, yet, they do not
            accept. They don't act like us, think like
            us . . . Forget enemies abroad—

The scene begins to morph, as do the present characters . . .

                                                DISSOLVE TO:

EXT. SUSA—HAMAN'S ESTATE—COURTYARD—DAY

473 B.C.

Peacocks shimmy about a large reflecting pool, undaunted by the numerous guests standing about. Every eye is on Haman's impressive house, where he addresses them from a portico.

                    HAMAN (O.S.)
                      (continuing)
            The true threat to our future is right here.

By the looks of things, Haman has grown insanely wealthy. He and his surrounding sons drip in riches, as does his lounging wife—who raises her cup for one of the many attendants to fill.

                    HAMAN
                      (continuing)
            We are like the flower, they like the
            weed, and I tell you, sirs, they are
            taking a strangle hold on our roots and
            obscuring the sun from our face. If we
            do not pull them soon, I fear we will
            be altogether overwhelmed.

From the crowd, one of the guests calls out.

> **HAMAN GUEST 1**
> Oh, I agree. I just came from Babylon where they are experiencing the same problem.

> **HAMAN**
> You're not the first to tell me. Babylon, Susa, Ecbatana, they seem to be everywhere but where they should be, and just like the treasonous Ionians, they could raise an insurrection at any time. In light of this, we cannot allow their numbers to further grow. The pattern, set years ago, continues unabated—they come, open their businesses, keep their services at minimal cost and thus undercut the rightful, native sons. Then they tell their brethren to come, join them, so as to share in the good fortune—and so on and so forth.

Another man speaks up.

> **HAMAN GUEST 2**
> A friend of mine lost his business for this very reason!

> **HAMAN**
> You see!

Then another...

> **HAMAN GUEST 3**
> Yes, my neighbor—he's a Jew and his property is larger than mine!

                    HAMAN
          I told you.

. . . and yet another.

                    HAMAN GUEST 4
          They don't participate in any of our
          rites!

                    HAMAN
          Do you seek shelter in a man's
          house and then refuse his way of
          living?

We now hear a number of disgruntled cries from the crowd . . .

                    HAMAN GUESTS
          They have no place here! They should
          be forced to leave! Make them go!
          Leave! Go!

                    HAMAN
          Agreed, and, one day, I hope to make
          them do just that.

                    HAMAN GUEST 1
          Why one day?

                    HAMAN GUEST 2
          Name it!

                    HAMAN
          Name it?

                    HAMAN GUEST 2
          Yes! So, in doing, you confirm it!

Haman is rather taken with the idea. He shares a look with his sons, who are just as enthused, before turning back to the gathered.

> HAMAN
> Then let the lots be cast!

> CUT TO:

EXT. SUSA—MARKET PLACE—DAY

Members of Susa's Jewish community are gathered before their businesses to talk. They are on the periphery of the bartering crowds, as it would seem they are being boycotted.

> SUSIAN JEW 1
> You can feel it in every look of disdain.

> SUSIAN JEW 2
> In every look not spared you.

> SUSIAN JEW 3
> It's like standing on the cliff's edge
> waiting to be pushed. Why doesn't the
> council do something—

> SUSIAN JEW 1
> Indifference. Besides, it isn't a crime to
> refuse business. It is a choice.

> SUSIAN JEW 2
> So, you think it's true?

> SUSIAN JEW 4
> That our gregarious prime minister has
> set a day for our destruction?

> SUSIAN JEW 2
> Yes. Do you?

> SUSIAN JEW 1
> Even if he has, the king would never
> allow it to pass . . . would he?

> SUSIAN JEW 3
> I can scarcely remember when it was he
> last visited.

> SUSIAN JEW 2
> There are rumors . . . that his mind is
> lost . . .

No one wants to believe this.

> SUSIAN JEW 4
> Rumors—only rumors.

> SUSIAN JEW 3
> Then why does he not come back?

> SUSIAN JEW 1
> Do not despair. He may yet come
> soon, yes?

> SUSIAN JEW 4
> Yes. We have not been abandoned.

We pull back, reinforcing the truth that these people are so few, among so many.

EXT. GREECE—ATHENS—RURAL THEATRON—DAY

Aristides sits with the charismatic PERICLES, 22, on one of the many wooden tiers of the theatron.

In the orchestra before them, members of the fifty-man CHORUS—STROPHE and ANTISTROPHE—prepare their cloaks and masks. Standing upon the stage, holding his own costume and pointing out instructions, is the famed father of Greek tragedy, AESCHYLUS, 52.

The sun beams off his bald head. Pericles laughs.

PERICLES
Aeschylus's brilliant mind.

ARISTIDES
Yes, I see. So, you're funding the production, Pericles?

PERICLES
(nods)
We hope to win the City Dionysia next year.

ARISTIDES
Why didn't you enter this year's?

PERICLES
I wondered the same thing, but Aeschylus . . . he has a message he feels must be conveyed. So, he continues to refine it so as to define it.

ARISTIDES
A message about . . . ?

PERICLES
Pride and humility . . . and those nuances in between. Though, a more simplistic view would be that it is merely about the battle of Salamis.

Pericles sees SOPHOCLES, 23, enter the theatron and take a seat on one of the upper tiers.

PERICLES
Ah, Sophocles! Greetings.

SOPHOCLES
Greetings to you, Pericles.

PERICLES
Come to see the master at work?

SOPHOCLES
Indeed.

PERICLES
(turning back to Aristides)
Sophocles is a rather talented bard himself. Who knows, in time, he might rise to the genius Aeschylus has.
(a beat)
I want to thank you for coming today. I know leading the confederacy keeps your days busy.

ARISTIDES
That it does.

PERICLES
But father and I agree, it has been exceedingly successful.

ARISTIDES
Beyond our expectations.

PERICLES
I doubt it would be so, had Sparta not relinquished control to us.

ARISTIDES
They didn't want to risk another one of their commanders being medized.

PERICLES
Do you really think Pausanias was corrupt?

ARISTIDES
Well, when Cimon and I were commissioned to Byzantium, we found his demeanor shocking. There he was, dressed like a Persian—being treated as if a king, and a despot at that. Soldiers were being denied rations, whipped . . . and when I complained of this to Pausanias, he turned to me with the most irate look and barked that he was not at leisure to talk.

PERICLES
Pausanias was trying to set himself up as dictator, yes?

ARISTIDES
That is the concern we relayed to the ephors. They recalled him and, though he was found not guilty, relieved him of duty. The allies were so desperate for a command change, that Cimon's equity and wise policy were all it took to win him the post.

PERICLES
Pausanias was brought before the ephors a second time, though, wasn't he?

ARISTIDES
From his place in Colonae.

PERICLES
Near Troy?

ARISTIDES
The same.

                    PERICLES
So, what were those charges?

                    ARISTIDES
Apparently, there was speculation that Pausanias was planning to incite the helots to revolt—which could not be proven. So, once again . . .

                    PERICLES
He was freed to go.

                    ARISTIDES
Returned to Colonae and, as far as I know, is still there.

                    PERICLES
But, you didn't answer the question. Do you believe he was—could still be—

                    ARISTIDES
Allied with Xerxes? I believe so, but without any proof . . .

Pericles shakes his head.

                    PERICLES
                    (rhetorical)
To go from the field of battle into the hand of the enemy . . . how could he do it?

                    ARISTIDES
Because there are some men who are allied, above all others, to their own self interests.

PERICLES
And those who assist them to that end
so as to thereby obtain their own.

Aristides mulls over this troublesome thought.

PERICLES
Aristides—

Pericles is cut off as Aeschylus CLAPS his hands and the rehearsal begins.

PERICLES
Ah, here we go.

IN THE ORCHESTRA

The chorus members, as one unit, take their places.

CHORUS
While o'er the fields of Greece the embattled troops/ Of Persia march with delegated sway/ We o'er their rich and gold abounding seats/ Hold faithful our firm guard; to this high charge/ Xerxes, our royal lord, the imperial son/ Of Darius, chose our honor'd age/ But for the king's return and his arm'd host—

ON THE STAGE

Aeschylus raises his hands.

AESCHYLUS
Stop! Hold on, hold on.

ON THE TIERS

Pericles shrugs.

> **PERICLES**
> Never satisfied.
> (a beat)
> My, these past few years have been interesting. We owe a great deal to Cimon.

> **ARISTIDES**
> Our forces could not ask for a better leader.

> **PERICLES**
> When I heard what happened on the Thracian coast . . .

> **ARISTIDES**
> Oh, when they besieged Eion?

> **PERICLES**
> And the Persian chief there burned the fortress to the ground—along with all those in it—rather than cede defeat . . . Yes. Terrible.
> (a beat)
> So, Cimon should be returning soon, no? I heard those Dolopian pirates who were harassing our ships in the Aegean have finally been denied their base in Scyros.

> **ARISTIDES**
> You heard correctly.

> **PERICLES**
> Wonderful news—

Once again, Pericles is interrupted by Aeschylus's CLAPPING.

> PERICLES
> Oh, here we go—I think.

ON THE STAGE

> AESCHYLUS
> (to chorus)
> Now, let us begin with strophe—On
> the line, "Now has the peopled . . ."

IN THE ORCHESTRA

The strophe section of the chorus take up their masks and begin to move before the thymele.

> STROPHE
> Now has the peopled Asia's warlike
> lord/ By land, by sea, with foot, with
> horse/ Resistless in his rapid course/
> O'er the realms his warring thousands
> pour'd/ Now his intrepid chiefs
> surveys/ And glitt'ring like a god his
> radiant state displays.

Now the antistrophe rally.

> ANTISTROPHE
> Fierce as the dragon scaled in gold/
> Through the deep files he darts his
> glowing eye/ And pleased their order to
> behold/ His gorgeous standard blazing
> to the sky/ Rolls onward his Assyrian
> car/ Directs the thunder of the war/
> Bids the wing'd arrows' iron storm
> (MORE)

> ANTISTROPHE(cont'd)
> advance/ Against the slow and cumbrous lance/ What shall withstand the torrent of his sway/ When dreadful o'er the yielding shores/ The impetuous tide of battle roars/ And sweeps the weak opposing mounds away? So Persia, with resistless might/ Rolls her unnumber'd hosts of heroes to the fight.

ON THE TIERS

Pericles turns to Aristides. He sees that his eyes are glossy.

LATER . . .

ON THE STAGE

We see the ATOSSA PERSONAE.

> ATOSSA PERSONAE
> . . . an eagle I behold/ Fly to the altar of the sun; aghast/ I stood, my friends, and speechless; when a hawk/ With eager speed runs thither, furious cuffs/ The eagle with his wings, and with his talons/ Unplumes his head; meantime the imperial bird/ Cowers to the blows defenseless. Dreadful this/ To me who saw it, and to you that hear./ My son, let conquest crown his arms, would shine/ With dazzling glory; but should fortune frown,/ The state indeed presumes not to arraign/ His sovereignty; yet how, his honor lost,/ How shall he sway the scepter of this land?

LATER...

SLIGHTLY OVERLAPPING

On the stage, Atossa is joined by the MESSENGER PERSONAE.

> MESSENGER PERSONAE
> Wo to the towns through Persia's peopled realms!/ Wo to the land of Persia, once the port/ Of boundless wealth, how is thy glorious state/ Vanish'd at once, and all thy spreading honors/ Fall'n lost! Ah me! Unhappy is his task/ That bears unhappy tidings: but constraint/ Compels me to relate this tale of wo/ Persians, the whole barbaric host is fall'n.

The chorus, united, begins to chant as we see a—

MONTAGE OF COALESCING FOOTAGE (SCENERY)

—Of Greece

—Of the Aegean Sea

—Of the coast of Asia Minor

—Rushing across the empire's diverse landscape, from mountainous forests, to desert, then fertile plains . . .

—Into the tense streets of Susa . . .

> CHORUS (V.O.)
> Wo; wo is me! Then has the iron storm,/ That darken'd from the realms of Asia, pour'd/ In vain its arrowy shower on sacred Greece . . .

                    STROPHE (V.O.)
          Through Susa's palaces with loud
          lament/ By their soft hands their veils
          all rent,/ The copious tear the virgins
          pour,/ That trickles their bare bosoms
          o'er./ From her sweet couch up starts
          the widow'd bride—

                                                    CUT TO:

EXT. SUSA—HAREM—BACK COURTYARD—DAY

Esther walks along the hedgerow, running her hand against the greenery as she goes.

                    STROPHE (V.O.)
                      (continuing)
          Her lord's loved image rushing on her
          soul,/ Throws the rich ornaments of
          youth aside . . .

The necklace slips from her neck and falls to the ground unnoticed.

Rain begins to fall.

                    STROPHE (V.O.)
                      (continuing)
          Her grief's not causeless; for the
          mighty slain/ Our melting tears
          demand, and sorrow-soften'd strain.

                                                    CUT TO:

EXT. SUSA—CITADEL—DAY

The rain continues . . .

                    ANTISTROPHE (V.O.)
          Now her wailings wide despair/ Pour
          these exhausted regions o'er

Mordecai stands beneath the treasury's overhang watching a litter being carried through the square.

> ANTISTROPHE (V.O.)
> Xerxes, ill-fated, led the war/ Xerxes,
> ill-fated, leads no more . . .

We realize that it is not Xerxes on the litter, but Haman.

CUT TO:

EXT. GREECE—ATHENS—RURAL THEATRON—SUNSET

All eyes are—

ON THE SKENE

Where the XERXES PERSONAE, dressed in rent robes, stands.

> XERXES PERSONAE
> Ah me, how sudden have the storms of
> fate,/ Beyond all thought, all
> apprehension, burst/ On my devoted
> head! O fortune, fortune!/ With what
> relentless fury hath thy hand/ Hurled
> desolation on the Persian race!

CUT TO:

EXT. PERSIA—THE ROYAL ROAD—SUNSET

We see the king's caravan en route.

> XERXES PERSONAE (V.O.)
> (continuing)
> Wo unsupportable! The torturing thought/
> Of our lost youth comes rushing on my
> mind/ And sinks me to the ground . . .

INSIDE THE KING'S CARRIAGE

The sight of the sun sinking into the horizon sparks in Xerxes' eyes through the window cover's narrow slit.

> XERXES PERSONAE (V.O.)
> Weep, weep their loss, and lead me to my house;/ Answer my grief with grief, an ill return/ Of ills for ills. Yet once more raise that strain/ Lamenting my misfortunes; beat thy breast,/ Strike, heave the groan; awake the Mysian strain/ To notes of loudest wo; rend thy rich robes,/ Pluck up thy beard, tear off thy hoary locks,/ And battle thine eyes in tears, thus through the streets;/ Solemn and slow with sorrow lead my steps;/ Lead me to my house, and wail the fate of Persia.

EXT. SUSA—CITY—DAY

We see one of the Jewish proprietors jovially approaching his peers.

> SUSIAN JEW 1
> It's true! The king returned last night.

> SUSIAN JEW 2
> Then may the reign of Haman finally come to an end.

EXT. SUSA—STUDY COURTYARD—DAY

Haman finds Xerxes, back turned, standing statuesque. Although he's been emboldened by the title of prime minister, in the presences of Persia's king, all presumption is lost.

Xerxes turns and Haman feels oh-so-small.

HAMAN
You—you're—your highness—you're back.

XERXES
Haman.

HAMAN
This, this is cause for a grand—

XERXES
Pleasantries are unnecessary—and, before you ask, my trip was fine.

HAMAN
Good—excellent.

XERXES
I just met with the council to review your dealings.

HAMAN
You did not find them satisfactory?

XERXES
No.

Haman shrinks further.

XERXES
(continuing)
On the contrary, all looks to be in order. You've done well in my absence.

HAMAN

(extreme relief)
Thank you. Thank you, my king. Now that you've returned—

XERXES
I don't know that I will be staying on
in Susa long. My son and I may go on
to Pasargadae. So, keep to what you've
been doing.

HAMAN
As though you're not here?

With a rueful, inward laugh and a rub of the brow, Xerxes turns; knowing all too well that, in all the ways that matter, he—isn't—'here'.

XERXES
Yes.

Spotting an object just peeking out from beneath the hedgerow, he goes to investigate.

XERXES
(distracted)
As long as there are no pressing issues, I
see no reason to upset the routine
you've all settled in to.

Meanwhile, Haman tries to work up the nerve to request the unthinkable. He has been waiting for this opportunity and, overcome by the fact that it is finally here, his entire demeanor changes; he suddenly looks as though this is the first time he has ever held audience with Xerxes.

HAMAN
(too quiet for Xerxes to hear)
Well, there is . . . there is an issue which
has been a cause of increasing concern,
which I feel can no longer be ignored.
(louder)
Now, it isn't anything that I cannot
handle, however, to do what is
necessary requires an official king's
decree. There is a certain people—

Xerxes picks the item up. It is Esther's necklace. He begins to brush the soil off of it and is transfixed by his emerging reflection.

> HAMAN
> (continuing; rambling)
> —dispersed and scattered among the peoples in all the provinces of your kingdom whose customs are different from those of all other people and who do not obey the king's laws; it is not in the king's best interest to tolerate them. If it pleases the king, let a decree be issued to destroy them . . .

Haman waits for Xerxes to say something, but he doesn't. Eager for approval, he takes a few steps closer to him.

> HAMAN
> . . . and I will put ten thousand talents of silver into the royal treasury for the men who carry out this business.

Xerxes, who has not listened closely, only registered the very beginning and the very end of Haman's appeal. He tucks the necklace in his robes, takes off his royal ring, and turns to face him.

> XERXES
> Keep the money and do with the people as you please.

Xerxes hands the ring to him and starts off. Haman is astonished that it has been so easily relinquished, for with this ring he can pass decrees as if the king himself. With a malevolent glint in his eye, he grins.

CUT TO:

MONTAGE—THE EDICT

—Dozens of scribes write down the dictation of Haman.

—Seated at a table, Haman applies the king's seal to copies of his own, malicious edict.

—Copies are passed to over one-hundred couriers.

—The couriers head off in different directions, riding across Persia.

—Haman, smug and reveling in power, sits at the head of the council hall's table.

—Hathach gestures for Esther leave her quarters and come with him.

—Xerxes, unaware of the tyrannical order that has been written in his name, remains secluded in his chambers. He appears anxious, waiting for Esther— and then changes his mind about seeing her at all. He opens one of the doors and speaks with the chamberlain.

—Before Xerxes' quarters, the chamberlain stops Hathach and Esther, notifying them of the change in plans. They turn around and walk away.

—Xerxes goes to the bed and lies down.

The following is heard over the montage:

> HAMAN (V.O.)
> Like the windswept seeds of a weed which corrupts the very soil it feeds on, there is an enemy scattered across the empire—an ever-growing presence which takes our land, but not our ways. This obstinacy is an insult, an offense, a treason and is soon to be put to an end. Let them not jerk their chins and snub us longer. The lots have been cast. The fates have spoken. The future is set. On the thirteenth day of the month of Adar, it is decreed that those of the nation of the Jews, whether man or woman, young or old, are to be destroyed and their estates seized. In the name of King Xerxes—so shall it be done.

INT. SUSA—XERXES' QUARTERS—NIGHT

Xerxes, still lying on his bed, is stirred from his thoughts by a KNOCK.

                    XERXES
               Come in.

Artaxerxes, now ten years old, but with the presence of one wise beyond their years, enters. Xerxes sits up.

                    ARTAXERXES
               You wanted to see me, father?

                    XERXES
               Come here. I have a question for you.

                    ARTAXERXES
               Well, may I then have the answer.

Xerxes directs his son to sit beside him.

                    XERXES
               Do you remember the story of
               Nebuchadnezzar? About his dream?

                    ARTAXERXES
               And the interpreter?

                    XERXES
               Yes.

                    ARTAXERXES
               I remember. Nebuchadnezzar had a
               dream about a glorious tree, from
               which one could see the whole world
               and whose branches offered shelter and
               comfort for a multitude, but an order
               was issued for it to be cut down,
               leaving only its stump and roots. When
                    (MORE)

ARTAXERXES(cont'd)
She asked the interpreter what it meant, he was told that he would be stripped of his glory and sent to wander in the wilderness for seven years.

XERXES
Like an animal.

ARTAXERXES
(trying to remember the exact words)
And he was told, 'the stump of the tree with its roots means that your kingdom will be restored to you when you acknowledge that Heaven rules.' And he was also advised—

XERXES
(more to himself)
I once dreamt, a long, long time ago, before the war, that I was crowned with a the branch of an olive tree. Its boughs grew till the whole world was covered by them and then . . .

ARTAXERXES
What, father?

XERXES
It just disappeared, right off my head. My magi told me it meant that I would rule the world over.
(a ponderous beat)
Go on, he was also advised?

Though a bit perplexed by his father's pensiveness, Artaxerxes continues as requested.

                    ARTAXERXES
            'Renounce your sins by doing what is
            right, and your wickedness by being
            kind to the oppressed. It may be that
            then your prosperity will continue.'

EXT. SUSA—CITADEL GATES—DAY

A hand slowly slides down the posted edict in Susa. Mordecai tearfully stares at the words and the king's seal. He can not believe Xerxes is capable of such treachery.

                    MORDECAI
            Haman . . .

He turns around to face those behind him: Jewish men, women and children. All, including himself, are dressed in sackcloth and covered in ash. Many are WEEPING. Others, gathered before the gates, try to enter, but are repeatedly pushed back by the guards standing duty.

                    SUSIAN JEWISH CROWD
            You cannot do this! Please! What have
            we done?! Xerxes!

                    GUARDS
            Get back! There is no entrance! Go
            back to your houses!

In the background, on horseback, is General Hydarnes. He is extremely disturbed by the sight, empathetic to the tearful. Protecting the king, however, is his duty. Consternated, he watches as the crowd continues to push and attempts to keep his soldiers level-headed.

                    HYDARNES
            Easy! Careful!

One of the guards pushes a WOMAN back with a little too much force. She falls to her knees.

> HYDARNES
> Soldier! Mind your muscle!

Mordecai assists her up. She puts her head on his shoulder and cries.

> JEWISH WOMAN
> Why is this happening? Why??

> MORDECAI
> Shh . . . Shh . . . Do not fear and
> doubt me not. We will be delivered
> from this.

He stares at the sky above.

INT. SUSA—ESTHER'S QUARTERS—DAY

Two of Esther's attendant girls are busy making her bed.

> ESTHER'S ATTENDANT 1
> You know that Jew official who always
> refuses to bow to Haman?

> ESTHER'S ATTENDANT 2
> (offers a laugh; nods)
> Surprising that he's kept his job—and
> head—all these years.

> ESTHER (O.S.)
> Perhaps because this . . . Jew . . . is the
> same man who once saved the king's life.

Both girls stop what they're doing, turn and, seeing the queen between the doors, bow.

> ESTHER
> (concerned)
> Why do you speak of him?

> ESTHER'S ATTENDANT 1
> My queen, there is a crowd outside the gate, all dressed in sackcloth and ash, weeping and wailing, and he is among them.

This news is clearly distressing to Esther.

> ESTHER
> Why? For what reason do they mourn?

> ESTHER'S ATTENDANT 1
> I know not.

Esther hurries out of the room.

EXT. SUSA—CITADEL GATES—DAY

At the behest of Esther, Hathach goes to find Mordecai, who he finds standing against the wall among a tumultuous sea of sorrowful faces.

Hathach exits the gate, descends the steps and tries his best to push through the frustrated guards who are still trying to keep the amassed crowd back. Even Hydarnes seems to be at his wits' end; preoccupied at the other end of the gate.

> HATHACH
> Let me through! Let me through!

He manages to pass the uniformed line and reaches for Mordecai across the shoulders of the distraught—

> HATHACH
> You, you there!

—and manages to draw him close enough to talk.

> HATHACH
> Are you the one they call Mar-duka?

MORDECAI
Mordecai—I am.

HATHACH
My name is Hathach. Hadassah has sent me to speak with you.

Mordecai is surprised that this man knows the true name of the queen.

MORDECAI
Hadassah?

HATHACH
Yes. She wishes to know what has happened.

MORDECAI
Haman has written a decree in the name of King Xerxes to destroy the race of the Jews. He even promised to pay ten-thousand talents to the royal treasury for it to be followed through.

Hathach, flustered with the ebb and flow of the crowd, tightens his grasp on Mordecai as the treasurer reaches up to the wall and rips down a copy of the edict posted there.

HATHACH
You can't—

Hathach sternly shakes his head as Mordecai tries to hand him the paper.

HATHACH
That is treason!

MORDECAI
It is, and that is why you must take it to her. Please. Take it to Hadassah, explain what has happened. Urge her to go before the king to beg for mercy and plead with him for her people.

Mordecai holds it out to him again and, reluctantly, Hathach takes it. The moment he does, he is seemingly swallowed back toward the gates, but never does he avert the 'what have you gotten me into' stare.

CUT TO:

INT. SUSA—ESTHER'S QUARTERS—DUSK

Esther sits on her lounge and observes the city.

> ESTHER (V.O.)
> All the king's officials and the people of the royal provinces know that for any man or woman who approaches the king in the inner court without being summoned the king has but one law: that he be put to death. The only exception to this is for the king to extend the gold scepter to him and spare his life. But thirty days have passed since I was called to go to the king.

CUT TO:

EXT. SUSA—CITADEL GATES—DUSK

Mordecai remains with the crowd, staring off at the prodigious buildings in the distance.

> MORDECAI (V.O.)
> Do not think that because you are in the king's house you alone of all the Jews will escape. For if you remain silent at this time, relief and deliverance for the Jews will arise from another place, but you and your father's family will perish. And who knows but that you have come to royal position for such a time as this?

INT. SUSA—ESTHER'S QUARTERS—NIGHT

Tears roll down Esther's face. She gasps and leans forward, cupping her own mouth to stifle the sound. Hathach regards her sympathetically her as he hands her a cloth.

> HATHACH
> To dry your tears.

She wipes her face and attempts to blink away the sting of her eyes.

> ESTHER
> They are not mine alone, though a
> thousand could be shed and not a thing
> they would do. They're worthless.

Esther looks around at the finery, the decadence of her surroundings. She observes the jewelry adorning her wrists, her fingers, the very robe she wears.

> HATHACH
> My queen?

She is a stranger to her own self, a dressed up doll. Lowering her face into her hands, she sighs before turning in her seat to face him.

> ESTHER
> Hathach, take word back to him. Tell him
> what he has asked of me, I will do, but I
> must ask something of him in return.

> HATHACH
> What is it?

> ESTHER
> Faith.

CUT TO:

MONTAGE—THREE DAYS AND THREE NIGHTS

—In secret, Mordecai speaks before a crowd of his kindred.

—The native citizens go about their daily routines in Susa.

—The Jewish pray and fast behind closed doors.

—In her room, a poorly dressed Esther turns away food.

—Haman is blissfully unaware of their plans, as he feasts, drinks and laughs with a group of nobles.

INT/EXT. SUSA—ESTHER'S QUARTERS—BEFORE SUNRISE

Standing on the balcony, Esther's pallor looks cool against the receding moonlight. She has not eaten or had anything to drink in three days and is quite weak. In lieu of her beautiful robes, she wears a simple shift. Her hair hangs messily about her face, looking as though it has not been combed since the fast began. The queen's tired eyes search the city in the distance as she tries to remember that, though she feels alone, there are many people counting on her to be brave.

Slowly, she relinquishes her hold on the balcony's railing and slides to her knees. Clasping her hands, she lowers her head and closes her eyes. She stays in this silent refrain for a while, till, finally, her eyes set their sights on the waning night sky and the twinkling stars above.

> **ESTHER**
> Please grant me courage.

Two female attendants, looking nearly as worn as she, enter the quarters and head for the balcony. One carries an exquisite gown, the other a brush. The latter puts a gentle hand on Esther's shoulder.

> ESTHER'S ATTENDANT 1
> My queen, might you not reconsider
> your visit? You have not eaten or so
> much as had a drop to drink in these
> three days.

> ESTHER
> Nor have you. Thank you.

> ESTHER'S ATTENDANT 2
> We are fine, but you intend to . . .

> ESTHER'S ATTENDANT 1
> Would it not be better to wait and
> regain your strength?

> ESTHER
> (standing)
> I am at my strongest now.

> ESTHER'S ATTENDANT 1
> What of his edict? He could—

> ESTHER
> I will go before the king today and if I
> perish, I perish.

Esther waveringly steps into the room, using the walls to support herself as she goes. With no more protestations left to utter, the attendants follow her.

INT. SUSA—XERXES' THRONE ROOM—DAY

Xerxes is reclined upon his throne, a leg draped over its arm and a hand at his brow. As if a baton, he slowly turns the scepter in his other hand, watching firelight dance off of it. The beams ricochet against his eyes with each twist.

The sound of FOOTSTEPS rattles him out of his lethargy. He sits up and sits tall, waiting to see who it is that has dared to ignore his law. The intrusion, it would seem, is not welcomed as the muscle of his jaw flickers bemusedly.

The footfall grows louder and he notes its discordant rhythm. Perplexed, he edges forward in his seat. Shadowed figures begin to emerge from the depths of the room. Then, all is revealed.

There, blanketed by torchlight, is Esther in all her royal splendor. The attendant girls flank her and, though unnoticeable to him, are holding her up from behind. Her eyes denote a suppressed fear as she is assisted to the throne. The young woman knows that the moment of truth is at hand and her mouth dries with each unsteady step.

Stopping before Xerxes, she forces herself to look up at him. What she finds is an expression that cannot be discerned. To her, an eternity seems to pass and she waits, hoping for one little sign of hope.

Finally, he stands, bathing her in his shadow. To her relief, he brandishes a heartfelt smile and extends the scepter in clemency. Weakly, she places a gentle kiss atop it before taking a wobbly step back to peer up at her husband.

Xerxes' smile diminishes as disorientation takes her, causing her eyes to flutter and her legs to slowly give way. The girls steady and keep her from descending to the floor, while the king edges forward.

Esther regains her strength, though he remains concerned.

We see, as their exchange progresses, that it is what they are not saying that speaks volumes.

> XERXES
> What is it, Queen Esther? What is . . .
> (increasingly overwhelmed by her presence)
> . . . your request? Even up to half the
> kingdom it will be granted.

She, too, is enamored.

>   ESTHER
>   If it pleases the king . . .
>   (a beat)
>   . . . let the king, together with Haman,
>   come today to a banquet I have
>   prepared for him.

Xerxes is puzzled by her invitation, but intrigued.

>   XERXES
>   (to one of the girls)
>   Bring Haman at once, so that we may
>   do what Esther asks.

INT. SUSA—PALACE—PRIVATE BANQUET HALL—SUNSET

Seated on couches around a table boasting an abundance of fine fare, Xerxes, Esther, and Haman drink wine. The latter looks so out of place, as husband and wife only have eyes for one another.

>   HAMAN
>   My king, it is a delight to be here.
>   Please allow me to extend my most
>   sincere gratitude for the invitation.

>   XERXES
>   It is the queen you should thank.

Wonder takes Haman over as he sets sights on Esther.

>   XERXES
>   (continuing)
>   She specifically asked for your
>   company.

                    HAMAN
Though I am humbled, may I ask, my
queen, what so fine a thing I have done
to be honored in such a way, for if it
will keep me in your good graces, I
shall always be mindful of it?

                    XERXES
I have been curious to know this, as well.

                    ESTHER
                 (to Xerxes)
He has worked so diligently since his
appointment and with such boldness,
that I felt his efforts should be—
                 (looking at Haman)
—recognized.

Placing a hand atop his heart, Haman tips his head in thanks. Xerxes holds up his drink. Esther, meanwhile, reaches into her robes and pulls forth the folded edict.

                    XERXES
And they are. You have done well,
Haman.

                    HAMAN
Your compliment is a gift in and of
itself.

                    XERXES
Speaking of gifts . . . There must be
something else you want.

Xerxes sets his cup down and takes Esther's hands—unaware of the bombshell held in her grasp. She is caught off guard by his touch and finds herself frozen by his stare.

                    XERXES
        Now what is your petition? It will be
        given you. And what is your request? Even
        up to half the kingdom, it will be granted.

                    ESTHER
        My petition and my request is this—

She takes in the sight of his hands atop her own. What she is about to say will very likely cost her everything.

                    ESTHER
        If the king regards me with favor and if
        it pleases the king to grant my petition
        and fulfill my request . . .

Esther glances at Haman, back to her hands—then back to her husband. If only they had more time . . .

                    XERXES
        . . . let the king and Haman come
        tomorrow to the banquet I will prepare
        for them. Then I will answer the king's
        question.

Xerxes raises her hands and plants a kiss on each.

                    XERXES
        Then tomorrow it is.

EXT. SUSA—CITADEL GATES—DUSK

Haman and his ensigns exit. Mordecai sits against the wall, still dressed in sackcloth, beneath another copy of the edict. There are guards posted, but since he keeps to himself, they let him be. Haman, however, is not so accommodating. He holds up a hand and brings everyone to a halt.

                              HAMAN
               Well, Mordecai, how pleasant to see
               you. So, still in protest, hmm?
                        (gesturing around)
               A lonely one at that.

                            MORDECAI
               Oh, but I am never alone.

Haman and his ensigns share a chuckle.

                              HAMAN
               Is that right? I don't see any of your
               rabble keeping you company. You
               should go share what time you have
               left together with them.

                            MORDECAI
               It is not in short supply.

                              HAMAN
               Then your memory must be. Look
               above your head and refresh it, why
               don't you?

Mordecai says nothing and this grates on Haman's nerves. He waves his men on.

INT. SUSA—HAMAN'S ESTATE—GREAT ROOM—NIGHT

Lounging around as if king himself, Haman speaks to his gathered family and associates.

                              HAMAN
               I am a wealthy man; in riches and in
               sons and in esteem.

DALPHON
You are elevated above all men, father, excepting the king.

HAMAN
Yes, and my greatest wish will soon come to be.

ASPATHA
To think, he trusted you so dearly, that when you asked for his ring, he did not hesitate to grant it to you.

ASSOCIATE 1
What is it like? To have it in your grasp?

HAMAN
To hold it, is to hold the world.

ASSOCIATE 2
It was difficult returning it, eh?

HAMAN
Oh, yes—slightly.

ASSOCIATE 1
What fortune has found you, Haman—to be held in such high regard by Xerxes.

HAMAN
And that's not all, I'm the only person Queen Esther invited to accompany the king to the banquet she gave. And she has invited me along with the king tomorrow.

Everyone is impressed.

> HAMAN
> Yes, I am, undoubtedly, a wealthy man, but . . .
> (grows grim)
> . . . all this gives me no satisfaction as long as I see that Jew, Mordecai, sitting at the king's gate. I loathe that man. I have all I want, but the mere sight of his defiant face is enough to make me think of nothing but wiping the smirk from it. Adar seems so long away.

> ZERESH
> That is because it is, husband. But . . .

> HAMAN
> What, Zeresh?

Zeresh drapes her arms around Haman.

> ZERESH
> In Mordecai's case, why wait?

> HAMAN
> You mean I should execute him?

> DALPHON
> Why not, father? He's broken the law by disrespecting you, hasn't he? Let his punishment be a preview of what's to come.

> ZERESH
> Yes, have a gallows built—

> PARSHANDATHA
> —fifty cubits high—

> PORATHA
> —and ask the king in the morning to
> have Mordecai hanged on it.

> ZERESH
> Then go with the king to the dinner
> and be happy.

The suggested plan of action and the eager encouraging looks of his family and friends prompts a smile from Haman.

INT. SUSA—XERXES' QUARTERS—NIGHT

Xerxes lays flat on his back, unable to sleep. He throws the covers off, grabs a robe, and leaves the room.

INT. SUSA—THRONE ROOM—DAWN

Xerxes sits on his throne, head propped atop his fist as two CHRONICLERS read the book of records to him. They are deep into its pages. This, coupled with their weary appearances, indicate they've been at this all night.

> CHRONICLER 1
> . . . the information submitted by
> Mordecai was confirmed, and the
> conspiring officers were consequently
> hung. The next record is dated—

The man begins to turn the page, but Xerxes sits up.

> XERXES
> Hold on.

> CHRONICLER 1
> Your highness?

> XERXES
> What honor and recognition has
> Mordecai received for this?

The chronicler turns the page back, then another.

> CHRONICLER 1
> Nothing has been done for him.

Xerxes is not happy to hear this. He looks up and, through the slightly ajar doors, sees the shadow of someone pacing back and forth.

> XERXES
> Who is in the court?

The second chronicler gets up and goes to see. He only has to take a few steps before recognizing who it is. He stops and turns.

> CHRONICLER 2
> Haman is standing in the court.

> XERXES
> Bring him in.

He proceeds to the doors and waves the prime minister in. As Haman approaches, Xerxes settles back in his seat.

> XERXES
> What should be done for the man the
> king delights to honor?

Haman, taking note of the book of records, assumes the king has been reviewing his work again and, therefore, comes to the conclusion that the man to be honored is none other than himself.

> HAMAN
> For the man the king delights to
> honor . . .

He is totally enthused and begins to thoughtfully pace.

> HAMAN
> . . . have them bring a royal robe the king has worn and . . . a horse the king has ridden, one with a royal crest placed on its head. Then let the robe and horse be entrusted to one of the king's most noble princes. Let them robe the man the king delights to honor, and lead him on the horse through the city streets, proclaiming before him . . .
> (stopping before Xerxes, hands up)
> 'This is what is done for the man the king delights to honor!'

Xerxes blankly looks at Haman, who waits for a response with bated breath. Finally, the king bobs his head.

> XERXES
> Go at once, get the robe and the horse and do just as you have suggested—

Haman could not be more elated.

> XERXES
> (continuing)
> —for Mordecai the Jew.

Haman could not be more deflated.

EXT. SUSA—CITADEL GATES—DAY

Finding Mordecai sitting in his usual place, Haman and his ensigns menacingly approach and encircle him. He does not spare them a look, however, nor does he show the slightest bit of fear.

> HAMAN
> You are to come with me.

MORDECAI
I am? By whose authority?

HAMAN
Xerxes'.

Mordecai peers up at Haman.

HAMAN
(almost unable to articulate)
He has ordered that you be . . .
honored . . . before all of Susa.

MORDECAI
Really? You expect me to believe—

HAMAN
It is your belated reward for informing
our queen of the assassins.

Haman snaps his fingers and an ensign hands him a beautifully designed tote. Mordecai doesn't know what to think of this; still suspicious of the situation.

HAMAN
(nearly choking on the words)
You are to put this on and then . . . be
led through the streets of the city for
everyone to see.

Remaining wary, he takes the sack and opens it, and to his surprise, finds evidence that Haman speaks the truth. He pulls out the king's robe and holds it before his face, amazed.

HAMAN
Well, are you going to get up? Or do
you prefer to insult King Xerxes by
choosing your tatters over his
graciousness?

CUT TO:

MONTAGE—THE PARADE

—Mordecai, wearing the king's robe, is led through the streets on a gorgeous, white horse. Haman leads the animal, smiling through gritted teeth.

—One of the palace attendants, HARBONA, walks past Haman's estate and sees the gallows being constructed beside it. The prime minister's sons oversee the work, and Harbona, who pauses at the sight, is in earshot of them.

—Onlookers watch as Mordecai's 'parade' continues.

—A rope is thrown up and over the gallows' beam.

—Haman stares sinisterly up at Mordecai.

—Esther and her attendants prepare dinner for the king in the palace's private banquet hall.

INT. SUSA—PRIVATE BANQUET HALL—NIGHT

A few attendants, including Harbona, stand by as Esther, Xerxes and Haman drink wine around a bountiful table, just as they did the night before.

XERXES
So, Haman, did Mordecai enjoy his day?

The prime minister nearly chokes on a piece of bread. Esther tilts her head, awaiting to hear his answer.

HAMAN
He did.

XERXES
Excellent. I regret that it has taken this long for his deed to be acknowledged.

               HAMAN
     Yes, well, it has now and I am sure if
     tomorrow were to be his last, he would
     go with a satisfied heart.

Esther's eyes narrow. Xerxes, unaware of what Mordecai really means to both her and Haman, grins and takes a sip from his cup.

               XERXES
     After such a feast as this, I am sure you
     would as well, eh, Haman?

               HAMAN
     Once again, my most profound
     thanks.

               XERXES
     And, once again, those should be
     directed to her.
          (turning toward her)
     But, will you now tell me what this is
     really all about?

She shyly looks away. He reaches for her hand.

               XERXES
     When you came to me, you did so
     under the impression that you were
     defying a law punishable by death. So,
     tell me, what was worth that risk? It's
     time.

Inhaling a breath as if attempting to draw confidence, Esther sits up on her knees and nods.

               ESTHER
     It is, but the words are reluctant to
     come.

> XERXES
> There is nothing to fear.

But she feels there is so much to lose. Like the night before, she gazes down at his hands holding hers.

He places a hand under her chin, making her look at him.

> XERXES
> Queen Esther, what is your petition? It
> will be given you. What is your
> request? Even up to half the kingdom,
> it will be granted.

Casting a glance at Haman, she can see he is completely baffled as to what is going on, but seems to recognize that it is not good for him.

Again, she locks eyes with her husband and draws a deep breath.

> ESTHER
> (increasingly emotional)
> If I have found favor with you, O
> king, and if it pleases your majesty,
> grant me my life—this is my petition.
> And spare my people—this is my
> request. For I and my people have been
> sold for destruction and slaughter and
> annihilation.

Xerxes is completely addled.

> ESTHER
> (continuing)
> If we had merely been sold as
> bondsmen, I would have kept quiet,
> because no such distress would justify
> disturbing the king.

XERXES
Who is he and where is he, who would
dare presume in his heart to do such a
thing?

Esther pulls a hand away from Xerxes to retrieve the edict from her robes and place it before him. Perplexed, he takes it as she points a finger at Haman.

ESTHER
The man who is our adversary and
enemy is this wicked Haman.

Xerxes trembles more and more with anger as he reads the edict. The prime minister can't believe what is happening and leans across the table.

HAMAN
What? I told the king my intent. I had
his approval. He himself gave me his—

Xerxes stands up, enraged.

XERXES
No. No, I would have never, never
endorsed such a horrendously
despicable thing as this! No man could!

HAMAN
But—but, you did! In the garden! You
gave me your ring! Don't you
remember?!

Xerxes looks down at his ring and, realizing Haman is telling the truth, glances from face to face before storming out.

INT. SUSA—PALACE CORRIDOR—NIGHT—CONTINUING

Xerxes marches through the halls of the palace like a madman, knocking over works of art as he goes.

EXT. SUSA—PALACE GARDEN—NIGHT—CONTINUING

Reaching the center of the garden, Xerxes frantically steps forward and back, clutching his head.

>   XERXES
>   (quietly mumbling)
>   What have I done? What have I done?!

He picks up a clay pot and, with tremendous force, hurls it toward one of the portico columns. Pieces of clay shatter and fall to the ground as he stumbles back a step, anguished and breathing rapidly.

This bout of rage is a catharsis of sorts, however, a means to alleviate the weight of all that has been keeping him down.

>   XERXES
>   (closing his eyes)
>   How did I lose my way? How did I . . .
>   (a beat; shaking his head)
>   Seven years . . . seven years, no rest;
>   from the day I crossed that bridge,
>   I have been wandering . . . seeking . . .

He sinks to his knees.

>   XERXES
>   . . . to be found.

A calm soon comes over him and he lifts his face to the sky. He stares at the stars, searching for an answer. Starlight fills his eyes. A shaky breath spills from his lips. He has had an epiphany and in his inspired stare, we can clearly see:

Persia's "Great King" is restored.

INT. SUSA—PRIVATE BANQUET HALL—NIGHT

Haman glares at Esther.

> HAMAN
> What games have you played with his mind? How did you twist it?

> ESTHER
> I didn't!

> HAMAN
> You did!! I had the king's approval. He gave me his ring! I did not go behind his back! I—

> ESTHER
> You used him! You used his grief! You preyed on it, scavenger!

> HAMAN
> You kept a secret all these years and you—who is Mordecai to you? Your father? Your—

> ESTHER
> He is my uncle, who raised me as his own—

> HAMAN
> (sarcastic)
> All the way to the throne.

He stands.

HAMAN
What do you know of me or the king!?

ESTHER
I know he has a heart, and no one who does could ever commit or allow such an offense against their fellow man.

HAMAN
Fellow man? The Jews??

ESTHER
How could you? Men, women and children?? How could you!?

HAMAN
Easily! They're all the same and—
    (pointing a finger at her)
—so are you!

He approaches her. The attendants are unsure of what to do.

ESTHER
Get—back.

Haman's contempt suddenly ebbs as the reality of the situation takes hold. He begins to shake, knowing that he has dug himself into a hole.

HAMAN
You have condemned me, you know?

ESTHER
Your hate has condemned you.

He nearly begins to cry.

HAMAN
When the king returns . . .
    (to himself; losing it)
He knew, he—knew!

Haman falls to his knees and pleadingly skirts across the floor toward Esther.

> HAMAN
> I am at your mercy now.

> ESTHER
> It is not mine to—

> HAMAN
> You can speak with him!

Mad with fear, Haman crawls atop her.

> ESTHER
> Stop! Get off of me!!

> HAMAN
> Please!! Please, I beg you!

Esther struggles beneath him, pushing with all her might at his twisted face. The attendants begin to advance. He doesn't even seem to notice, so terrified by the prospect of punishment that all rationale has been abandoned. This attempt to be absolved has only sealed his fate.

> XERXES (O.S.)
> Will he even molest my own wife
> while she is with me in the house?

Everyone freezes. Esther turns her head and sees Xerxes standing in the doorway, bristling at the sight of this so-called 'noble' atop her.

Hydarnes arrives and joins the king's side. A few guards filter past both of them into the room. Before Haman can utter a word, he is seized and his head is covered by a sack, which silences and masks his terror.

Xerxes casts Esther a comforting look, but their connection is severed by Harbona, who approaches to speak with him and the general. What he has to say further incenses the king.

                         XERXES
                 A gallows fifty cubits high?

Harbona backs away and nods. Xerxes spares the subdued Haman one last look and turns to Hydarnes.

                         XERXES
                    Hang him on it!

The tone of the order demands immediate action. Hydarnes directs the guards to come and, despite his muffled protestations, Haman is promptly removed from the scene without so much as a second glance from Xerxes.

The kings eyes are, instead on his wife. Esther slowly stands as he proceeds into the room and heads straight for her.

                         XERXES
                  So, you're a Jewess?

                         ESTHER
                         (nods)
                  Mordecai is my uncle.

                         XERXES
                Is Esther even your name?

                         ESTHER
                Yes, but one others saw fit to call me,
                that I grew into . . . not the one I was
                born with.

                         XERXES
                    Which would be?

                         ESTHER
                       Hadassah.

Xerxes crosses his arms as he addresses Harbona.

>   XERXES
>   Find Mordecai.
>   CUT TO:

INT. SUSA—THRONE ROOM—NIGHT

Mordecai, still in sackcloth and ash, and a tearful Esther stand in front of Xerxes, who sits formally upon his throne.

>   XERXES
>   (to both; eyes set on Esther)
>   Because Haman attacked the Jews, I
>   have given his estate to Esther, and they
>   have hanged him on the gallows.

He turns his sights on Mordecai and, despite the man's dreary appearance, recognizes him as a hero who has not only saved his own life, but stood up for those of his kindred. The respect he has for him is plain to see.

What is not seen—on Xerxes' finger—is a certain adornment.

>   XERXES
>   Now write another decree in the king's
>   name in behalf of the Jews . . .

Mordecai peers down at his own closed hand and, curling his fingers back, beholds the king's signet ring.

>   CUT TO:

MONTAGE—COUNTERING HAMAN'S EDICT

—The royal scribes take the dictation of Mordecai.

—We see the king's seal applied.

—Couriers race across the breadth of the empire.

EXT. SUSA—PALACE BALCONY—BEFORE SUNRISE

Xerxes stares off into the distance. Esther quietly stands behind him, his ring in hand.

>   ESTHER
> My king.

He turns. She holds out the ring. He takes it and slips it back on.

>   ESTHER
> Do you wish for me to gather my
> things now?

A long, considerate pause follows. Xerxes twists and gazes at his ring.

>   XERXES
> Do you remember when I asked you
> what you knew of me?

>   ESTHER
> I do.

>   XERXES
> Of all the titles you mentioned, the most
> important is that of guardian. Still,
> despite myself and all my ideals, I left the
> empire vulnerable. I should have listened.
>   (a beat)
> A dear, wise friend once told me that
> one could not look to the past without
> turning away from the present, but I
> did anyway. I neglected what was right
> in front of me and, in so doing,
> jeopardized the future.

>   ESTHER
> Its path has yet to be set.

He finally looks at her and reaches for her hand.

> XERXES
> A path I want you to walk with me.

> ESTHER
> You mean . . . I have retained your favor?

> XERXES
> And my respect.

> ESTHER
> But, I kept from you the whole of who I am—

> XERXES
> I don't care.

> ESTHER
> And though you may not care, there are those who will, and they will never accept a Jewish girl—an orphan no less—as their queen.

He moves behind her and, as he does so, pulls her necklace out of his robes.

> ESTHER
> (continuing)
> I know that the wants of your subjects you hold above your own. Surely they will demand I be—

She stops short, feeling the chain slide around her neck, amazed that it's been found.

> ESTHER
> I thought it was lost forever. Where did you—

> XERXES
> Beneath the hedgerow. I have been meaning to return it to you, but its clasp needed mending.

He closes it. She turns.

> XERXES
> Tonight, you proved that you were willing to die for your—our—people. So, no one can deny that you, Esther, Hadassah,—my wife—are Persia's rightful queen.

As the sun crests the horizon, they kiss.

INT. SUSA—COUNCIL HALL—DAY

Xerxes is in a meeting with his advisors. While the men are pleasantly surprised by the fierce confidence he exudes, they also don't quite know what to make of it.

> CARSHENA
> But what about the Greeks?

> XERXES
> The garrisons abroad, if confronted, may respond however they see fit. Should territory be relinquished, so be it. Our mainland borders are secure and our focus must be dedicated to the nations held within them.

> MERES
> But, O king, to defend this Jewish minority against the native people—

XERXES
We talk of unity, yet we are always so eager to define and divide. Minority? Native? According to our beliefs, these words should mean nothing, but I tell you, there is a great disparity between peace and war; love and hate. So, let me say this plainly. I am issuing our satraps to provide protection against anyone who would do harm to their neighbor. If a man chooses to take up his arms, he does so knowing that they will be met.

SHETHAR
But if that man is one of your friends?

XERXES
I am a friend of the right. It is not my wish that the weak should have harm done him by the strong, nor is it my wish that the strong should have harm done him by the weak. The right— that is my desire and it will stand.

CUT TO:

MONTAGE—THE DAYS OF ADAR

—Jews across the empire assemble to defend themselves against their enemies.

—In Susa, the ten sons of Haman raise a mob of just under a thousand men to attack the Jews.

—We see various stages of battle, from Babylon to Egypt, and even Jerusalem.

—Back in Susa, the sons of Haman lead a charge through the streets, but are shocked by the sight of the Immortals, led by Hydarnes, coming to the Jews' defense.

—All ten sons swing dead on a gallows.

—Across the empire, the feast of 'Purim' is celebrated.

—At Susa's citadel gates, Mordecai stands before a celebratory crowd, dressed in royal garments of blue and white, a large crown of gold and a purple robe of fine linen.

—Alone on a balcony, king and queen stand in one another's arms, basking in the moonlight and the joyous sights and sounds of the capital.

INT. PARSA—DARIUS'S ESTATE—GREAT ROOM—DAY

Darius, despite having been deposed, is not without wealth, and his house is far from modest. The interiors are reminiscent of the palace. Pillars mark each end of the room. Tapestries and carpets line the walls and floor.

Darius's fingers loudly tap atop the desk at which he is seated. The source of his agitation is an opened letter marked with Xerxes' seal. An attendant girl tries to soothe him with an embrace, but he indignantly shrugs her off.

> DARIUS
> Leave me!

Stung by his words, she hurries out of the room—just as Amestris enters. Though impeccably dressed and made-up, the former queen's lovely features are overshadowed by a spiteful aura, one she shares with her son.

> AMESTRIS
> (spotting the letter)
> Who is it from?

> DARIUS
> The 'king'.

She did not expect to hear that.

AMESTRIS
What does his majesty want?

DARIUS
He's coming to Parsa.

She was not prepared to hear this, either.

AMESTRIS
Then we will leave the city and go
elsewhere for the duration of his stay.

DARIUS
He wants to see me.

AMESTRIS
See you? To what? Put your grievances
to rest?

Darius rises from the desk. Amestris keeps her eyes trained on him as he skulks around the room.

AMESTRIS
You aren't considering unburdening
him of the past, are you?

DARIUS
Have you ever considered that I am
also tired of bearing the weight??

AMESTRIS
Darius, he acknowledges you now
because he wants to forge ahead in his
new life with no ties of guilt to his old.
He seeks the only thing you can offer
him—absolute absolution—and if you
grant him it—

DARIUS
Oh, I can't.

AMESTRIS
Then why do you talk as if you could?

Darius stops and, like a child throwing a tantrum, wildly gestures as he rants.

DARIUS
I was born to be king, not some civilian nobody! This was not my destiny!!

AMESTRIS
Nor mine—but so it is. We were robbed by an unapologetic thief who masks himself as fair and generous, and do not think for a moment that you are above mistaking his lies for sincerity!

DARIUS
But he may be ready to give me back my birthright!

AMESTRIS
And he may also be ready to forsake his queen and take me back, as well.
(coldly)
Darius, he needs but one son, one heir, and he has him.

A subtle flicker of sadness crosses her face.

DARIUS
Artaxerxes is only a child! If anything were to happen to fath—Xerxes, he is incapable of taking the throne!

                    AMESTRIS
                And you are?

She begins to circle him.

                    AMESTRIS
                You think you'll go there and, upon
                seeing you, his precious first born, he
                will fall to his knees, beg your
                forgiveness and give you back your
                dignity.

                    DARIUS
                I want it back.

                    AMESTRIS
                And as entitled to it as you are, of this
                you can be sure—it is not by
                ingratiating yourself to his appeasement
                that you'll get it.

                    DARIUS
                Are you suggesting . . . ?

She stops in front of him, and he can see the answer to his unfinished question in her icy stare.

                    DARIUS
                No. No! I could never do such a thing!

                    AMESTRIS
                Couldn't you?

Leaving her dumbfounded son to consult his conscience, Amestris backs off and departs into the shadows.

EXT. PERSIA—ROYAL ROAD—NIGHT

The king's caravan is at a standstill due to poor weather. Tents have been raised; each under guard.

INSIDE THE ROYAL TENT

Xerxes is going over plans—construction plans. He glances back at Esther, who sleeps in a small nook, then to Artaxerxes, who sleeps in another. He smiles, thankful for the peace he has found, and returns to his work.

A guard enters, damp from the rain.

>   GUARD
> Your highness?

>   XERXES
> What is it?

>   GUARD
> There is a small caravan approaching
> from Pasargadae, mostly merchants and
> the like, but one of the men with them
> has been recognized as Artabanus.

Xerxes sits back.

>   XERXES
> If you can confirm it's him, bring him
> to me.

LATER . . .

Artabanus is ushered into the tent, shrouded beneath a cloak, which he promptly removes. The man revealed, unassuming in both attire and presence, is not one Xerxes recognizes.

>   XERXES
>   (to guard)
> You may go.

He leaves.

XERXES
Sit.

Artabanus slings his cloak over an arm and, spotting Esther and Artaxerxes, quietly proceeds to take a seat.

XERXES
I must say, I never thought I would lay eyes on you again.

ARTABANUS
If I may ask, why do you do so now?

XERXES
Because I don't believe this to be a coincidence. It's not, is it?

ARTABANUS
No, it's not.

XERXES
Why are you here, Artabanus?

ARTABANUS
I knew you would be traveling to Parsa, but I did not anticipate it would be at the same time as I.

XERXES
You're on your way there, as well?

ARTABANUS
A journey I decided to take in hopes of holding audience with you, yes.

XERXES
Well, it looks as though your venture was not in vain.

ARTABANUS
That it does.

XERXES
What do you want?

Artabanus glances at Artaxerxes again.

ARTABANUS
My, he has grown. How old is he now?

XERXES
Nearly eleven.

ARTABANUS
He looks a great deal like Tigranes did when he was a boy.
(looks back to Xerxes)
He's the reason I'm here . . . he and Tritan both.

Xerxes uncomfortably shifts, expecting to be accused of their demise again.

ARTABANUS
I have been a poor father. I took for granted the days we had together, failed to offer support in those apart, and so bitter with grief over what befell them . . . I refused to honor their memory. In truth, I did all I could to belittle it. I have spent these past few years paying the penance and it was just that I did.

XERXES
We all seem to have our own guilt to bear . . . some more than others.
(a beat)
(MORE)

> XERXES(cont'd)
> I sent word to Darius, though a reconciliation is doubtful and not something I intend to force. His wounds run deep and it will take more than time to heal them.

> ARTABANUS
> I wonder, might ours be mended?

> XERXES
> They might, yet.

INT. ATHENS—AGORA—DAY

470 B.C.

The center of Athens has been blocked off by wood rails, leaving ten entrances for the citizens to use, based on their 'phyle'. They are casting their ostrakons today.

In every hand, a piece of earthenware, etched with the name of choice, can be found.

We see them deposited before nine presiding archons, Aristides among them, and the Athenian council (the Boule). Themistocles anxiously watches the proceedings with his peers.

> STATESMAN 1
> You look nervous Themistocles. Don't worry. You'll keep your wealth and, in ten years time, you may return to your estate.

> THEMISTOCLES
> Should I be the one. It could be Cimon, Aristides, Xanthippus—any of us who have obtained a bit of recognition.

                    STATESMAN 1
And power. Yes, so don't take it
personally . . . should you be the one.
These ostracisms are a merely a means
to appease the common man's sense of
equality; to temper, through exile, the
presumption of men who have risen
too high.

                    THEMISTOCLES
Yes, makes one think it preferable not
to aspire to anything at all. The low
always tend to go unnoticed and
unchecked.

Themistocles walks away.

EXT. COLONAE—PAUSANIAS'S ESTATE—NIGHT

A courier tucks a sealed letter into his satchel as he exit's the former regent's house.

INSIDE . . .

Though regally dressed and surrounded by wealth, Pausanias does not appear to be sound of mind. He sits at a desk, one hand buried in his mussed hair, the other alternating between furious scribbles and a cup of wine.

Two SERVANTS stand in the background, observing him.

                    SERVANT 1
                (noting the other's dismay)
It's only your second day. You'll find
yourself used to it soon enough.

                    SERVANT 2
This is normal?

SERVANT 1
He has been like this for years. There was a girl he desired in Byzantium, named Cleonice, who he horribly wronged. He has desperately sought her reconciliation ever since.

SERVANT 1
Oh, so is that who he's writing?

SERVANT 2
He has been writing many letters as of late, but, no, none for her. There would be no courier willing to relay a message, anyway.

SERVANT 1
Why? Where is she?

SERVANT 2
In the earth, long buried.

SERVANT 1
You mean he—

SERVANT 2
By accident. He went to the oracle at Heraclea recently and claims he saw Cleonice and that she told him, should he return to Sparta, he would speedily be freed from all evils.

SERVANT 1
So, is he going to go?

SERVANT 2
(affirming)
He decided on it today.

Back on Pausanias as he continues to write . . .

> PAUSANIAS (V.O.)
> It was sorely distressing to hear of your ostracism. I sympathize, as I know just how it feels to be used and discarded. They lift you up only to tear you down for jealousy. This is our thanks, but, while they've denied us our proper due, I will see to it that they get theirs.

INT. SPARTA—COUNCIL HALL—DELIBERATION ROOM—DAY

The courier who left Pausanias's estate stands before the ephors as they review the letter he has brought.

> PAUSANIAS'S COURIER
> I was to deliver it to a noble in Asia Minor, but no courier he has sent with a letter bearing this seal has ever returned. So, I opened it and, as you see for yourself . . .

> EPHOR 1
> He was informing the Persians of his continuing efforts to stir a helot uprising.

> EPHOR 2
> Finally, confirmation.

> PAUSANIAS'S COURIER
> Pausanias has already left for Sparta.

> EPHOR 1
> Well, we will be sure he receives a proper welcome.

EXT. SPARTAN ACROPOLIS—DAY

Pausanias, accompanied by guards and servants, proceeds through the dense main street, feeling the eyes of passersby upon him as he goes.

Ahead, he sees a group of ephors standing upon the steps of the council hall. One of them salutes.

> EPHOR 1
> Hail Pausanias!

Flashes of armor glint through the crowd, momentarily blinding an increasingly paranoid Pausanias. Regaining his sight, he sees his courier in the presence of the ephors. He realizes that the Spartans know his secret and he is about to be arrested.

He runs. A mob forms and apprehends his men, while others chase him to a temple known as the ATHENA CHALCIOECUS.

He absconds inside, but his pursuers stop before the entrance.

INT. SPARTA—ATHENA CHALCIOECUS—CONTINUING

Pausanias, panicked, paces back and forth before the open door.

> PAUSANIAS
> You cannot take me from here! To do so, to cross this threshold, would be a defilement!

An OLD WOMAN is ushered to the front of the crowd.

> OLD WOMAN
> Pausanias! Pausanias!

Beholding her, he freezes and his eyes well.

> PAUSANIAS
> Mother . . . Mother, tell them! Tell them they cannot do this to me. Not after all that I have done for them—for you. I am not the betrayer. I am the betrayed! Please, tell them!

Her silence perplexes him, as does the rock she holds in her hand.

> PAUSANIAS
> Mother? What—what are you doing?

She places the rock down in the entrance way and turns to leave.

> PAUSANIAS
> Don't leave me. Don't—mother?
> Mother!!! You can't leave your son!!

Another person steps forward, places a rock down and leaves—

> PAUSANIAS
> No! No!!

—then another and another—

> PAUSANIAS
> Please! Don't do this. Don't do this!!!

—blocking Pausanias—and his cries—up inside.

INT. GREECE—ARGOS—THEMISTOCLES' HOUSE—DAY

Just inside the door of his sparsely furnished dwelling, Themistocles speaks with an ATHENIAN MESSENGER.

> THEMISTOCLES
> (confused)
> So, you have been sent from Athens,
> here to Argos, just to tell me that
> Pausanias has—

> ATHENIAN MESSENGER
> No, sir. I have come to inform you of
> the charges being leveled against you.

THEMISTOCLES
Charges? By whom and for what?

ATHENIAN MESSENGER
By the Lacedaemonians. Documents were found rendering you suspect in Pausanias's dealings.

Themistocles finds this preposterous.

THEMISTOCLES
You're serious?

He finds confirmation in the messenger's earnest expression.

THEMISTOCLES
The man sent me letters. He did entreat me to join in his enterprise, but I adamantly refused to take part. I refused!

ATHENIAN MESSENGER
Sir—

THEMISTOCLES
You do believe me, don't you?!

ATHENIAN MESSENGER
(nods)
But what I believe makes no difference.
(a beat)
Sir, Athens has been called upon to respond to these allegations. Should they cede, you will be arrested and prosecuted by an allied synod for treason.

EXT. ATHENS—BOULEUTERION—DAY

The council members are entering the building. Aristides walks with Cimon.

> ARISTIDES
> Themistocles may be guilty of many things; egocentricity, impetuosity . . . and, if he is brought in and convicted, it will be for these crimes, not for being a traitor.

> CIMON
> Well, he certainly has his share of detractors.

> ARISTIDES
> You and I among them, but in this case . . .

> CIMON
> I'm surprised he hasn't run.

> ARISTIDES
> He hasn't because he still has a shred of trust left in the people. Sadly, that, I fear, is about to be ripped away.

CUT TO:

INT. GREECE—ARGOS—THEMISTOCLES' HOUSE—DAY

ATHENIAN OFFICERS burst inside the abandoned residence.

CUT TO:

INT. THEMISTOCLES' LITTER—NIGHT

Themistocles is concealed within the curtained carriage. Its rocking lulls him to sleep. He begins to—

DREAM

A snake is coiled upon his stomach. It slithers to his neck and, upon reaching his jaw, turns into an eagle. He is cuffed by its wings. It begins to take flight and we see—

THROUGH ITS EYES

It climbs and flies above the clouds, which then part, revealing . . .

The completed GATE TO ALL NATIONS, the mammoth gateway to Parsa's citadel.

                    XERXES (V.O.)
          I used to think all things that came to
          pass were destined to—

We move from behind the eagle's eye, to see the complex reflected in it—then the just the eye itself—which then morphs into a horse's eye.

EXT. PARSA—PLAIN—DAY

465 B.C.

Earth flies off of its galloping hooves. The animal rears as its rider launches a spear. The weapon embeds itself into a makeshift target.

                    XERXES (V.O.)
                    (continuing)
          —that what was fated to be was
          dictated by time and would happen
          granted enough of it. But the future?

From the terrace above, Xerxes stands and claps along with other CHEERING onlookers, including Esther.

The horse is reined in. The mysterious spearman dismounts and is revealed to be . . .

                    XERXES (V.O.)
            It is a matter of—course—.

... Prince Artaxerxes, now eighteen.

                                        CUT TO:

EXT. PARSA—TACHARA—THRONE ROOM—DAY

Father and son stand before the relief of the 'Great King'.

                    XERXES
            Choose yours wisely, and you will find
            time is what you make it . . . not what
            it makes you.

                                        CUT TO:

INT. PARSA—XERXES' THRONE ROOM—DAY

The king's court and security silently standby as Artabanus privately addresses him.

                    ARTABANUS
            He claims to want to speak with you
            concerning affairs which are of great
            importance and has agreed to submit
            himself to your laws.

                    XERXES
            Yet he would not tell you his name?

                    ARTABANUS
            To that question, he answered that it
            may not be imparted to any man
            before the king himself.

                    XERXES
            I will see him.

Artabanus gestures to the guards posted at the doors. They open them and the MYSTERY GUEST's shadow strikes the floor.

We follow him as he approaches the throne, and his near-immobilizing anxiety is palpable.

Upon reaching Xerxes, he falls down in reverence and remains fixed in place.

>   XERXES
> What say you, stranger?

He keeps his head low. The pace and inflection of his words indicate he is speaking a language foreign to him.

>   MYSTERY GUEST
> I come with a mind suited to my
> present calamities, O king; prepared for
> favors and for anger; to welcome your
> gracious reconciliation, and to
> deprecate your wrath. Should you spare
> me, you spare your suppliant. If not,
> you destroy an enemy of the Greeks,
> who have banished me from my own
> nation.

>   XERXES
> What is your name?

The guest finally looks up, revealing his face.

>   THEMISTOCLES
> O king, I am Themistocles the
> Athenian.

Everyone is stunned, but Artabanus's reaction is the most extreme. He takes a step forward, intending to go after him, but is stopped by a raised hand—Xerxes'—who is finding it hard to trust his own eyes and believe that his great antagonist, no longer a mere name, has, after all these years, surrendered.

INT. PARSA—OUTER COURT—MORNING

Themistocles sits between two guards, uncertain of his fate. The doors to the throne room open. He is roughly directed to stand and enter on his own.

INSIDE THE THRONE ROOM

Themistocles' fingers fidget at his sides and each step is reluctant. Though the king's guards stand at attention, he can feel their scornful eyes upon him as he passes by and is nearly stopped cold in his tracks by the insult one issues under his breath.

>   GUARD 1
>   You subtle Greek serpent. The king has
>   brought you to heel.

Culling his courage, he continues to the throne and obeisantly falls before Xerxes, whose thoughts are masked behind a piercing gaze. Silences stretches. Tension mounts, then . . .

>   XERXES
>   I am now indebted to you two-
>   hundred talents.

Themistocles looks up, confused. A slight smirk tugs at a corner of the king's mouth.

>   XERXES
>   The proposed reward for whosoever
>   brought me Themistocles of Athens.

EXT. PARSA—HADISH—ATRIUM—DAY

Xerxes and Hydarnes (whose attire is more befitting a satrap than a general), sit on opposite lounges. Once again, the king has architectural plans with him, but they have been abandoned in favor of conversation.

XERXES
It is a great irony, isn't it? That in the end, he would look to his nemesis, and find his only friend.

HYDARNES
What determined your decision to grant him refuge?

XERXES
I admired his courage. For the past year, he has been off learning our laws and traditions.

HYDARNES
Will he be here tonight?

XERXES
I don't believe so, but it isn't an impossibility.

Hydarnes acknowledges the papers.

HYDARNES
Still more plans?

XERXES
Oh, there will always be more plans.

HYDARNES
May your beautiful works preserve you.

XERXES
These? No, they are but stone and cedar and any inscription or tale they may bear is mute if there is no one to give them a voice.

An attendant approaches.

> ATTENDANT
> King Xerxes?

> XERXES
> Yes?

> ATTENDANT
> Your son wishes to speak with you.

> XERXES
> Let him come.

Xerxes turns back to Hydarnes. The attendant, though wanting to say more, chooses not to interrupt and goes.

> XERXES
> Artaxerxes will be pleased to see you.

> HYDARNES
> As will I be to see him. The last time I did, he was just here to my shoulder.

> XERXES
> The years go by quickly, don't they? He's a young man now, with so much promise, but then, I have always seen that in him.

Hydarnes' attentions are drawn upward.

> HYDARNES
> Darius.

> XERXES
> I regret that I never took the time to look.

> DARIUS (O.S.)
> You might now.

> XERXES
> Darius?

Xerxes turns and is awestruck. Darius, like the prodigal son, has finally returned.

Antsy and wavering in confidence, he takes a breath, goes before his father and, like a shamed child, kneels beside his lounge.

> DARIUS
> I just arrived from Ecbatana and was—
> I thought . . .
> (a beat)
> It's been so long. I don't know what to
> say, what to call you. I just wanted
> to—

Interrupting, Xerxes directs Darius to look at him and marvels.

> XERXES
> You've come home. My son . . . my
> son has come home.

Darius was not expecting to be so warmly received.

They both stand just as Artaxerxes appears on a nearby portico. He and Darius lock stares. Xerxes waves for his younger son to join them.

> XERXES
> Artaxerxes, your brother—he's returned
> to us.

The siblings awkwardly move to greet one another. Darius extends a hand.

> DARIUS
> Brother.

Artaxerxes, skeptical of this sudden reunion, gingerly takes it.

MONTAGE

—Nobles and satraps from throughout the empire ascend the steps to the Gate to All Nations.

—Bearing gifts, the guests are ushered between the colossal bulls guarding the entrance to the Hall of One-Hundred Columns.

—The guests weave through the pillars, deposit their tributes to the magistrates within, and—

—exit through another set of bulls onto the tiered stairs which lead to the courtyard of the completed Apadana.

—Inside the building, there is a party goin' on.

INT. PARSA—APADANA—PRIVATE ROOM—NIGHT

The room is adjacent to a master balcony and reserved for the king and his court.

Darius, the subject of many HUSHED WHISPERS and sideways glances, stands with Artaxerxes. Both keep an eye on their father, who sits in a corner with Hydarnes.

>   DARIUS
>   So, you haven't asked.
>
>   ARTAXERXES
>   Asked what?
>
>   DARIUS
>   About our mother. She's well. I
>   arranged for her to stay in the city.
>   Perhaps you might meet with her—

ARTAXERXES
Why, after all these years, have you
finally decided to forgive father?

DARIUS
It was time. I was wrong to keep my
distance. No good came of it.

ARTAXERXES
Or would if you continued to do so.

DARIUS
My, aren't you cynical?
    (slightly louder)
I am your brother, Artaxerxes. I want
us to be a family.

This draws the stares of Artabanus and a few others. Artaxerxes leans in to maintain discretion.

ARTAXERXES
For your sake, I hope you're being
sincere.

INT. PARSA—APADANA—BALCONY—LATER

Xerxes stands before a sea of admirers. Behind him, out of the audience's sight, are his sons.

XERXES
My friends, you've journeyed from across
the empire to honor me with your
presence; to pay tribute to your king. This
banquet was to be a thank you; a show of
appreciation in return for yours . . . but
tonight is better defined as a reunion.

In the background, the brothers briefly look at one another.

> XERXES
> Just as a father recognizes himself in his
> children and is, in this way, preserved
> by them, so, too, is a king found in
> and kept by his people. Tonight, I
> stand with my sons . . .

Xerxes directs the young men to show themselves. The sight of Darius elicits wide-eyed stares from the crowd.

> XERXES
> . . . those beside me, and you before.
> Of all your gifts, this moment—it is
> the greatest.

INT. PARSA—APADANA—PRIVATE ROOM—LATER

While members of the court wait to be seated at one of the newly set-up tables, Darius approaches the small group with which Artabanus and Hydarnes are keeping company.

> ARTABANUS
> (wryly)
> Darius, how good it is to see you.

> DARIUS
> I had heard you'd been taken back into
> the fold. Having now seen for myself, I
> finally believe it. Took awhile for you
> to reestablish yourself in the royal
> court, though, eh?

Artabanus is almost amused—almost.

> ARTABANUS
> Despite your father's idealistic musings,
> some 'sons' must prove themselves
> more than others, as his guilt only
> endears so many.

He pats Darius on the shoulder and walks away.

>   HYDARNES
>   (uncomfortably)
> Well, then . . .

>   DARIUS
> Oh, I'm not concerned about him. It's
> my father I worry about.

>   HYDARNES
> What do you mean?

>   DARIUS
> Artaxerxes. The instant he saw me
> earlier, his expression turned so dark
> and ominous.

>   HYDARNES
> You think he feels threatened?

>   DARIUS
> I am the first born. He knows that,
> despite the rift between my father and
> I, that title was never taken, nor could
> it ever be.

>   HYDARNES
> Your brother loves the king.

>   DARIUS
> Then shouldn't he support our
> reconciliation? It's what father wants—
> has wanted—for years.

Both men look to the far back of the room, where a curtain has concealed the king's table from the rest.

BEHIND THE CURTAIN

Xerxes sits with Artaxerxes who, spying on his brother through a slit, is brooding.

>   XERXES
> Artaxerxes?

>   ARTAXERXES
>   (turning to him)
> Father, it's just . . . I know we are
> brothers, but he may as well be a
> stranger. Where has he been all this
> time? What business has he dealt in?
> What friends does he keep—

>   XERXES
>   (calm)
> Stop, stop, stop. You growing to be
> strangers is not the fault of Darius.
> That blame is mine—

>   ARTAXERXES
> And my fear is that, contrary to what
> he claims, he intends to hold you to it.

>   XERXES
>   (still calm tempered)
> Enough.

Darius pokes his head through the curtain.

>   DARIUS
> Father?

>   XERXES
> Darius, come, sit.

He enters, carrying two drinks.

>   DARIUS
> Drink?

Xerxes doesn't hesitate to take it.

                        DARIUS
                (offering the other)
               Brother?

Artaxerxes casts a look at his father. Compelled by his urging nod, he turns back to Darius, takes the drink and offers a silent toast before taking a sip.

                                              CUT TO:

MONTAGE

—Miscellaneous party footage.

—Xerxes feasting with his sons and friends

INT. PARSA—APADANA—LINKING HALLWAY—LATER

This corridor is the main artery which accesses the king's private room, the women's banquet hall, and an exit. It is currently empty, save for two people.

In the humming torchlight, Xerxes, pretty tipsy at this point, and Esther steal a moment alone to talk.

                        XERXES
         (looking at the doors to the private room)
         I still cannot believe he's here.

He turns back to Esther and stumbles a step forward. She steadies him.

                       ESTHER
            My king, are you alright?

                       XERXES
            Dizzy with joy.

ESTHER
Or might it be the wine?

He playfully takes her by the wrists and cajoles.

XERXES
No.

The look in his eyes implies the return, 'Maybe it's you.' He leans in. They kiss.

XERXES
So, how are your guests?

ESTHER
Pleasant company.

XERXES
As are mine, though I do prefer yours.

He casts another suggestive look, but it soon turns serious.

ESTHER
What?

XERXES
I was wondering if I should let you in on a secret.

ESTHER
Oh, a secret?

XERXES
Mm-hmm. Can I trust you to keep it?

ESTHER
Beyond question.

XERXES

From my earliest memory, I have wondered what mark would I leave on this world. Every king desires to be remembered as having been loved by his subjects . . . and while I am no different, whether I am or not, what I do know, from the depths of my heart, is that I will be remembered for having loved you.

She is moved beyond words. He reaches for a flower from a nearby urn.

XERXES

The future may speak of wars and intrigues, transform myths into facts, lies to truth . . .
    (placing the flower in her hair)
. . . but we, my queen? We shall transcend them all.

ESTHER

In love we are redeemed.

XERXES

Yes.

They kiss again. Pulling back, he teeters a bit.

ESTHER

Are you certain it is only joy which overcomes you?

XERXES

Perhaps a little wine. I think I'm going to retire for the night. So, go back to your guests, make your excuses and then meet me.

> ESTHER
> I won't be long—but, if you're sleeping?

> XERXES
> Then wake me.

> ESTHER
> Should you open your eyes only to drift right back to sleep?

> XERXES
> Then my dreams are assured to be beautiful, for I will carry with me that glimpse of you.

They share another kiss, one that lingers.

They finally pull back and she reluctantly moves to leave, her hand remaining in his for as long as possible.

Upon her exit, Xerxes turns to find Darius holding another two drinks.

> DARIUS
> (offering one)
> Father?

> XERXES
> Oh, ah . . . alright, one more.

He takes it and starts drinking.

> DARIUS
> Did I hear correctly? You're leaving?

> XERXES
> Once I locate my escor—

                         DARIUS
                  I'll walk with you.

The eager-to-please look on Darius's face is endearing.

                         XERXES
                    I'd like that.

INT. PARSA—APADANA—PRIVATE ROOM—LATER

Artaxerxes, worrisome, parts through the crowd and, finding Hydarnes, pulls him aside.

                       ARTAXERXES
             Hydarnes, have you seen my father?

                        HYDARNES
             A bit ago. He went to speak with the
             queen and then I believe he left.

                       ARTAXERXES
                  Where's Artabanus?

                        HYDARNES
             He mentioned something about a
             minor security matter.

Artaxerxes is all the more unsettled.

                        HYDARNES
                    Is there—

                       ARTAXERXES
             Excuse me, I have to go.

He hurries away.

INT. PARSA—HADISH—KING'S HALLWAY—NIGHT

Darius assists his father to his chambers. Xerxes stumbles a lot, mostly due to the wine, but also because he cannot stop staring at his son.

> DARIUS
> Is something the matter?

> XERXES
> I don't want you to disappear in a blink.
> (a beat)
> Darius, you—I. I treated you so poorly and that you're here at my side now? There is no way for you to know, for me to articulate my regrets, but I will find a way to convey to you how much your forgiveness means to me.

Darius can see the sincerity in his eyes. His own suddenly sting.

> XERXES
> (continuing; alluding to his inebriation)
> Perhaps not tonight, but—you are here to stay, aren't you?

An ache in his throat nearly renders Darius mute.

> DARIUS
> I . . . I am, father.

They proceed to enter—

XERXES' CHAMBER

Darius helps his father to the bed.

> XERXES
> What a night it has been.

                        DARIUS
                    (lowering him)
                Easy. There we are.

                        XERXES
                We'll talk more tomorrow.

Xerxes extends his hand and waits for Darius to take it. The sight of the ring has transfixed him, though.

                        XERXES
                Darius?

Darius looks at him and the spell is effectively broken.

                        DARIUS
                Yes, father.

He clasps his hand.

                        DARIUS
                Till tomorrow.

Darius begins to let go, but Xerxes holds on a moment longer.

                        XERXES
                Darius. Thank you . . .

A tear rolls down Darius's face. For him, a 'thank you' from his father is tantamount to an admission of love.

He turns to leave before the moment can be ruined, but is stopped just short of the entrance by Xerxes' wine-laced words.

                        XERXES
                And Artaxerxes—if his guard is up, it is
                only because he was only a boy when you
                left. The years are so fleeting, aren't they?
                He is a young man, now; a fine, young
                man and he will make such a fine king.

A fire ignites behind Darius's eyes—his anger renewed.

On the bed, Xerxes pulls off his ring and, regarding it, contentedly smiles. A shadow stretches over him like a dark cloud. The ring drops to the floor.

INT. PARSA—HADISH—KING'S HALLWAY/XERXES' CHAMBER—NIGHT

As Artaxerxes approaches his father's room, something curious catches his attention. One of the doors is ajar. Panicked, he runs and enters.

> ARTAXERXES (O.S.)
> Father, no. No!

A dreadful, sorrowful CRY emanates from within the room. It is abruptly strangled by a surprise attack. Two shadows crawl the length of the wall as the men they mimic collide. ITEMS CRASH to the floor and, soon, so does one of the opponents—who then scurries out of the room—unidentified.

Silence falls over the scene. The man left standing looks at an object protruding from his torso and the truth of the matter is revealed . . .

INSIDE XERXES' CHAMBER

Artaxerxes' pulls a dagger from his side. He grits his teeth, but doesn't stop to tend to the wound. Mustering his strength, he goes to the balcony and cries out into the night.

> ARTAXERXES
> Security!!! Someone!! Somebody!!

> XERXES (O.S.)
> Artaxerxes.

The prince forces himself to turn to the bed and is anguished by the sight of Xerxes paling atop its ever-darkening sheets.

ARTAXERXES
Father.

Artaxerxes falls to his knees and clutches his hand.

ARTAXERXES
Father, you're going to be alright—

XERXES
I have always been in such awe of you.

He tries to sit up a bit.

ARTAXERXES
Father, no. Just be still—

XERXES
So . . . proud of you.

Artaxerxes can see his father slipping away. He feels utterly alone and helpless. In desperation he goes to the—

HALLWAY

—and screams through his tears.

ARTAXERXES
Somebody!! Somebody help me!!!!

A group of guards come rushing up.

ARTAXERXES
One of you go get the physicians! My father has been attacked. Go! Hurry!!

One of the men bolts away as the others join Artaxerxes.

> GUARD 1
> Sir, who has done this?

> ARTAXERXES
> I didn't get a good look at him. He went the back way.

> GUARD 1
> (noticing Artaxerxes' wound)
> You're—

> ARTAXERXES
> I'm fine! He may still be in the palace. Go!

Then men do as ordered and no sooner do they disappear around the corner, than Esther and her retinue approach. The sight of her despairing step-son speeds her steps.

> ESTHER
> What is it? What has happened?

He tries to keep her from going in.

> ARTAXERXES
> No. No, don't—

She won't be stopped.

DARKNESS

> ESTHER (O.S.)
> Xerxes, wake up. Please, wake up. Open your eyes. Please.

Through his eyes, we see the shadowy form of Esther looming above him, the necklace dangling, just like in his past dreams. The sight slowly sharpens and becomes lucid.

XERXES
(holding on)
You're here. You are so beautiful. Do you know, before you ever asked me to share your wishes—I think you were already sharing my dreams.

She tries to hold back her tears.

ESTHER
Was I?

XERXES
Watching over me as you are now—like an angel.

He begins to lose consciousness.

ESTHER
Xerxes? No—you're, ah—you're drifting off.

XERXES
I can't seem to stay awake.

ESTHER
Please. Just—just awhile longer.

XERXES
Just long enough for one last kiss good night.

She leans down, pressing her lips to his. A tear escapes through her lashes and rolls down his face.

He is no longer kissing back.

Xerxes has passed on.

The flower he placed in her hair earlier comes loose and lands beside him as she sits back.

ESTHER
Goodnight, my king . . . my husband.

IN THE DOORWAY

Artaxerxes watches, silently crying. The guard he spoke to earlier has returned. He places a hand upon his shoulder.

GUARD 1
Prince Artaxerxes.

CUT TO:

INT. PARSA—HADISH—BACK HALLWAY—NIGHT

Artaxerxes quickly rounds a corner into the corridor with the guard. He sees the others standing in a semi-circle around two figures, one crouching, the other sprawled out.

ARTAXERXES
What happened?

The guards part and he sees Artabanus on bended knee, hunching over someone.

ARTABANUS
I had heard the king left without security. I was just to the corner when I heard you calling for help and he came running—holding his chest and rambling that he'd done the unforgivable. He proceeded to draw a weapon on me and so I . . .

Artaxerxes takes another few steps forward as Artabanus turns the unconscious 'assailant's' head.

ARTABANUS
I didn't know it was Darius until I'd
already knocked him out. As soon as
the guards arrived, I sent one to get
you.

The guard spots something glinting beneath Darius's curled fingers.

GUARD 1
What's that—there in his grasp?

Artabanus takes the object and, realizing it is Xerxes' ring, proceeds to place it in the palm of Artaxerxes' trembling hand.

ARTABANUS
Is the king alright?

The young man makes a fist. Bringing it to his heart, he stares off, deadpan.

ARTAXERXES
Close the gates. No one enters or
leaves. As for my brother, take him,
find out whether or not he acted alone
and then . . . hang him.

DISSOLVE TO:

EXT. PARSA—PROCESSIONAL WAY—NIGHT

A stream of firelight, with seemingly no beginning or end, flickers through the street as Xerxes, enshrouded, is conveyed on a gold carriage by eight-white steeds to the Mount of Mercy, where he will be entombed beside his father.

EXT. PARSA—RAQS-E-ROSTAM—NIGHT

Mimicking the scene in part 1 exactly, except for the different characters—

Isolated, Artaxerxes sullenly stands before the foot of the mountain, staring up at a magnificent tomb cut into its face. Standing in the periphery is Esther, Hydarnes, Artabanus, the rest of the king's court and guards—even a teary-eyed Themistocles.

A multitude of MOURNERS are also gathered, people of all social classes. The surrounding plain looks as though it could be the night sky, dotted by torch and candle light.

DISSOLVE TO:

INT. PARSA—XERXES' THRONE ROOM—NIGHT

SEVEN MONTHS LATER

The throne is empty. Artaxerxes leans against a wall, holding his father's ring, waiting for a special guest, who is soon ushered in by guards.

It is Amestris, clothed in tatters.

> ARTAXERXES
> Dismissed.

The guards leave.

Artaxerxes slowly approaches his mother. She doesn't know what to make of him. This is the first time she has seen her youngest since Xerxes expelled her all those years ago.

> ARTAXERXES
> Amestris.

> AMESTRIS
> My son, you—

ARTAXERXES
Whatever you imagined our reunion to be, prepare to be sorely disappointed.

She shuts right up.

ARTAXERXES
When Darius was apprehended, I sent for you to be brought before the court. You, however, had run. Where to remains a mystery, the why—quite obvious. But, I find myself in a quandary when pondering another 'why'. Why, having absconded to safety without leaving a trace behind, would you venture to seek my clandestine audience these many months later?

AMESTRIS
Because I cannot stand the grip on my heart a day longer.

ARTAXERXES
Your heart? I wasn't aware you had one.

AMESTRIS
Artaxerxes—

ARTAXERXES
Silence!

In tears, she sinks to the floor before him.

ARTAXERXES
You knew! You knew what Darius was going to do, which makes you complicit in my father's murder.

                    AMESTRIS
          You're right, but I am not the only one.
          We did—we plotted against Xerxes,
          and in turn, we, too, were betrayed—
          used. I tell you and you must believe—

                    ARTAXERXES
          Must I?

                    AMESTRIS
          Yes. It was not your brother's hand
          which committed the crime.

Artaxerxes tightens his hold on the ring.

                    ARTAXERXES
          You gave me life, so I will spare yours,
          but you better tell me everything you
          know. I mean everything.

She breaks down and bows at his feet.

                    AMESTRIS
          Everything, my son, I will tell you
          everything.

EXT. PARSA—ROYAL COURTYARD—DAY

Immortals stand at attention before a formally armored Artaxerxes. Their GENERAL surveys the front line and takes his place at the end, where Artabanus, wearing a cuirass similar to Artaxerxes', waits.

                    GENERAL
               (to Artabanus)
          They're ready, regent.

                    ARTABANUS
          Your highness.

Artaxerxes nears the line and directs Artabanus to proceed along side him as he surveys the men himself.

          ARTAXERXES
I have come into some information regarding my father.

          ARTABANUS
Really?

          ARTAXERXES
Darius wasn't acting alone.

          ARTABANUS
But—

          ARTAXERXES
I know you personally saw to his questioning, but it turns out to have indeed been a conspiracy.

          ARTABANUS
Who has told you this?

          ARTAXERXES
I cannot say—but I have been told that my brother crossed my father only to then be crossed himself. Makes an intriguing tale. The long-lost, first born son finally returns to make amends with his father, the king, for his whole court to see . . . and to cast doubt on his younger brother, who has not yet been—officially—named heir to the throne.
    (shakes head)
Darius, with no time left to entertain his conscience, was set to play the
          (MORE)

ARTAXERXES(cont'd)
lamenting hero; his ally would do what he himself could not—take my father's life. The guards would find him beaten in the hall, having desperately tried to defend the king and suspicion would be cast upon me as having masterminded it.

ARTABANUS
Doesn't make sense to have it all happen in the span of one night. Why didn't he try to better convince the people of the reconciliation by initiating it much sooner?

ARTAXERXES
For the very reason I stated—he only finally decided to go through with it because he'd run out of time. My succession was to be confirmed. As far as he knew, it could have happened as soon as the next day.

ARTABANUS
But why would any one believe him over you—until that confirmation, your claim to the throne could be contested.

ARTAXERXES
All he had to do was say that, before the attack, the king had promised him the throne.

ARTABANUS
Again, why would any one believe him over you?

                    ARTAXERXES
          Because his ally would come forward
          and vouch for him—someone who
          had, through the years, done his all to
          earn the trust of the court.
                    (a beat)
          Unfortunately for Darius, he was
          merely a pawn in a scheme which had
          little to do with imperial ambition.
          No, it was not a coup to which my
          father fell prey. It was simply revenge
          and it's not yet finished, either—is it?

He abruptly stops.

                    ARTABANUS
          Artaxerxes—

                    ARTAXERXES
          Everyone looks to be in order, but, I
          must say, my armor—it doesn't seem
          to fit quite right. Artabanus, you're
          around the same size. Let me wear
          yours.

Artabanus doesn't budge. Artaxerxes points at him as he addresses the men with a humored grin.

                    ARTAXERXES
          I think he's being much too modest.

He turns back to Artabanus and snaps.

                    ARTAXERXES
          Take it off. Now!

Artabanus has no other choice. He removes the cuirass, revealing a scar on his chest.

                    ARTAXERXES
            You would have finished Darius off
            right there and then in the hall had the
            guards not come upon you. As it was,
            you barely had the time to frame—

                    ARTABANUS
            Xerxes took everything from me! My
            sons, my title, my dignity—

Artaxerxes turns away from him and draws his sword.

                    ARTAXERXES
            No. There is still one thing left to
            take . . .
                    (he turns)
            . . . your life.

He twirls the sword in hand before running Artabanus through.

                    ARTAXERXES
            Now, it is done.

EXT. PARSA—TERRACE—GATE TO ALL NATIONS—NIGHT

While staring out across the sprawling edifices of the city, a tear slides down Artaxerxes' face. Esther stands by his side.

                    ARTAXERXES
            I used to feel so small next to my
            father. Yet, now . . . Oh, how infinitely
            smaller I feel without him by my side.
            I can't believe he's . . . gone.

                    ESTHER
            No. I still see him.

With a gentle hand, Esther coaxes him to look at her.

He leans into her touch.

> ARTAXERXES
> What . . . what do I do now?

> ESTHER
> You step out from the shadow and be a light.

Artaxerxes knows she's right.

He walks further out on the grand terrace. Stopping between two fire baskets, he opens his hand to reveal his father's ring and, finally, slips it on.

Taking hold of the wall's edge, his ring and gold wrist cuffs glittering brilliantly, Persia's new king peers into the night in anticipation of a new day.

We hear a few Middle Eastern influenced GUITAR NOTES . . .

DISSOLVE TO:

EXT. PARSA/PERSEPOLIS—TERRACE—GATE TO ALL NATIONS—DAY

The moon descends and the sun rises. Wrists are no longer cuffed in gold. Instead, we see a black cuff watch—and a hand holding a steel pipe railing.

This is no longer Artaxerxes.

Where the city once was, is now a barren plain and, as a CHARTER BUS crests the horizon, the subtle instrumental kicks up into Metallica's *Wherever I May Roam*.

The mystery man presses the 'pause' button on a walkman and pulls his headphones back an inch.

ON THE BUS

—are about ten TOURISTS. Because of Iranian law, the women wear head scarves and modest attire, while the men sport nothing less than trousers and the casual, short-sleeved dress shirt.

All attentions are on the GUIDE standing at the head of the bus.

> GUIDE
> After Xerxes' assassination in 465 B.C., his son, Artaxerxes, ascended the throne. One of his most notable actions as king was issuing a decree which allowed for the walls of Jerusalem to be rebuilt and his name can be found in the Biblical books of Ezra and Nehemiah. Plutarch has also credited Artaxerxes with signing the Peace Treaty of Callias—which basically stated that, so long as Athens agreed not to interfere with Persian interests in Asia Minor, the Delian League's independence would be respected.

One of the younger tourists raises a hand.

> GUIDE
> Question?

> TOURIST 1
> Yeah, uh, what became of Them— Themistickle—

> GUIDE
> Themistocles?

TOURIST 1
Yeah, that's it.

GUIDE
Well, after being embraced by the Persians, he settled in Magnesia, located in present day Turkey, where he actually served as satrap until his passing.

Another tourists begs the guide's go-ahead to speak. It's granted with a nod.

TOURIST 2
What about Esther? What became of her?

GUIDE
That . . . we don't know, but there is a mausoleum here in Iran, in Hamadan, formerly Ecbatana, recognized as the tomb of Esther and Mordecai.
    (to everyone)
If you're interested in further concentrated study, there are many sources you can look to for more information on the Achaemenid kings. Um, let's see, the Bible, of course; a number of ancient writers, including Herodotus—again, Plutarch—um, Diodorus, Thucydides, Xenophon, Ctesias, Aeschylus, Justin—

TOURIST 3
    (laughing)
He lucked out in the name department, didn't he?

GUIDE
Oh, yes. Yes, he did. Um, there are also more contemporary works available, too, so . . .

The bus comes to a stop. The guide looks out the window.

     GUIDE
Look who's already here.
   (turns to tourists)
Ok, we're going to go out now, walk around the perimeter of citadel and then, you are going to meet with one of our most popular guides, Malik. Don't worry. He speaks English. In fact, he happens to be from the States. So, are we ready?

     TOURISTS
Yes! Ready!

     GUIDE
Alright then, let's go.

EXT. PARSA/PERSEPOLIS—OUTER WALL PERIMETER—DAY

The guide leads the tourists along the southern façade. We see the columnar ruins above.

     GUIDE
In 330 B.C. the Persian Empire, more powerful than any preceding it, fell to the Macedonian, Alexander the Great.
   (a beat; turning to group)
Now, before carrying away its riches, which, it's written, took over twenty-thousand mules and some five-thousand camels to do, he dubbed Parsa, 'Persepolis,' which means 'the place of the Persians'. As you'll see, during Alexander's occupation, the
     (MORE)

GUIDE(cont'd)
king's likenesses were defaced, which lends even more credence to the subsequent razing of the citadel being a direct means of reprisal against Xerxes for destroying the Athenian acropolis over a century before. The irony is that the fire contributed in the site's preservation. It wasn't identified, however, until around 1620 and scientific excavations did not begin until 1931 when the Berlin-based professor, Ernst Herzfeld, was commissioned by the Oriental Institute of Chicago. Now, you'll find among the many bas-reliefs inscriptions in Elamite, one of which can be found on Xerxes' Gate to All Nations.

As the tour group proceeds to follow the leader, two girls hang back a few steps.

TOURIST 4
Maybe there will be at least one 'portrait' of the king left.

TOURIST 5
Curious, huh?

TOURIST 4
You know the Greek historian, Herodotus, that the guide mentioned earlier?

TOURIST 5
Yeah. Sorta. Well, no, but pretend I do.

> TOURIST 4
> Well, in one of my college courses, we've been studying his writings and there's this quote where he's describing the Persian army and he asserts . . .
>> (pacing self to remember the exact words)
> '. . . among all this multitude of men, there was not one who, for beauty or stature, deserved more than Xerxes himself to wield so vast a power.'

> TOURIST 5
> Wow, that's some compliment. Too bad this is all . . . ruined.

She points at the ruins.

> TOURIST 4
> Yeah . . . he was probably freakin' hot!

The tour guide begins walking backwards as they approach the western side and the Gate to All Nations.

> GUIDE
> Ok, listen up, everyone! We're approaching the stairs to the terrace and our friend should be waiting for us at the top—and we are going to issue a greeting befitting "The Malik"—that's what we all call him, because his name—

> TOURIST 1
> Means something in Persian?

> GUIDE
> Well, not Persian, but in Arabic it means king. So, when we reach the base, you all stop and . . .

EXT. PERSEPOLIS—GATE TO ALL NATIONS—DAY

MALIK, remaining a mystery, continues to wait on the terrace. He's resumed listening to the Metallica song and, leaning back against the guard rail, drums his fingers atop it.

BELOW, before the center of the double-ramped staircase, the tour group has gathered. The guide holds up a hand, then signals the tourists to do their thing.

Palms are placed over hearts, heads are lowered in reverence and they shout—

> TOURISTS
> All hail, The Malik!!!

AT THE TOP

He pulls his headset down, though the music continues, and he turns.

To those below, he is backlit, so they can't initially see him.

> MALIK
> S'up, my people?

They move closer to the facade and gradually make out his short hair, the sunglasses he begins to remove, and that he is clean shaven.

As we hear the lyric—

Carved upon my stone, my body lie, but still I roam. Yeah! Yeah!

—the glasses are pulled off and we behold a modern day Xerxes—proof that stone works and inscriptions are not the only creations of Persia's "King of Heroes" that have endured through the centuries . . . his line has, too.

THE END

FADE TO BLACK

Courtesy of the Oriental Institute of the University of Chicago

SOURCES

LITERARY

- The Bible, *Books of Daniel and Esther*
- Herodotus, *The Histories*
- Ctesias, *History of the Persians*
- Aeschylus, *The Persians*
- Plutarch, *Lives of the Noble Grecians and Romans*
- Thucydides, *History of the Peloponnesian War*
- Marcus Junianus Justinus, *Epitome of the Philippic History of Pompeius Trogus*
- Diodorus Siculus, *Bibliotheca Historica*
- Xenophon, *Anabasis*

IMAGES

- Persepolis photos courtesy of the Oriental Institute of the University of Chicago. *http://oi.uchicago.edu/OI/default.html*
- Map of the Persian Empire courtesy of the Perry—Castaneda Library Map Collection. UT Library Online: *http://www.lib.utexas.edu/maps*

For more information on Xerxes, please visit:

http://www.renahakim.com